Labor Pains

Labor Pains

KATE KLIMO

CROWN PUBLISHERS, INC.
NEW YORK

To my beloved coach, Harry

Published by Crown Publishers, Inc.,
225 Park Avenue South, New York, New York 10003
and represented in Canada by
the Canadian MANDA Group.
CROWN is a trademark of Crown Publishers, Inc.
Manufactured in the United States of America
Library of Congress Cataloging-in-Publication Data
Klimo, Kate
Labor pains: a novel / by Kate Klimo.
     p. cm.
     I. Title.
PS3561.L47L34 1988
813' .54—dc19   87-37964
                              CIP

ISBN 0-517-56941-8

Design by Deborah Kerner

10 9 8 7 6 5 4 3 2 1
First Edition

Labor Pains

L A M A Z E · · *The First Lesson*

Two by two, they filed into the occupational therapy
room on the seventh floor of Hudson River General Hospital, the men looking uniformly squeamish and out of
place, the women, as they shed their winter layers, casting furtive looks at the size and shape of each other's
bellies.

Someone had pushed the three long, low, wheel-chair-
height Formica tables back against the wall. Still, the
counters and shelves bore the unmistakable evidence of
the room's daytime function: exercise grippers, rubber
balls for squeezing, color-coded nesting blocks, and the
like. On a pale green blackboard that retained the chalky
remnants of some medical student's chemical equations,
someone had written in large block letters the words:

PSYCHOPROPHYLACTIC METHOD
OF CHILDBIRTH

Two by two, they found seats facing the blackboard. A
tall attractive blonde in a maternity business suit shared
a couch with her husband, who had the stocky build and
broken nose of an ex-wrestler. A small woman with a Nef-
ertiti-style haircut and about whom everything was
round—her belly, her breasts, her face, her clear green
eyes, the curves of her elbows, and the curves of her
knees—lowered herself gingerly into the room's only
chair, leaving her husband no choice but to sit elsewhere,
stand behind her, or squat on the carpet at her feet. A
puckish-looking fellow, he chose to stand, still wearing his
expensive shearling coat, working a therapy ball in one
hand while glancing about him, as if for a means of
escape. Over by the windows, a pretty redhead with a
persistent cough and her black-haired husband held

hands and looked into each other's eyes as if gathering some secret sustenance.

Through the swinging doors a woman burst, her rippling mane of golden hair cascading over a bright patchwork coat. "Hi!" she said, looking around her with determined cheeriness. "Oh, good! I'm not late."

The others instinctively found themselves looking over her shoulder for the mate of this striking woman. As if she had read their thoughts, she doffed her coat and stood before then, all in black, statuesque in her pregnancy, and announced as if in triumph, "Don't bother looking for him, folks, he won't be coming. I'm the token Single Mother."

The other three couples absorbed this information in awed silence and were relieved by the entrance of a second lone female carrying a metal clipboard, her strawberry-blond hair cut sensibly short, her hospital nametag obscured by a red cardigan sweater worn capelike.

"Good evening!" she said briskly, looking around at each face. "How's the world outside? Believe it or not, I haven't set foot out of this joint since six this morning."

"It's snowing again," the single woman volunteered, as if the others' status as couples had robbed them of their powers of observation.

"Oh, well. Good news for skiers, I suppose. My name is Josephine Maxwell, but most people call me Maxi. I'm an obstetrical nurse here at Hudson River General, where I have assisted in over two thousand births. I am also the mother of three children—two vaginal and one cesarian," she added, again scanning their faces, "so I guess you could say that I've experienced childbirth from every possible angle. I'm here to do everything I can to help you prepare yourselves for this momentous experience.

"Before I summarize what we'll be covering in the five lessons scheduled between now and your big day, I'd like to go around the room, have you introduce yourselves, tell us a little about yourselves, and answer one question: Why are you here tonight?" She pointed to the ash blonde in the business suit. "Why don't you start?"

Impatiently blowing her bangs off her forehead, she had the look of a woman squeezing this in between two other meetings; the look of a woman uneasy in the company of other women unless the pretext was business. "My name is Carleen Donovan. I'm editor-in-chief and co-publisher at Grantley House. I'm forty-one years old and this is our first child. My mother gave birth five times without any medication. I don't see why I can't do it once." She turned to her husband. "Bill?"

"Right. My name's Bill Donovan." He grinned bashfully, as awkward as his wife was poised. "I'm a sportswriter, so I figure I'll make a great coach. No, seriously, I've seen what Carleen's gone through these past months, and if I could give birth to this kid instead of her, believe me, I would. But since I can't, I figure the next best thing I can do is be there to help her in any way I can."

Carleen patted his shoulder fondly.

"My name's Louise Rosen," the little round Nefertiti spoke up. "I'm a homemaker and mother of three. I'm also the originator of a successful line of infant and toddler wear."

Eight months ago, doubtless no one in the room would have particularly cared, but, with babies on the brain, everyone perked up and leaned forward at the very mention of *infant wear*. Louise Rosen probably would have gone on playing to their interest had not her husband tapped her lightly on the shoulder.

She gave him a narrow look but went on. "I've never had too much trouble giving birth before, but for some reason this time I'm nervous. So Shelly—he's my doctor—"

"Dr. Sheldon Berry," the nurse explained, "for those of you who don't have him: the heartthrob of the OR."

"He suggested I take the full course, instead of just the refresher, to, kind of, you know, maybe put my fears to rest."

"And what about you, Mr. Rosen?"

His wife turned to him, an eyebrow arched in warning.

Continuing his bruising massage of the rubber ball, he shrugged and said, all in a single breath, like a reluctant student: "Marty Rosen, I own and manage a food store, and I have absolutely no idea what I'm doing here."

Into the embarrassed silence that followed, the single

3

mother poured herself bravely. "I'm Kendra Madison, I'm a sculptor and painter, and I know exactly what I'm doing here. I'm in this thing alone, and I need all the help I can get."

"Have you arranged to have a coach?" Maxi asked. "A girlfriend maybe? Your mother?"

Kendra chuckled. "My mother...you have no idea how funny that suggestion really is. My mother finds the notion of natural childbirth déclassé. 'Natural' is for peasants and nursing is for cows. My girlfriend's volunteered, but she's out of town right now."

"Well, in the meantime," Maxi said, "I'll be your partner. And what about you two?" she said to the couple by the window.

"My name's Frank Rapasardi," he said, stroking his black handlebar moustache. In his red-plaid flannel shirt and dungarees, he looked like a romanticized version of a lumberjack. "I'm a landscaper. This here's my wife, Mary Beth. We have a six-year-old son at home and, knowing what Mary Beth went through to have him, I would never, and I mean never, think of letting her go through anything like that alone."

"Did you have a particularly difficult time, Mary Beth?" the nurse asked gently.

"It's like this," the woman said hoarsely, pausing to cough. "I didn't take a Lamaze class before. I know that sounds pretty dumb, but I'm an ob-gyn's daughter and I guess I thought I knew it all."

Maxi nodded quickly. "Go on."

"I mean, I grew up with all these strange women calling my house at all hours. Water breaking. Contractions. Spotting, mucus plugs, you name it. I remember there was even one woman who had her baby on her kitchen floor. The stories my father used to bring home! On the one hand, I guess you could say I was pretty blasé about it. On the other, I was petrified. Anyway, my own labor was a nightmare. Remember, honey?" She turned to her husband. "At one point, I really lost it. The bed started shaking and I was afraid I was going to die. I remember thinking: It's a good thing my dad isn't alive. He'd be so ashamed."

4

Maxi regarded her thoughtfully but not without compassion. "Your father wasn't by any wild chance Liam O'Mally?"

Mary Beth nodded, fingers working a shredded piece of tissue in her lap.

"He was a wonderful man," Maxi said quietly, then flipped her clipboard closed. "Well! I guess this is going to be it."

"Are the classes usually this skimpy?" Kendra wanted to know.

"Not at all. You should see our April/May batch. Just like at the zoo, springtime is baby time. You're to be congratulated for being brave enough to give birth in February." She checked her watch against the clock on the wall. "There's one more couple registered." She read their names off her list. "Would anyone know anything about these folks? If there's a chance they're coming tonight, I could—"

"She won't be coming," Kendra said. "In fact, I'm surprised she didn't cancel ages ago."

"Did she transfer to another hospital?"

Kendra looked around at the others as if unsure how to answer. "No, not exactly," she said slowly. "Actually, she lost the baby."

Maxi made no immediate attempt to dispel the pall that suddenly fell across the room. They might have been a military unit mourning a fallen comrade. Then she marched over to the blackboard and jabbed a finger at the lengthy phrase written across it.

"Psychoprophylactic," she said, biting off each syllable. "Prevention or lessening of pain through psychological and physical means." She turned to face them. "And I am here, ladies and gentlemen, to help you learn to stand up to your worst fears and deal with them. Now, shall we get on with it?"

PART I

Conception

Jill

Jill and Warren English lay side by side on their king-size platform bed, an island in the party-debris-strewn triplex, their eyes on the small, color portable on the swivel stand at their feet. They were watching a late-night rerun of "Dallas." Mallomars for the eyes, Jill called it. As usual, she was asleep before the first commercial break, awakening briefly in the flickering blue light to hear that Warren had switched to the Cable Sports Channel. A Knicks-Celts game.

"Go, go, go," he urged on the Knicks through clenched teeth, his enormous bulk rocking the mattress beneath them. He could sit for hours in front of the TV watching sports. Basketball, football, baseball, tennis...anything with a ball. And then, some time later, the screen black and silent, she felt the weight of his hand, like a warm ham, resting on her back.

"Hey, Jillsie. What do you say? My pecker's got amnesia, it's been so long."

Not speaking, she groped him to see if he was hard. Some vestige of memory obviously having lingered, he was. He rolled over on top of her and stuffed himself inside, letting out a grunt of satisfaction once in. Then he butted into her repeatedly, as if she were something frail but stubborn that refused to give way.

Was this really the same man, she marveled? Was this the partner in the investment firm of Barton, Martin & Thurman who, less than three years ago, had stood above her drafting table, fit-looking if not exactly dashing in his three-piece Brooks Brothers, pretending to look at her layout for the Annual Report but really just scoping her cleavage? Was this the same Warren English who, after six weeks of failing to get her to come out on a date with him to the Ocean Club, or to Regine's, or to the Mudd Club, or to some other trendy Manhattan mecca, had cornered her after-hours in her tiny viewless office and made love to her as she sat on the low counter between the hot-wax machine and the paper cutter?

Or was it Jill who had changed? She certainly didn't feel any different from the woman who had talked her way into the senior design position at Barton, Martin & Thurman with nothing to back her up but her experience, over ten years earlier, on the Smith College yearbook and some phony freelance projects. Perhaps Warren, like his personnel director, had been deceived by her résumé and her packaging. For she was not, as her former roommate and best friend, Kendra Madison, used to point out to her every morning as she gulped her instant coffee, slipped on her high heels, and headed for the subway to Wall Street, your Average *Cosmo*-sung New York Working Gal.

It had been immediately after graduation that Jill and Kendra, all set to take on the entire New York Art Establishment, had leased the big, funky, battleship-gray-painted loft three stories above the Bowery. The Lower East Side was a long way from the New England campus of Smith, but, after all, wasn't that a part of the artist's gritty rite of passage?

At first it had been an adventure. Since neither of them was taking money from her parents, they had to get part-time jobs, Kendra as a nude model at Cooper Union, the more modest Jill as a barmaid at a pub on University Place. They both had been able to arrange their hours so that they were free to paint mornings and midday, when the light was best. Afternoons they worked, and nights they spent sitting up late drinking coffee or wine and talking about art, or roaming the bars of Soho and Noho in search of other artists, preferably male and as horny as they were. Weekends they did the galleries, both uptown and down, usually sharply critical, but sometimes achingly envious, of their more successful fellows.

Five years into their Bowery life, they began team-painting, collaborating on the same pieces, and, looking back, Jill would always think of it as the most exhilarating phase of her short-lived career as a painter, combining the pleasures of friendship with those of creation. They had even had a professional photographer come to the loft and take slides of the resulting series of big, bright splashy canvases. In their pleasing use of color and their regular interplay of pattern, they sometimes looked more like stretched yards of exotic textile than painted canvas. Confident that the work was good and salable, they had taken turns making the rounds of the galleries to show their slides: Castelli, Paula Cooper, Greene Street. A typical response was "too decorative," or "pretty but essentially vapid," or "lacking that conceptual *je ne sais quoi.*" When it was Jill who toted the portfolio, she would come back to the loft stung and seething and ready to quit, whereas Kendra—big, blond, hearty Kendra— seemed totally unfazed. "What do they know about painting?" was her way of shrugging it off. "They're merchants and speculators at best, parasites and whoremasters at worst."

It occurred to Jill that Kendra could go on for years painting in the loft on the Bowery and living with rejection. For Kendra, who had grown up a millionaire's daughter in a millionaire's world, was not in this for the money and recognition it might one day bring; whereas Jill, product of a more hungry, lower-middle-class suburban environment, could not help but dream of one day living in a sleek, gleaming loft on the corner of West Broadway and Spring, or, better yet, a refurbished barn in the Hamptons, and reading her praises sung in the pages of *Art News* or *Art Forum* or in the Sunday *Times* Arts and Leisure section.

When it hit her that the odds against such a thing ever happening were staggering, the dinginess of her Bowery existence began to seep into her consciousness, dampening her morale and undermining her energy to paint. The thrift-store clothes they wore, the bodega-bought groceries they ate, the cheap red wine they drank, the sweltering weekend subway rides out to the beach at Coney Island every summer when their classmates were already making enough to rent houses on Fire Island, all began to drag Jill down. For this was New York City, the consumer capital of the world. And everywhere they looked, from the glossy pages of *New York* magazine to the clothing racks in Soho boutiques, to the golden views through the windows of Greenwich Village carriage houses, there was evidence of what money could buy: not only security but Beautiful Things. A steady hunger began to gnaw at Jill until one day, over ten years after coming to the Bowery, it was necessary for her to do something about it. Borrowing a thousand dollars from her older sister, Cheryl, she went down to Orchard Street and purchased the basis of a working woman's wardrobe. Then she began to study the *Times* Help Wanted section every morning and to plot her strategy.

Kendra had looked on the entire venture with a combination of wry amusement and morbid curiosity. Would her Bohemian roomie be able to pass in the Straight World? It didn't surprise her when Jill came back from only her third interview having landed a twenty-thousand-dollar a year job. She had seen Jill in college bluffing her way through courses for which she had never so much as opened a book. But it had surprised her when Jill actually hung on to the job and flourished.

"Design is fun," Jill said. "It's like painting, only in the service of something." She began to look at ads in magazines and newspapers, at the lettering on awnings and in neon signs with a new analytical eye toward function as well as form. At the office, they were more than pleased with her work.

But Jill had been unable to give up all the trappings of her former life. With her Albert Nipon suits, she enjoyed wearing blouses with daring necklines, and pieces of flamboyant, sculptural jewelry, the work of artist friends.

Among other women in the office, who were either secretaries or junior associates, in their own versions of dress for success, she felt herself to be a true exotic, something not quite of the same soil and climate. The men in the office sensed that she was different, too. She felt the desire she spawned in them and it thrilled her, gave her a sense of power she had not felt since she was an adolescent showing off her young breasts in her sister's hand-me-down mohair sweaters.

When the office's most coveted bachelor began asking around about her, she realized for the first time what it was that had brought her down to "the Street" in the first place. She was here to find a husband. Before he had ever said three words to her in a row, she knew that Warren English was it.

"Describe him to me," Kendra had asked.

"He wears a suit," she said.

"And the pope wears a dress, but tell me something I don't know."

"He's jockish," she went on. "His secretary told me he played football at Dartmouth."

"Dartmouth!" Kendra blurted out. "I never met a Dartmouth boy who wasn't repressed."

"Kendra, all businessmen are repressed. That's what makes capitalism go 'round."

"Well, *ugh*," was all Kendra could say.

Then there came the night he had finally made his move. She had come home to the loft that night disheveled and hicky-pocked and said, "That thing I said before about *repressed*? Forget it."

From that point on, Jill's office life took on a dimension right out of *Fanny Hill*. She never knew when Warren would come upon her and take her: in the conference room, in the office kitchen, in the supply closet. One late night they even made it on the desk of Sherman Martin himself, Warren getting a boyish charge out of staining the old man's desk blotter with his semen.

She began to spend most weeknights and every weekend in his West Village triplex, their agenda consisting of

making love, eating out, going to movies, and shopping—
the former and the latter taking precedence over all else.
He liked to take her down to Soho and spend unholy
amounts on her in boutiques whose price tags had, in the
old days, made Kendra and Jill chuckle in derision. For
himself he bought ties, cuff links, and expensive toys that
he rarely ever played with: a video camera, a capuccino
maker, a spear gun, an electric towel-warmer. Only once
had Jill made the mistake of taking him into an art gallery. Sensing there things he would never understand,
and not interested in buying, he walked quickly, expres-
sionlessly, from one end of the gallery to the other and out
the door, strictly passing through. Later, he had asked her
if her own work, which he had never seen nor asked to
see, looked anything like that, and when she had said,
"Not really," his response had been a strangely belligerent
"I hope not."

As their relationship deepened, they made the kinds of
confessions all lovers make. Warren told her about his
first true love and about the Mt. Holyoke freshman he
had gotten pregnant. His father had paid for the abortion
but had made him work two jobs that summer to pay off
the debt. Hesitantly at first, Jill told him about her four
abortions and he was always careful after that, as if her
confession had been a warning, to wear a condom when
they made love, which was fine with her since she could
then stop taking the mini-pill. She took him out to Long
Island to meet her father and stepmother. Her father,
having long since given up on his daughter's ever making
a sensible match, was touchingly pleased with Warren.
What wasn't to be pleased with? He was, after all, Prime
Husband Material. Warren took her to Philadelphia to
meet his parents. "Please don't wear any of that clunky
jewelry" had been his only spot of coaching. If Jill read
them correctly, Warren's parents had approved of her, and
she even overheard Warren's father, the banker, congratulating his son in decidedly unbankerish terms: "A definite
cut above the usual bimbo you march out to meet us."

And, of course, the inevitable day came when Kendra
had to meet Warren. Kendra had suggested inviting him

up to the loft. But Jill, knowing that Warren would not understand her bachelorette pad any more than he had that Soho art gallery, orchestrated a Sunday brunch on neutral turf in a Greenwich Village restaurant instead. It was, predictably, a disaster. Kendra found Warren spoiled, insufferable, and an expert on too many subjects. Warren found Kendra a screwy ball-buster, albeit a piece of ass.

Later, Jill had defended her fiancé to Kendra.

"Well, of course he's spoiled. All executives are spoiled. They can't help it. They make all this money, so they figure they have to be smart, and they're surrounded by secretaries, coolies, and colleagues who treat them like pashas—"

"You forget," Kendra cut in, "my father is the King of the Pashas. I know all about it."

But it was not Kendra who was marrying Warren, it was Jill. And Jill, crowding thirty-five, with her biological clock ticking away, had already made up her mind. They were married in the English family church in suburban Philly. Warren's brother, Claude, also a banker, was best man. Kendra was maid of honor. Claude and Kendra shared a joint and wound up making it in the choir loft, much to Jill's consternation. At the reception, Warren's mother, a whippet-thin, blue-haired Main Liner with all the warmth of a Strawbridge & Clothier house detective, had cornered Jill as if she had just palmed a lipstick. Smoking a slim, pastel-tinted designer cigarette, holding a small tin ashtray so close to her chin she looked as if she were about to eat it, she had warned her daughter-in-law:

"Don't expect him to be ready for fatherhood. He's nothing but a big baby himself. And my baby always has to come first," she added, supremely proud of her creation.

After two weeks' honeymoon in Bermuda, Jill returned to the office only to be told, much to her surprise, that now that she was Mrs. Warren English, it would be best for her to resign. Nepotism, unless it was of the Old Boy variety, was not encouraged there. Within months of her resignation, their sex life, now relegated to home and without the aphrodisiac ambience of the office, went from Baroque to Bauhaus. These days she was lucky if she got so much as a kiss by way of foreplay.

With nothing to do with her days but swim laps at the local health club and shop, Warren having told her that any salary she could earn would only be a tax liability, she eventually returned to painting. She staked out a corner of his basement gym as her studio. But something about her painting infuriated Warren. In one of a run of bitter arguments, she finally pinpointed the source of his irritation. Artists, unless they were successful—hence millionaires, hence *businesspeople* like himself—were simply not worthy of his respect. Artists, like people who marched in favor of nuclear disarmament and to save the whales, were objects of ridicule to him. And he was damned if he was going to be married to a joke.

Eventually, she packed away her paints and rolled up her canvases, her muse frozen out. At his prompting, she took up gourmet cooking. He sent her to cooking classes, where she showed considerable flair, consoling herself that at least cooking was creative. Warren praised her work in the kitchen, bought her food processors, blenders, grinders, fancy carving knives, and excessively expensive French cookware. These days he kept her busy entertaining partners and associates regularly at dinner parties. Jill's culinary feats had taken the place of Jill's cleavage as the talk of the office. There was only one problem: The more accomplished she became, the fatter her husband grew. His weight having risen from an athletic 190 pounds to a fat boy's 267, she now had to avert her eyes when he undressed. Who was married to the joke now? When she ventured to suggest to him that he might have a problem, he would heave his beefy shoulders and say, "Hey, I'm a married guy now. Who cares?"

But Jill cared, especially when he was on top of her, plugging away, as he was now. Jill cared intensely. She felt smothered by his flesh, crushed by his bulk, baffled by his hugeness. She was just about to cry out in protest, which he would no doubt mistake for passion, when he stalled out inside her. Was he finished or merely winded?

16

With a grunt, he rolled off her and padded downstairs to the bathroom spa to wash. She listened to the sound of the fine needle spray emanating from three shower heads and shook the numbness out of both arms. Then she felt it, sticky and warm on her inner thighs, the unmistakable trail of his semen. He had forgotten to wear a condom! She thought of dragging herself out of bed to douche, but, having cooked a Mandarin banquet for twelve tonight, she didn't have the strength. Besides, she had the irrational conviction that his sperm, like the man himself, were fat, sluggish, and out of shape, hence no threat to her prodigious fertility. As she drifted off for the second time that night, she was dimly aware of his getting back into bed beside her and switching on the TV to catch the kickoff in a South American soccer match. Anything with a ball.

Mary Beth

Mary Beth O'Mally Rapasardi looked up over the rim of her teacup and saw her lover making his way across the Palm Court toward her. He was wearing a brown corduroy suit and a maroon knit tie and his shoes were suede, the same soft brown color as his eyes, which never left hers from the time he entered the room. Cup and saucer began to rattle uncontrollably as she hastily set them down and held out her cheek for a chaste public kiss.

"Hi," he said, his voice low and husky.

"Hi," she said shyly.

"Sorry I'm late."

"I thought I was early. My meeting was over quicker than I thought."

"Let me get this out of your way."

He took the dove-gray leather portfolio that rested against her legs beneath the table and propped it against the side of his chair. He liked to brush her knees with his as they sat and sipped their ritual cup of Constant Comment before going upstairs to the room.

"Don't let me forget it," she said. "There are four thousand dollars worth of little duckies and bunnies in there."

He frowned. Mary Beth illustrated children's books for a living. Her lover did not approve when she belittled her career. In order to regain his approval, she added hastily:

"My last book got a good review in the *School Library Journal*." With trembling fingers, she removed from her handbag the tearsheet she had just picked up at her publisher's and passed it across the table to him.

As he read, he plucked absently at his left eyebrow. Ten years ago, when she had studied under him in college, his eyebrows, thick and unruly, had turned her on almost as much as his voice, gravelly from nicotine as he read aloud to the Freshman English seminar, Matthew Arnold's "Dover Beach."

Ah, love, let us be true to one another!

"That's very good." He looked up at her tenderly. "I'm proud of you."

"The reviewer liked the text as much as the pictures," she pointed out. "I guess I have you to thank."

She had illustrated several books before, but never written any. She had shown him the rough draft of her first effort. Mercilessly, he tore it apart, as once he had critically dismantled her freshman term paper on John Ruskin, bringing her to tears. Later, for the first time, he had kissed away the tears, locked the door, and made love to her on the floor of his campus office. There was never any question that their affair was something to be viewed in the short term. He was married to a prosperous trial lawyer, the mother of their twin sons. The affair had ended junior year when she went abroad to Florence to study art. Less than a year ago, she had run into him on the steps of the New York Public Library. He was still married. His twin sons had a little sister three years old.

But now they were on more equal footing. No longer the love-stricken college girl, she was an established free-lance illustrator married to Frank, a successful landscape architect. They lived in a cute Tudor-style home in lower Westchester. Their five-year-old son, Denny, was the joy of her life.

As he poured his cup of tea, he grazed her knee with his and said: "Oh, I can think of a perfectly lovely way you can say thank you."

She shivered, already so close to the edge, and he had scarcely even touched her yet.

They always took the same room, a suite overlooking the fountain and the park. He enjoyed being extravagant with his teacher's salary, since his wife's, as a partner in a major firm, was in the middle six figures. Wryly, he referred to himself as a kept man. No sooner was the door closed than he pinned her against it, kissing her deep and long. Dizzily, she felt all the air rushing out of her and into him as he began to peel off her clothing.

"You're shivering," he said, sounding surprised.

Over his shoulder, she looked out the window and saw the haze of green buds hanging over Central Park. When they had first taken this room, the azaleas were in full bloom. Almost a year of monthly trysts had passed since then. She shivered again. She always found spring an un-expectedly chilly season. But his hands were warm as he pulled her sweater over her head. Now all she wore was a lemon-yellow push-up bra, the briefest of bikinis, garter belt, and stockings. He had ordered the matching set for her from Victoria's Secret, the sexy mail-order catalog. Slowly, he slid the bikini down her hips, touching her between the legs as if by accident. His fingers felt searingly hot. He was still fully clothed.

"Lie down," he ordered her.

Meekly, she complied. He stacked the starched white pillows high so she could sit up and look at him.

"Spread your legs wide," he said, backing away and leaning against the door, eyeing her critically.

"Now," he said, "lick your fingers."

Blushing, she sucked on the fingers of both hands.

"All right," he said, "now give yourself pleasure."

She hesitated.

"Go on. Do it the way I taught you." That hint of impatience in his voice always made her want to pull her legs together and cry.

She had once confessed to him that she had never learned to masturbate. "Until you learn to give yourself pleasure," he had said, as if delivering a lecture on the Pre-Raphaelites, "you can't expect others to do so."

Before long he was tearing off his clothes, his body pale, soft, hairless, contrasting so sharply with her husband's, yet so much more sensitive to her touch. He lay on his back and pulled her astride him as she sank him deeply into herself. His hardness seemed to touch her very core. She kneaded his chest. Waves of heat broke over her as she began slowly to move herself up and down. How had she gone without this for a month? This was sex as she had always dreamed of it. Self-emolation. A thing worth dying for.

Later, on the 4:05 to Pelham Park, wedged between the early commuters, her body was convulsive with sobs. Back at the Plaza, she had stripped off the lemon-yellow lingerie, showered, and put on her plain white cotton underwear.

"What's wrong?" he finally asked when she came out of the bathroom already dressed.

In a silver bucket by the bed, a bottle of expensive champagne stood unopened.

She took a deep, shuddering breath, unable to meet his eyes. "I think I have to stop seeing you."

He did not put up a fight. It had been agreed, when they first began seeing each other again, that if either of them cried Uncle, the other would let go without a fuss, without a lot of messy questions.

"I'm sorry to hear that," was all he said.

"It's just—" Her voice caught. Talking hurt so much.

She looked at herself in the dresser mirror: Her curls stood around her head in a soft red halo, her freckled cheeks blazed. She didn't look like an adventuress.

"Just what?" he said kindly.

"I'm not enjoying being with Frank anymore. All I want is you. All I think about is you."

"I'm flattered, naturally."

"But I don't like that! Don't you see? I love Frank. He's my husband. He loves me. He'd do anything for me. I—" She broke off again, unable to go on.

"I know . . . I know," he said.

"No, you don't know!" she said plaintively. "I thought I could handle this. I thought I could have the best of both of you . . ." She shook her head. That was the trouble with affairs. It was so difficult to avoid talking in clichés. Perhaps that was why so many affairs were nonverbal, conducted so much more eloquently on a strictly physical basis.

She was crying again. Mercifully, he hadn't moved to touch her.

"I think," he said quietly, "it would be easier if you left first."

Later, she stood in the doorway, lipstick on, hair combed, portfolio once more in hand, and attempted a feeble joke.

"Do me a favor and stay away from the New York Public Library, okay?"

"Okay," he said sadly, as if her request had been put to him in earnest.

As soon as she opened the front door, Denny came running to meet her, clutching a picture he had made in kindergarten.

"I made a robot, Mom."

She took the piece of coarse white paper and forced herself to look at it. He wanted to be an illustrator, just like his mother. "What are these squiggly lines?"

"Freeze rays, Mom, can't you tell?"

She set down her portfolio with the duckies and the

bunnies inside, and her handbag hiding Victoria's Secret, and admired the picture as she stooped and wrapped an arm around him.

"It's beautiful, sweetheart," she whispered into his hair.

He frowned and pulled away. "It's not beautiful, Mom."

"It's not?"

"No, it's *cool*."

"Oh, of course! Yes, it's very cool."

"Did you bring me a present, Mom?"

Now it was her turn to frown. "Would I go into the city and not bring you back a present?"

She reached into her handbag and brought out a wind-up toy to add to his vast collection of wind-ups: false teeth and penguins and dinosaurs and mice and King Kongs and pink sneakers with nobody inside them.

"What is it?"

"It's a wind-up sushi. I think it's a California roll."

"Neat, Mom!"

She had spied it on her art director's desk this afternoon. It intrigued her that people who worked in offices invariably kept toys on their desks.

"It's not neat," she told him, "it's cool."

"Hey, Dad!" He dashed into the living room to show his father his wind-up California roll. Mary Beth doubted he even knew what sushi was, much less a California roll.

Frank Rapasardi sat with his bare feet up on a leather hassock, watching the end of "Live at Five," sipping from a bottle of Beck's. He had showered and put on the bottom half of the white Dior pajamas she had given him last Christmas. His muscular chest was already coffee brown from working shirtless out in the sun since early March. Talcum powder clung to his curly black chest hairs. As he folded her into his arms, asking her how it had gone in the Big Dirty, she reflected bleakly how he had the most beautiful body she had ever seen. It was so much more beautiful than her lover's—her ex-lover's—she didn't understand why it didn't arouse her more.

"I got a good review," she said.

"Yeah?"

He pulled back to look at her. His smile faded.

"Baby, are you okay? You been crying or something?"

Oh, God, she thought. It shows. It's all over my face.

She withdrew from him quickly and went into the kitchen to start supper. She heard Frank changing the channel from news to a situation comedy, and saying to Denny: "Stay here and watch 'Different Strokes.' I'm going to talk to Ma."

"Tell her to stop being so sad all the time," Denny called after him.

He came and stood behind her, hands resting gently on her shoulders. As she packed the ground sirloin into patties, the tears trickled down her cheeks, hot and guilty.

"What is it, Mary Elizabeth? What's wrong?"

The first time she had met Frank was a week after her father's funeral. A prominent Park Avenue obstetrician, Liam O'Mally had died of a stroke on the court of the New York Tennis Club. She had emerged from her mourning to go to the supermarket. When the man at the meat counter snapped at her for asking for boneless chicken breasts, she broke down. Frank had been there laying in his weekly bachelor supplies. Strangely, she wasn't too distraught to notice the handsome, broad-shouldered, black-haired man with the glistening handlebar moustache, dressed in a plaid flannel shirt, jeans, and work shoes. As he reached for a package of chicken wings, he asked her if she was all right. When his concern only caused her tears to fall more freely, he hustled her out of the supermarket to a nearby bar and later to his house. They slept together that night. He had been a soothing and considerate lover.

"What can I tell you?" he said sheepishly the next morning. "Sympathy always makes me horny."

Now, he wiped the ground sirloin off her fingers with a dish towel and sat her on the stool by the window. Outside, a well-pruned hedge of forsythia shielded their home from the neighbors'.

"Please talk to me, Mary Beth." He knelt before her, peering anxiously up into her face.

"There was this man," she began. Oh, God, she thought. It's happening. I'm splitting open. It's all going to come spilling out of me now. Everything. Remember that teacher in college I told you about? The one I had an affair with who broke my heart? Well, he's done it again.

"What man?" he asked for the second time, his face hardening, his hands curling into fists.

"In Grand Central," she said, the lie unfolding itself in front of her like a dark road before headlights. "He was following me around whispering filthy things. He kept flashing me. Finally, he cornered me. Pushed me up against the wall. I could feel him rubbing himself against me. It was horrible!"

"Son of a bitch!" He slammed his fist down on the butcher-block counter. She expected to see it crack and split apart.

"I screamed and a policeman came."

"What did he do to the fucker?"

"Shhhh! Denny will hear you. Nothing. He ran away ... down into the subway tunnel."

"If I could just get my hands—"

"Please!" she cried. "I just want to forget all about it!"

"I'm sorry," he said, rubbing his face with both hands. "You don't need my macho bullshit right now. Come on." He rose and pulled her gently to her feet. "Upstairs."

"What about supper?"

"I'll take Denny out to Pizza Hut. You lie down."

Upstairs in their bedroom, with its view of the budding cherry tree out the window, he helped her off with her clothes and then lay down on the bed beside her and held her in his arms, stroking her.

"Everything's gonna be fine now, baby. There's nothing to be afraid of. Nothing to be sad about. You're home now, with me."

Through the loose, thin cotton of his pajamas, she felt his erection growing.

Distractedly, she began to fondle him.

He cleared his throat. "Sorry about that. You know how sympathy works on me."

"Don't be sorry," she whispered, untying the drawstring and moving her hand down the length of him. What was wrong with her? Only hours ago she had been in the arms of her lover. Maybe it was spring fever—or maybe she was losing her mind. All she knew was that suddenly she wanted to make love with her husband more than she had in months.

"Isn't this your dangerous time?" he whispered.

For an instant, her passion cooled. Frank had always kept better track of her cycle than she did. He was a gardener. He knew instinctively when to plant, when to reap, and what was ready to flower. But she didn't care about any of that right now. All she cared about was having him inside of her.

As she slipped him into her with ease, she thought of her late father's favorite expression, *In for a penny, in for a pound,* and whispered back, "It's too late to do anything about it now, isn't it?"

Kendra

"Think of it," she said, leaning over to pull open her bedside table drawer and taking the familiar shape of the Prelude II vibrator into her hand, "as a *ménage à trois.*"

He paused mid-thrust, his hands tightening on her hips, his pale blue eyes narrowing on the machine as she switched it on. To look at him, you might think it was a buzzsaw.

"Sorry," she said, applying its humming pink tip to her clitoris. "But it's really the only way."

"Whatever you say." He relented as the vibrations racing through her caused the muscles of her vagina to grip his shaft.

"*All right!*" she said, shutting her eyes, throwing her head back. "That's the way! That's sooooooo good. You know something?" Exquisite spasms ran through her as she called out to the near-total stranger deep inside of her. "You're really a very sweet man!"

The alarm clock went off. Without removing the black satin sleeping mask she wore to shield her eyes from the glare of the Bowery's streetlights and the tawdry all-night fluorescence of the flophouse across the street, Kendra Madison rolled over and groped on her bedside table for the thin glass tube: the basal body temperature thermometer. It rolled into her hand, as if as atuned to this routine as she was now after five weeks of taking her temperature and recording it every morning at five minutes to seven. Finding the right end, she stuck it beneath her tongue and lay back with her cheek against the pillow, letting herself doze with the thermometer warming in her mouth, knowing that in five minutes her snoozer alarm would go off.

While she slept she had a dream—or was it a continuation of last night's?—one of those vivid cinematic flashes. She is up at the cabin on Lake George sitting on the dock sketching Jill, who is sunbathing naked, her body gleaming with baby oil. The sketch is coming along beautifully. Kendra can feel the familiar exhilarating impulse as it shoots up her right arm, across her chest, and upward to her brain.

"Whatever you do, Jill, don't move," she says in a cautious, excited whisper.

Then Lane calls out the kitchen window, "Anyone for tequila?" in the shrill party voice she never uses around men.

"Jillsie?" Lane shouts. "What about you? There's a little wormy-worm in the bottle and everything."

Suddenly, Jill sits up. "I get dibs on the worm!" And dashes off the dock into the house.

"Shit." Kendra looks down at the sketch pad. The drawing isn't as good as she thought. In fact, it's dreadful. Mercifully, it vanishes from the page. Then, one by one, they both vanish: first Lane, then Jill, leaving Kendra all alone on the dock.

The alarm went off again. She remembered the dream for only an instant before it faded like snowflakes on a dark sleeve, and just as quickly she analyzed it. They had both gotten married, first Lane, right after college, then Jill, only two years ago. It didn't take Sigmund Freud to figure that one out. She sat up and slipped the mask off. The first sight that met her eyes was the big print of Georgia O'Keeffe's lavender orchid that hung over the stove, spattered red across the bottom with old bubbled-over marinara. She took the glass stick out of her mouth and blinked blearily at the little numbers. 97.2.

"Now, do I know my body—or do I know my body?" she asked the empty loft.

For the past ten days since her period began, her temperature had been running around 96.7. Yesterday, it had dipped to 96.5, and today it shot up almost seven-tenths of a point. She had pinpointed it exactly, having ovulated sometime yesterday.

She reached down and felt between her legs. She was still moist and sticky. The clear mucus stretched elastically between her fingers like airplane glue, the better to conduct sperm upward into her womb. She was sticky, too, from his semen. Usually, she liked to wash a man out of her, but this morning she would refrain from bathing just in case any errant sperm might still be wriggling their way up the gluey corridor.

She set the thermometer down and reached for her old chenille robe, wrapping it around her as she scampered across the cold floor to the sink and filled the kettle. Late May sunlight tinged the dingy mesh-covered windows yellow, but not until noon, when it beat down through the twin skylights, would the loft be comfortably warm. She turned on the radio. WBAI crackled as she set the kettle on to boil, having to light the burner with a match. The pilot had been out since December when the spaghetti water boiled over. Last night she had meant to ask him to take a look at it. Anything that had to do with gas or electricity gave her the willies. It was no way, she realized, for a woman living alone to behave. Learned Helplessness. They gave courses in practically everything these days. Maybe the New School offered a seminar in Overcoming Learned Helplessness: everything from re-igniting a pilot light to changing a flat.

She spooned instant into a chipped delftware mug and, while waiting for the water to boil, slipped into a pair of paint-smeared dungarees and man's gray V-necked sweater that hung over the back of the kitchen chair. Not until she poked her head through the neck did she see the note lying on the table, written on the stationery her mother had given her for her last birthday; pale blue with dark blue engraving: **KENDRA MADISON • SKYLOFT • 125 BOUWERIE**. It had been her mother's idea to give this seedy loft a pretentious name. Her mother liked to name everything: houses, boats, cars, horses. She had plenty of all four, thanks to the Madison Millions, of which Kendra had not taken a penny since graduation. He had written the note with a stub of charcoal. She hadn't realized he had even left a note, only that he had left. After the last time they made love, she had fallen asleep, waking briefly to him leaning over and kissing her good-bye, apologizing that he had an early flight to catch. His leather jacket had smelled of fresh saddle soap.

She studied the note. He had nice handwriting—another plus. Was neat penmanship genetic or acquired? She had neat writing and so did her mother—or had she merely grown up imitating her mother in this if in no other respect?

> Kendra—
> Wow!
> This is a more than fabulous
> sendoff for me. You and your
> mean little machine were
> fan-fucking-tastic.

Fan-fucking. She didn't care for that. His speech was sometimes too trendy. What did she expect from a man she had picked up in the Broome Street Bar one night three weeks ago and seen only three times since? There was always something that kept her from completely accepting a man. She was never at a loss to detect those little things that, given enough importance, could undermine a relationship before it even began. But there was nothing wrong with the way he looked. He was tall —over six feet, a nice match for her lanky five-eight— with the kind of gold-streaked brown hair beauticians charge hundreds of dollars to create artificially, pale blue eyes, and a body that got its tone from work rather than working out. As a rule, she didn't like vain men. And he was smart. She knew that, too. He had graduated from Yale Drama, where he'd majored in set design. So he was creative, too, as well as good with his hands. Although she had never come out and asked him, she figured he was in his late twenties. A YUM. Now in her thirties, Kendra reluctantly conceded that most men she met in bars nowadays qualified as YUMs, young unattached males, as opposed to their wizened counterparts, MOMs, much older males, and MOMAs, much older males, attached. Then there were DORKs, drugged-out rich kids, and DOGs, drugged-out geezers. Sometimes, the acronyms were deceptive. For instance, BOD signified not a superior physical specimen, but bag of dirt, and SAP didn't mean a soft touch, but short abusive prick. Considering the categories, YUM was downright complimentary. And this YUM had the added virtue of being on his way out of town, leaving for Rome en route to the Spoleto Festival, and from there on to some extended gig in Asia. She might not see him for a year. She might not, in fact, ever see him again. He fit the profile perfectly.

She poured boiling water into her mug and added a few drops of condensed milk. Then she strolled across the loft to inspect the painting she had been working on yesterday just before she went off to the Broome Street Bar in her knock-me-down-and-fuck-me shoes and her slinky Norma Kamali that showed off the early tan she had picked up at the lake in March.

She was pleased with yesterday's work. Recently, she had formulated this theory that the work she did when she was ovulating was somehow better. She was developing a new technique: stretching canvas over three-dimensional armatures made out of forked branches, then slathering the canvas with layers of oil paint. She had filled the back of her old Saab with interesting sticks she had gathered up at the lake. The canvas stretched tautly over the wood often took on bold and primitive shapes, like ancient shields or banners. This one had a more graceful, peaceful conformation. She wondered what it was. Then, as the phone rang, she realized exactly what it was: the Stone Age Venus of Willendorf, one of the oldest fertility symbols in existence.

"So? How did it go?"

"Jill? Aren't you up early!"

Since the Bowery now depressed Jill, and Warren's triplex oppressed Kendra, they sustained their friendship primarily over the phone.

"Yeah, well, I got up to throw up."

"Sounds like you're 'pregnant and lovin' it,' " said Kendra, quoting the title of one of Jill's pregnancy self-help books that particularly tickled her fancy. "Also sounds like you're eating for the first time in weeks."

"I am. Saltines. You're supposed to eat right after you puke. Isn't that special? That way the vitamins get into your bloodstream before you puke them out again."

"I wasn't aware that saltines had any vitamins."

"Are you going to read me a lecture on nutrition or give me the YUM report?"

"Not if the Fat Boy's panting on the extension."

"The Fat Boy gets out of the house as early as he can these days. Preferably before my first wretch of the day. Apparently, he finds the impulse contagious."

"Parallel puking. A new phenomenon."

"He's so parallel, any day now I expect him to start showing."

"Tell me about it. That boy started showing months ago."

"You know the type. Two days after the first missed period and he's off to Mothercare for the works."

When Jill's home pregnancy test came out positive two days after her missed period and thirteen days after making love without birth control, Kendra was the first person she told. From that moment five weeks ago, Kendra had made up her mind to get pregnant herself. That she had no husband—not even a remote prospect—seemed beside the point.

"So how did it go with the GAS?"

Kendra could hear Jill crunch her saltine.

"The what?"

"You know, genetically acceptable specimen."

"Terrific. We did it three times."

"Three times!" Jill echoed wistfully. "I can't remember the last time we had a triple header. It's all Warren can do these days to lick it once, shudder, and shove it in. Then it's strictly Trickle City."

"Obviously, a trickle is all it took."

"I guess even his sperm are experts. So what do you think?"

"I wouldn't know. I've never seen his sperm."

"We're talking about the YUM, not the Fat Boy. Do you think it took? Are you knocked up? I want you to know that I have no intention of going through this thing without you."

Kendra glanced across the room at her own rendition of the Venus of Willendorf and said, "I'd say it's in the bag. Or should I say womb?"

$\mathcal{L}$ouise

Louise Rosen tried to make herself heard over the rising chaos in her kitchen: the five-year-old riding his hot rod scooter around and around the table, the three-year-old up on the counter banging the top of the microwave with wooden spoons, the littlest, naked, waving her shit-smeared diaper over her head like a victory flag and screaming at the top of her eighteen-month-old lungs. It was the au pair's day off, and the housekeeper's sister was in the hospital for surgery.

"I said *two percent!*" she shouted into the receiver, plugging her free ear with a well-manicured forefinger. "Last time you brought home whole milk and I can't drink whole anymore. It tastes like cream!"

"Jeez, Louise, what's going on over there? It sounds like the Mau Mau uprising."

He was only teasing her, still, tears pricked the backs of her eyes. The headache she had awoken to this morning had only worsened.

"It's Francine's day off, remember? I'm here alone?"

"Yeah, well, whose fault is that?"

He had offered to bring in somebody to spell Francine on her one day off, but Louise had refused. She felt pampered enough as it was compared to her friends in the park, most of whom had at least two kids and no help whatsoever, even from their husbands. Here she was, with two live-ins, a French au pair and a Portuguese housekeeper, and a husband who offered to pick up groceries on the way home from work. Of course, it helped that he owned a food store. Louise had trouble imagining what life for her park friends must be like—life without help.

"Yeah," Marty had once pointed out, "but they don't have Irish triplets."

Irish triplets: three kids in three years. Was it her fault that her husband had an inexhaustible sexual appetite, emissions that exploded even industrial-strength condoms, and she was allergic to every form of birth control on the market? Pills, foams, creams, tassaways, diaphragms, five different varieties of IUD—she had tried them all. Now she was back on the diaphragm again. She kept three of them in the medicine cabinet and alternated them. Since her husband could be depended upon to want sex with her at least once a day every day of the month except for the first day of her period, when her flow was so heavy even he drew the line, she once calculated that there were only about eight hours during any given month when she did not walk around with that wet, spermicide-reeking sneaker inside her.

"Just don't forget the two percent," she said weakly, "and a dozen oranges. Zack's getting another cold and he's been eating them all morning."

"Sure thing, Weezie. Gotta go now. I got a complaint here about some arugula with frost spots. I'll try to be home on time."

She hung up knowing it was doubtful he would be home before nine o'clock. Over the last four years, he had transformed a single storefront deli into a three-storefront, two-story gourmet-food emporium with the insufferable name of Truffles-n-Stuff that was, on the Upper West Side, the only rival to Zabar's. Selling both retail and wholesale to the finest restaurants in the five boroughs, the store had been written up in everything from *Esquire* to the *Voice* to *Food & Wine* to *Travel & Leisure*, and he himself had been touted as the Boy Wonder of the Fancy Food Trade. He was thinking of opening branches in San Francisco and in Boston's Fanueil Hall. "Not bad," he liked to say, "for a kid who started out in the Rag Trade."

Louise had met Marty Rosen seven years ago when they were both starting out at New York's Fashion Institute of Technology. He had founded a punk clothing business with two seniors called Street Smarts and had sold out to his partners on graduating for over a million dollars. He was working on his second million when he asked Louise to marry him. By the time Zack was born, he was well into his fourth. Louise's father, Barney "Top" Topolsky, the Toyota salesman from Valley Stream, liked to say with more than a hint of grudging admiration, "The kid's got the friggin' touch."

As Louise put a pot of water on to boil, she reflected on her good fortune. Her kids ate hand-stuffed tortellini and pâté, whereas she had grown up on Chef Boyardee and chuck meat loaf. They owned a seven-bedroom apartment on Riverside Drive with a drop-dead view of the river and twenty-four-hour doormen to help her unfold and load the double stroller. They had a house in Bridgehampton and went to Bermuda every Christmas. She even had a VIP membership to the Vertical Club, where three times over she had managed to restore her five-foot-five voluptuous body to its former tone. And for their fifth anniversary last year he had bought her a mid-calf-length sable coat which she was too embarrassed to wear anywhere but out to dinner once a week with him, somewhat inappropriate since Marty eschewed the type of gourmet restaurant his store catered to in favor of low-key bars that served up a good cheeseburger, chili, and fries. Why, Marty had even offered to set her up in her own business. After Bruce was born, she started sewing appliqué pictures on kids' sweatshirts. Dragons and alligators and little train engines. Through Marty's contacts she had sold some orders on consignment to Bendel's and to small shops in Soho and Chelsea, all of whom had sold out and reordered. After Mary was born, she didn't have the energy to meet the orders until about ten months ago when she had started a new line—Weezie's Wonderwear—this time buying white goods down on Orchard Street and dying them herself in bright candy colors. But she had had to stop when winter set in because there was not a

34

single week when one of the kids did not come down with a cold, or the flu, or the pox. And when Francine succumbed to mono just after Christmas, she had nearly caved in.

"Let Francine take care of Francine," Marty had said when he came home at the end of the day to find her gaunt and haggard from waiting on a household of invalids all day.

But in many ways Francine, only eighteen, was a kid herself: a five-foot feather-weight gamine with a tough, wistful way about her that only made Louise want to mother her, too.

"You're too easy on her," Marty would say. "And too hard on yourself."

"Mary, leave your ear alone, sweetie pie."

Sitting in her highchair, Mary, with straight brown shining bangs and wide-spaced green eyes, was a pint-sized replica of her mother. After the third ear infection this year, the pediatrician had inserted a plastic tube to drain off the fluid. It seemed to be working, except that Mary was forever fussing and batting at it. Louise didn't blame her. She set down a bowl of tortellini before her, hoping food would distract her.

"Look, sweetie pie, 'leenies. Dig in."

Ever so delicately, as if selecting hors d'oeuvres from a tray at a very fancy affair, Mary picked one and nibbled at it thoughtfully.

"Cut it out, Zack."

Zack was busily inserting a tortellini up his nose to get a laugh out of his little brother, who was giggling and clapping.

"Look, Brucie. Boogers. I'm gonna eat my boogers."

"I said stop it, Zack."

It was hard to stop Zack once he had his audience going. Ever since Louise could remember, the kid would do anything for a laugh. Marty called him the Henny Youngman of Riverside Drive, which wasn't far from the truth. Now he was trying variations: a tortellini moustache, earrings, and eyes.

"Try eating it, huh, Zackie?"

She pushed Bruce's booster seat farther back on the chair. Last month it had slipped off and Bruce's upper lip had split on the table edge, requiring three stitches. Louise turned her back on the three long enough to look at the To Do's scrawled on today's calendar for June 1: *pediatrician* (to remove Mary's shunt and check to see if the white spots on Bruce's chest were fungus or just dry skin); *Bloomies* (for sneakers for the boys and summer clothes for all three, then up to the toy department for a present for the birthday party Zack was invited to this Saturday. Naturally, she would wind up having to buy all three of them a little something to assuage their jealousy.) Then across to the park for the requisite daily fresh air and home for children's tea. It had been Francine who introduced children's tea to the Rosen household. Francine had done a stint as an au pair in London the year before emigrating to America. The idea of feeding children separately at four-thirty so that they could be bathed, read to, and tucked in before the grown-ups sat down to eat in peace was, to Louise, the height of civilization.

"Mommy, Mommy!" Zack shrieked and Louise spun around.

"Look at Brucie! He got a tortellini stuck up his nose!"

Louise stretched out in the extra-long apricot tub just off the master bedroom, sipping Dry Sack and depressurizing from the day's insanity, compounded by a side trip to the emergency ward at St. Luke's-Roosevelt Hospital to remove the shredded tortellini from Bruce's right nostril. Fortunately, her headache had disappeared in the excitement. She had just done forty-five minutes of Advanced Janes in front of the VCR. Francine's day off was the only day of the week she didn't make it to the Vertical Club, and she was always conscientious about exercising on her own. She had been interrupted only three times by Bruce and Zack alternately popping out of bed with requests to pee, get a drink of water, and remove the toy Godzilla from the top shelf, where it cast menacing shadows across their ceiling. With Magda off tonight, Louise was serving Doxsee Clam Chowder doctored with canned baby clams and left-over boiled russets, and club sandwiches. Of course, not just any club sandwiches but club sandwiches the way they were served at the Savoy in London, where they stayed last spring when Marty had gone to inspect Harrod's world-famous food halls. She was grateful that Marty, surrounded as he was all day with the world's most exotic foods, was an undemanding eater.

She took another sip of sherry, closed her eyes, and leaned back in the tub. Yes, she was a very lucky woman. A warm, loving husband, three beautiful healthy kids, the youngest soon to be out of diapers. Three was the perfect number. At least that was what Marty thought. She could just as easily go on to have four or five.

She loved babies, loved their smell, like fresh laundry; loved their noises, like exotic birds; loved the feel of their soft, smooth skin and the weight of them riding on her shoulder or her hip. She even liked being pregnant: the way her body swelled by the day, the feel of those first finny kicks growing harder and bonier by the day. And her labors had all been relatively easy and uncomplicated—"by the book," Dr. Berry called them—each lasting no longer than eight hours. She could easily have more babies. But Marty was adamantly set against it, having been the fourth and last child himself and feeling as if he were his parents' afterthought. When she asked him very nicely if, that being the case, he would consider having his tubes tied, or whatever it was men did to stem the flow of sperm, he said *no way*. The guy who did his books had had that operation and hadn't been able to get it up ever since.

Louise contemplated the soggy diaphragm resting on the edge of the tub. She was twenty-six years old. If she was anything like her mother, menopause wouldn't come until she was at least fifty-five. Thirty years—no, she calculated silently, make that 10,590 days—of walking around with a wet sneaker between her legs? It was enough to drive a woman to tie her own tubes. But Marty was against that, too. What if, God forbid, something should happen to one of their kids?

Louise sighed, drained her sherry to the dregs, and, feeling pleasantly tipsy and rosy from her bath, emerged to pat herself dry with an apricot bath sheet. As she regarded herself in the full-length mirror on the door, she was not dissatisfied. Three times her body had been taken over, and not a single stretch mark or residual bulge betrayed her. She might even be able to fit into her string bikini this summer. Just out of curiosity, she went to her top dresser drawer and took out the black bikini bathing suit she had picked up in Martinique on their honeymoon. Slipping it on, she was pleased to see that she looked better in it now than she had then. Before she married, she had never worked out a single day in her life, but 1,800 visits to the Vertical Club later...

She struck a few *Playboy* poses in the vanity mirror, swaying her back and sticking out her breasts.

"Not bad," she said aloud to her reflection.

"Are you kidding?" Her husband stood in the doorway, unbuttoning his shirt. "You're the best there is."

She spun around in surprise. "Marty! You're early!"

"Surprise," he said, coming toward her. He was a smallish man, only an inch taller than she, with a nice build, curly hair like a faun, and a prick that belonged on a porn star. "I was hungry."

"I'll get dinner," she said, but he backed her up against the vanity table.

"I think I'm in the mood for hors d'oeuvres first."

He slid down the strap of her bra and took her erect nipple into his mouth. "Mmmmmmmm," he said, "bing cherries. Red and ripe."

"Marty!"

He moved aside the elastic on the crotch of her bikini. "Mmmmm. I think I'll browse for truffles."

Next thing she knew, she was sitting on the glass top of her vanity table, legs flung over his shoulders.

"What makes you so delectable?" he asked.

"What makes you so horny? You'd think you hadn't had it in a month."

"Guess it's a vicious cycle."

"Oooooooh!" Louise leaned back against the mirror, no longer coherent. Over a thousand times they had made love and still, he had that power over her.

"We're going to break the mirror, Marty."

"I don't care. I'm crazy about you."

She found herself thinking again of her friends in the park, whose husbands sometimes went for months without touching them. Forget the beach house, forget the mink coat, forget—at this moment—even the kids. This was why she was such a lucky woman. Because after seven years of sleeping with her, Marty Rosen still wanted her tonight as much as he had that first night he had taken her virginity in the dark on the couch in her parents' living room.

She felt her body temperature rising, fogging the mirror beneath her, behind her. If one of the kids should wake up and come in right now, if the building caught on fire and the entire fire brigade came rushing in, if the doorbell rang and all three phones started ringing at once, she wouldn't care. All she wanted was to be filled with him, bursting with him, just like this.

"Seven years' bad luck!" she reminded him breathlessly.

"Who cares?" he gasped. "Isn't it worth it?"

She heard a crack as the glass gave way beneath her.

"Shit!" she said.

"Don't worry," he panted, "it's six inches away from your gorgeous ass. You're still safe."

"That's what you think," she said.

He stopped moving inside her.

"I forgot to put in my diaphragm," she added in a small voice.

He pulled away from her and slapped his forehead. "Jeez, Louise! You're kidding."

"Marty, honey, would I kid about a thing like that?"

Carleen

At a certain point, it became impossible for Carleen Donovan to concentrate on the manuscript in her lap. The conversation between the two women sitting across from her in the waiting room eventually drove her to lift her head and eye the source.

Both women were huge with child—about to pop, as Carleen's own mother, herself the mother of five, liked to put it. The woman dominating the conversation couldn't have been petite even under normal circumstances, but now she was grotesquely enlarged, reduced to wearing an extra large set of gray sweats, whose seams she strained.

"Twins," she explained to anyone who stared at her too hard.

"Better you than me," was the usual response.

"How do you think my husband feels? We've got four at home already, the oldest in fifth grade. They can't wait." She shifted her enormity and groaned. "Me, neither."

"Listen," the woman next to her said, "count yourself lucky. You've got four—six—healthy kids. My sister-in-law, she just had her sixth miscarriage. Count 'em."

"Six! God almighty. Why doesn't she give up? I had one at eight weeks and another in my second trimester, and I can tell you it was no fun. I had to have a D and C, the works."

"Four of the six come out dead," the other went on. "They did an autopsy on the fetuses. There was something wrong with them, know what I mean? If you ask me, those two just aren't meant to have children. I have another girlfriend . . ." The woman rattled on.

Carleen shook her head and looked back at the manuscript. What was it about the waiting rooms of obstetricians that gave rise to such horror stories? It was as if these women, bursting with the life growing within them, felt irresistibly drawn to discuss deformity, catastrophe, and death.

"You think *that's* bad," the mother of twins put in, "my girlfriend, she had two misses in the fifth month. The third time, her doctor sewed her up."

"I heard of that. They stick a plug in you, don't they?"

The other woman nodded sagely. "She had to lie down for the last four months. Four months on her back with her husband waiting on her. The kid came out okay, but gee, sometimes you wonder, maybe the Lord just didn't mean for her to, you know..."

How many times had Carleen turned to Bill after feeling the twinges that signaled the onslaught of her period, or after returning from the bathroom, having thrust up that first burningly dry tampon, and said, "Maybe it just wasn't meant to be."

Carleen Donovan was forty years old. She and her husband had been trying steadily for over seven years now to conceive a child. As editor-in-chief and co-publisher at one of the most successful small book publishers in New York, she had experienced so far more happiness and fulfillment in her job than most women—and many men— could expect to in a career lifetime. If it were up to her, she would have given up on having children years ago. But Bill was determined.

They had been to dozens of specialists. She had been poked, prodded, examined, analyzed, worked-up, and counseled by the best of them.

It had started out simply enough. She charted her basal body temperature every day for a year. She seemed to be ovulating regularly. Then she submitted herself to an internal exam two hours after she and Bill had made love to find out whether her mucus was "hostile" to Bill's sperm. As it turned out, her mucus and Bill's sperm were on friendly terms. Then she checked into the hospital and underwent an excruciatingly painful test called the hysterosalpinogram, during which dye was injected through her cervix into the uterine cavity and out the Fallopian tubes while an X-ray was taken to detect abnormality in the uterine cavity or fibers in her Fallopian tubes. On successive occasions, she had subjected herself to a laparoscopy, an endometrial biopsy, a serum-progesterone test, a thyroid profile, a serum FSH and LH test, and ultrasound. Nor had her husband escaped the scrutiny of specialists and the cold eyes of technicians. Over half a dozen times he had been required to masturbate and ejaculate into a sterile glass vial, whereupon his semen was evaluated for sperm count, sperm motility, sperm viability, sperm morphology, clumping, and, last but not least, agglutination.

After every work-up, Carleen found herself praying they would find something wrong, if only so it could be fixed, or not fixed if that were the case...just so they could *get on with their lives!* But as far as any of the tests could reveal or any of the specialists could determine, there was absolutely nothing wrong with either her or Bill and no reason why they couldn't have children.

Unless maybe it just wasn't meant to be.

Finally, early last spring, she had jumped up and run out of a pre-sales meeting. In the ladies room she found a bloody mess in her panties: Her period had arrived two days early. She burst into tears, unable to return to the meeting. Eventually, they sent one of the secretaries in to see what was the matter. "There's nothing the matter," she told the concerned young woman. But she had wanted to add, "I just can't seem to get pregnant. And it's ruining my life."

That night she came home and told Bill she was abandoning Operation Baby Donovan. But Bill, a sportswriter at the *Times*, pleaded with her to hang in there just a little while longer. There was, it turned out, one specialist in New York they had not yet tried. A guy in his office recommended him. The guy and his wife had been trying for ten years before they went to Dr. Sam Fitzwater, an infertility expert who specialized in artificial insemination and worked in a group practice with several garden-variety ob-gyns. Now they had a beautiful baby daughter. "The guy claims he has a green thumb," Bill said. "A likely story," Carleen said. But she agreed to go see him. Today was the third month in a row they were trying AIH, artificial insemination by husband, as opposed to AID, artificial insemination by donor. If it didn't work this time, they would have to consider trying something even more complicated and expensive.

In one of the many little offices in back, her husband now sat flipping through the pages of a coffee table book on Chinese erotic art in an attempt to arouse himself. The previous two times he had used *Penthouse.*

"No wonder the insemination didn't take," he had joked last night. "I summoned pervey sperm. This time we can't miss. We're a class act."

With the best intentions in the world, Fitzwater had told Carleen she could go into the little room with Bill to "help" him. But she had demurred, knowing it would make her feel tawdry and pathetic, like a convict's wife on visiting day.

Bill didn't mind going it alone. In fact, he seemed to enjoy it. "Kind of takes me back to my youth. Annette Funicello, where are you now?"

Poor Bill, Carleen reflected. He was so sweet. Such a good sport.

"Mrs. Donovan."

The receptionist had slid open the glass window and stuck her head into the waiting room.

"It's your office, again," she added with a smug smile. "You can come take it in here."

The other women in the waiting room stopped talking and stared at Carleen as she got up to take the call. "It's your pimp," the receptionist might have said. Didn't any of these women work in offices? Had the Women's Movement been only a dream?

"Thanks." Carleen sat in the straight-backed chair next to the receptionist's desk and unclipped her left earring.

"Carleen Donovan here."

All around her young women in crisp white jackets bustled to and fro, carrying file folders, transporting vials of urine and test-tube trays of blood, thick and oily as perfume.

"I'm sorry, Carleen."

It was Randy, her assistant of five years.

"Don't be sorry, Randy." It was only the second time he had called her in the last half hour.

"It's Mitch Michaelman again."

"Why aren't I surprised?"

Two months ago, Carleen had managed to lure the best-selling author of spy thrillers away from the competition. From the day they had started contract negotiations, he had been nothing but trouble.

"It's limousines this time."

"Limousines," she repeated dully. "Last time it was masseuses."

"He says he wants a stretch limo—with a wet bar, TV, video recorder, and phone—at his disposal twenty-four hours a day every day he's on his book tour."

"We discussed this. I told him it wouldn't be a problem."

"Yes, Carly, but he wants it *on paper.*"

"And did you explain to him that my esteemed co-publisher refuses, on principle, to make such guarantees *on paper?*"

"I explained, I explained." Randy sounded bored.

Carleen sighed. "Tell him I'll put it in his contract." She was beginning to rue the day of her big coup, when she had taken Mitch Michaelman out to lunch at Le Cirque and flattered him shamelessly through appetizers, four courses, three whiskey-sodas, and two truly noxious Cuban cigars.

"But what about—"

"I'll deal with Hugh tomorrow. He's the one who wanted Michaelman in the first place. He's got to understand that if he wants stars on his list, he's got to roll out the red carpet. Anything else before I wax into yet another cliché?"

"Nothing important."

"Come on, Randy."

"Well," Randy began reluctantly, "Harmon was just in here."

Harmon Josephs was her brilliant but highly temperamental art director.

"And?"

"He threatened to quit if he has to design another convention booth this year."

"Was he staging a fit or did he sound like he meant it?"

"Sounded sincere to me. He says Simon and Schuster uses an outside vendor."

"Did you remind him that we did, too, three years ago, and the results were disastrous?"

"He said if you give him the fifty-thou you pay a vendor, he'll be happy to do it."

She couldn't let this one ride. "Tell him to come to my office for tea this afternoon. Order those fancy cookies he likes and make sure we have that tea he drinks that tastes like old smoked saddlebags."

"Roger Willco, but I thought you were going to be tied up, so to speak."

Randy knew all about her insemination.

"It's not major surgery, Rand. I can come back today... if necessary." She hung up and stared at the phone. If this is how everyone behaved when she was out of the office for a single morning, how would they survive when she was on maternity leave? She wiped that unlikely possibility from her mind as she looked up and found Sam Fitzwater standing before her, beaming.

"There she is! And here I went all the way out to the waiting room to fetch her personally. I should have known she was on the phone."

"Hi," she said, feeling suddenly queasy.

"It's that magic time again, Carleen!"

Dispirited, she followed him into his mahogany-paneled office with its Braque print flanked by five framed diplomas. He sank into his brown leather Eames chair and folded his arms behind his head, Iacocca-style.

"Well, your boy Bill really outdid himself today, Carleen. You might say," he added with a chuckle, "he rose to the occasion. We're washing his sperm right now."

She resisted the impulse to ask him if they were dirty. Instead: "Is he still around?"

"No, he had to get back to the office. The Mets are playing the Cubs this afternoon," he reminded her.

She never saw Bill in the office during these visits. It was as if Fitzwater deep down wanted to keep them separated, as in some kind of tribal mating ritual when the couple must be kept apart a given amount of time in order for the magic to work.

"We did a split ejaculation today, Carleen," he went on. "But he seems to have quite a lively count in both batches, so..." He stopped and looked at her kindly. "How are you feeling, Carleen?"

Had she met Sam Fitzwater at a cocktail party, she would have considered herself his equal, each having attained a certain standing in their respective fields. But because this was his field they were playing in now, she felt humble, stupid, stripped of her dignity.

"A little discouraged."

"Now, Carleen," he chided her, "we've spoken about this before. You know my philosophy. A is E."

"Attitude is everything," she said before he could.

"Why don't you go and get ready? I'm going to give you a few minutes to yourself before I come in."

"To work on my attitude?"

"No," he laughed shortly, "I've got a woman in hysterics waiting for me to phone her back. I can tell you why because I know you're level-headed enough to take it the right way. I successfully inseminated her last year with her husband's sperm and now she's claiming I used the wrong sperm because her kid isn't smiling on schedule."

"Is that possible? I mean, that you could inject someone with the wrong sperm?"

"Anything's possible, Carleen." He smiled roguishly. "Including getting you pregnant."

Carleen lay on the table, naked from the waist down, with her legs spread, her feet already in the stirrups, and a white paper sheet over her knees. She stared up at the mobile of brightly colored birds revolving slowly in the soft warm breeze blowing in through the air duct. It was not unlike a crib toy. Were women, in the eyes of the medical profession, nothing more than big babies, to be coddled and distracted by brightly colored mobiles?

"That hardly constitutes improved attitude," she scolded herself, just as Fitzwater and a nurse bustled into the room. The nurse carried a tray which held a catheter tube and a vial full of viscous liquid. Fitzwater and the nurse were discussing the procedure. Carleen returned her attention to the birds. She didn't need to hear it. She knew it so well that, if called upon, she could probably assist as efficiently as the nurse. He wheeled up a low stool, switched on the lamp, and directed it between her legs. She felt its heat, like a small sun. The speculum was cool, a far cry from Bill's fingers.

"Good girl!" he told her. "You're nice and relaxed."

She found herself thinking of a story she had heard over lunch last week with one of her authors, a gay man. It seems a couple of lesbian friends of his were having a baby, using the donated sperm of another gay man.

"They inseminated her on the kitchen table—with a turkey baster. It was strictly a do-it-yourself operation. But it worked!"

"Okay, now, Carleen," Fitzwater was saying, "I'm inserting the tube."

She felt a small pinch. Maybe a turkey baster would be more effective and less uncomfortable.

"And now I'm injecting Bill's semen into your cervical canal. Say 'welcome' to the little fellas."

She felt a coolness down there, a sensation of rushing as when she douched. She kept her breathing shallow and regular, wanting her muscles down there to remain receptive to Bill's "little fellas," even though the progesterone in his semen had brought on cramps.

"Today," he went on, "I'm going to insert a small cap or plug. It's got a string attached to it, like a tampon. This afternoon, oh, around five o'clock, you may go to the little girls' room and remove the cap yourself. By then, Bill's little guys will have had sufficient contact with your cervix."

He removed the speculum and switched off the light, handing the discarded tube and vial to the nurse.

"Just lie here now and listen to Bach. Twenty minutes should do it."

He had asked her what music she would like to have today. Last month she had complained of having to lie there through twenty minutes of Easy Listening. Brahms, she had requested. Thoughtfully, he had gone out and bought her a tape of the Brahms Symphony No. 4 in E Minor, Opus 98. He really wasn't a bad man. Just a little patronizing.

"It's Brahms," she patronized him right back, "and thanks."

"Well, Carleen." He grinned and snapped off his sheer rubber gloves. "I don't want to get your hopes up or anything, but I want you to know that I'm feeling mighty lucky today."

PART II

First Trimester

Louise

It was a Saturday morning in June. The kids were out in Bridgehampton with Francine and Magda. Marty Rosen rolled over expecting to find the usual warm, moist welcome between his wife's legs and was disappointed to find she had barred the way with one hand.

"Marty, please," she said. She couldn't explain it or understand it, but ever since she had found out she was pregnant, it hurt to have sex.

He sighed and rolled off her onto his back. "Boy, oh, boy."

They both stared down at his insistent erection. "Any brilliant ideas, Weezie?"

"Maybe we could try it the way we did the other night?"

"Okay." He sounded discouraged.

Louise dutifully took off her nightgown and lay on her back while Marty straddled her, his penis resting between her breasts. He began to move up and down, squeezing her breasts together tightly.

"Ouch, Marty," she said after a while.

"What? What?" He opened his eyes and stared at her, having been dragged down from a considerable height.

"You're resting your full weight on me, my breasts are very tender, and you're hurting me. That's what."

"Okay, how about this?"

He rose up on his knees and nudged her lips with the tip of himself. Slowly, inch by inch, she took him into her mouth.

"Oh, yeah!" He began to move in and out of her, bracing himself on the carved oak headboard. "Suck me. Suck me hard, baby. Easy now. Tongue the tip. That's it. Now give me some teeth. Not too much. Just a little. Nibbles, yeah!"

She followed his instructions to the letter, her eyes wide open and terrified.

"Here it comes!" he announced. "Oh, baby, here it comes!"

As he spent himself in her mouth in a series of quaking spasms, Louise began to gag on the warm metallic-tasting slime. She pushed him off her and made a run for the bathroom, where she threw up last night's ribs and fries, which hadn't been sitting any too well to begin with.

"Jesus!" she heard him say from the other room. "I'll sure be glad when this is all over."

Louise raised her head from the bowl and leaned over the sink, splashing cold water on her face. She stared at her flushed reflection.

"And speaking of which," he went on, "have you made that appointment yet?"

"No," she said, making a nasty face in the mirror, "I haven't."

"Better do it soon, Weezie. The longer you wait, the harder it will be...on all parties concerned. You hear what I'm saying?"

"I hear you," she said. But she had no intention of calling the abortion clinic to make an appointment. If he wanted to get rid of this baby so badly, he could pick up the phone and make the call himself.

Jill

It was on a sparkling day in the second week of June that Jill ventured out of the apartment for the first time since early May. When she had gone to ground five weeks ago, the flower boxes along West 12th had been filled with daffodils and tulips, stiff and bright as lollipops. Now they were stocked with impatiens and lush banks of rose geraniums. This morning the tiny postage-sized lawns shone like emeralds and the freshly hosed sidewalks glistened in the sun. Only when she passed the open door of a restaurant from which there emanated the smell of stale beer, cigarette smoke, and disinfectant did her stomach begin to rise. But she took deep breaths, fought it down, and kept right on walking. She had an appointment at the midwife clinic at eleven o'clock. Having had to break two previous appointments because she was too ill to get out of bed, she was determined to make this one. After all, according to her calculations, she was nine weeks pregnant—and it was high time to have it validated.

She spied her reflection in the plate-glass window of a beauty parlor: a small, dark woman with curly hair worn in the style of a Thirties movie star, bounding along in a pair of size-eight jeans, turquoise silk tunic, and gold gladiator sandals, a hot-pink shawl flung over one shoulder. She hadn't been able to fit into a size-eight anything in five years. It seemed strange, being pregnant and having shed over ten pounds. But it was not surprising considering that there had been days over the past weeks when she had thrown up no fewer than a dozen times. Although she was now down to a single dizzy dry heave first thing in the morning, her stomach muscles were still tender to the touch and her ribcage felt frail and insubstantial. When she had called the clinic to cancel, she reported her impressive statistics and was told, "No problem. Nothing to worry about. For some women, this is normal." Throwing up every hour on the hour, normal? Warren had come home from the office one day to find her in the bathroom and bellowed his congratulations through the keyhole.

"Ben Thurman's wife's doctor says the more you throw up, the better. It means the thing's taking."

"That's easy for Ben Thurman's wife's doctor to say," Jill gasped, staggering back to bed, making sure that none of his pillows had fallen onto her side. Warren's pillows smelled of stale beer and sometimes all it took was an inadvertent whiff to send her hurtling back to the tile chamber. Still, it seemed puzzling to her that the other four times she had been pregnant she had never felt so much as a hint of queasiness.

"It's because your body knows this one's for keeps," Warren explained to her cockily, cracking open a Stroh's and settling down to watch the Mets.

The midwife clinic, one of the first and best in the country, was part of the ob-gyn Department of Hudson River General Hospital. As she made her way through the labyrinth of disinfectant-stinking halls, following the endless little arrows and numbers, directing her this way and that, she tried to close down all her senses save sight. Ever since she was a little girl, Jill had hated hospitals. She was eight years old when her mother first came down with headaches so severe she would have to lie down in a darkened room with a cold cloth over her eyes. When Jill was ten, her mother was rushed to the hospital one day while Jill was in school. Two days later, after school, her big sister Cheryl had taken her to Ray's Place for a milkshake. Sixteen, with a gorgeous figure, a wardrobe of mohair sweaters, and a boyfriend in college, Cheryl was a regular at Ray's.

"Mommy's got a lump in her brain the size of a walnut," Cheryl explained. "It's growing every day and as it grows it puts pressure on her skull."

"Why can't they just take it out?" Jill wanted to know.

"What do you think she's doing in the hospital? Getting a nose job? They're going to try." Somebody had put Dion on the jukebox: "My Little Runaway." "But maybe they won't be able to get it out. Or maybe they'll get it out but it will grow right back like weeds."

"What then...?" Jill's coffee milkshake had long since turned to watery suds.

"Then"—Cheryl smiled sadly—"let's look up."

In the days that followed, when Jill had to explain to her friends what was happening to her mother, she found the phrase *Let's look up* came in quite handy. If she or anyone else mentioned the word *die* or *death* in connection with her mother, she was guaranteed to cry. And crying in public was not something she was willing to do.

It was easier for Cheryl. She was practically a grown-up herself and would be moving out of the house in a couple of years. It couldn't be soon enough for Cheryl. Ever since Jill could remember, Cheryl and her mother had fought: over boys, over school work, over clothes, over the amount of time Cheryl spent on the phone or in the backseat of her boyfriend's Bel-Air.

"Count yourself lucky," Cheryl always used to say after she and her mother had had a major round. "By the time she gets to you, all the fight will be out of her."

Jill remembered the daily visits to the hospital. Many times, her father, who struggled along in the city as a salesman, would have to work late and would call home to tell the girls they should go on to the hospital without him. Cheryl, who had her learner's permit, would drive them illegally in the family station wagon to the hospital, where they were not, according to the rules, allowed to visit without adult supervision. Somehow, going against the rules made the whole routine more bearable, raising it to the condition of adventure. It wasn't the cancer killing their mother that was the enemy. It was the cops if they caught them on the road, or the nurses if they caught them in the hall. Giddy with fear and excitement, Cheryl and Jill would sneak up the echoing stairwell to the fourth floor, tiptoeing down the long buffed linoleum corridors the color of bruised banana, smelling of disinfectant and the flatulence of the sick. They would tiptoe past the open doors where shrunken old men lay propped up on pillows, moaning through parched lips; where fat women in bandages wept like babies, begging absent doctors for painkillers. Jill always tried her hardest not to look, to keep her eyes straight ahead on the double swinging doors at the end of the corridor. But Cheryl would tug at Jill's sleeve and drag her over to stare at some particularly wretched specimen. Once, it had been a man, not much older than a boy, with no legs, lying on his back waving his gauze-wrapped stumps in the air like feelers. The gauze on one stump was bloody.

When they came to the nurses' station just before the swinging doors, they had to duck and crawl past the counter, hoping that the nurses had their attention on the charts or medications. Once, years later, Cheryl had told Jill that the nurses almost always saw them but let them pass anyway, taking pity on the two daughters of the woman who lay dying in Room 418.

They never came without bringing something—papers from school, drawings, photographs of themselves, little bouquets of flowers from their mother's own garden, which they were trying their best to keep weeded, and always prunes or some other dried fruit, for she claimed the hospital diet constipated her. Lying sunken into the pillows, their mother looked wasted, her head shaved and swaddled in a lopsided turban of bandages, her voice tiny and faraway sounding. She would tell the girls to take good care of their father, ask about their grades and their friends. Once, when Cheryl left the room to get ice for the water pitcher, her mother asked Jill if Cheryl was still seeing that college boy.

"Oh, no!" Jill reassured her fervently, the lie coming so easily to her now that she knew her mother would never get out of the hospital to discover it. "They broke up ages ago."

At the bedside, her small hand sweating in her mother's cool, dry one, Jill prayed for the visit to be over with. They never lasted longer than ten minutes. Her mother tired easily and there was always some nurse coming in to take their mother's blood pressure or to give her pain-killers. Yet they seemed to Jill to go on forever, especially toward the end, when her mother's head had swollen to the size of a beachball and her once big beautiful blue eyes blinked sightlessly at the fluorescent lights above.

After their visit, Jill and Cheryl crept back down the hall and downstairs to the telephone booths near the gift shop, where Cheryl liked to call her boyfriend in his dorm room and flirt with him. Cheryl's boyfriend had taught her how to make free calls. By taking a razor blade and slicing through the thin plastic sheathing of the receiver wire and then touching the exposed metal to the metal edge of the coin-return slot—presto!—you got a dial tone. When her boyfriend was out with friends or at the library, Cheryl called her best girlfriend, who had moved away the year before to Tucson. Jill usually dialed her own best friend, a mere local call, and always felt it was a shame that she didn't know someone who lived farther away— Paris, for instance, or Moscow—so that she could dial for free and say to them, "Hi, I'm here at the hospital. My mother is dying." She imagined herself crying into the receiver, her forehead pressed to the glazed yellow-brick wall so no one would see her.

The day her mother died, Jill sat on the living room couch while her father wept into a dish towel, unaware that his elder daughter had gone out for a long ride with her boyfriend. That night, Cheryl crawled into Jill's bed and confessed that she had, that very day, lost her virgin-ity. She proceeded to relate to Jill every detail of her de-flowering. From that day on, it would always be hard for Jill not to associate death with sex. "You and Woody Allen," Kendra liked to say. "The hymen and the shroud."

* * *

The midwife clinic was an oasis within the dingy green-walled desert of the hospital. On the freshly painted white walls hung matted black-and-white photographs of nude women proudly patting their enormous distended bellies, nude women panting and sweating in labor while their husbands supported them with pillows, and babies slithering through their mother's vaginas into the world. She couldn't imagine Warren being anything but grossed out by these pictures.

"Just fill out this form, Mrs. English. Let me know if you have any questions." The woman at the receptionist's desk was only in her early twenties, but dressed in an indigo Indian-print shift, she looked like a fugitive from the Sixties. There wasn't a white uniform in sight.

"There's also a reservation form in there."

"Reservation?" Jill echoed.

"For Lamaze classes. You'd be surprised how quick they fill up. And they like to keep them small. We recommend Maxi."

"Maxi?"

"Nurse Josephine Maxwell, but most people call her Maxi. Everybody likes her. She's the best."

"Thanks." Jill took the form with her to the waiting room. It was a large open room painted egg-yolk yellow, filled with plants hanging in macrame holders and standing in hand-thrown pots. The leaves looked healthy and scrubbed. Jill chose a seat near the window overlooking the Hudson and settled down to fill out the three-page form, giving her medical history, ticking off yes to German measles, no to heart disease, no to kidney disease, no to diabetes, no to sickle-cell anemia, and so on. Drugs taken: none. Family history: mother deceased, aged forty-one, malignant brain tumor; father remarried, three children. She took a deep breath before the section on menstrual and reproductive history. She had been dreading this. Sure enough, there was not sufficient space for her to list her four abortions. In a tiny cramped hand she set down the specifics of each and found herself, not for the first time in her life, feeling the shadow of shame, the words of self-defense forming on her lips: "Abortion was an automatic option in those days. Simply *everyone* had one."

Later, Jill sat in the cheerfully cluttered office of the woman who was the head of the midwife program and author of no fewer than three midwifery textbooks. Jill watched the woman's eyes as she scanned the form and, calculating when she would have reached the reproductive history section, cleared her throat and ventured a question:

"All those abortions...they couldn't have an adverse affect on my pregnancy, could they?"

The woman looked up over her half-glasses and frowned thoughtfully. "Were any of them what you might call traumatic? It says here the first two were illegal."

"And plenty traumatic," Jill put in readily. "The first, I was only in high school. This friend of my big sister, he was a med student from France. The girls all called him Paul la Pipette. Basically, what he did was insert a catheter and suck on it." Jill blushed, remembering that he had also put the moves on her almost immediately afterward.

"Charming," the woman mused. "To introduce suction into the uterine cavity." She didn't seem particularly shocked, only bitterly nostalgic as she shook her head and said, "Those really were the bad old days, weren't they? I gather you miscarried?"

"The next day." Jill remembered the fever she had run —over 104. Cheryl had wiped her down with rubbing alcohol and begged Jill to go to the emergency ward of the nearest hospital. Since what they were doing was illegal, Cheryl could not go with her without risk of being nabbed as an accessory. With what was left of her strength, Jill had risen from the sweat-damp bedclothes and protested. "No!" She would not go to a hospital, not under any circumstances. She would die first. Luckily for her, the fever dropped.

"The second one was even more grisly," Jill went on. "I tried quinine, castor oil, turpentine, scalding baths, and lifting heavy furniture for eight days before I went to an RN who inserted something up me."

"Ouch." The midwife winced sympathetically.

"Within eighteen hours, I ejected whatever it was she had put up me plus the fetus. It was very painful. I guess like labor."

"Only nowhere near as rewarding. Well, it doesn't seem to have affected your ability to get pregnant. I see here that you didn't terminate your fourth pregnancy until the seventeenth week?"

"Yeah," Jill said, fiddling with the fringe on her shawl. "I wasn't sure about that one. I mean, I sort of wanted to keep it." But her boyfriend at the time had freaked out and insisted that she have an abortion, borrowing the money from his roommate.

"Well!" the woman said brightly. "You seem to have no doubts about wanting to keep this one."

"Oh, no!" Jill reassured her. "I want this baby very much." *Desperately,* she wanted to add. Instead, she said, "My biological clock is ticking."

The midwife flashed a knowing smile. "Ah, yes! These days the maternity wards are teeming with women responding to the ticking of their clocks. And what about your husband?" She glanced quickly back at the form to make sure there was one. "How does he feel?"

"He wants it, too," Jill assured her. Which happened to be true. Now that she was over the morning sickness and he was used to the idea, he was downright bullish. It was, if nothing else, an opportunity to buy a new kind of toy: electronic baby minders, talking teddies, automatic baby swings...the selection of equipment guaranteed to give you bigger, better, smarter babies was endless. He had even started to diet and to work out at the health club, as if the prospect of her swelling was encouraging him to shrink. Maybe Warren's mother was wrong. Maybe fatherhood was just what the man needed.

"You know, we welcome—indeed, encourage—husbands to come along."

"I realize that, but he's tied up at the office today. I promise I'll bring him next time I come."

"Very good. Supposing you go into the room across the hall and undress. I'll be with you in a few moments, to give you a general physical, a pelvic and a breast exam. I'll also need a sample of your urine and two blood tests. The nurse will show you how to prepare for the urine specimen. We need what's called a 'clean catch.' Three swipes with the antiseptic swab; it's for a culture. Afterwards, Jill, I'll ask you to dress and rejoin me in here, where I'll go over in detail exactly what we here at the midwife clinic have to offer you."

"Thanks," Jill said gratefully, feeling that she already had been given something very important: reassurance, if not absolution.

"Midwives! Jesus H. Christ! Midwives? We're living in a city that's host to the finest medical minds in the western world and you want to put yourself—and our kid—in the hands of midwives! Why not witch doctors and faith healers, for crying out loud!"

Jill had expected him to poke a little fun but not to freak out. She pushed her plate away and leaned back in her chair, feeling suddenly exhausted from the day: the trip to the midwife clinic, then down to Bigelow's to fill her prenatal vitamin prescription and jostling with the mob at Balducci's to buy ingredients for tonight's dinner. She had felt like celebrating. Now, as she looked around the table at the plates laden with chicken pesto, dill potato salad, artichoke hearts and tomatoes vinaigrette, then at Warren's face, red and bloated with anger, all she felt like was puking.

"Gee," she said weakly, "you'd think I was proposing to have our child squatting on the dirt floor of some hut."

"You might as well."

"Oh, come on! You speak of *medical minds* as if giving birth were brain surgery. It's not an operation at all, it's a natural process during which, if all goes well, only a minimum of medical intervention should be necessary."

"And what if it is necessary, Jill? What do you do then?"

"No problem. The midwives are smack dab in the middle of the hospital."

"Yeah? So they go to the OR and say, 'Pardon me, fellas, can we borrow your stuff?' Don't give me that, Jill. Midwives don't even have admitting privileges at hospitals. Midwives aren't jack shit in the hospital hierarchy. Midwives are nothing but doctors' lackeys."

"They're associated with the head of the ob-gyn department. I think he should have some pull in the OR," she rejoined haughtily.

"Yeah? And who is this guy? Have you done any research on him? Do you know what kind of track record he has? Supposing, just supposing, something should go wrong with the delivery. How acquainted with your case is he going to be? Wouldn't you rather have the guy who takes care of you in an emergency be the same guy who's taken care of you all along from the very get-go?"

"And who says it has to be a guy?"

"Come on, Jill, don't try to dodge the issue. You know what I'm saying."

"I know exactly what you're saying," she said coldly. "You're saying you'd feel safer in the bosom—excuse my expression—of the male medical establishment—"

"Than with a bunch of flakey female para-professionals? You bet your ass I do. And if you were thinking with your brain instead of with your ovaries, so would you."

"I'll have you know that midwifery is one of the world's oldest professions."

"Yeah?" he said meanly. "Along with what else?"

"I refuse to dignify that with a reply. The practice of midwifery is accepted all over Europe."

"Sure it is. And have you looked at the statistics for infant mortality in those same countries?"

"No, I haven't," she said flatly. "And what's more, neither have you. You're only guessing."

"Ah, but there's a difference. I'm guessing right. I bet you a hundred bucks—no, two hundred bucks—that the countries that use midwives have a higher infant mortality rate than those that use doctors."

He grinned and thrust his huge paw across the table, ever the jolly aggressor in a wager.

Ignoring his hand, Jill got up and went to the bathroom to wretch.

Mary Beth

Hanging on the wall of Dr. Dina Lassiter's Number 2 examination room between the blood pressure gauge and the rack of pamphlets was a framed calligraphed lesson, courtesy of an infant-formula company. "Children Learn What They Live" was the title. Mary Beth concentrated on its insipid message as Dr. Lassiter peered between her legs, then reached up inside her vagina with one hand while pushing against her abdomen gently with a fist.

"Oh, yes!" she said, withdrawing her hand and peeling off the transluscent rubber glove. "I'd say you're very pregnant."

Mary Beth closed her eyes and a single tear trickled down the side of her face and into her ear. For weeks she had known it. Still, hearing the words said out loud made her feel that much more sorry for herself. "Thanks, Dina," she whispered.

"Mary Beth O'Mally Rapasardi," the doctor said sternly, "you don't sound one bit happy! Don't you and Frank want more kids?"

"No—I mean, yes. I mean, it's just that we didn't exactly plan this."

"Oh, well!" Dina made a few notations on Mary Beth's chart. "If that's all. You ask me, there's entirely too much planning going on with some couples these days. Whatever happened to good old serendipity? Get dressed, kiddo, and we'll talk."

Kiddo. Mary Beth's father had always called her that.

Dina Lassiter had been in practice with Liam O'Mally for the last ten years of his life. Having graduated first in her class from Cornell Medical and after putting in her internship at a hospital in Norfolk, Virginia, Dina Lassiter came north to Hudson River General to serve her residency in obstetrics and gynecology.

With his flowing mane of white hair, his Irish patrician good looks, and his fey sense of humor, O'Mally was one of the more popular attending physicians at Hudson River Medical and the junior partner in a thriving Park Avenue practice. From the first time he saw her at work, Liam liked Dina's style. She was smart without being snooty, funny without being flip, a demon of a hard worker, and had the best bedside manner this side of the silver screen. She was a looker, too; pretty enough to be a movie doctor.

When her three years of residency were up, O'Mally invited Dina to join his practice. Mary Beth remembered the change in her father brought about by Dina's joining the practice. Before, he had been tired and often short-tempered with the children, the joy he had once taken in his work being worn away by long hours and no vacations. But now he was his old whistling, cheerful self, calling his patients, as in the old days, his "ladies."

Mary Beth's mother, grateful for the change in her husband, often invited Dina and her dates over to the house for dinner, even though those dinners seldom went uninterrupted by a call from the service that one of the "ladies" was having early spotting, or water breaking, or contractions only two minutes apart.

When Liam, who had never been sick a day in his life, dropped dead on the tennis court, Dina had been very nearly as devastated as Mary Beth. And when Mary Beth found herself, not long afterward, pregnant with Denny, there had never been any question as to who would be her obstetrician. It had made Frank a trifle uneasy, knowing he would have to drive her, when the time came, into New York City. Weren't there plenty of competent obstetricians practicing in Westchester? But if it was too late to have her own father deliver her firstborn, she would have the next best. Mary Beth had always considered herself far luckier than so many other women who complained that their obstetricians were martinets, cold fish, creepy, or downright incompetent. Mary Beth's relationship with Dina was far closer and more sustaining than the standard patient-doctor relationship.

In the little bathroom off the examination room, Mary Beth filled the plastic specimen cup and then got dressed, doubting their relationship was so close she could confide in Dina that she had carried "good old serendipity" to a rather reckless extreme. Not only had she not planned this baby, she hadn't the slightest idea who its father was —her husband, Frank, or her lover, Daniel. It was a dilemma most modern women would easily have solved by having an abortion. But Mary Beth had been raised a Catholic and to her abortion was not an option.

"Well, you're looking perkier now," Dina said when Mary Beth sat down across the desk from her. "Maybe it's just the weather has you down."

Outside the office window, rain pelted the wide, smooth sidewalks of Central Park West. It had been raining almost steadily for fourteen days. Every morning Frank got out of bed, looked out the window, and swore. The seeds and the seedlings he had worked so hard putting in earlier in the spring would be drowned.

"I guess I'm getting used to the idea," Mary Beth said, forcing a smile.

"Audrey will be pleased." Dina was filling out a prescription for vitamins.

"My mother treats every new grandchild as if it were the first."

Audrey O'Mally had a dozen grandchildren, the other eleven by Mary Beth's three brothers, who had all married good Catholic girls. Audrey was one of those grandparents who peer into the bassinet for the first time and launch into an investigaton: Who does it look like? The mother? The father? The maternal grandmother, Wilma? Or the paternal uncle, Fred? When Denny was born, Mary Beth had snappishly dismissed such talk. "I think he looks like himself," she insisted. It seemed so stupid to her. All babies looked alike. It was only later that traits of their parents began to surface so unmistakably. For instance, Denny had his father's big brown, downward-turning eyes and his perfect heart-shaped face. Who would this baby wind up looking like?

"Remember, no processed flour," Dina was saying. "Stick with whole-wheat breads, bran cereal. No empty calories, no junk food, lots of green leafy vegetables, and one small glass of prune juice before you go to bed at night. As I recall, those vitamins tended to bind you a bit. Drink lots of milk, of course. Any questions?"

"None that I can think of. Thanks, Dina." Mary Beth took her file from Dina and wandered out to the receptionist to make her next appointment. What she really meant was none that she dared to ask.

As soon as Mary Beth stepped out of Dina's office into the rain, she began to cry. How could she have been so stupid? She walked right past the doorman, who might have succeeded in hailing her a cab, because she didn't want him to see her tears. How could she have been so careless? She stepped up to the curb and raised her hand. The wire trash basket on the corner was brimming with soggy newspapers and a discarded umbrella lay in the gutter like a broken bird. The taxis coming down Central Park West were all occupied. Of course they were. Everyone knew it was impossible to get a cab in the city when it rained. Her own umbrella, which Denny had used to parachute off the top of his playhouse, had a bent rib, and the rain came trickling down her upraised sleeve.

"Taxi!" she cried, spying a "vacant" light as a cab turned the corner of 73rd. But a businessman who had just emerged from beneath an awning dashed out and claimed it.

How could she have done this to Frank? Dear, sweet, unsuspecting Frank. Surely he would know sooner or later if the child wasn't his. Would he divorce her as she deserved? Or simply go on living with her, silently reproaching her?

66

To escape the torrent, she ran into a rank-smelling phone booth and came face to face with the graffiti: "If you want to suck my pussy and fuck me till I come, dial this number." But that was not the number she found herself dialing. She didn't expect him to be there. It was the end of June—the term was over—and usually he and the family rented a place on Fire Island for the summer.

"Hello."

Hearing his voice for the first time in over a month, she realized why she was calling him. Not only could she not stand being separated from him another day, but he was the only person in the whole world to whom she could tell her problem.

"Hi," she said.

He was quiet for a long time. She swallowed hard. What if he was angry with her?

"Christ," he said at last, expelling a long-held breath. "It's been absolutely no good without you. Where are you?"

"In a phone booth," she said. "On the corner of Seventy-second and Central Park West."

"Stay there," he told her. "I'll be right down to get you."

"Thanks."

"I love you, Mary Beth."

"I love you, too."

"You always did look good in the rain."

It had taken him fifteen minutes to lock his office, claim his car from the garage, and drive down there from Broadway and 120th Street. His hands burrowed beneath her raincoat, her sweater, her blouse, her bra, massaging her tender nipples. His lips were everywhere—brushing her eyelids, tasting her lips, traveling down her neck.

"I swear I could take you right here in this front seat." He pulled back and looked at her. "Please don't cry," he said in a voice far gentler than any she remembered hearing. "I know it's been hard. It's been hard for me, too."

"No," she said, shaking her head, "that's not it. I'm—I'm pregnant."

He turned away from her then and sat with his hands

on the wheel, looking straight ahead through the flooding windshield as if he were driving. "I see."

"I think it must have happened that last time . . . the last time we were together."'

"Well! Well! Well!"

She pressed onward, ignoring the strange note in his voice. "But you see, it's not even that simple. The thing . . . the thing of it is . . . I slept with Frank, too, the night I came home. So you see—"

"You really believe in covering all your bases, don't you?"

She stared at his profile, too stunned to say anything.

"Okay!" he said at length, almost cheerfully. "It seems to me that there's really only one thing to do. There's a very chichi abortion pavilion near our place. I've seen lots of mink-clad matrons coming and going. We can go there this afternoon. Don't worry if you haven't brought your checkbook. I hear they take Visa."

A high, wounded cry escaped Mary Beth. Grasping the door handle, she fled back out into the rain. Up Central Park West she ran, down 73rd, her body aching with the hurt, a grapefruit-sized lump lodged in her chest blocking the tears that might have at least given vent to her pain.

"Mary Beth!"

He caught up with her just as she hit the intersection of Broadway and 73rd, grabbing the back of her raincoat as if she were a runaway child.

"Let me go!" Her voice came out a sort of outraged howl.

"I'm sorry, Mary Beth."

"Sorry?" She wheeled on him, rage getting the upper hand. "*Sorry?*"

"I don't know what came over me. When I was sixteen, my girlfriend got pregnant." His face had turned very red, his eyes suspiciously damp.

"So suddenly you turned sixteen again?" Mary Beth said heartlessly.

"I was so angry with her, you see. I blamed her. I took precautions. I covered my end. If she got pregnant, I figured it was her fault. Or another guy's fault. I can't help it. I was angry with you, Mary Beth. These are the Eighties. Women don't have to get pregnant if they don't want to."

"Not even *Catholic* women?"

"Jesus Christ." He covered his face with both hands and stood there in silence a few moments. At last, he uncovered his face and said, "It's only just beginning to dawn on me what a horse's ass I am. Come on," he said, taking her arm, "let's get you out of the rain."

She remained absolutely rooted where she was, waiting for the light to change from Don't Walk to Walk so she could get away from him. When he wouldn't let her go, she said in an icy voice, "I'd appreciate your driving me to Grand Central."

"Mary Beth, how many times are you going to make me beg your forgiveness?"

"I don't want to hear you apologize. I want to get out of this rain and go home to my husband and son."

"You and I have to talk. You can't just come back into my life, drop this bomb, and run the hell back out again. Come, let's go down to the Plaza."

"I don't want to go down to the Plaza," she said through clenched teeth, "ever again."

"Okay," he said, "then I'll take you someplace else."

"No hotels," she warned.

"No hotels," he said. "I promise."

She let herself be led back to the car.

It was a studio apartment in a brownstone just off Amsterdam in the 80s. Shedding her sopping raincoat, she wandered along the bookshelves reading the spines—Lytton Strachey, Virginia Woolf, *The Last Romantics*—and eyeing the things hanging on the walls—a framed page of a letter from James Joyce to Leonard Woolf, a page from the original manuscript of *Waiting for Godot*, an eighteenth-century engraving of Covent Garden in full swing.

"Gifts," he said quietly, standing behind her, "from my beloved wife."

She flinched when he touched her and moved away.

"You're soaked to the skin," he said. "Let me help you off with your things."

Stiffly, she stood there and let him remove her clothes, telling herself that if he made the slightest sexual move she would scratch his eyes out. He must have sensed this latent violence, for he kept his fingers attentive to the business of buttons and snaps. When she was naked, he rubbed her with one towel and wrapped her hair in another.

"I think I have some herbal tea in the cupboard," he said. "Would that be all right?"

She nodded. "Does your wife come here?"

He laughed shortly on his way to the small galley kitchen. "The last time she came here she was in law school. It was my bachelor apartment then. For some reason, I've never let it go."

She wondered, fleetingly, if he ever brought women here these days. But looking around, she doubted it. It had a distinctly monastic air. She knew why he had kept it. So he would have someplace to come when he wanted to be alone, to get away from his family. Wrapping herself in his raincoat, she curled up on the studio couch with its brown corduroy cover and waited for her tea. She had to admit she felt better now that she was out of the rain and relieved of her wet things. If only it had all been a bad dream: breaking up with Daniel, and getting pregnant and fighting in the car. If only she could say a prayer, fall asleep, and wake up to find everything back the way it had been.

Jill

"So? Tell me how it went."

"Dismally," said Jill.

"Come on," Kendra said, "Sheldon Berry's one of the top G-men in the business. He warms the speculum and gives his patients bunny slippers to wear in the stirrups. He's written books, been on TV—didn't Johnny Carson dub him the Sensuous Gynecologist? How dismal could it be?"

"I don't know about you, but good-looking G-men make me nervous. Those bunny slippers only make you feel like you're visiting a pederast instead of a physician. And with Warren standing there swapping baseball stats with Berry while he sticks his hand up my zorch, you're asking me how dismal it could be?"

"He didn't!" Kendra said. "You're just saying that to shock me."

"I'm not. I swear I'm not. Something happened to Warren as soon as he set foot in that waiting room and got a load of all those pregnant women and all those baby magazines. All of a sudden, he wanted to talk about guy stuff. He even talked sports with the receptionist. Wrestling. Oh, it was special, all right."

Kendra chuckled at her end.

"You think I'm kidding?" Cradling the phone between cheek and neck, Jill was transplanting a pot of blooming zinnias into a window basket. She wished she were someplace far out in the country where she could have a whole garden to dig in. As it was, she had gone over to the flower district and ordered a garden's worth of potted plants: poppies with shiny bright petals, giant velvety irises, vats of daisies, and, for outside on the terrace, big pots of peonies, rhododendron, and azaleas.

"No," Kendra said, laughing, "I can actually picture it: Warren and some no-nonsense dame in white stockings discussing Hulk Hogan and André the Giant."

"And the worst part was when the two of them—Berry and Warren—ganged up on me."

"No!"

"On the form—Christ, I filled out one just like it only three weeks ago at the midwife clinic; I was really sick of it by now—where it says how many abortions have you had, I only put down two."

"How come?"

"How come? I figured it was none of Berry's fucking business," she said truculently. "Besides, how do I know if I tell him today, it won't wind up in some book tomorrow?"

"Or on Johnny Carson, yet."

"When we sit down in Berry's office—and you should see Berry's office; he's got enough art in there to fill a small wing of MOMA—Warren is reading the form upside down while Berry reads it right side up. So he says to me, 'Jill, haven't you forgotten something?' Yeah, I wanted to tell him. I forgot to leave your ass at home. 'Is there a problem here?' the Sensuous G-man wants to know. 'No problem, Doc,' I say. 'Jill,' Warren says, 'if you don't tell him, I will. As your physician, the man has a right to know.' Well, I just stared at him like he was shit that's suddenly sprouted lips. So he says to Berry, 'My wife's had four abortions, not two. Before I ever met her,' he adds. *Before I ever met her!* Like he wants to completely disassociate himself from me and my slatternly past. I cannot tell you how humiliated I was."

"So what did Berry do, make you stand in the corner with a speculum on your nose?"

"No, he just took down the data. I made sure I recited everything in graphic and gory detail just to make Warren really squirm. The problem was, I was the one who felt bad. I was practically in tears by the time I finished."

"Poor baby," Kendra said.

Remembering, tears again flooded Jill's eyes. "All I kept thinking of was that midwife clinic and how wonderful and supportive and cozy it all was."

"I'm sure Berry's plenty cozy, Jill. Bunny slippers and all."

"I'm sure he is, too, but it just won't be the same."

"You never know. Maybe it will be better."

"Do *you* think it's better to go to a doctor than to a midwife? Are you going to go to a doctor?"

"Inasmuch as I'm about two minutes pregnant," Kendra said, "it's a little early to be making these decisions."

"Yeah, but when the time comes, you'll go to a midwife, you'll see."

"I probably will," Kendra admitted.

"You're so lucky. When there's a decision to be made, you'll just make it. You won't need to consult with your mate, or do research, or compile statistics, or debate. You'll just do what you want to do. It's all going to be so much easier for you."

"I doubt," Kendra said heavily, "that it is going to be anything like easy for me."

"God, listen to me! Of course it won't be easy for you. Forgive me, Kendra. I'm a prize asshole."

"Yeah," Kendra said, and Jill could practically hear her grinning, "but you're *my* prize asshole. And I love you."

Carleen

"Hey, Carleen, you're beginning to show already."

Carleen looked at herself in the ladies' room mirror. She was wearing a short-sleeved Armani jacket with a pleated floral-print skirt. Except for an infinitesimal thickening in her waist and an extra sheen in her straight, shoulder-length ash-blond hair, she didn't think she was showing. How could she? She was less than eight weeks pregnant. It irritated her that it had gotten out so soon that the third insemination had been a success. She had not intended to announce it until after the results of the amniocentesis sometime in October. Her assistant, Randy, had been able to trace the leak to one of the assistants in Personnel/Compensation. When Carleen called the head of the department to complain, all she got was a blithe congratulations. It didn't matter to this woman that Carleen had no wish to share every second of her gestation with every woman in the firm. Bill told her to relax and go with it—Bill's solution to just about everything. "You mean this is just the beginning of my body belonging, not just to medical science, but to the entire world?"

As she brushed her hair, Carleen looked at the other woman in the mirror, who was reapplying her eyeliner. Her name was Angela something-or-other and she was the comptroller's secretary.

"Don't feel bad," Angela said, "the minute I'm pregnant I show. And by the end, I'm out to here. Last time, my husband got me one of those shirts—you know, the ones with the big arrow pointing down? 'Baby'? Funny guy. I needed that like I needed a hole—"

"*Last time?*" Carleen repeated. She was not used to the ladies' room and coffee-station chitchat she had run into since the news got out. Small talk didn't come especially easily to her. But she was curious in spite of herself. "Exactly how many children do you have?"

"Four," the woman said modestly.

"Four!" Carleen sputtered. The woman couldn't have been older than thirty.

"My mom's a doll. She looks after the kids, thank God. Speaking of which, are you coming back after?"

"Of course," Carleen said, not that it was any business of hers.

"I guess you'll be having to find a nurse or something."

"Nurse?" Carleen echoed.

"Well, it being a test-tube baby and all, won't you have to find specially trained help?"

Carleen reeled out of the ladies' room. That would teach her to open her mouth. Test-tube baby, indeed! On the way back to the conference room, no fewer than three people who normally would have passed her with a simple "hi" or a smile stopped to ask after her health.

"Much better, thanks," was her standard reply.

She felt, in fact, absolutely vile. While she hadn't actually thrown up, she was constantly dizzy and disoriented. Normally she was the first out of bed in the morning, but now it was Bill who made the coffee and breakfast—Melitta drip mocha java and a fresh bran muffin with red currant jam—bringing it to her on a tray. Only after downing the coffee and nibbling at the muffin could she even set her feet on the floor.

The conference room was already full. The director of sales and his assistant, the director of marketing, the three East Coast regional sales managers, the comptroller, the art director, the two executive editors, and, occupying the head of the table, delicately sipping tea from a Wedgewood cup and saucer, her co-publisher, Hugh Grantley III.

"Close the door, will you, Carly? I think we're ready to roll." Hugh Grantley exuded the confidence bred of four years at Deerfield, another four at Harvard, and two at Wharton. He was, simply put, a star. It seemed to Carleen that he strode through life as if ignoring a storm of paparazzi's flashbulbs. When he signed off on contracts it was with a flourish, as if he was giving his autograph. His most casual remark sounded prepared; his laughter, canned. And yet Carleen found him oddly loveable. They were about the same age, she and Hugh, but with a difference. Hugh was the grandson of the founder of this publishing company, groomed from birth to take over from his father, Hugh Junior. Carleen had worked her way up over fifteen years from editorial assistant. While he respected her editorial acumen, Hugh—or "The Third," as he was fondly called—never let it be forgotten that he *was* Grantley House and that she, Carleen, was merely a faithful retainer.

"I've saved a seat for you, Carly." Nelson Whitehorn, one of the executive editors, patted the chair next to him. Nelson, who was nearing retirement age, had been Hugh Junior's right-hand man. She took the seat between him and Hugh. Harvey Morstein, the director of sales, sat at the other end of the table, drumming it with nails bitten to the quick.

Randy had supplied her with a legal pad, three sharpened pencils, a cup of cappuccino, and a neatly typed list of the calls that had come in yesterday after three when she had left the office early, too dizzy and groggy to hold out any longer. She scanned the list. A handful of authors, agents, and editors: Posy Martin, the features editor of *Publishers Weekly,* wanting to interview her; Mitch Michaelman, wanting to know what she thought about his three opening chapters. His courier had dropped off the 150 pages of manuscript yesterday at two o'clock, and already he wanted to hear her reaction.

She swallowed nervously. She was over 1,500 pages behind in her reading. She had been running behind for weeks. She didn't understand it. Her concentration was flighty and fragmented. Fighting nausea and panic, she took a sip of coffee.

"Shouldn't you be laying off that stuff?" Elton Norwood, the other executive editor, leaned across the table, wagging a finger at her. She looked at him and blinked. Elton's wife had, six months earlier, given birth to their first child. For all Elton had shared his experience with everyone in the office, one would have thought that Elton himself had undergone the forty-three weeks of gestation culminating in thirty-six hours of labor, epidural anaesthesia, and forceps delivery of their nine-pound-three-ounce Elton Junior. Elton had come to them from the competition, where he had been quite the Young Turk, having acquired a small but growing list of what Carleen called Punk Novelists. They were all young, some barely out of college; drugs, sex, and nightlife nihilism was their bag. It wasn't Carleen's but, as Hugh liked to say, "It has the virtue of selling."

"It's decaffeinated," she told him, irritated with herself for lying. What business was it of his if she drank caffeine or absinthe?

Hugh cleared his throat. "All right, Harv. This is your meeting."

Harvey nodded curtly and reached for his package of Kools.

"Harvey," Hugh said, "I wonder if you could chair this meeting without the benefit of your usual nicotine orgy?"

"Okay, okay, okay," he snapped, slapping the pack back down on the table, giving Carleen a grudging nod.

Great, thought Carleen. He resents me as it is for being a Woman. Now on top of that, he'll resent me for being a Breeder.

"It's time we talked about the sales conference in December. I'd like to throw out a few things. Number one, I'd like your guarantee"—he pointed to Hugh with a nicotine-yellowed finger—"that the jacket art we see there ain't necessarily going to be graven on a tablet."

Harmon Josephs leaned forward in his chair, his fair

complexion suddenly riddled with blotches. "What exactly is he saying, Carleen?"

"Let him finish," Carleen said gently.

"I mean," Harvey went on, "last year a few of the reps had some pretty constructive criticism to offer and the Prince of Pasteup over here not only refused to listen to them, he flounced out of the room before the pitch was even over."

Hugh, who had been out on the tennis courts at the time, looked to Carleen for confirmation.

"I think that saying that a cover is a 'piece of shit' doesn't exactly constitute constructive criticism, Harvey. There is such a thing as tact."

"Fuck tact," Harvey rasped. "They were right."

"I don't have to listen to this." Harmon started to rise.

"There he goes again." Harvey grinned, pleased. "Flouncing out."

"Harmon, please sit down. Harvey, stop baiting him. I have a suggestion to make." Carleen took a deep breath before continuing. "Harvey, if you or any of the reps have any objections to any cover art or design, may I suggest that you put them down on paper in the form of a memo to me? Your reps do know how to write a memo?"

"Cute," Harvey said.

"And we'll take it under consideration. But, as I recall, John Froebisch's objection to last year's *Diet and Sex* jacket was that he hated the colors pink and gray. I assure you, neither Harmon nor Hugh nor I ever base our judgment of covers on personal likes or dislikes. Now, if you were to say that the title didn't read, or that the colors popped, or that a certain composition lacked shelf visibility..."

"Okay, okay, okay." Harvey reached instinctively for his cigarettes, then recoiled as if he had been slapped by an invisible hand.

"I'd also like to add," Carleen put in smoothly, "that I must receive your *constructive criticism* no later than Christmas. Otherwise, I can't guarantee that the proof the reps carry around in their sales kits will be consistent with the final cover. And we all know the importance of consistency."

She made a note on her pad. "Don't worry, Harv, I'll drop your reps a memo and remind them about the date, okay?"

Next to her, Nelson muttered a muted "Bravo." Over the years she had learned how to deal with Harvey. How to push him, but not to the point where he lost his temper. Harvey losing it was not a pretty sight. Her personal nickname for him was Rumpelstiltskin, the little man who, when angered, jumped up and down until one day he stomped his way clear through the floor.

"What's next on the agenda, Harv?" Hugh said, making a gallant effort to hide his boredom.

"One-on-ones."

"And what, pray tell, are *one-on-ones?*"

"I'd like you guys to divvy up the sales force among the four of you—Hugh, Nelson, Elton-baby, and Carleen—and schedule meetings, say half-hour sessions, with each of the reps."

"Whatever for?" Hugh looked pained. "We will have had ample opportunity to talk shop over cocktails at the various parties and banquets."

"This would be intensive," Harvey said. *"One on one.* Get it? You'll be able to talk up future product, listen to their beefs, make them feel part of the Grantley family."

To his credit, Hugh refrained from shuddering. The idea of treating men who wore heavy gold chains, monogrammed sunglasses, and suits that looked as if they'd been made from tablecloths as "family" had to be repugnant to him.

"If you think it's a good idea, Harv," Hugh said doubtfully, "I'll have my girl coordinate it."

"Why don't you let Randy take care of it?" Carleen suggested brightly. Hugh's "girl"—the Wheatley School and Briarcliff—found anything beyond making restaurant reservations as complicated as a moon launch.

"Okay! What's next, Harv?"

* * *

79

Nelson stopped her in the hallway after the meeting.

"What are you doing taking on all this responsibility, Carleen?"

"It's my job, Nelson," she said, weary of his relentless paternalism.

"I realize that, love, but you'll be *seven months* pregnant by sales conference."

"So?"

"Well, perhaps things have changed since my Martha was with child, but it seems to me that pregnant women in their third trimesters are not supposed to fly. Something about the air pressure in the cabin. And in your case, especially—"

"I know all about my case, Nelson."

"And it's all right with your physician?"

"I haven't actually discussed it with my physician... yet." All she wanted to do was get through the amniocentesis. If the baby she was carrying around inside of her wasn't a Mongoloid, then she'd worry about the rest of the pregnancy.

"I have to go," she said to Nelson. "Hugh wants to talk to me."

"I'd start to prepare him now if I were you, Carleen. Having to handle the sales conference on his own will be quite a shock to that young man. I'm afraid you've spoiled him."

When she got to his office, Hugh Grantley was already lounging at one end of a long, aged leather couch beneath the life-size portrait of his grandfather. Although the family resemblance was undeniable, the iron had been bred out of the jaw of the younger. Hugh was what could most charitably be called "boyishly attractive," not necessarily an asset in a leader.

"Carly!" He patted the cushion next to him. He seldom sat at his desk. Like the President of the United States, he used it on ceremonial occasions or when posing for photographers.

"What's up?" She remained standing in the doorway. She had to go to the bathroom—again!—and she didn't want to get caught up in one of his hazy, open-ended, clubby chats while the pressure in her bladder mounted.

"You really gave it to old Harv." He chuckled. Then, more seriously, "Is everything okay, Carleen?"

Carleen sighed. *And if it weren't?* "Of course. Everything's fine, Hugh. I just have a lot of work to do."

"How's it going with Michaelman?"

"Fine."

"And the photos in that exercise book?"

"Fine."

Unlike everybody else in the company, he would ask her about everything but her state of health. Although she had gone and told him as soon as the gossip had risen to a dull roar, he had taken it with surprising equanimity. Almost as if he hadn't really let the news sink in.

"Harmon will be all right, don't you think, Carleen?" He was fidgeting with a small pre-Columbian statuette, failing to meet her eyes.

"Harmon will be fine."

"He's used to Harv."

"Aren't we all?"

"So. What do you think of these one-on-ones?"

"I think we'll have to wait and see."

"And you're going to have Randy handle the scheduling?"

"As soon as we know which days are free, I will."

"Great." He set down the statuette.

"If that's all, Hugh, I really do—"

"Actually, Carleen, that's not all. I just wanted to make sure. That is, I was just talking to Nelson, and he seemed to feel that, what with your impending, uh, that is to say, you realize, don't you, what a watershed this coming sales conference is going to be?"

"I realize that, Hugh. It's the fiftieth anniversary of Grantley and the first with the newly organized sales force."

"Right you are! And I just want you to know...that Grantley is counting on you, Carleen Donovan, as never before."

Carleen nodded, feeling a surge of nausea, knowing that, regardless of her physician's orders, there was no way she could miss this conference. And if there had been any doubt about that before, the next words out of Hugh Grantley's mouth only served to confirm it.

"Elton has already gone on record as saying he'd be pleased to pitch in—"

"What?" Carleen cut him short. "And deprive you of a tennis partner? I wouldn't dream of it. Don't worry, Hugh. I'll be flying down to Puerto Rico with you and the boys. I wouldn't miss it for the world."

Kendra

Angus, the groundskeeper of the Madisons' Old Greenwich estate, Whispering Laurels, climbed out of the war surplus British Land Rover, just like the one he had driven when he served in North Africa with Field Marshall Montgomery, and waved Kendra through the front gates.

"Good day to you, Miss Kendra." He saluted her with a broad, gold-toothed grin. "You're lookin' bonnier all the time."

"Have the rabble all arrived, Angus?"

"Aye, Miss. They're up at the big house snooting their martoonis. Better hurry yourself along. You wouldn't want to miss one minute of this bonny day."

"Guess the weather must have been hard on your garden, eh, Angus?"

"Aye, Miss, that it was. I lost my dahlias for sure, and the roses have all dropped their drawers. Poor loves never stood a chance."

"I'm sorry, Angus. Maybe the rest of the summer will be kinder."

"Aye, Miss. It's for sure we have it comin' to us."

Kendra hesitated before driving on. In the old days when she came home from prep school or college, she always used to stop off at Angus's cottage for a spot of tea and talk, feeling it necessary to sustain herself with his colorful, rolling brogue before mounting the hill to the thirty-five-room stone manner house where everyone, including the maids, suffered a bad case of Greenwich Lockjaw.

"Nice to see you, Angus."

"Nice to see you, too, Miss Kendra."

Reluctantly, she drove on up the rise. On one side of the road, on immaculate rectangles of lawn surrounded by neat white rail fencing, a few bay mares and their colts gamboled. On the other side, the open fields were carpeted with daylilies which seemed to have thrived on the excess of rain these past weeks. But as she crested the hill, she saw what Angus meant. His rose gardens lay in ruins, shriveled petals of pink and red and rusted white littering the lawns.

"Poor Angus," she sighed as she swung into the laurel-bordered driveway and found a place to park her 1950 Saab between a hunter green Jaguar and a Silver Cloud Rolls.

"Permit me to say that it has been entirely too long since we have seen you." Perkins, the butler her father had inherited from the president of the Greenwich Savings & Loan over twenty years ago, bowed to Kendra as she tried to sneak in the front door.

"You're permitted. Hey, Perky, I've missed you, too." She gave him a peck on the cheek and watched with pleasure the delicate blush steal up to his snowy hairline.

"You're too kind, Miss."

"Where is this sock hop, anyway, Perky?"

"They are currently in the solarium, Miss. Soon to repair down to the bathhouse for the festivities."

The "festivities" was the annual Madison Bastille Day

Barbecue and Fireworks Fete, for which occasion her father not only bribed the city fathers and obtained a permit from the fire commissioner, but hired three members of the world-famous pyrotechnical Grucci family, leased a hundred-and-fifty foot barge, and purchased a hundred thousand dollars' worth of rockets, pinwheels, flares, and aerial salutes.

It was the one family occasion, next to Christmas, that was impossible for Kendra to wriggle out of. Gun-shy from an early age, she found the prospect of twenty minutes of bombs bursting in air nearly as harrowing as having to see her parents again.

"Hello, Dolly." Dolly, short for "darling," was the only name Kendra ever remembered being called by her mother. Nora Alicia Madison—Nana to her children—broke away from her guests and floated forward to greet her only daughter. She was wearing a long, flowing caftan of sheerest something beneath which her perfect tan and her white studded leather bikini were enticingly visible.

"Hiya, Nana. Sorry I'm late. The Saab got temperamental on I-95 and I had to pull into a rest stop and sweet-talk her."

"Goodness, Dolly, if only you'd let us buy you a car. Something small and feminine. One of those darling little Japanese cars, perhaps."

"I like my Saab."

Nora Alicia's artfully lifted features took on a look of gallantly borne martyrdom. "Of course you do, Dolly. Loyalty has always been both your great strength and your great weakness. Have you met our guests?"

Her mother proceeded to propel Kendra about the high-ceilinged, glassed-in room where the rubber trees sought jungle heights and the parrots and toucans had been taught to defecate on a tray. One by one, they were introduced to Kendra, the upper-echelon management types who worked for Pepsi, IBM, the big Wall Street firms, and the even bigger shipping lines—all wealthy enough to be able to afford to live by the water and belong to the yacht club.

"I haven't asked you what you're drinking."

"Nothing, thanks, Nana. I'm not drinking."

The first inkling of suspicion crossed Nora Alicia's face. "Really?" she said thoughtfully. Usually, Kendra started in on the Chateau Latour the moment she stepped over the threshold and generally carried her glass out to the car with her when she left.

"Where's Poppy?"

"Where else? Down on the beach making sure everything is shipshape. Here is your brother. Grady, go fetch your sister something nice and *soft* to drink, will you? She's not drinking." She cocked an ironical eyebrow.

Grady Madison was older than Kendra by nineteen months but they could have been twins. Both were tall and slender, with thick golden hair, green eyes, and tawny complexions. At thirty-eight, he was a vice president at Greenwich Maritime Trust ("Underwriters to the Maritime Industry"), the investment bank of which their father was president and founder.

"Since when have we become temperance, Keddy?" He took his sister's elbow and moved them toward the bar.

"Since a couple of months ago, Grade."

"You always were a creature of extremes. What kept you? Nana almost popped her tucks."

"My car broke down."

"Still driving that old heap? Pepsi, please," he told the bartender. "You're really serious about this?" he asked dubiously, handing her the soda and requesting a martini for himself.

"I thought sobriety would be a novel experience."

"I can't say that it's done you any harm. You look smashing. And where did you get that item? You're putting these Greenwich matrons to shame."

Kendra twirled around to show off the shimmering silk summer frock dappled with a pattern of gold and purple pansies. "St. Marks Thrift Shop, nine-ninety-five bargained down to six-fifty. So, tell me, speaking of pinching pennies, how goes it at Money Grubbers Anonymous?"

He sighed theatrically. "The pits. But I've just put down money on a house in Westport. On the beach. Four bedrooms, four baths, each with its own sunroom, sauna, and whirlpool."

"Sounds like a real hovel."

"Don't be such a snob, Keddy. It's not the Bowery, but it will do in a pinch."

Grady had suffered his brush with poverty and art. After graduating from Carnegie Mellon, he had gone on to do a bit of acting in Off- and Off-Off-Broadway productions, living in a basement apartment over in Alphabet Land, on East 9th between Avenues B and C. He had been burgled three times and mugged twice, the last time losing his picture-perfect God-given front teeth. Losing the teeth had finally done it. He gave up and accepted their father's long-standing invitation to join him at the bank. Both Grady and Kendra were disappointments to their parents in that neither of them had yet married and settled down. For Kendra, it was a matter of never having found the right fellow; for Grady, she knew, it was a case of being gay, and so cramped in the closet his hands shook and he found it difficult to get through a day without downing numerous dry martinis.

Smiling glassily at their parents' guests, brother and sister gradually worked their way across the room, onto the terrace, and out onto the front lawn.

"Thank God it's stopped raining. I was beginning to sprout *moss* behind my ears." Loosening his tie, Grady led the way down the wide, verdant aisle bordered on either side by high, glossy-leafed laurels and flowering rhododendrons. Their view extended clear to a small saltwater pond and the Long Island Sound beyond. The bathhouse, a miniature of the big house, was situated on the spit of land between pond and Sound.

"I don't know," Kendra said. "I've sort of liked the rain. Being holed up in my loft with lots of materials, listening to the pitter-patter on my skylights."

"Doing good work?"

"The best ever. You've got to come down sometime and see it."

He took her hand and swung it easily. "I will. Who

knows? Maybe I'll commission something for my new house." He stopped and looked at her, his shoulders slumping. "At least one of us is fulfilling herself." He shook his head and looked quickly away. His conservatively cropped hair had once been as long as hers, trailing down his back in a single thick golden braid. The hole piercing his left ear had long since closed up. He looked so dejected and hopeless, she felt she had to tell him.

"Grady, dear...I wanted you to be the first to hear this: I'm pregnant."

He turned swiftly, his pale green eyes pooling with tears. "Oh, Keddy, that's the best news I've heard in...I don't know how long. I'm so happy for you!" He flung his glass into the bushes and hugged her hard. "A baby in the family! Who's the lucky man?"

"Oh," she said casually, "he's no longer exactly, as they say, on the scene."

"Hmm...I guess he's not so lucky, after all. Do Nana and Poppy know? What am I saying? Would you be out here enjoying sweet freedom if they did?"

"I've been seriously considering not telling them until after the baby's born in February."

"You'll never get away with it. Even if it doesn't show now, there's still Christmas. No, you'd better tell them now. Give them some time to have their cardiac arrest and get it over with."

"Give them some time to *interfere*, you mean. But I suppose you're right," she said ruefully.

"Have you thought of *when* you're going to tell them? After all, timing is everything."

"I figure after the show tonight."

Grady threw back his head and laughed. "Talk about *fireworks!*"

"Don't be absurd, Kendra, the baby has to have a father. It wasn't the Immaculate Conception."

Ainsley Madison paced the terra-cotta tile floor of the bathhouse living room, his fists balled in the pockets of his white flannels, his scarlet ascot skewed. Out on the darkened beach, Angus was rounding up the last of the guests and loading them into the Mercedes station wagon to drive them up the hill to their own cars. Beneath the chintz couch on which Kendra sat, a polished cotton pillow gathered to her middle, Lady Cristobal, Nora Alicia's dim-witted Afghan hound, still suffered the after-effects of the pyrotechnical display. Every so often, she would let out a sigh or a whimper. Kendra didn't blame her; she felt the same way.

Kendra's mother posed by the open French window, her caftan mingling with the curtain billowing in the evening breeze. Over by the door stood Grady, grave and passive as a palace guard, having promised to stick around in case his sister needed support.

"I'm only saying, Poppy"—Kendra measured her words with care—"that the father and I are not all that close."

He snorted. "You managed to get close enough, didn't you?"

"Ainsley." Her mother's voice held a quiet warning.

Ainsley dry-washed his face with both hands. At sixty-two, he looked like he had just stepped out of a Dewar's Profile. With his helmet of silver curls, his rich man's tan, and his presumption of nobility because he had money, he had always reminded Kendra of a strutting, aging, spoiled move star. "What about his people?"

The Madison obsession: *Let's check the pedigree.*

"I don't know anything about his people, Poppy. This isn't the Junior Cotillion, and neither he nor his people have any idea that I'm carrying this baby."

"And when do you propose to enlighten them?"

"That's just it, Poppy. I don't. I've decided to do this on my own."

At this, Ainsley turned to his wife for support or explanation, but she remained standing impassively by the window, staring out at the water.

"That's the way she wants it, Pop," said Grady.

Ainsley whirled on his son. "And I suppose you find the whole thing humorous?"

Grady shook his head slowly. "But I do think it's wonderful."

"It's been so long," Nora Alicia said dreamily, "since we've had a baby in the house."

"Well, that's just hunky-dory!" His voice rose. "She's bringing somebody's little bastard into the world and you two go all ga-ga on me. What do you propose to call this little bastard?"

"Madison has always been good enough for me," Kendra said quietly.

With that, of course, he was powerless to argue, so he tried another tack. "And how do you plan to feed and clothe it?"

"I've been selling several pieces to some private collectors. North Eastern Bank, as you know, has been steadily buying up my work, at least one piece a year. That gallery down on Greene Street may be mounting a show for me this spring. I've always been rather good at getting along on rather little. And if all that isn't enough, I can always go back to modeling at Cooper Union."

"In your condition?" Now it was her mother's turn to show outrage. "Do you really think that's *seemly*, Dolly?"

"I will not have it!" Ainsley bellowed. "Do you hear me? I will not have my daughter parading around in the buff showing off her—her—"

"My swelling belly? Well, it's *my* belly, and if I want a bunch of life-drawing students to see it, that's my business, not yours."

Ainsley sat down abruptly as if he had been pushed. Nora Alicia came up behind him and began to massage his shoulders.

"Perhaps it won't come to that, Ainsley." She spoke to him gently, as if neither child was present. "Perhaps for the sake of the baby, she won't be averse to our helping her out a bit. Perhaps she won't even be averse to coming up here to stay with us for the duration."

"No way!"

"Just until the baby's born," she pleaded.

"You know, Keddy," Grady put in, "it's not the worst idea in the world. I mean, is the Bowery any place for a pregnant woman or a newborn child?"

She shot him a reproachful look that said, *You're sup-*

posed to be on my side. "Haven't you people ever heard of gentrification? There are babies popping up all over the Bowery these days."

"Bums having babies?" said Grady. "What next? Bag ladies throwing benefits?"

"Very funny. My neighbors, some of whom come perilously close to being Yuppies, are beginning to have children."

"But what's happened to you, Kendra?" her father rallied. "What's happened to my daughter who's always gone out of her way not to conform? If everyone else is having babies, I'm surprised you aren't running out to tie your tubes."

"Call it a natural urge, Poppy. Call it time running out on me. I'm not lucky like you and Nana. I haven't been able to find a mate I can be happy with."

"You think it's been easy?" he started up again. "You think we haven't had to make our share of tough compromises? The problem with you is you refuse to compromise."

"Would you rather I pulled a Jill? Married a man without loving him and used him to have babies?"

"Frankly, yes. At least it's by the numbers."

She smiled sadly. "You know me, Poppy. I never liked to paint by the numbers. I'll tell you what: I'll offer you a compromise. If you promise not to con me into coming back here to live, I'll let you buy your grandchild's layette. How's that?"

Ainsley grumbled, Grady burst into diplomatic applause, and Nora Alicia's face took on that faraway look she always got when she began to mentally draw up her shopping list. Kendra hoped she wouldn't live to regret this.

Louise

On the walls there hung a series of framed posters of old *Life* magazine covers. Louise wondered if the people in the clinic were aware of the intense irony of that word, repeated everywhere she looked: Life, Life, Life, Life, Life.

"I asked you if you skipped lunch, Mrs. Rosen."

The white-jacketed receptionist spoke without looking up from the clipboard riding her hip. On the clipboard was a five-page form containing Louise's complete medical history.

She nodded. She had made Marty a ham and Swiss for lunch, but she couldn't have eaten anything, even if permitted. Sitting next to her on the couch, Marty gave her hand a reassuring squeeze. Most of the women occupying the waiting room had come without men. She wondered if they were unmarried or simply going it alone. Some of the women flipped idly through magazines. Others sat staring into space or drumming their fingers on the arms of their chairs, not bothering to conceal their nervousness.

"Will you be wanting a record of this procedure sent to your regular physician? If so, I need his name and—"

"His address is right there on page three." Marty thumped her clipboard rudely and flipped through the sheets. "See it, miss? *Dr. Sheldon Berry.* Is the doctor ready for us, miss, or are you going to continue to flaunt your incompetence at my wife's expense."

The receptionist gave Marty a sharp look. "The D and E is scheduled for two-thirty, Mr. Rosen. Your two o'clock is a counseling session."

"Counseling session? What kind of counseling session, miss?"

"With a social worker, sir. She will explain the procedure in full. And give you some information on birth control," she added pointedly.

Marty grinned. "Look, lady, we know all about the procedure, and believe it or not, we know all about birth control, too. In fact, me and Louise could write a book on the subject. Can't we just get on with this? Making my wife wait like this is cruel and unusual."

"Marty." Louise tugged at his sleeve. The other women were staring at them. "We'll be happy to see the social worker, miss," she said sweetly.

Glad that at least one of them was sensible, the receptionist retreated behind the door.

"Get a load of Frau Brucker there." Marty spoke to the room at large. "Ladies going through what you're going through ought to be treated with kid—and I mean *kid*—gloves."

Louise was grateful when three minutes later the social worker, a tall, cool-looking blonde in a pale blue seersucker suit, appeared at the door and said:

"Mr. and Mrs. Rosen? We're ready for you now."

They followed her down a long, beige-carpeted hall with doors on either side. Behind one closed door, Louise heard a sound not unlike a vacuum cleaner. D & E: *dilation and evacuation.* She wondered whether, that very minute, some woman's baby was being sucked out of her womb into the bag of some medical Hoover.

The blonde held open the door to a small, very neat office in which there was room only for her desk and chair and two other chairs facing it. She invited them to wedge themselves into seats.

"Well!" she said, scanning the form. "It looks like we've got everything we need here. I see you have three fine, healthy children. How nice."

"Save your congratulations, miss," Marty said. "Let's get on with it."

She directed him a look that sized him up as a troublemaker, then returned her attention to Louise. "Today, you'll start by giving us some urine and some blood."

"How come?" Marty asked.

She smiled tolerantly at him. "To check her hematocrit and hemoglobin to see if she's anemic. Her blood will also be tested for syphilis, but don't worry, Mr. Rosen, it's nothing personal, just routine." She returned to Louise, who had worked her hand free of Marty's and sat kneading the arms of her chair with damp, sweating palms. She felt nauseated and claustrophobic in this cramped little office.

"You'll be having a local anaesthesia to numb your cervix. Once you are on the table, the doctor may feel it necessary to give you a tranquilizing injection to help you relax. You'll receive that in an IV which will also contain pitocin, a hormone that helps the uterus contract to its original size. I'm sure you're familiar with pitocin, Mrs. Rosen, following the birth of your three children?"

Louise nodded dumbly. A roaring sound had risen in her ears. It was hard for her to catch everything the woman was saying to her. "Vagina...antiseptic... paracervical block...injected into the cervix...then dilated...for the aspirator to enter the uterus...heavy pulling sensation, followed by mild cramping. As the uterus is emptied of the fetus, it will contract.

"Are there any questions?"

Louise shook her head and turned to look at her husband. Since the beginning of the recitation, he had remained uncharacteristically silent and had, in fact, gone rather pale.

After a few words about vital signs, recovery, and possible complications, she got to the part she had clearly been waiting for.

"Now, we come to birth control. Have you two decided on a method?"

"We had a method," Louise said. "The diaphragm."

"Oh, no!" Marty held up both hands. "No way."

"What do you mean, 'no way'?" Louise said stubbornly.

"I mean diaphragms can be forgotten, Louise, just like

you did—no offense. What we need, miss, is something a little more foolproof. A little more permanent. What kind of IUDs you got available?"

He might have been asking a store clerk to show him a line of running shoes.

Louise groaned. "It doesn't matter what they've got, Marty. I've tried them all and they all hurt me."

"Wait a minute." He rested a hand on her arm. "Let the lady make her pitch. Maybe they've cooked up something new. You haven't tried an IUD in a couple of years. Maybe it'll work this time."

"The Cooper T is still the one with the best track record and the fewest recorded complications or side effects," the social worker said, holding up the IUD in its clear cellophane wrapper.

"Hey, that doesn't look so bad," Marty said.

"The Copper T gave me cramps and ten-day periods." Louise scowled and turned away, unable to bear the sight of that gadget. It had always reminded her of a fishhook.

"Miss," Marty appealed to the social worker, "don't you think there's a strong psychological element at work here? I mean, who knows, maybe I'd get cramps too if I thought about having this little dingus up my giggy, but we've got to be practical, Weezie, and face it, you don't want to have to go through this again."

"No," she said levelly, "I don't want to go through this again. But I'll stick with the diaphragm, thank you very much. Unless you'd be interested in a vasectomy?" She raised a menacing eyebrow.

"Fine," said the woman, clearly not expecting to have been caught up in a family squabble. "The diaphragm it is. And might I suggest that in the future, you *both* take responsibility for making sure the device is in place?"

The roaring was still in her ears, now so loud she was surprised the nurse didn't hear it, too. She lay on the table and held out her arm for the blood pressure cuff. The nurse frowned at the gauge over Louise's shoulder. "You're a little high," she said. "We'll have to watch that."

Then she left the room again. At least they had let her keep her sundress on. They had asked her to take off only her sandals and her underpants. It was a small, coffin-shaped gray room with none of the questionable amenities of a regular gynecologist's exam room: no mobiles, no cute sayings on the wall, no vapid drawings of kids with big heads and tiny eyes too close together that always find their way into doctors' offices.

"Good afternoon! So, I hear your blood pressure's a little high." The doctor came in briskly, switched on the lamp, and rolled his stool up between Louise's legs. There were a lot more like her waiting their turn and he obviously had no time for small talk or bedside banter.

Reaching two gloved fingers into her, he felt her uterus from the outside. "Eleven weeks, I'd say." He spoke to the nurse, not to Louise.

Eleven weeks. It took only thirty-six weeks to make a fully formed baby. That meant that her baby was almost a third done. She thought of the pictures she'd seen of babies in utero. At eleven weeks, it would no longer look like a fish. It would have eyelids and tiny fingers and even fingernails. In the middle of last night, she had wakened convinced she had felt a faint flutter. Then she thought of Zack and Brucie and Mary: the look of them when they first came out, frog-eyed and dazed, yet so completely themselves. The faces she looked at across the breakfast table were identical to the faces she had seen on the delivery room table in those first few moments after birth.

The doctor held up a large syringe.

Louise sat up.

The nurse put a restraining hand on her shoulder. "It's all right, Mrs. Rosen. This is to numb your cervix."

The roaring sound in Louise's ears was louder than ever. She could just make out her own voice, rising above the din. "I don't want my cervix numbed."

She took her feet out of the stirrups, kicked off the sheet, and swung her legs around. "I don't want my cervix numbed, or my cervix dilated, or my baby vacuumed out of me like a dust ball. I want to keep my baby and not you, or my husband, or anybody else is going to make me do any different. Where are my shoes? I'm getting the hell out of here. Get me my damn shoes!"

The roaring had stopped. She didn't bother to take in the expressions on the faces of the doctor and nurse as she pulled down her dress and marched out of the operating room.

"Mrs. Rosen!"

The nurse came running down the beige-carpeted hall after her.

"You leave me alone," Louise said, leaning against the wall to slip on her sandals. "You can't make me do this. No one can make me do this. Do you hear me? This wasn't my idea in the first place, and I tell you, I'm not going along with it." She gestured wildly, her underpants clutched in one fist. The nurse took a step backward as if Louise were deranged and possibly dangerous.

"You forgot your pocketbook," she said meekly, looking as if she were about to cry.

"Thanks." Louise took her bag and stuffed her underpants into it.

"And, Mrs. Rosen," the nurse added in a whisper, "good luck to you."

"Have you completely fucking lost it, Louise?"

"No," she said, "I just don't want to lose this baby."

"Since when have you become such a rabid right-to-lifer?"

"This isn't about movements, Marty. This is about me and the life I feel growing inside of me."

"This is about marriage, Louise. About partnership. And I thought we decided—"

"No," she said, "*you* decided on this abortion, not me. We never even threw open the floor to discussion. You're the one who made the appointment. You're the one with the crazy obsession with the number four. Well, this is a *baby* inside of me. A living thing. Not some sort of good luck—or bad luck—symbol to be done away with at your superstitious whim."

He braked the car suddenly as a flock of jaywalkers drifted across Park Avenue, and leaned on the horn. Louise covered her ears with both hands. He reached over and yanked her hand away.

"You're not listening to me, Louise. I said you're having enough trouble coping as it is."

"I cope very well, thank you very much. I cope with their needs and I cope with your needs. And if I can cope with three little kids and one big fat one, I can damned well cope with four little kids and one big fat one. And if I ever—and I mean *ever*—hear you saying anything to this kid or around this kid that would make it feel that it was unwanted in any way, I'll kill you. Do you hear me, Martin Rosen?"

"Hormones," he muttered.

"What?"

"You're the victim—*I'm* the victim—of your hormones. You don't know what you're saying. Tomorrow you might feel different about the whole thing. Maybe we'll go see Berry. Maybe it was a mistake taking you to one of these clinics. Maybe with Sheldon you would have been more relaxed and accepting."

"Sheldon happens to think this child is a wonderful idea. He thinks women like me were made to have babies and more power to us."

"Christ!" He braked at a yellow light and banged his head repeatedly on the wheel. "It's a conspiracy. A fucking conspiracy."

"Did it ever occur to you that you're not the only victim around here? Did it ever occur to you that serving your sexual needs day in, day out, night in, night out, has victimized *me*?"

"I thought you enjoyed it!"

"Of course I enjoy sex with you. But twice a day every day? After a while it gets to be like torture."

"Well, thanks a whole hell of a lot, Louise. What an ego massage you turned out to be."

"And another thing. Dr. Berry thinks maybe it's not a great idea for us to have intercourse for a while."

"And why not?"

"Because it hurts me, that's why. He thinks maybe my body is trying to tell me something."

"'No more babies!!' That's what your body's trying to tell you. You just refuse to listen."

When she glared at him, he said, "Fine, fine! I can see right now there's just no way to reason with you. You're going to have this baby and I'm not going to have any more nookie for nine months. Fine, we'll just have to be creative. A few blow jobs." He sighed. "I'll muddle through."

"Blow jobs make me throw up."

"Swell. Then hand jobs it is."

"In that case, I think you might as well take care of it yourself, don't you?" she said coldly.

"Oh, sure!" he said. "A real pleasure. For years now I've been itching to get my hands on myself. Where do you think you're going?"

When he stopped for the light at the corner of Broadway and 115th, she opened the door and hopped out. "To the drugstore to get my vitamin prescription filled. I knew there was a reason I didn't throw it out. Then I'm taking the four-thirty jitney out to Bridgehampton to be with the kids. Can we expect you?"

"I've got stuff to do," he said, rubbing his eyes. "I don't think I'll be able to make it out till next Saturday."

She slammed the door.

"Bye," she said, leaning in the open window and beginning to feel a tiny bit sorry for him.

"Bye."

"I'll call you."

"Fine."

"The kids'll want to say hi."

"Yeah."

"There's lots of food in the fridge."

"Great."

"Are you going to be okay, Marty? Listen, I'm really sorry about this, but it really couldn't have turned out any other way."

"Oh, yes it could have, but obviously you don't want to hear that."

"Are you going to be okay?"

"Who, me? Hey, don't worry about me. I'll be just peachy." He held up his right hand and flexed it. "Me and Miss Mary Five Fingers are old friends. We'll make out just fine."

"Could you picture us living in one of these houses?" Warren asked casually as he steered his BMW sedan through the tree-lined streets of the posh Flower Hill section of Port Washington. They were on their way to a barbecue at the Crawfords'—Lane and Bruno.

"Never," Jill said sullenly, eyeing the crewcut shrubs, the golf course lawns, the neocolonial mini-manses with the cast-iron eagles hammered up over the front doors. "It doesn't look like any kids live here. It's the next right."

"Of course kids live here. Lane and Bruno live here and they have kids. This is suburbia. They grow kids here. Look at the size of these places. There's kids here all right."

"Yeah, well, how come I don't see any evidence? Any bicycles at the curb. Any toys strewn over the lawns. Any strollers. And look at these lawns. They'd be fantastic to roll on. Do you see any kids rolling on these lawns?"

"Maybe they do their rolling in back."

Jill shrugged. "I still don't like it. It lacks life. It lacks character."

"The trouble with you," he said, pulling into the long,

curving blacktop driveway, "is you mistake slovenliness for character. Just like your rich girlfriend Kendra."

Jill didn't have time to retort. Lane burst out the red front door of her brick colonial and came walking briskly down the driveway, frosted gin and tonic held high in her hand as if she were toasting them.

"Hi, Mom!" She hugged Jill and put her hand on her still-flat belly. Jill felt odd. After all, Lane was the one deserving of the name Mom. Was she being inducted into some sort of club?

"Hi, Dad!" Lane waved to Warren as he got out of the car. "Congratulations!"

"It was nothing." He blinked with false modesty, handing her a bottle of Bootles and kissing her cheek.

"The boys are around back," Lane told him. "If you don't mind, I'm going to spirit the little mother off to the kitchen with we women folk."

"Be my guest." Warren lumbered around back as Lane led Jill up the immaculate front walk into her picture-perfect suburban home.

From the kitchen, the "little mother" could see the men sprawled out on the patio, each with a drink in his hand, while Bruno played with the fire. They were clad in the leisure suit of the upper crust: khaki, kelly green, or fire-engine red Bermudas and Lacoste shirts. At the far end of the yard, a bunch of kids—four of Lane's and some belonging to the other guests—were noisily swarming over a duplex treehouse and a large custom-built wooden jungle gym complete with tire swing, rope bridges, slides, and tunnels—not unlike something you might find in a Sutton Place pocket park. The pool was covered.

"Is the pool sick or something?" Jill asked.

"Don't remind me." Lane rolled her eyes as she chopped up fruit for a salad. "It's got some kind of algae or fungus we can't get rid of. It looks like lemonade and it smells like—"

"It's just as well," Jill said as she sat at the table sipping a ginger ale and watching the other women prepare dinner. "Warren wouldn't let me take my suit. He said pools aren't safe for pregnant women."

"Men!" sputtered Hatty, Lane's next-door neighbor, as she tore greens for a salad. "They'd like to put us in a bubble for nine months."

"You want to know why?" asked Sheila, who lived down the block. "Because we're carrying the seed of *their* loins."

"We're mere vessels," Lane added with a smirk.

Jill felt as if she were suddenly plunged into a Fifties musical comedy, the kind where all the men are on one side of the stage singing about dames and all the women are on the other, throwing up their hands and singing, "Men—can't live with them, can't live without them." If, fifteen years ago, someone had shown her a preview of the scene, she never would have believed it.

Lane had been Jill and Kendra's suitemate junior and senior years. Next to Kendra, Lane, a poli-sci major, was the biggest iconoclast Jill had ever met. She was always on the cutting edge. The first freshman to join the sit-in during the Vietnam war moratorium, the first to campaign in favor of legalizing abortion, the first to experiment with psychedelic drugs. She had worn her strawberry-blond hair long—falling almost to her waist —and her blue jeans elaborately embroidered. Senior year, she had met Bruno, a Columbia law student, and surprised everybody by marrying him a week after graduation. While he completed school, she supported them by doing research for CBS News. But as soon as Bruno passed the bar, she quit her job, got pregnant, and became a full-time housewife. Over the next fourteen years, she would give Bruno four children. She now wore her lovely hair in an altogether too perky Dorothy Hammill style and dressed, like her own mother in Garden City, as if she had just stepped out of a golf cart.

"Mom, we're boiling out there. Can we go swimming?" It was Lane's second son, Brian, standing in the kitchen doorway, droplets of grimy sweat sliding down the sides of his face.

"Of course you can't go swimming. You know we're still waiting for the pool doctor to visit. Say hi to Aunt Jill."

"Hi, Aunt Jill," he said grudgingly. "At Robby's pool, I meant."

"But Ben and Sheila are here. There's no one over there to watch you."

His face lit up as if with a brilliant idea. "Can't *you* come over and watch us, Mom?"

"Of course I can't. I'm in the middle of getting dinner ready. Maybe after dinner, if it's all right with Sheila, we can go over and take a dip."

His face fell. "You're no fair."

"Of course I'm no fair," Lane admitted evenly, "I'm a mother." As the boy shambled out, Lane winked at Jill. "Bet you can't wait."

Jill smiled wanly. "At least I'm over the morning sickness."

"With Teddy," Lane said, having moved on to toss a three-bean salad, "I was sick as a dog for all nine months."

"You think that's bad," Hatty put in. "With Donna, I had morning sickness, plus I had pains."

"Pains?" Jill gulped. Did yet other forms of discomfort lie in wait for her?

"Pains," the woman assured her. "Sharp, shooting pains all through my stomach. I went to the doctor and he says, 'Well, there's no telling, of course, but you'll probably miscarry.' Miscarry! Great, thanks for the encouragement. It wasn't till I started asking around that I discovered other women had pains, too."

"Like *Rosemary's Baby*," Sheila added with a fiendish grin.

"Gee," Jill said. "I'm beginning to feel lucky I had only nausea. You should have seen me..."

But no one seemed to be listening to her. All three women had begun chattering at once, none of them listening to anything the others said. Perhaps it was a disorder that came from spending too many hours of the day with children, who all chattered at once and never listened either. Any other time, Jill would have turned her back on them and gone out back to talk to the men. At New York parties, men and women mingled and talked. There wasn't this sexual segregation, like at a junior-high dance. But at least at a dance, the boys eventually got up the nerve to ask the girls to dance.

They ate outdoors at a long stone picnic table, the girls on the side nearest the kitchen in case anybody needed anything, the boys on the side nearest the fire and the bar. On a blanket beneath the jungle gym, the kids ate burgers and hot dogs. The grown-ups' steaks were thick and deliciously rare, but everybody but Jill was too drunk to appreciate them.

"So, Jill," Bruno said. "I hear congrats are in order."

Fifteen years ago, Bruno had tried to get Jill involved in a ménage à trois with him and Lane. When she refused, he went and successfully recruited Kendra. Ever since then, she had not trusted him. She looked into his dark, sleepy, sexy eyes and said, "Thank you, Bruno."

He smiled and added slyly, "Warren here tells me he won the Battle of the Midwives."

She glared at Warren, who, looking instantly contrite, was diving for a beer. "I keep forgetting," she said with mock sweetness, "that men are even bigger gossips than women."

"Let us in on it," Lane said gleefully. "What's this about midwives?"

Jill's voice was level, grim. "I wanted to go to a midwife clinic instead of an obstetrician. But the father of my child wouldn't let me. End of story."

"Gee," Sheila said, "I thought midwives went out with chastity belts."

"There's an extremely reputable clinic associated with Hudson River General," Jill said. She couldn't believe she was actually participating in this discussion. The only consolation she derived from it was the prospect of relating it to Kendra later, in all its grisly detail.

"Really?" Hatty marveled. "And you wanted to go to it? How brave!"

"Bravery doesn't have much to do with it."

"Hah!" said Hatty. "Wait'll labor kicks in. Bravery has everything to do with it."

"Whip out the medals, boys," Neil, Hatty's husband, spoke up. He was a florid man with a paunch and red fuzz growing on the back of his fingers. "The gals are going to start talking childbirth again."

"Honey," Hatty said, covering Jill's hand with her own, "I had three C-sections. Believe me, when I needed that doctor, it was nice to have him right there. You just never know."

"My doctor's a real Nazi," Sheila went on. "But if there's ever a problem, I know he can handle it."

"That's what I told her," Warren said. "I said what if something goes wrong. I'm not saying it will, but *what if.* Won't it be nice to have that doctor around? And face it: You're in a hospital anyway. In the hospital the doctors call the shots."

"Not if you're under a midwife's care and it's a routine birth," Jill maintained stubbornly.

All three of the women burst into harsh laughter. "Oh, Jillsie," Lane said sadly, "as you'll find out soon enough, there is no such thing as a routine birth."

Mary Beth

"I'm afraid of hurting you," he said.

Mary Beth had never seen Daniel's face like this. Before, there had always been a hint of hardness about his mouth, of cruelty in his eyes. But there was a softness here now.

"You're so beautiful," he said. "It breaks my heart how beautiful you are."

Naked, he lay beside her and stared into her eyes. As her lashes fluttered, he moved in and kissed her softly on the lips. She sighed and nestled into his arms, feeling the softness of his skin against hers, the hardness of his penis as it pressed against her thigh. Suddenly, she wanted him very much. She reached down and guided him inside her. She was wet, as she had been since the last time she saw him. He moved in her slowly, carefully, never losing contact with her eyes.

She felt ripe, tingling as if a thousand extra nerve endings had come alive with the embryo growing inside of her. It required no passionate thrusting to push her over the edge. This gentlest of friction was all it took. "It feels so good!" she said.

"I'm glad," he whispered. "Because from now on I want you to feel nothing but good things. You're so, so precious to me."

"Oh, my goodness," she said, amazed. "I'm coming!"

And crying out, like a small boy who doesn't want to be left behind, he lurched after her.

When he dropped her off at Grand Central Station an hour and a half later, they had still not had that serious talk he suggested on the rainy street corner four weeks ago. They now met every week instead of every month, as had been the routine before, at his bachelor apartment off Amsterdam instead of at the Plaza. He had even given her the key, which she took care to slip into her portfolio as soon as she retrieved it from the station locker before boarding the train for home.

When she got home, she found her guys in the flagstone foyer, where Denny was helping his father repair a windowpane in the front door. Her guys. She used to call them her "boys." But when Daniel noticed, he had given her one of his superior looks and said that she must not have much respect for her husband if she called him "boy." Heatedly, she had defended herself, saying that "boy" was, to her, a term of endearment. "It's a term of belittlement, whether you're conscious of it or not," he told her, so she made up her mind then and there to start calling them her "guys" instead.

"Hi, guys!" she called out as she came up the front walk.

"Mommy, Mommy, Daddy got mad and busted a window."

The euphoria that had suffused her body all afternoon began to ebb.

"What happened?"

Frank's face was grim as he worked the caulking gun.

"What Denny said," he replied shortly.

"Denny, honey, take my portfolio upstairs to my studio, will you?"

"Sure thing, Mom. Umph! It's heavy." He grunted as he lifted the case, which was nearly as big as he was, and staggered with it toward the stairs.

"Are you okay, honey?"

"'Course I'm okay," he said, not taking his eyes off the job. "Any reason why I shouldn't be okay?"

She fought panic. Dear God, what if he knows? What if a neighbor had seen Daniel dropping her off at Grand Central this afternoon? But no, she told herself, such a coincidence was highly unlikely. Taking control of herself, she said, "Are you going to tell me what happened to the window?"

"Oh, just that I got a call this morning from a customer who blamed me for the weather we had all July. Instead of bitching her out, or tearing the phone out by the roots, I chucked my keys at the door. The window broke. There, are you happy now?"

She took a deep breath and reminded herself of her new credo: She could keep them all—Daniel, Denny, Frank, herself, the baby growing inside of her—if only she remained calm and centered. She came up behind him and wrapped her arms around his middle.

"As a matter of fact," she whispered, "I'm very happy." She waited, hoping he would ask why. When he didn't, she went on. "I went to see Dr. Dina today."

It was a lie. It had been weeks ago, but how was he to know?

"Yeah? And how is Dina doing?"

"She's fine. But I'm even better. She had some news for me."

"Yeah?"

"We're going to have a baby."

He turned and set down the caulking gun, the anger draining from his face.

"You're kidding! When?"

"Oh, around February. February fourteenth, as a matter of fact. Valentine's Day." She grinned at him. "Happy Valentine's Day, sweetheart. Now, are you happy?"

"Happy? Holy Toledo!" he exploded. "That's terrific! Let it rain for forty days and forty nights. We're going to have us a baby!" He picked her up in his arms and whirled her around and around, stopping abruptly. "Hey, are you feeling okay?" He carried her into the living room and set her down gingerly on the couch.

"Of course I'm okay." She laughed, smoothing his dark hair back from his forehead. "Why shouldn't I be okay? I'm going to have your baby." And for that moment, it was necessary that she believe that statement with all her being, in order to meet his eyes.

Kendra

It was hot and overcast the day she returned from Whispering Laurels to the city. Kendra was tired—tired from the constant confrontations with her parents and from three weeks spent in the bathhouse guest room, where the sounds and smells of the beach, once so familiar to her, made her restless and on edge and unable to sink into a really satisfying sleep.

Finally finding a parking space between two rent-atrucks on Bond Street, Kendra made her way down the garbage-strewn sidewalk to the corner bodega for milk and juice. On the ride down, she had perspired profusely and now felt dehydrated and wrung out. Standing on line at the counter, she held her damp face to the faint breeze coming from the oscillating fan on the shelf behind the register. Fat flies skated across the greasy Formica and swarmed over the contents of the smudged display case: three pale, mealy tomatoes, a couple of nibbled-looking Kaiser rolls, a sprouting onion, a half-dozen brown lemons, and a package of melting lard.

"Put it on my bill," she told the man behind the counter. She had the cash but not the energy to dig into her bag. Out on the sidewalk, a bum lay propped up against a standpipe with the stump of his amputated foot wrapped in a soiled ace bandage. He wore, as all vagrants seemed to wear, even in the dead of summer, a heavy woolen coat. He lifted a blackened palm.

"Spare a quarter, lady? I'm trying to make the down payment on my house in the Hamptons."

Ever one to reward a panhandler for using a little imagination, she rummaged in her wallet for a quarter and dropped it into his palm, moving off briskly down the street before he could strike up a conversation. She realized now why she had welcomed the rain earlier in the summer, and the days of enforced isolation up in her loft. Pregnancy had boosted her customary sidewalk paranoia to soaring heights. Every stranger was a potential mugger, every stray piece of trash threatened to trip her, even the grillwork on passing cars had taken on a menacing look, as if at any second they might jump the curb and run her down. Years of living on the outskirts of urban civilization had made her a cautious woman, but this was ridiculous.

Looking quickly to her right and to her left, she inserted the key into the lock, turned it, and shoved the door open with one hip. He must have come from across the street, or from behind a parked car, but he seemed to loom out of nowhere: stinking of defecation and rotting flesh, black hair a riot, beard encrusted with yellow scales, the whites of his eyes wild and furious in his sooty face.

"Give us a kiss, Goldilocks," he growled, taking her roughly and depositing on her cheek a slimy gift. Elbowing him away with a disgusted cry, she managed to squeeze in the door and bolt it behind her.

"Whassamatter, Goldy, you don't believe in foreplay?" He banged on the door a few times and went off cackling maniacally.

She was shaking all over, her body bathed in cold sweat, her cheek sticky where his lips had been. She felt violated, contaminated, and more frightened than ever before. She had experienced run-ins with bums before. She had always shoved them away or kneed them in the groin. But she couldn't do that now. What if one of them got it together to kick her back? Right in the stomach? Shuddering, she flipped through the mail that had accumulated in her absence. There were no mailboxes here. The mailman had the key to the front door and left the mail for everyone in the building in a hasty heap on a wooden bench in the entryway. The stairs were steep and listing to one side. Taking a firm hold of the humid bannister, she pulled her way slowly, slowly up the three long rickety flights. What was it the midwife had said? *Avoid climbing stairs?* What was she supposed to do for the next few months? Rig a hoist?

Stopping to rest twice, she was at her door in three minutes, panting, her head throbbing, wanting that shower so badly she could taste it. Open up the three locks, shove open the fireproof door, relock the three locks, and she was home!

She dropped her bag, her groceries, and the mail in a pile by the door and made a beeline for the shower, shedding her clothes as she went. She didn't want to stop and take too hard a look at this 2,500-square-foot space she called home. She doubted it would hold up to scrutiny very well in the dingy light of this August day, especially after the sumptuous and sheltering beauty of Whispering Laurels.

She stood under a hot shower for ten minutes: first

shampooing, then soaping off the sweat and the bum's kiss; then five minutes under a cool rinse, taking deep calming breaths. Her hands traveled down to her breasts. Her nipples were hard and enlarged, having turned a dark tannish color. She felt a small soft mass just over her pubis bone where the baby was nestled and patted it protectively. Then her fingers made their inevitable way between her legs and felt the slippery moistness that awaited her there.

She turned off the water and wrapped her hair in a towel, rubbed oil into every inch of her skin, powdered beneath her armpits, her breasts, and between her legs, and walked out into her loft: a woman resurrected.

After she put the milk and juice away in her noisy, often cantankerous bar-sized refrigerator, she took up the mail and lay down on her bed to sort through it. The sheets felt cool and soothing against her skin as she tore open the envelopes and read through the invitations to lectures, to gallery openings, to play showcases. As she read, she reached over, unthinking, into her bedside table drawer and got her vibrator. Switching it on, she put it between her legs and was surprised to find herself having a quick, sweet orgasm in a matter of seconds. She switched off the machine, a little unsettled, and went back to the mail. She came to a postcard from the island of Capri. That blue, blue water looked so refreshing. Expecting to find a message from one of her old schoolmates on the other side, she was surprised to see the handwriting that had grown so familiar to her in so short a time.

Kendra!
We all came down here from Spoleto for a bit of sun and fun. Yes, the water really is this color. Wish you were here so we could go swimming in the nude and then make love under the stars. Perhaps absence makes the heart overly fond, but I keep thinking you're the best I've ever had. Mean machine or no.
Love, Morgan.

The mean machine was back on again, between her legs, as she found herself riding off on one tiny orgasm after another, pursuing fantasies of swimming in picture-postcard blue waters and making love beneath the stars with a man named Morgan.

arleen

Bill Donovan, captain of his college wrestling team, always looked uncomfortable in a suit. But as a concession to The Four Seasons, he wore a white linen jacket and a sky-blue silk tie that matched his eyes—the one that Carleen had tucked in his stocking four Christmases ago. When he saw Carleen trailing the maitre d' around the fountain, he rose and bowed boyishly.

"Hi," he said shyly.

Carleen kissed him quickly on the cheek, avoiding meeting his eyes. They were here to celebrate getting through the first trimester, but before they left the apartment this morning they had had the umpteenth quarrel about her flying to Puerto Rico for the sales conference in December. Through an editorial board meeting, an author lunch, a cover meeting, and a tough contract negotiation session with an agent, their exchange echoed in her mind.

"Eight years, Carleen! Eight years of trying and failing and hoping and praying and you're willing to flush it all away on a gamble!"

"It's not a gamble, Bill. It's my job. Have you any idea how eager Elton Norwood is to rush in and help?"

"Elton Norwood is an asshole."

"Elton Norwood is an *ambitious* asshole who has taken to playing tennis every Tuesday with Hugh."

In order to get away from him, she had taken her coffee and muffin out onto the terrace. They lived on the forty-first floor of an East Side high-rise. Through the inverted air, she could just make out the Twin Towers swimming in the smog.

"Then I'd like to know what you'd call it?" He followed her out and stood behind her, where she perched on a white wrought-iron chair that was gritty with soot and urban fallout.

"Fitzwater says it's a *calculated* risk," she said.

"*And* he advises against it."

"No, he does not. He says we'll have to wait and see how I'm doing when the time comes. It's three months away, Bill. I'm feeling stronger and better every day—"

"Have you thought about what we've been through getting you pregnant? The financial investment alone..."

He was pacing back and forth in his stocking feet, pounding the iron railing. Watching him, Carleen was thinking how glad she would be when they found a new apartment. The terrace was simply too dangerous, the railing too low and flimsy.

She imagined carrying her baby out here, saw herself tripping, losing hold of the baby, and watching it fall forty-one stories to the street. They had been living here for almost fifteen years and the rent was, relatively speaking, cheap for a two-bedroom. They had just begun to make the rounds with a realtor. The price people wanted for their three-bedroom condos was laughable but Bill and Carleen had no choice, they needed more space; they needed to raise their baby in an apartment closer to the ground.

"I've never really thought about it as an *investment*, Bill."

"If you can't think about the money, think about the *emotional* investment. Remember how depressed we always got watching couples with babies in the park? Sure, we never said anything about it, but it cast a shroud over our entire lives. I've been so happy this summer. When I think of losing that happiness . . ."

"I think that's what having a baby is all about," Carleen said thoughtfully, "having something you can lose. You might as well get used to it, Bill. This is the way it's going to be from now on."

He stopped pacing and looked at her, his polo shirt already discolored at the armpits from perspiration. It was going to be another beastly August day. "If anything happened to this baby because you went to P.R."— he took a breath as if unsure as to whether he should go on—"I don't know if we could go on living with each other."

"How was your day?" Carleen asked formally, flipping open the menu and glancing at the appetizers. Now that she was inside an air-conditioned space, she was starved.

He laughed shortly. "I've had better."

"It's the heat," she said. "It's getting to everyone. Our air conditioning konked out this afternoon and we can't even open our windows. The fan kept blowing my papers all over. Tempers were very short. I think we need to get away. We haven't gotten away all summer. You think you could grab a week in September? We could go up to the Vineyard, eat lobster, and lie in the dunes. How does that sound?"

She reached across the table and laid her hand over his, a first gesture of reconciliation.

"No problem." He eased his hand out from under hers and took up the menu. "I can get a week. I can get two weeks. Three weeks even! Hey, why the hell not?"

She looked at him closely. There was a strange, reckless light in his eye. "Are you all right?"

"Sure!" he said. "I'm fine. Listen, Carleen, I'm really sorry about what I said this morning. I guess I got a little hysterical. It's just that I feel so powerless sometimes. I mean, it may be our baby but you're the one who's carrying it. I think if I had my way, I'd lock you in a padded room. But I don't guess that's possible."

"Or practical. But you're worried. I understand."

"And I just want you to know, if Fitzwater says it's okay for you to fly in December, I've got no problem with it."

She leaned back in her seat as the waiter came and filled their water glasses. Bill raised his. "Let's drink. To your First Trimester."

"And to getting through the other two," she added, grinning, clicking her glass with his. She shook her head at him, baffled. "William Bartley Donovan, you never cease to amaze me. Pulling a one-eighty like that in the course of a single day."

He shrugged and shifted his eyes away from her. "A lot of things can happen to a guy in a single day."

"Oh?" She leaned across the table to brush a lock of his light brown hair out of his eyes. "Such as . . . ?"

"Oh," he said evasively, "such as a guy could find himself out of a job, for instance."

At first she thought he was kidding. Then the look on his face told her he wasn't.

"As of when?"

"Two weeks from today."

"Why?"

"Carleen, when I took this job, we both knew it might be short-term. Finley's feeling healthy enough to come back to work. Finley's got seniority. Donovan's out. That's all there is to it. It'll look great on my résumé. Short but oh, so sweet."

Carleen nodded slowly as it dawned on her. "So that's why you're suddenly no longer so dead set against my working the sales conference!"

He flexed his fingers on the tablecloth, his face having turned a deep red. "I guess . . . maybe . . . I don't know."

"We can't afford to have me sit it out now even if I wanted to. Even if I *had* to."

"I'm sure I'll be able to line something up by then."

"Oh, really?" Carleen couldn't keep the note of panic out of her voice. "You said yourself things are very tight out there."

"I'll squeeze in somewhere. Or I'll freelance. We'll be fine."

"What about our plan to buy a bigger apartment without a terrace?"

"I guess that'll have to wait. Hey, what are we complaining about? A guy at the *Times* and his wife live with three kids *and* the nanny in a six-room railroad. New York's getting to be more and more like Moscow!"

"Shit!" she said, not realizing until then just how much she was counting on this new apartment. "I guess if I was one of those women who got pregnant every time she lay down, we could scratch this one and try again later—at some more *convenient* time." Her eyes filled with tears. She felt sorry for Bill for being on the beach, sorry for herself for having to bring in the bread *and* carry the baby, sorry for them both that they wouldn't be able to afford that expensive new nest.

"Are you ready to order now?" The waiter stood over their table.

"Suddenly, I'm not feeling very hungry," Carleen said in a choked voice.

$\mathscr{L}$ouise

"I can just see Marty's face when you told him to beat his own meat." Agnes laughed so hard she spilled her Pouilly-Fuissé down the cleavage of her black and gold maillot.

"Poor guy! You gotta feel sorry for him." Patsy lay face down, the sun glinting on her oiled back.

"Poor guy, nothing!" Agnes rejoined. "If you ask me, Louise has spoiled Marty rotten, spreading her legs every time—"

"Do you really think I've spoiled him?" Louise sat up

and pushed her sunglasses down on her nose to stare at her two friends. Her beach friends differed from her park friends in two respects: They were rich and they were idle. The three of them lay side by side on rattan lounge chairs on the deck of Louise's house in Bridgehampton. Far down the beach, out of sight, where the pounding of the surf was a distant rumble, their children were being looked after by au pairs, nannies, and lifeguards. The air was dry, the sky cloudless, the breeze scattering a fine veil of sand. If it weren't for the seagulls wheeling overhead and the smell of salt, they might have been in the middle of the desert.

"*Spoiled* isn't quite the word," Patsy said thoughtfully. "I mean, if Hal wanted to have it off with me every night, *I'd* be the one who considered herself spoiled." Patsy had married a very busy, very successful plastic surgeon and had the face and body to prove it. The traces of her three pregnancies had been expertly obliterated by a series of strategic tucks and implants, the scars of which not even her leopard-skin bandeau bikini revealed. She had, Louise had always thought, the body of a woman who had sold her soul. She flipped over onto her back, oiled her perfect belly and her perfect thighs, took a sip of her frosted margarita through a straw, and surrendered herself once again to the sun's rays. "Hal is happy doing it once a month. And if he forgets, I'm the one who has to remind him. I hate that. I feel like a charity case."

"That's nothing," Agnes said. "I haven't had sex in so long, I probably need a refresher course." Divorced two years ago, Agnes, a tall blond Swede who had custody of four tall blond children, preferred to be celibate rather than risk contracting AIDS or herpes. Her ex-husband, an internist with a thing about cleanliness that rivaled that of the great Howard Hughes, had taught her just enough about the World of Germs to make her socially wary, if not downright paralyzed.

"I think it comes back to you"—Louise yawned up into the sun—"like riding a bike. I have to admit, though, I don't miss it a bit. It's been weeks, and for the first time in years I feel like I'm really on vacation."

"You are on vacation, lovie," Patsy reminded her. "Look around you."

"I mean from sex."

"I never did it very much when I was pregnant," Agnes said. "Kroger was afraid to."

"Afraid?"

"Infection."

"Oh! Naturally. Well, Hallie and I did it all the time. Something about that big, sleek gut of mine really made him horny. He used to rub baby oil into my tummy and then one thing would lead to another and—"

"Weren't you afraid of getting the baby oil inside?" Agnes asked with characteristic anxiety.

"Why do you think they call it *baby* oil, lovie?" Patsy cracked.

"I always enjoyed sex," Louise said dreamily. "Before ...when I was carrying the others...if only because it was the only time I didn't have to worry about birth control. But this time...I don't know what it is...I'm really turned off."

"Every pregnancy's different, that's what my doctor used to say," Patsy said. "Of course that's pretty much their explanation for everything."

This one was different all right. Only fourteen weeks gone and she was already wearing a maternity bathing suit. Usually she didn't begin to show in a big way until the twentieth week. She had always prided herself on how neatly and lightly she carried. But less than halfway there and she had gained over twenty pounds. She felt sprawling, sloppy, and totally undesirable.

"Don't worry about it," Dr. Berry had told her the last time she went in to see him. "It's summer and you're retaining a lot of water. You'll level off."

"Aren't you afraid he's going to seek outside help?" Patsy asked.

Louise sat up and chugged the rest of her ice water, holding up her strapless bathing suit with one hand. Her breasts were enormous and sweaty in the sun. "You mean a shrink? Marty would never in a million years go to a shrink. Even if he needed to."

"I think he's got a treatable condition," Agnes said. "It's called priapus or something like that. It's the male version of a nympho."

"I don't mean a shrink," Patsy said. "I mean *other women.* Marty's a very attractive guy, and I've seen the little doll babies he hires to work the cash registers at Truffles...mighty cute morsels they are, too. I don't know, Louise."

Louise felt herself growing hot and flustered. "Marty wouldn't do that!" But as she said the words, she was no longer so sure.

"Of course Marty wouldn't do that." Agnes batted the thought away. "He's a nice Jewish boy. Jewish men are notoriously faithful. I think the impulse to run around and chase skirt was removed at birth...along with their foreskins."

"You really think so?" Louise lay back down. But she was not altogether reassured.

That evening as the sun set, they barbecued hot dogs and hamburgers out on the grill while the children sat at the picnic table and colored; or rather, Zack colored, Bruce scribbled, and Mary nibbled delicately on a red crayon.

"I don't think you look so big," Francine said righteously, swatting a strand of long silver-blond hair out of her eyes as she tended the hamburgers on the grill. "I think you look lovely."

"Big as a house," Louise said, slicing tomatoes on the marble chopping board. They were blood red and sweet. For days, Louise had been eating them whole and sun-warmed, like apples. "That's what Marty said last weekend. 'Weezie,' he said, 'you're as big as a house.'"

"Maybe that's because he doesn't get to see you every day like we do," Francine maintained.

"I think maybe I should go on a diet."

Francine was Louise's height and maddeningly slim in a pair of short shorts and a halter top. In a dyed pink Mexican wedding dress, Louise felt like Miss Piggy.

"Don't diet," Francine cautioned. "You really mustn't. It

isn't good for pregnant women to diet. Besides, it's not you who are big. It's the baby. You are skinny everyplace else."

"Then what am I doing carrying such a humongous baby? Zack and the other two came out under seven pounds. I'm little, Marty's little..."

"Remember what Dr. Shelly said: 'Every pregnancy's different.'"

"I don't know. I think I'll phone Marty and ask him to bring me out that little kitchen scale this weekend. Maybe if I exercise portion control, I'll level off. I promise I won't starve myself."

She didn't *feel* as if she was overeating. She ate three sensible meals a day and never snacked. Still, every morning when she climbed, naked, on the scales, she seemed to have gained another pound. She had always felt so in control of her body. Even when pregnant, she never gained more than eighteen pounds. What was wrong with her? Was it the lack of sex? Did sex really burn up calories like they said it did?

"I think I'll call him now," Louise said resolutely. She'd have him bring out the scale and start weighing her portions and have sex with Marty again and everything would be okay.

It was cool and dark inside. In the kitchen, Magda was making ice cream from fresh peaches and cream. Louise had been looking forward to dessert all day, but now she decided to forego it. As she passed Magda, she fanned her face with one hand to show Magda how hot it still was. Magda stopped churning and stared at Louise with dark, disapproving eyes. Magda had been in the States for a year and a half and got by on very little English. If it weren't for Francine, who spoke Spanish and a smattering of Portuguese, Louise would have had to communicate with her housekeeper in sign language alone. Before she knew what she was doing, Louise dipped a finger into the bowl of the ice-cream maker and was sampling a hundred and fifty calories' worth of peach ice cream.

"Fantastic!" she said a little too loudly and Magda

pursed her lips. Louise shrugged and continued on her way.

How she loved this place: a big sprawling English-style cottage sided with cedar shingles weathered to the silver of driftwood, and covered with climbing roses. The rooms were large and airy, the gleaming teak floors rugless, the furniture chintz- or provincial-upholstered wicker and built-in banquettes covered with off-white duck to resist the wet bottoms of bathers. From the family room phone, she dialed the store. Marty's assistant picked up, sounding harried. "Marty? He went home with a headache."

"Really?"

"How is it out there?" he asked. "It's stinkin' hot in here. Air conditioning don't begin to help."

"It's hot but gorgeous and breezy. No rain for three weeks and not a cloud in the sky."

"You're making me very jealous, Louise. You mind trying to get your old man to spend a little more time out there? He's been walkin' around here with a six-inch rod up his—excuse me—he's been a real bear."

"I'll see what I can do," she promised, ringing off.

While she was dialing home, Zack ran in to show off the picture he had just colored.

"Look, Mom. I did a picture of all of us. Here's me and Francine and Brucie and Mary and Magda. That's you with your new little baby in your arms. It's all born and outside of you and everything. Aren't you happy?"

"I'm very happy, Zackie, but where is Daddy?"

"Oh, Daddy was too busy to be in the picture. Daddy was at the store."

A woman answered the telephone in their apartment.

"Hello?" All of a sudden, Louise's heart was beating like a jackhammer. "Is this the Rosen residence?"

"It sure is."

She sounded very young. Like one of those "cute morsels" who worked in the store?

"Is Marty there?"

"Yeah, he is."

"Can I speak to him, please?"

"He's in the shower right now. Any message?"

Marty, in the shower, with another woman in their apartment? Maybe Patsy was right. Maybe she had driven him to seek outside help. Maybe it was too late to make everything better.

"No," Louise said tightly, holding her hand to her belly, where she felt now, unmistakably, the first kick. "I'll call back later."

PART III

Second
Trimester

Jill

The beach at Cape May Point was beautiful after the season, the ocean a frosty blue, uncluttered by summer debris and unplagued by the jellyfish that had kept bathers out of the water most of July and August. For two weeks in September, Jill and Warren rented a Victorian tower cottage across the street from the dunes and down the way from St. Mary's-by-the-Sea, the rambling turn-of-the-century resort hotel that now served as a retreat for an order of Philadelphia nuns.

Jill liked the tower the best, a small circular room at the top of the house with a three-hundred-and-sixty-degree view of the ocean and dunes, the surrounding houses, the lighthouse, and St. Mary's. Papered in a black floral print, it was bathed all day long in pale salt-diffused light and at night permeated by the sea's dampness like the cabin of a boat. She and Warren spent many peaceful hours in the tower room; he, having rigged a telescope on a tripod, eyeing the passing parade of boats and ships and an occasional school of dolphins, she, reading and dozing in a big white wicker chair. Every night they ate fish and fresh vegetables, and every morning Jill rose at dawn for her daily constitutional. While Warren still slept, she slipped out of bed, donned her bikini bottom and a tank top to conceal her swelling belly, and padded barefoot down the street past St. Mary's. As she passed the porch she heard the high, sweet sound of the sisters singing Matins, mingled with the shrieking of the seagulls as they wheeled and dipped over the red roofs, carrying their prey in hooked beaks.

She walked about two miles down the shore, which was

deserted except for fishermen surfcasting from the beach or, if the tide was high, out on the breakwaters trying their luck in deeper waters. When she came to the last breakwater, she walked all the way out to the end and, slipping into the sea-weedy dark waters, began to swim the two miles back to the beach in front of Tower Cottage. Her strokes were slow and regular, almost languorous, as she felt her longer muscles lengthen. Her mind, except for a fleeting projection of the sealife swarming beneath her, was a perfect blank. One morning at the end of the first week of their stay, as Jill was swimming past the high red roofs of St. Mary's-by-the-Sea, she felt a sudden sharp pain pierce her lower abdomen. Thinking that it was perhaps a swimmer's cramp, even though she hadn't yet eaten her breakfast, she calmly headed into shore on her back, propelling herself with legs only.

On the beach three nuns were preparing to take their morning dip. Even when they were out of their habits, it was easy to spot the sisters from the modest necklines, long skirts, and dark conservative print of their bathing suits. They were also among the few remaining women to wear bathing caps.

As Jill emerged from the surf, the pain gradually fell away.

"How is it?" one of the sisters asked, tucking her cropped gray hair into a bathing cap.

"Perfect," said Jill, catching her breath and looking back at the breakers, as if the cause of her pain were still out here somewhere.

"You're a lovely swimmer," said another. "I was just saying to Sister Carmella here, 'She's a lovely swimmer, isn't she?' Like a little fish."

"Excuse me," Sister Carmella said uneasily, pointing at Jill's legs, "but it looks as if you might have gotten your period."

Jill looked down. A trickle of watery blood ran down her inner thigh and pooled at the back of one knee.

"That's impossible," she said, panic gathering deep in her stomach. "I mean it just can't be!"

* * *

Jill scrambled down the beach to Tower Cottage. Maybe she had unknowingly cut herself on the breakwater rocks. Maybe she had a bleeding hemorrhoid. Maybe the dye in her bathing suit was running. She dashed down the narrow wooden walk spanning the beach grass in the front yard and banged open the kitchen screen door. Warren, cooking his usual breakfast of bacon and three eggs, turned to say good morning. Ignoring him, she ran past him into the bathroom, pulled down her bathing suit bottom, and sat on the john. The white cotton crotch was faintly tinged with blood. She wiped herself. Only the palest pink there, too. The cramp she had experienced out in the water was clearly past. She leaned back and closed her eyes. Everything would be fine. Everything had to be fine. Had to be, she told herself. *Had to be!*

"Is that blood, Jill?"

Jill opened her eyes. Warren stood over her, a spatula in one hand, a dish towel worn like an apron over his madras Bermudas.

"It ain't tomato juice," she cracked.

For a minute, fear passed across his face like a shadow before the Expert took control.

"Get out of that wet suit, Jill, and get in bed. We'll call Berry."

"We will not call Berry."

"What do you mean, Jill? You're bleeding. We're calling Berry."

"It's probably just a false alarm."

She peeled off her suit and tank top and climbed into the shower to wash off the salt and blood.

"False alarm or no, he should know about this. If you won't call him, I will. Shit!" He bolted from the bathroom. She heard him in the kitchen cursing loudly and smelled hot grease and burning bacon.

Putting on a fresh nightgown, she got into bed. Through the gauzy curtains hanging across the bedroom windows she could make out the gentle slopes of the dunes, and the early beachgoers, with umbrellas and beach bags, setting up for the day. She felt like an invalid.

Downstairs she heard Warren dialing and speaking on the phone. Although she couldn't make out the precise words, his tone was subdued and anxious. Then she heard him clumping up the stairs. He entered the room, his mouth set in a grim line, and sat down heavily on the bed.

"Berry says stay in bed and take it easy." He spoke to his Weejuns.

"Did Berry say pregnant women spot like this all the time and there's nothing to worry about?"

"Not *all the time*, Jill," he said pointedly. "In the first three months he said it's a lot more common. But with someone as far along as you ..."

"It's not a good sign," Jill finished for him, cupping her hands protectively over her stomach.

Warren nodded ponderously. "He told us not to fuck."

Jill laughed shortly. They hadn't had sex since the night she conceived.

"What else did he say?"

"He wanted to know if you had any pain?"

"One cramp."

"And whether the blood was brown or red."

"Actually, it was sort of pink."

"I think that means red."

"Is that a good sign or a bad sign?"

He sighed. "It's better if it's brown. It means it's old blood." He looked stricken. She had to remind herself: *This is happening to him, too.*

Jill nodded slowly. "I'll try to bleed brown next time."

Warren got up and walked over to the window. "I blame myself," he said, punching his palm.

"Why?"

"I *knew* ... I just knew I shouldn't have let you go swimming."

Four days, Jill stayed in bed and watched her underpants for bloodstains. When none showed up, she got up and began to resume her normal daily routine minus the swim, which meant that she went back to sitting in the tower room in the big white wicker chair, reading and dozing, while Warren peered through his telescope. When the early-morning breeze sometimes carried to her the sound of the nuns singing Matins, Jill found herself missing her daily walk and swim—and longing for a time when she lived her days without fear of losing her baby. Two nights before they were to leave, Warren took her out to dinner at a barge restaurant where she ignored his warning and ordered lobster.

"I'm sure I read somewhere that pregnant women aren't supposed to eat lobster."

"Oh, please!" She ordered a glass of white wine to spite him further. While she was breaking open the tail, she was seized by a pain so sharp she dropped both cracker and tail and let out a scream, clutching her abdomen. When the pain passed sufficiently for her to be able to stand, she made her way slowly to the ladies' room, walked into a stall, pulled down her underpants, and saw blood. Not brown blood, not pink blood, but fresh, bright red blood, and lots of it. In a strange way, the sight of the blood came as a relief to her for, from the day Sister Carmella first saw it trickling down her leg, Jill had never really doubted that she was going to lose this baby.

"I blame myself," Warren said as he drove her from the restaurant to the emergency room of Cape May Hospital.

"Why is that?" Jill asked, having just come down off a long and jagged contraction, her underwear stuffed with toilet paper to sop up the blood and clots that suddenly seemed to be pouring out of her. "Because you let me eat lobster?"

"No," he grumbled, "that's not why."

"Forget your reasons, Warren, my love," she said, tensing up as another wave of contractions picked her up. "You know as well as I do that you'd never dream of blaming yourself. You blame me."

"What," asked Jill, laying back weakly against the hospital pillow, "is an incompetent cervix?"

The doctor, younger than Jill by at least three years,

had been called away from his son's seventh birthday party in order to perform the D & C on Jill earlier this morning. Jill, who had been up all night in painful and fruitless labor, was not overly sympathetic.

"A normal cervix," he explained, "dilates only in labor to expel the baby. But in some cases the cervix is unable to hold the contents of the fetus and it opens prematurely."

"Is a person born with an incompetent cervix, Doctor?" Jill wanted to know.

"It's hard to know. Some women do suffer a congenital weakening of the cervix. We know you've had no previous traumatic delivery. A resulting cervical tear sometimes causes incompetence. But we do know that you've undergone several abortions, possibly traumatic. And it's possible—indeed, probable—that you may have suffered repeated forceful dilations of the cervix that have contributed to this weakening."

"I see." Jill plucked at the flimsy hospital blanket. "Does my husband know about all this?"

"Your husband and I have already talked."

"So he knows about my incompetent cervix," she said slowly. No wonder he hadn't been in to see her since post-op. "Well," she said, her voice high and brittle, "I appreciate your help, Doc. Why don't you get back to your son's party. Your work here is finished."

Carleen

"Any history of congenital heart defect?"
Carleen shook her head.
"Any history of Mongoloidism?"
Again, she shook her head.

"Any stillborn deaths in the family?"

"No."

The geneticist, an elegant Chinese woman by the name of Dr. Hoo, was using a small, strangely shaped ruler to draw up the schematic representing Carleen's family history. Bill looked on, his tree having already been completed.

"If it should happen that the test turns up negative results," Dr. Hoo went on, "have you and your husband discussed what you would do in that event?"

"Of course," said Carleen, looking out the window over the rain-lashed rooftops of the Bronx, "we'd terminate it."

This struck Carleen as a singularly stupid question and reminded her of the conversation she had had in the ladies' room the other day with the head of Grantley's accounts receivable.

"This way if, God forbid, something's wrong with the baby, you have a few months to prepare."

"Prepare?" Carleen had asked the woman. "For what?"

"You know. Arrange for a home. Or in-home care for it."

Why in the world would she go through the ordeal of having a long, nasty six-inch needle inserted into her belly if she intended to keep the baby regardless of the test's results?

"I assure you," Carleen had told the woman, "if there's something wrong with this baby, I'll have an abortion."

"After all the trouble you and your poor husband took to conceive it? Well"—the woman shrugged—"you never know. By the time you get the results, you'll really be feeling the life inside you. You might be whistling a different tune then."

"I doubt it," she said crisply.

Never in her career had she so fervently wished she had a private bathroom.

The twelve couples waiting for the amniocentesis sat on couches that had been squeezed into the hallway, along with filing cabinets and a water cooler, outside the genetic counseling office and the tiny suite of rooms in which the procedure was performed. Although they had all been thoroughly counseled and had even seen a film detailing the steps of the procedure, not a single woman there—and quite a few men—looked altogether unwilling to pack up and forget the whole thing.

One woman began to pass the time by polling the others as to who wanted to know in advance the sex of her child and who didn't.

"I, for one," she was saying, "want to know. I mean, the thought of that doctor of mine knowing and me not makes me crazy."

"Really?" Carleen said. "I'm not asking. I figure life holds so few genuine surprises for us. Why spoil it?"

"Me, neither," another woman said. "I've got three daughters. If I found out this was a fourth, I just might be tempted to take a tumble down the old stairs."

The other women stared at her in horror, but she waved her hand and grinned to show she was just joshing.

"We're not asking to know," a bearded man in embroidered denim said. "As it is, we lay so much shit on our kids. People find out the sex, they name the kid, they form a whole idea about who the kid is before it's even born. I say, let the kid be, without laying on all these egocentric preconceptions."

"Here, here." Bill applauded, then quickly froze mid-clap as the women in the hallway all stared at him.

"I'm not asking to know," yet another woman said, "but not for that reason. They told a girlfriend of mine hers was a boy. Well, they screwed up and it wound up being a girl and she had a devil of a time bonding with the kid. Couldn't shake the idea that there had been a mix-up at the hospital and they'd given her the wrong baby. Creepy."

"If you've ever given birth, you'd know that could never in a million years happen," the mother of three daughters reassured her. "Once you see that kid's face, you never ever forget it."

"It's called imprinting," Carleen put in.

"I had a feeling," the woman across from Carleen spoke up, "the genetic counselor here approves more of *not* asking."

"Genetic counseling!" the woman next to Carleen

snorted. "Sounds like something out of Orwell. Next stop: genetic engineering." They were sitting flanked by their husbands, Bill reading the *Times* Help Wanted section even though he knew any job he would want would not be listed, and the other woman's husband, in a three-piece suit, nonchalantly flipping through the *Wall Street Journal.*

"Brave New Baby," Carleen said ruefully. "Still, I for one am grateful the technology exists."

"I don't know," the woman said. "Did you see how little they can tell? I mean the test really isn't all that conclusive."

"It's conclusive about Down's syndrome," Carleen said. "And spina bifida, and some congenital lung diseases and a few other grisly disorders I'd be just as happy to avoid inflicting on a child of mine."

"I suppose you're right. I just hope I don't end up with the problem my girlfriend had."

"What was that?" Carleen asked, not really wanting to hear. This might have been an ob-gyn waiting room for all the grim statistics being bandied about.

"Her test turned up a *bent* chromosome."

"Bent? Not broken?"

"They didn't know what it meant. The doctors were in the dark."

"Did she go ahead and have the baby?"

"Oh, sure."

"And the baby's fine?"

"The baby *seems* fine, but every time she looks at it, she wonders about that bent chromosome."

"Mr. and Mrs. Lavin!" Dr. Hoo stood outside the procedure office holding a manila folder.

"That's us," her neighbor said, rising.

"Good luck," Carleen told her.

If her manner had been cocky up until now, she now looked as nervous as she felt.

"I'm sure the anticipation is worse than the thing itself," Carleen said as, hand in hand, the couple walked toward the little suite of rooms down the hall.

"Listen," the woman across from Carleen said, "don't

worry. I've had it twice, and compared to giving birth, it's a piece of cake."

"Open-heart surgery's a piece of cake compared to giving birth," another woman chuckled.

From the amnio room there emerged another woman followed by her husband, the former looking almost humpbacked with pain.

"How did it go?" someone asked her. The woman lifted her hand and made a weak circle of her fingers, smiling wanly. "At least it's over."

"It really didn't look so bad to me," her husband said, helping her to settle on one of the couches.

"What do you mean?" his wife rallied with sudden spirit. "You didn't even see what was going on!"

"I thought they let your husband stay and hold your hand," Carleen said.

"Not when they're actually sticking the needle in. They make him stand across the room. The doctor has to be there instead and there's really not enough room for both."

There was a slight commotion in the amnio room. A white-jacketed assistant came hurrying out and went over to the cooler to draw a cup of water.

"Is there a problem?" Bill asked him.

The assistant smirked. "Not really. We got ourselves another fainter."

"The poor woman," Carleen said.

"No," the man said, "her husband. Took one look at the needle and keeled right over."

There was tittering up and down the hall.

"So Mr. *Wall Street Journal* fainted," Bill mused. "It just goes to show you, you never know."

"Jump up and down, Mrs. Donovan."

Carleen stared at the nurse, momentarily puzzled.

"Didn't they tell you you'd have to jump up and down?"

"Oh, yes, of course." Carleen jumped up and down a few times in order to shake the fetus down to the bottom of the amniotic cavity. Then the nurse helped her to lie down on a padded table. They rolled down her waistband and pulled up her top. Then the sonogram technician applied a cool, clear gel to her stomach and began to run a rubber comb across her belly in search of the baby.

It was at this point that Bill, who had been asked to wait outside while Carleen was prepped, was allowed to come into the little room.

"I'm glad they let you keep your clothes on," he said, watching the technician at work. "Makes the whole procedure seem less radical somehow."

"There's the little cutey now." The technician, a gawky man with wire-rim glasses, tapped the screen.

It looked like a transmission from one of the early space shots. The baby might have been some species of extraterrestrial.

"See the head?"

By manipulating a dial on the side of the sonogram machine, the technician was able to indicate the head by means of a moving white arrow.

"Hey, yeah!" Bill said. "It *is* sort of cute."

The young man moved the white arrow further down. "See that there? That's the tibia bone." He measured it. "Seventeen weeks, five days."

"You can tell exactly?" Carleen said. "All from a tibia bone?"

"All from a tibia bone," the technician said.

"Someone said you can get a photo of the sonogram if you ask," she said.

"Yep. And if you go to the hospital up in Westchester that performs this procedure, you can have an actual videotape. One of my neighbors has one. They showed it at a dinner party. Whatever turns you on, I say."

"On second thought," said Carleen, "forget about the photo."

"Here we are!" A spry, jolly-looking fellow in a white coat entered. "Good morning, all!" He shook Bill's hand. "My name is Dr. Timky."

"Good morning," Carleen said uncertainly. He looked, perversely enough, like a man who enjoyed his work.

135

"I think I've got it, sir," the technician said, moving the arrow to indicate a black space, a gap between the baby's body and the placental wall in the amniotic cavity. The idea was not to poke the baby with the needle.

"Is there a danger that the baby will move once you've picked the spot?" Carleen asked.

The doctor shook his head, still staring at the screen. "Try a little over to the left, will you, Todd?" The technician moved the arrow over.

"That-a-boy," the doctor said, sounding pleased.

"That would be right about"—the technician marked Carleen's belly with a betadine-soaked cotton swab— "there."

"Can I ask you to stand over there, sir?" the doctor said to Bill. "I need me a little elbow room."

Bill backed off, letting go of Carleen's hand. The sonogram screen went black, but Carleen found herself staring at it anyway. If she looked over at Bill, she would see what the doctor was doing, see the size and length of the needle, and she didn't want to do that.

"I'm going to give you a little Xylocaine to numb the spot," the doctor said. "You'll feel a little pinch, then numbness. Don't move now."

Carleen felt a tiny pinch. She realized she had stopped breathing. She felt dizzy and lightheaded while they waited a few seconds for the anesthetic to take effect.

"I'm going in now with the needle. You'll feel a slight pulling sensation as I withdraw the fluid, and some cramping. Whatever you do, don't move."

Carleen remained still, wiggling only her toes.

"Feel some cramping?"

Carleen nodded, wiggling her toes more vigorously. A thin glaze of sweat formed on her upper lip.

"All set!"

She looked over at the syringe in his hand. It was full of a yellowish cloudy liquid, the medium in which her baby floated. It served as a temperature regulator, a shock absorber, even as a source of nutrition, since the baby sometimes drank it. It also contained cells shed by the fetus.

When set to grow in a culture for two to four weeks, those cells would tell other technicians the sex of the baby, its exact age, and whether it was genetically sound.

"You're all taken care of, Carleen!" the doctor said, moving aside to let Bill in. "You're to be congratulated, young man! You didn't even faint!"

Carleen returned to the couch in the hall, where she had been told to sit for fifteen minutes before walking out to the car. She felt nauseated and definitely premenstrual, as if she were about to lose her baby. Wouldn't it be ironic, she reflected glumly, if the baby was fine but the procedure caused her to miscarry anyway? Hazards of modern medicine.

Bill squeezed her hand and asked her if she was all right.

She nodded. The room kept fading in and out. She thought she might actually faint.

"You look so pale," he said.

"Believe me," Carleen managed to say, "I feel pale."

"Was it that bad?" one of the women still waiting asked.

Carleen focussed on the young woman's worried face. For her sake, she ventured a smile. "Not so bad." It actually hurt to speak. "I'm glad it's over, though."

"Is this your first?" another, older woman asked.

Carleen nodded.

"Well, you know what my mother always said."

"No," Carleen said, "what did your mother always say?"

"Kids are like waffles."

"Really?" Carleen said, dreading what would come next. "And why is that?"

"You have to throw the first one away."

Kendra

"I don't think I realized until I lost it just how much I wanted that baby."

"Of course you wanted it!"

"And now I feel so empty. Honest to God, Kendra, I don't know what I'm going to do with myself."

"Give yourself time to rest. Heal. Then, who knows? Maybe you and Warren could try again."

"I'm not sure that's such a hot idea."

"How come? You said Warren was gung-ho about it."

"Yeah, but lately he's been acting weird."

"Weirder, don't you mean?"

"No, really. He's being very nice—"

"Of course he is. His wife's just gone through hell."

"But he's also very scarce. He spends all his free time these days at the health club rediscovering physical culture. He's losing weight. He seems very happy."

"That's good, isn't it?"

"I don't know. *Too* happy, if you ask me."

"Now you're being paranoid."

"Am I? I haven't exactly been a barrel of Bozos to live with these days."

"No one expects you to be. You had a second-trimester miscarriage, Jill. Go a little easy on yourself."

"Yeah, and if I hear one more person say, 'It's nature's way,' or 'It's probably for the better,' I'm going to tear his tongue out."

"People can be thoughtless assholes. Why don't you come up here to the lake with me?"

"No, a nice radiant pregnant lady like you doesn't need a shriveled bitch like me around."

"Stop it, Jill!"

"What I would like is to stay in the loft for a while, if it's all right with you."

"Of course it is. But do you think it's a good idea for you and Warren to be apart right now?"

"I honestly don't know. All I know is that the sight of him getting his body back in shape is almost as revolting to me as his Fat Boy Phase."

"Somehow, I understand."

"I just need to think things out."

"Of course you do."

"And Kendra?"

"Yeah?"

"Forgive me."

"Forgive you for what?"

"In the hospital, after the miscarriage, I found myself hoping, with all my heart...that you'd miscarry too."

"Jill!"

"I mean, we had this pact, to go through the thing together. It just didn't seem right or fair that you were going ahead without me when it was my idea in the first place."

"I guess I understand."

"There you were, without a husband, a steady job, a nice place to live, any of the requisite support systems, going through with it. You're so strong, so beautiful. God, how I resented you."

"Not to change the subject, but was the doctor in Cape May able to tell you why you lost it?"

"Sure. Simple. It was my shady past...catching up with me. The ghosts of my four aborted babies wreaking revenge."

"Cut it out!"

"Actually, one of my abortionists probably screwed up."

"Really?"

"Yeah. Who would have thought I'd be paying for my reckless ways lo these many years later?"

"Jill, that's horrible. But can't you get another opinion? I'm sure there—"

"Don't you see? I don't want another opinion. And I

139

certainly have had it with doctors for the time being. I've had it with just about everybody, in fact. Now do you see why I'm not fit company? Now do you see?"

Kendra saw, all right. And by the time they hung up, both women were in tears.

The first few days up at the lake, Kendra awoke every morning to the fall foliage at the very height of its splendor. She had converted the master bedroom, with its picture window fronting on the lake, to a studio and found herself mixing pigments to match the leaves falling all around her: fiery red, mellow pumpkin orange, shrill yellow, and a range of burnished browns and ochres. There was no TV, no radio, and, except for the one sad call from Jill and an occasional wrong number, the telephone didn't even ring.

Each morning at dawn she rose and fixed herself a cup of herbal tea and a slice of cinnamon toast. She had her breakfast sitting out on the dock. Then she took a brief turn around the lake in the canoe, paddling easily but working up a sufficient sweat to take a skinny dip off the dock on her return. Tingling and fortified, she dressed in overalls and went to her studio, where she worked, either stretching or priming or painting, until about one o'clock, when she fixed herself a salad and ate it sitting at the big table in the dining room with its birchbark-paneled walls shimmering with the water's reflection. After lunch she went back to work until the light faded, when she treated herself to the day's only vice, a single glass of chilled white wine, while preparing her supper. She alternated cooking chicken breasts and lean sirloin steak, which she ate with a single baked potato and steamed spinach or broccoli.

After dinner she took a cup of camomile tea out on the dock and sipped it slowly, waiting for it to make her drowsy. Then she would change into a flannel nightie— for although the daytime temperature sometimes reached seventy-five, the nights were near freezing—and climb into the goose-down bed she had slept in as a little girl.

One night she awoke to a flapping sound in the eaves above her head. Sometimes birds on the roof made such a racket it sounded as if they were inside the house. But then the flapping came even louder and she felt a cool fanning sensation against her face. She sat up quickly and switched on the light.

This time she saw it winging low over her head. At first she thought it was a baby bird that had accidentally flown in the open door and now was trapped inside the house. But it was too late in the year for baby birds. Next she thought it was a big black butterfly or moth. Then, as it landed on the windowsill and crawled toward her, all sharp white fangs and black leathery wings, she knew what it was. It was a bat.

Of all her childhood fears, bats were the most prevalent. At an early age she had learned never to go swimming after dark, for that was when the bats came out to feed. Grady would tease her with stories of young girls who had gotten bats trapped in their long hair and had their brains clawed out as the creatures tried desperately to escape. Even now, whenever she walked in the woods after dark, she always wore her long hair tucked up in a hat. But if Grady was a merciless teaser, so was he her only savior. The few times bats had gotten into the house, it had been Grady, heroically donning a pith helmet— which came to be known as the Bat Hat—and arming himself with a tennis racket, who had gone and routed them out.

As Kendra lay cowering beneath the covers, too frightened even to reach out and turn off the light, she sent a telepathic message to Grady to come in the Bat Hat and rescue her. But, alas, Grady was hundreds of miles away, his telepathic line busy, and she was all alone in the house with a bat. Pitifully, she began to cry.

Her ability to concentrate on her work thoroughly undermined by the presence of the bat in the house, Kendra was lying on top of the boathouse sunbathing nude when a large, cold shadow passed across her sun.

"Well, hello to you, too."

Starting, Kendra sat up and reached for her dungaree jacket, blinking up at her visitor.

"I didn't mean to scare you."

Grinning, Morgan squatted beside her and unburdened himself of a large, serious-looking backpack.

"What happened to Spoleto?" Kendra asked him, moving swiftly to cover her nakedness.

"All over," he said.

"What happened to Asia?"

"The gig was canceled. Some hassle with the State Department. I've got something lined up with Joe Papp, but that doesn't start for another six weeks. When I called the loft, your friend Jill seemed to feel you'd appreciate the company."

Kendra pulled on a pair of cutoffs.

He pointed at her belly. "She didn't, um, mention anything about that. If," he added sheepishly, "that's what I think it is."

Self-consciously, Kendra buttoned her jacket over her swelling stomach.

"Yes, well, she doesn't exactly approve of the father," she said evasively.

"Is he up here, too?" Morgan looked around.

"Oh, no," she said, "he's down in the city. He's an investment banker," she added, thinking it was a nice touch.

"Gee, then, I guess I'll fill up my canteen and hitch on back to New York."

Kendra thought of the bat she had been sharing the house with for the past week. All he would need to do is stay the night to get rid of the bat. Maybe she could get him to carry in some firewood while he was at it.

"No, please," she said, "there's no sense in your hitching all the way up here only to turn around and head back. Stay the night at least."

"Won't your old man—?"

"Don't worry about my old man," she told him. "My old man and I have an understanding."

Mary Beth

"I don't understand why you have to go into the city every single week."

"I told you, honey, it's this new art director. He's very insecure."

"If he's so insecure, why doesn't he send a messenger for the sketches? Doesn't he realize a woman in your condition has better things to do—"

"We need to go over the sketches, face to face, and there are plenty of women 'in my condition' who go into the city five days a week."

He shook his head, ran one hand through his hair, and grinned sheepishly.

"I'm a real pain in the ass, aren't I?"

"Daddy said ass!" Denny sang out.

"Don't tattle," said Mary Beth. "Who wants another half an English muffin?"

"I do!" Frank and Denny chimed.

Splitting it, Mary Beth handed the halves to Denny to pop into the toaster.

"You think the new baby will like English muffins, too?" Denny wanted to know.

"I don't see why not," she said. "It's probably in the Rapasardi genes."

"Good," said Denny, "'cause that way there won't be any more halves left over."

"Good going, Den." Frank looked up from the *Mt. Vernon Record* spread out next to his breakfast plate. "Little guy's a mathematical whiz."

"Also in the Rapasardi genes?" Mary Beth raised an eyebrow.

"What are Rapasardi jeans?" Denny wanted to know. "Jeans like Dad and me wear?"

"Like Dad and *I* wear," she corrected him.

"*You* don't wear jeans anymore, Mom," Denny said judiciously, " 'cause the baby won't fit into them."

Frank left for work early. It was, next to spring, the busiest time of the year for him, the time to put in bulbs, clean up nature's mess of fallen leaves, and mulch the beds.

"Come on, Den," Mary Beth said as soon as they had waved Frank off in his sleek black Toyota pickup, "let's try on your costume one more time."

"Okay!" Denny said brightly, following her into the house.

This year's costume, which Mary Beth had designed and Frank had executed from wire lathe and papier-mâché, was even better than previous years', which had been, successively: a strawberry, a Chiquita banana, an apple with a worm in it, and, last year, in a radical departure from the edible, Wicket the Ewok. This year they were making a glorious return to their perennial theme with, what else but an artichoke?

"I bet nobody in the whole first grade has a costume like mine," Denny said proudly.

"I bet nobody in the whole school ... maybe even in all of Westchester," Mary Beth added.

"Maybe even the whole universe!"

Mary Beth carefully lowered the nest of painted lacquered leaves over her son's head and adjusted the two green suspenders that held it on.

Watching him parade proudly around the living room in the ridiculous costume, Mary Beth shook her head and said, "Will you please tell me how in the world you got to be so cute?"

"Simple, Mom." He stopped and faced her, holding his hands palms up. "You made me that way. You *and* Dad," he amended thoughtfully. "I sure hope the new baby is as cute as I am."

"I don't see how it can miss."

" 'Cause if it isn't," Denny went on with a five-year-old's grave sympathy, "I'm going to feel awful sorry for it."

"I have to leave a little early today."

"Mmm. How come?"

"I promised Denny I'd take him around trick-or-treating before dark."

Daniel rose up on an elbow, his chin glistening. "Is today Halloween?"

"Of course it is!" She regarded him curiously. How could a man with three young children not know it was Halloween?

"You forget that we are denizens of the city, my dear," he said, a certain defensiveness creeping into his voice, "where little children get razor blades in their apples for treats."

Mary Beth shivered and sat up, pulling the corduroy coverlet over her knees. "Yes, but they get to wear costumes, at least, don't they? I mean, we've been planning Denny's since, gee, August."

"And what did you plan?" he asked, stroking her thigh.

"Well, it was a toss-up between a peapod and an artichoke. Denny likes artichokes better, so he finally settled on that."

"An artichoke!" He chuckled softly. "You're such a good little mother." He patted her stomach.

She frowned fiercely and pounded her knee with one fist. *I am not a good mother.*

"But you are. You're like one of those cute little kindergarten teachers, marking off the years in holidays. You make doily hearts and homemade chocolates on Valentine's Day and trim baskets at Easter time. You make your kid's Halloween costume—not just some thrown-together thing, either—and at Christmas, you deck the halls and make gingerbread houses that are architectural marvels. Why, I'll bet you even leave out milk and cookies for Santa."

She stared at him blankly. "Doesn't everybody?"

"No, my dearest," he said fondly, "everybody does not. You'll probably be shocked to know that for Christmas, we take the kids out shopping and let them pick out their own presents."

"That's no fun!"

"Ah, but it is eminently more practical—and my wife is nothing if not practical. But it takes more than practicality to make a good mother. It takes planning, hard work, imagination, and a sense of fun. And for all these things, I love you. Now, may I please get back to the business at hand? Or was it at mouth?"

"Not just yet." She scissored her legs together and slid off the studio couch. "I have to go to the bathroom," she apologized, blushing.

"For a change," he said dryly.

"I'm sure it's nothing," he said, angling his way through the traffic going downtown.

Not having an orgasm is not nothing, Mary Beth said silently. Never before in all their times together had she failed to come at least once. She felt let down and cheated, as if she had taken a great deal of money into a wonderful department store and failed to buy a single thing. On the sidewalks, children just out of school in costumes—the flimsy, Day-Glo dimestore kind—wormed their way in packs chaperoned by parents or older children. Store windows were festooned in black and orange crepe paper, skeletons, and arching black cats. Jack-o-lanterns grinned through apartment windows and from fire escapes. How could you not know it was Halloween? It was in the very air.

"It's because you felt rushed today," he added. "From the moment you came in the door, I sensed it."

He never liked it when she came to him weighted down with baggage from her other life. To him, their meetings were exercises in isolationism—any intrusion of the outer world he considered to be in slightly questionable taste.

"Well, it's true I don't want to miss the three fifty-five. I promised Denny—"

"For pity's sake. The kid's got all evening to go begging for sweets."

Mary Beth frowned at his profile. She didn't like it when he called Denny *kid*. The lack of tenderness in his voice when he spoke of children—including his own—saddened her. When it came to Denny, Frank seemed to have an inexhaustible store of patience and gentleness. And yet, to be fair to him, Daniel seemed to feel *something* toward the baby growing inside her. Was it because at this stage it was still a part of her? An extension of their love affair? Would he still feel the same way after it was born? Or would it become just another *kid?* Last week, after drinking a cup of brandy-spiked tea, he had woven for her an elaborate fantasy about the seven of them— Daniel and his three children, Mary Beth and her two— all going to live together in a big house by the sea. The University of California at Santa Cruz had just offered him a position as department head, and it was this that had prompted the fantasy. Mary Beth found herself listening to him, entranced, actually able to picture them all living happily together. Mary Beth would have a studio in the house through whose skylights there poured shafts of luminous beach light. The bigger kids would help take care of the littler ones. Hadn't Denny always wanted an older brother or sister? She pictured herself beachcombing with the new baby—symbol of their love for each other—bundled into a backpack while Denny rode one of the twins piggyback. She saw herself nursing the baby in the light of a beach bonfire. He must have seen the glow in her eyes, for he said, "Christ, listen to me! I ought to be horsewhipped for carrying on like that. How irresponsible can I get?"

"Frank's beginning to object to me coming in every week," she said as he turned off Fifth Avenue and headed east.

"He can't very well forbid it, can he?"

"No, but he worries and I don't want him to worry."

"Doesn't sound to me as if the man trusts you very much."

She shot him a look. "There's a difference between concern and distrust."

He reached over and took her hand. "You and I both know that it was his paternalism that attracted you to him in the first place. You transferred, virtually overnight, from your father to Frank. And obviously, in many ways, Frank feels more secure thinking that you're a creature in need of sheltering than a smart, self-reliant, self-supporting—"

"What's wrong with him worrying about me!" Mary Beth blurted out. *Don't you ever worry about me?* she wanted to add. But she didn't. Because she knew deep down that she wasn't worthy of either man's concern. She had betrayed them both. It was only a matter of time before God saw fit to punish her for her treachery.

Sensing her distress, Daniel reached over and laid a hand on her knee. Mary Beth recoiled. Where once his touch had inflamed her, now it only served to make her feel foolish. She was ridiculous. Look at her: In her kelly-green maternity overalls and her bright red frizzy hair, she looked like a clown. In the old days, she used to feel so romantic riding the train in to meet her lover. But lately —over the last few weeks, as her body thickened and became obviously pregnant—she only felt absurd. Certainly no one's idea of the sexy lover on her way to a tryst.

He turned down Vanderbilt into the side entrance of Grand Central Station and stood in line behind a row of taxis. Putting the car in park, he turned to her and took both her hands in his.

"Remember." He kissed each of her slightly swollen knuckles in turn and stared kindly into her eyes. "The power is in your hands. All you have to say is 'Uncle.'"

$\mathcal{L}$ouise

With his curly blond hair, slow blue eyes, square jaw, and air of almost Olympian fitness, Dr. Sheldon Berry looked like Central Casting's idea of the Society Baby Doctor. His book, *Harken to Your Body!*, a collection of informal patient-doctor questions and answers, had been on the trade-paperback bestseller list for over twenty months. He had served on the committees of several balls to raise funds for everything from unwed mothers to AIDS research. He had been a guest on Johnny Carson three times and *Today*, Donahue, and Oprah twice. The vanity plate on his Porsche 911 read STORK. Still, for all his astonishing looks and overwhelming good fortune, he was, the women who were lucky enough to be his patients agreed, an uncommonly good doctor. While his behavior was always of the highest professional order, he was unquestionably and avowedly a lover of women and, as such, brought to the job something that even some women doctors lacked: total and unconditional sympathy.

"How are the kids, Louise?"

"Great," Louise said, lying on his examination table like a beached whale with bunny slippers, her huge lemon-meringue yellow maternity sweatshirt pulled up to reveal the shining dome of her pregnant belly. "The kids are having a ball with this belly of mine. They pat it and talk to it and Zackie even tells it jokes."

"And Marty?"

"He hates it. He tries to ignore it. But, as you can see, it's getting a little difficult to do that."

"Marty'll come around in time, don't worry about him."

Berry felt Louise's stomach with both hands.

"I doubt it," she said glumly. "He's always wanted three kids and I've always been happy to have more. It was bound to come to this sooner or later."

"Oh, I've seen this kind of thing before, Louise." He put on his stethoscope and began moving the cup around her stomach.

"A fat belly, you mean?"

"No," he said, after a bit, "a preconceived notion as to the right size family. Usually, it's the women who have it. They see themselves with two kids. Since they're eight, ten years old, they've had this mental image of themselves as the mother of two kids, and they aren't about to let reality screw that up. By the same token, I've seen women who want five kids. They've had four complicated C-sections and I tell them to cool it. But nothing will keep them from fulfilling their dreams. With some it's two, others five ... with Marty, it's three: that mystical number three. Otherwise, the guy's perfectly rational."

"I think mostly he hates the number four," Louise said.

They were both quiet for a couple of minutes while he continued to harken to her belly.

"Well." Berry straightened and removed the stethoscope from about his neck. "In that case, I don't really see that we have a problem, Louise."

"How do you mean?"

"I had my suspicions last month."

"What suspicions?" Louise rose up on her elbows, alarmed.

"We're not talking 'baby,' here, Louise."

"We're not?" Her eyes widened. "You mean it's twins? No wonder I'm so fat!"

Berry frowned thoughtfully. "Of course I'll have to do a sonogram to confirm, but unless my ears are going bad, I am picking up three distinct heartbeats."

"Then it *is* twins!"

"That's three heartbeats, apart from your own, Louise. We're talking trips, Louise. We're talking that mystical number three all over again. Triplets! I'd say you—and Marty—have really hit the jackpot this time."

Mary Beth

That crisp November evening, the Rapasardis' dinner guests were greeted at the front door by a scarecrow leaning rakishly against a shock of corn, dressed in a straw hat and an old shirt and patched overalls of Frank's. Vases of bitter-sweet and dried flowers were set throughout the house, along with attractive arrangements of gourds and dried leaves, and fresh fruit and nuts. The eggplant dip was deli-cious, but the guests went easy on it, knowing what awaited them for dinner: roast venison in a black currant sauce, wild rice, and green beans and toasted almonds. While the grown-ups stood around talking with steaming cups of hot mulled wine, Denny went rushing about showing off his latest toy—the Stay-Puft Marshmallow Man from the movie *Ghostbusters*—and a drawing he had done in school of a Pilgrim holding a blunderbuss standing next to a smil-ing turkey.

"How come the turkey looks so happy?" Dina Lassiter held Denny's drawing at arm's length.

" 'Cause," Denny said, grinning at his own cleverness, "the Pilgrims decided to have spaghetti instead."

"Good answer!" Dina mussed his hair.

"My dad shot the deer we're eating tonight, you know," he told her.

"So I heard," Dina said, winking at Mary Beth.

"It was a twelve-pointer. Dad got him three weeks ago when he went hunting with my uncles."

"Guess that deer wasn't as lucky as your turkey."

"Dad said he might have starved over the winter anyway —and that's the honest truth."

"Maybe," Dina said. "In any case, I've never been one to

turn my nose up at breast of Bambi." This was addressed more to Denny's mother than to the boy himself, who had already moved on to show Dina's date the drawing and the toy.

"Every year Frank says he's going to stop those macho hunting weekends," Mary Beth said. "But every year my brothers manage to bamboozle him into it."

Mary Beth, in an elegant black silk maternity shift, her red curls pushed back from her face with two silver combs, spoke with her eyes riveted on her husband, who was standing across the room engaged in conversation with her editor. These dinner parties had evolved into an annual tradition, falling midway between Halloween and Thanksgiving. Most of the guests were Frank's biggest clients; it was his way of thanking them for their business. In the last couple of years, Mary Beth had taken to inviting some of her own business associates: her editor, the publicist who handled her books, some of the authors whose work she illustrated. Only Dina was a mutual guest.

"I said Denny seems very happy and adjusted to the coming Big Event," Dina repeated gently.

"What?" It wasn't until this afternoon that it had hit her like a bucket of ice water. What if Frank made some mention to her editor about her weekly trips into the city? Frank was laughing easily, handsome in a turquoise flannel shirt, chamois vest, and red plaid tie. She had to get over to them and break them up.

"Are you all right, kiddo?" Dina asked. "You seem nervous."

"I just want the evening to go well," she said faintly.

"Your evenings always go well. Come on, Mary Beth, 'fess up."

Mary Beth blushed. "I guess I'm feeling a little jealous."

Dina looked completely nonplussed. "You mean Megan ...and *Frank!* You've got to be putting me on. Frank worships you. And he's dog loyal."

"You know how insecure pregnant women sometimes get, Dina." She bit her lip. "Would you do me a real favor?

I have to go check on the roast. Go over there and break those two up, huh?"

Dina cast Mary Beth a skeptical look. "I hate to encourage your bizarre delusions . . ."

"Please? As a special favor?"

"Well, all right, but only because jealousy causes undue stress, and you're my favorite patient."

He came up behind her as she bent over the roast, and she let out a scream.

"Jesus, Mary Beth, but you're jumpy!"

"Sorry, honey, you scared me. Give me a hand getting the roast on the cutting board, will you?"

"Sure." Casting her an uncertain look, he lifted the roast out with two forks while Mary Beth held down the pan with two asbestos-gloved hands.

"That dip was something."

"I'm glad."

"The house looks terrific."

"Good."

"Denny's behaving really well."

"He is, isn't he?"

"Megan said you haven't been in to the office since late August."

Mary Beth felt the blood drain from her face. She turned quickly away from him and groped for the wooden spoon.

"Get those dishes out of the oven for me, will you?"

She stirred the string beans with one hand and shook the pan holding the wild rice to make sure it wasn't sticking.

Frank opened the other oven and went to reach for one of the serving dishes she had put in to warm.

"Use a potholder!" she warned him, but it was too late. Burning his fingers, Frank dropped the bowl on the floor, where it broke into three neat pieces.

"Shit, shit, shit!" He sucked on his fingertips.

"Is everything all right in here?" Dina poked her head in cheerfully, took one look at their faces and the broken bowl and said, "I think I'll collect dirty cups," leaving them alone.

"Not since August, Mary Beth," he repeated through clenched teeth. "You mind telling me what the fuck's been going on with you?"

Mary Beth felt her face grow hot, her uterus tighten around the baby. "I—" Her voice sounded small and weak. How could she have been so stupid as to have invited her editor here tonight? This was punishment she deserved.

"She also said there is no 'new' art director. They've got the same old art director on board. 'What's with this new A.D.?' I ask her, and she looks at me like I'm nuts. Imagine how I felt, Mary Beth. I felt like a total jerk, that's how I felt."

"I can explain," she said. The tightening in her uterus increased by the second. It was like a metal band around her hips, a tightening corset... the hand of God coming for her baby.

"I'd really like it if you could."

Mary Beth bent over painfully to pick up the pieces of the broken bowl.

"I've been going in... to the library... to sketch," she gasped.

"Mt. Vernon has a perfectly fine library, Mary Beth."

"You don't understand." She rose shakily, not knowing what to do with the jagged pieces in her hands, not knowing what to say next. The pain in her stomach was such that she couldn't think straight. He took the pieces out of her hands.

"Try to make me understand, Mary Beth." The pleading in his voice hurt her, exacerbating the pain in her midriff. I'm in labor, she thought. I'm going to lose this baby because I've been unfaithful to my husband. It's God's punishment. Then, her more rational side took over and she thought, no, what I'm feeling is the accumulated tension of all these months of lying. Maybe if I just tell him the truth, the pain will go away. *And the truth shall free them.* She opened her mouth.

"I'm waiting, Mary Beth."

"It's just...that I've been feeling...trapped."

"Trapped?" He was incredulous. "By what? By me and Denny? By this beautiful home we've made together? Trapped by what?"

"I don't know!" she said. "By the idea of having to sit home with this new baby for months and months. You don't understand what it's like. You get out every day, but unless I make an effort, I wind up stuck here day after day. Going out shopping is a big production. And instead of looking forward to it, I dread it. Don't you understand, honey?" Her tears were beginning to blind her. What did any of this matter when she was about to lose her baby? "I was turning into a shut-in. So I forced myself to go on the train every week and sketch in a carrel in the library. I'd—oh, forget it, I knew you wouldn't understand! I knew you wouldn't—"

His arms were around her, his lips in her hair. "Hush, baby! Hush. You're getting hysterical. Of course I understand. It's all right. You can stop crying. Mary Beth, please. I'm sorry I bullied you. My God, what is it? You're white as a ghost. Mary Beth! Jesus! Hey, Dina!" he yelled. "Get in here quick!" Mary Beth felt his arms around her as her legs buckled beneath her and her kitchen faded to a dull-red glow.

She was lying at the bottom of a deep, silty lake, her head and limbs swollen, gigantic. Every time someone shut a door or spoke in anything louder than a whisper, she felt her body rise as if stirred by cannonballs.

"Am I losing it?" Mary Beth lay upstairs on her bed, a quilt covering her. Dina stood by the side of the bed, smoothing her hair away from her forehead.

"I think any danger's past. Luckily, my bag was in the trunk of my car. I've given you something to relax your uterus. You were having some premature contractions, that's all, kiddo."

"Where's Frank?"

"Downstairs, presiding heroically over a table of very

155

worried guests. Most of them wanted to take off as soon as you fainted, but I wouldn't hear of that gorgeous meal going to waste."

"Is he ... mad at me?"

Dina eyed her strangely. "Of course not. If anything, he's mad at himself. He blames himself."

"No." Mary Beth shook her head. The relaxant made her breathing slow and shallow. "It's not his fault. It's my fault."

"Do you think you're ready to tell me what's up with you, Mary Beth?"

"I can't," she said stubbornly. "You'll hate me."

Dina laughed softly. "I doubt it."

"It's too terrible. I didn't even tell at confession."

"What's terrible is holding it in like this."

Mary Beth closed her eyes and felt herself floating.

"I've been having an affair," she heard herself say, as if in a dream.

"How long?" Dina asked, sounding calm and cool and far, far away.

"About a year and a half. This man—I met him years ago, in college, he's older than me. I had a crush on him then. I ran into him, by accident, ten years later and—I don't know—we just started up all over again."

She opened her eyes and stared at Dina.

"This is going to sound like a stupid question, but are you in love with him?"

Mary Beth nodded. "I'm in love with the way he makes me feel. I'm addicted to it in a funny way. But I'm in love with Frank, too, in a different way. With Daniel, it's like a drug, like getting high on a drug. With Frank, it's, I don't know, calmer, sweeter. I feel like I need both kinds of love."

"And you don't want to have to choose between them."

"Oh, I couldn't ever!" Mary Beth's eyes filled, her throat ached. "But the problem is, Dina, either of them could be the father of this baby."

Dina let out a nearly silent whistle. "Move over and make room for Dr. Dina. This isn't the sort of conversation I can have standing up."

Mary Beth moved into the middle of the bed as Dina sat beside her on top of the quilt.

"So you don't hate me?" Mary Beth asked.

"Of course I don't hate you. I sure as hell don't envy you, but I certainly don't hate you."

"Is there some way...after the baby's born...to find out who the father is?"

"Before I answer that question, is there any reason why you'd want to know? I mean, do you intend to do anything about it? Like tell either your lover—Daniel, is it? —or Frank, or, one day, the child itself?"

Mary Beth shook her head. "I think *I'd* like to know."

"A paternity investigation is a relatively simple procedure, which I could conduct with a certain amount of discretion. We know your blood type and Frank's. All we need to know is Daniel's. Of course, if you or Daniel, or Frank or Daniel, has the same blood type, it gets a little more complicated, but it can still be done. But I think you ought to give the matter serious thought before you give me the go-ahead."

"I guess you're right." Mary Beth sighed, her mind reeling. "Maybe it's better not to know. Oh, Dina, what must you think of me!"

"Mind if I tell you a little story about myself?"

"Go ahead." Mary Beth snuggled beneath the quilt and took one of Dina's hands in hers.

"Once upon a time when I was a lowly resident, I fell in love with an older man."

"What was he like?"

"Oh, incredibly handsome, smart, successful, sexy, and very, very, very much married. I was crazy about him."

"Was the feeling mutual?"

"He said—and I believed him—that he loved me more than any woman he had ever met."

"More than his wife?"

"More than his wife. But, in those days, men like him didn't just pick up and leave their wives of thirty years for a younger woman. So I did what I had to do: I became his mistress."

"Did you have trysts?"

"We even had a love nest. Over on the far West Side in a little Georgian townhouse not much wider than our queen-sized bed. We'd meet there every chance we could steal. He was a wonderful lover. Yes, being with him was like being high on a drug. Every aspect of my life—my work, my appearance, my every waking minute—was enhanced by the feeling he gave me."

"And there was no chance he'd ever leave his wife?"

"None whatsoever. And, after a while, I got so that I convinced myself that it was better that way. That if he ever did leave his wife and we got married, it couldn't possibly be as wonderful as it was when we were lovers. Maybe I was fooling myself but, to this day, I still believe that."

"So what happened? Did you break up?"

"No," she said, "he died...playing tennis...at the New York Tennis Club."

Mary Beth sat up and stared at Dina. *You mean you and my father...?*

Dina nodded. "So you see," she went on calmly, "I'm hardly in a position to judge you, am I? But I am in a position to give you a little friendly—and doctorly—advice. I believe that even if it can be worked out, lovers seldom make the transition to spouses. The more ecstatic the love affair, the less likely it will convert to a good marriage. It's like trying to sustain a dream in waking life. I don't think everyday life can support it. And I do know that what you've got downstairs is a warm, generous, truly sweet man who loves you with every ounce of his being. He's *real*, Mary Beth, not a dream. And right now you need to embrace that reality with a hundred percent of yourself. Because living this double life of yours is obviously schizzing you out. Schizzed-out, you won't be much good to anyone—not to Frank, not to Denny, and particularly not to this baby. I think it's time, Mary Beth, that you set your priorities straight. Doctor's orders."

158

Louise

"I think you simply must tell him!" Francine brushed the sand off Mary's apple slice and sent her toddling back to the sandbox.

"I've tried to." Louise blew on her gloved fingers and held the sketch pad up to the thin, gray November light. "What do you think?"

"I think it is a very charming giraffe, but you are avoiding the discussion."

"I'm putting it on the yellow T-shirt that goes with the safari jacket."

Since August, Louise had three seamstresses and a silk-screen operator working five eight-hour days a week to produce Wonderwear for over a dozen major accounts.

"Splendid, Louise, but you have known that you are carrying triplets now for almost three weeks. Marty, too, should know this. It might make him—"

"All the more angry with me for not getting that abortion," Louise finished for her. "I mean, one unwanted baby is a nuisance. Three's a major invasion. Zackie! Stop licking those chapped lips!"

Her eldest son stood at the top of the slide, his hood flapping in the wind, his lips surrounded by an angry red circle where his tongue traced a nervous path every few minutes.

"Okay, Mom!" Zack licked his lips and proceeded down the slide on his belly, bumping into his little brother, who sat at the bottom, gleefully shoveling sand onto the foot of the slide and then spitting on it for good measure.

When his brother collided into him, Bruce jumped up and ran to his mother. "Zackie knocked my brains out."

"No, he didn't," Louise answered, brushing the sand out of his hair. Only the hardiest mothers and nannies had ventured out this fortnight before Thanksgiving, when an Arctic cold front had swept down from Canada, sending the temperature down into the teens. Francine, wearing boots, a ski parka, and pants, kept moving to stay warm. Beneath her mink coat, Louise felt the warm tangle of tiny arms and legs that was her triplets.

How many times over the last weeks had she tried to tell Marty he was three months away from becoming the father of triplets? But he had been so busy, what with the onset of the holidays and trying to set up a branch of the business in Boston. He worked at the office late almost every night. While she tried to stay up to talk to him, she almost always fell asleep by nine, tired out by the extra weight she lugged around with her all day, and by the demands of her own business. There were the trips down to the silkscreener's on Avenue B to check to make sure he was maintaining the level of quality her customers expected, then over to the apartments of her seamstresses to deliver them dyed good and materials, or prototypes of the new designs. In the top drawer of the room designated as the new nursery, she had begun to store her favorite designs in triplicate. Last night Francine had deliberately gone out as soon as the kids were tucked in, in order to give Louise an opportunity to tell Marty. When Marty came home at ten-thirty, Louise was in the kitchen in her robe and nightgown and fuzzy slippers, waiting for him.

"I thought you'd be asleep by now," he said, making for the refrigerator.

"I thought I'd wait up. We need to talk, Marty." It was like striking up a conversation with a stranger, as if, having broken their sexual bond, all other forms of communication had been sundered along with it.

"You want to talk?" Marty stood at the open refrigerator door, rolling sliced Virginia ham and stuffing it into his mouth. "So talk."

"I'd be happy to make you a sandwich," she offered quietly.

"Don't bother. Sit. Keep the load off your feet."

"It's no strain, Marty. I like to do things for you."

He laughed bitterly and shook his head. "Tell me about it," he said.

"You just don't seem to let me anymore, that's all."

"So this is about what *I'm* not doing, eh?"

"No." She swallowed dryly and began again. The well-rehearsed words came out haltingly. "Marty, this is going to sound crazy to you, but late last summer I called you here at the apartment from Bridgehampton. They said you'd gone home from the store with a headache."

He colored and began to chew more slowly. "Yeah?"

"Well, Marty, this girl answered the phone. Here, in our apartment. A *girl*."

He looked relieved and disgusted at the same time. "Midge!"

"Midge? Midge Rodriguez?"

"Jeez, Louise, she's only a two-hundred-fifty-pound Puerto Rican bull dyke. We had a swell time fucking on the kitchen floor, Louise. You really should have been there. And afterwards we sat around naked and went over the floor plan for the spring remodeling. Thanks for trusting me, Louise, thanks a whole bunch."

Louise was so happy she took to her feet and went to him. "I knew it was something like that. You know how crazy those hormones can make us."

"Tell me about that, too," he grunted.

"I miss you." She touched him lightly between the legs. At least she felt him stirring as he stuffed yet another piece of ham into his mouth.

"We got any cheese?" he asked.

"In the right-hand bin," she whispered. "I mean, I really do miss you, Marty."

Slowly, she unzipped his fly and took him out of his trousers. Even semi-tumescent, he was huge and warm in her hands.

She dropped to her knees before him. "You're so big," she said huskily.

"Come on, Louise." He leaned against the refrigerator door. "Francine..."

"Francine's out." She took him into her mouth. He really did feel wonderful, swelling inside her like old times.

"Then what about the kids, Louise? And Magda?"

"Asleep," she whispered, tonguing him. "Asleep. They're all asleep."

He yanked himself away from her and tucked himself back in his trousers. "What are you trying to do to me, Louise?"

"Marty, I—"

"I hate this, Louise. I hate what's happening to us! I hate it, I hate it, *I hate it!*" He spun around and slammed his fist into the refrigerator, then stalked out.

Unable to rise gracefully to her feet, Louise remained on her knees staring helplessly up at the dent he had just made with his fist. Later, she had gone into her new nursery, burying her face in the fragrant piles of Wonderwear, crying until the early-morning hours.

"Besides," Louise said to Francine as they sat on the park bench, "I've missed my chance to tell him this week. He left for his Boston trip early this morning."

"That's just perfect!" Francine said.

"Why is that perfect? He won't be home till Thanksgiving."

"Because," she said impishly, "you can go up there, surprise him in his hotel room, have yourselves a hot old time, and then you can tell him the good news."

"What about you and the kids?" Louise said doubtfully, but it was beginning to sound good. Maybe Francine was right. Maybe alone together in a hotel suite in another city, he would forget his anger and disgust with her.

"I'll invite my girlfriend Laurie over. You know she loves the kids."

"And it wouldn't drive you crazy being saddled with them—?"

"What drives me crazy," said Francine, "is looking at your face day after day and seeing you so miserable when, by all rights, you ought to be the happiest woman in the world."

The drive up to Boston on I-95 was surprisingly relaxing. She took the Mercedes sedan because it had the soft leather seats and the best stereo system. All the way up, she played the music she and Marty had listened to while they were courting: Steely Dan and Elton John. Seeing her face in the rearview mirror, minus the swollen body, she could almost believe she was that young girl Marty Rosen had fallen for at the first freshman mixer of the year. Driving through the streets of Boston, there seemed to be young people everywhere she looked: students revving up for the Thanksgiving break. She remembered the first time she had brought Marty out to Valley Stream to meet her parents, Thanksgiving of freshman year. She had been so nervous, wanting her parents to approve of the young man she had chosen to marry. Her father and Marty had taken an instant liking to each other, retiring to the TV room to watch football and argue Carter politics. In the kitchen, Louise's mother had loaded the dishwasher, her lips pursed.

"So what do you think of him, Mom?" Louise couldn't resist asking.

"Very attractive."

"He is cute, isn't he?"

"Very bright."

"Oh, yes!"

"And a real go-getter, that much is clear."

"His business is really taking off."

"But he's trouble, that one—mark me, Louise."

"What do you mean, trouble?"

"I mean it won't be easy to keep a man like that happy day after day, year after year. A man like that's got one thing written all over his face, in capital letters, Louise. HUNGER. Lots of luck keeping him satisfied."

* * *

163

The lobby of Boston's posh Ritz Carlton was crowded with computer salesmen in for their annual sales convention. She had to wait on line at the desk while the six conventioneers standing ahead of her registered.

"I'd like to know what room Marty Rosen's staying in," she asked when at last she came to the front of the line.

"Suite 311, ma'am," the man said, "but I'm afraid you won't find him in this evening. Would you care to leave a message?"

Louise's heart plummeted at the thought of spending the evening after her five-hour drive in a crowded lobby full of noisy conventioneers.

"I wonder if it would be possible for me to wait for him in his room?" She would take a nice, long, hot bath, put on the sexy negligee she had bought just for the occasion, and be waiting for him when he got in. Surprise!

The man standing behind the desk took in her mink coat and the condition it barely concealed. "If you'd like," the man said, "I can dial his room and check with his wife."

Louise swayed slightly. "With his wife?" she whispered. "But I'm—"

"Yes," he went on, "Mr. Rosen indicated on his way out earlier that Mrs. Rosen would be staying in tonight. I believe she's having dinner in. I know because she ordered a bottle of French wine that is not on our list and we had to send a man out for it. If you like, I'll ring her."

Louise broke into a sweat. "Don't bother," she said between clenched teeth. "I wouldn't want to disturb her."

"It's a mistake. The concierge made a mistake." Francine stood at the stove heating Louise a pan of milk. Louise had driven back all the way from Boston nonstop and arrived at two o'clock in the morning to find Francine and her girlfriend watching the original *King Kong* on the Late Late Show.

Francine had made Louise take a hot bath and then change into her maternity granny nightie. Louise sat in the kitchen, seething.

"I'm sure it isn't a mistake," Louise said. A girl picking up the phone here was one thing; a girl stashed in his hotel room, quite another.

"But of course it's a mistake!" Angrily, Francine flung her hair out of the way as she poured the hot milk into a mug and mixed in a teaspoon of honey.

"She even likes fancy French wine," Louise said, taking the mug between her hands. "I wonder if she's pretty. What am I saying? Of course she's pretty. Probably gorgeous. A walking, talking wet dream!"

"I do not believe it!" Francine maintained. "I will go to him myself and ask him."

"Don't you dare!" said Louise. "I'll handle this my own way. Whatever that is. Besides, that would only piss him off, your interfering. Maybe he'd even fire you. And I happen to need you right now...more than I need him."

"Oh, Louise!" Francine's long eyelashes were beaded with tears. "This is too, too terrible."

"Don't you get upset, too. I suppose I shouldn't be surprised," she said, more to herself than to Francine. "It would be one thing if I kept his baby against his wishes and went on satisfying him in bed. But I crossed him *and* I cut him off, cold turkey. I mean," she went on, "I told my own husband to jerk off...literally! A man with Marty Rosen's libido is not going to be satisfied for long with Mary Five Fingers."

"Who is this Mary Five Finger? I will speak to her!"

Louise laughed shortly. "No, now is not the time for confrontation. For the time being, I'll just have to get myself used to the idea—that there's at least one other woman. I mean, there's not a hell of a lot I can do about it right now. But when I'm back in fighting trim...*look out, Marty Rosen!*"

"What does this mean?" Francine asked. *"Look out?"*

"I'm going to hit him with the biggest, messiest divorce suit in the history of the Upper West Side, that's what it means."

Francine frowned.

"What, you don't think he deserves it?"

"No, I don't think that you deserve to be a single mother of six. Alimony or no alimony. I think you should try to work it out."

"Gee," said Louise, smiling bitterly as she sipped her warm milk, "I guess this is what they mean by a no-win situation."

"You're looking good, Jill."

"Thanks, Warren, you're not looking so bad yourself. Like your old svelte self as a matter of fact."

They were lying side by side, naked, on the king-size platform bed on the night of Jill's return from her stay on the Bowery. Warren's naked thigh was hooked over hers, his semen evaporating between them. Perhaps it had been the months of abstention, but the two of them hadn't made such hot love in a long, long time.

"That was pretty good, wasn't it?" he said, voicing her very thought.

Jill grinned at his profile. "It was downright bullish, English. Hungry?"

"No," he said, stroking her hair, "let's just stay here and not move for a bit."

"That's fine with me." Jill sighed contentedly. She thought of how she had spent the last weeks—going to movies by herself, reading Oriana Fallaci's *Letters to a Child Never Born*, doing a little painting, and a lot of thinking—basically gathering herself to herself once more. It had done her good. She felt strong and cleansed, and although a certain sadness lingered it was no longer enough to tear her apart or make her lash out at the world.

"You know," she said, running a hand up and down his muscular bicep, "before, when I guess I was still under the influence of hormones, I had this crazy idea you were in love with somebody else."

He frowned, a single deep crease cleaving his brow.

"I had this wild theory all worked out. I figured *she* worked at the health club since you were spending so much time there."

He swallowed, his Adam's apple bobbing. In the bluish light from the streetlamp, she saw his eyes well with tears.

"Hey, Warren." She nudged him playfully with her foot. "Like I said, it was a theory, a figment of my hormones. I was just looking for ways I could feel even more sorry for myself and..." She trailed off. His body had gone suddenly tense and dampish. Abruptly, he swung away from her and rolled over to his side of the bed, his big back to her like a smooth white wall.

"Hey, look," she said to the wall, as lightly as she could. "I'm sorry I brought it up, okay? I just wanted you to understand one of the things that was making me so bitchy before. I didn't mean to ruin our lovely reunion. I'm sorry, Warren. Really—"

"Why in hell should *you* be sorry?" His voice, muffled in the pillow, sounded cracked, adolescent. Jill's heart stepped up a beat.

"Warren, what is it?"

He turned to her almost violently, his cheeks slick with tears.

"I knew I couldn't hide it from you much longer. As soon as you got it back together, I figured, you'd guess."

Jill sat up, the air suddenly cold on her nakedness. "Hide what?" she asked, feeling sick as she got up and went to retrieve the flannel shirt he had stripped off her when he couldn't get his hands on her naked breasts soon enough.

He heaved himself up in the bed, pulling the duvet up to his waist.

"Her name is Wendy."

"Her name is *Wendy?*" Jill had an irrational urge to giggle.

"And she teaches advanced aerobics. She's in terrific shape," he added inanely, "she really is."

Jill sat down on the edge of the bed.

"And you and this terrifically fit Wendy person have been getting it on for quite some time now?"

"It started when I had to stay at the office too late to make the advanced class. It was the last class of the day and the best. She offered—she's really a nice girl, Jill, you'd probably like her even though she's only twenty-two, but she's not snotty or shallow at all—she offered to give me a private class after the club closed."

Jill didn't need to hear any more. She covered her ears with her hands and leaned her elbows on her knees, rocking back and forth wearily. The effects of her convalescence fell away like scabs too quickly formed. She could just see them doing it on the Nautilus equipment, on the exercycle, on the health-food bar, in the hot tub. No wonder he had been walking around so cheerful these past weeks! She uncovered her ears.

"I don't want to hurt you, Jill. Wendy doesn't want that, either. She's pretty sensitive—"

"Christ! Could we please not talk anymore about how young and pretty and thoughtful and sensitive this Wendy is?"

He flinched. "Sorry."

"Me, too," she said hollowly. "Me, too." And she found herself wondering. After he divorced her and married Wendy and made her quit working because her salary was a tax liability, would their health-club-enhanced sex life go from Baroque to Bauhaus in a matter of weeks? Then, again, that wasn't her problem, was it?

Kendra

Nora Alicia's father, a prominent Saratoga lawyer and breeder of racehorses, had built the lake cabin with his own hands as a wedding present for his wife. It was a large, rambling Ponderosa-style log-and-mortar structure nestled in a cove and sheltered by a grove of white birches that leaned gracefully toward the lake. Kendra's happiest childhood memories were of summers spent here with her grandparents and her brother and all the cousins, the kids all sleeping together in a dorm stacked with bunk beds known, because of its one wall of glass facing the lake, as the Fishbowl. When her parents died in the early Sixties, Nora Alicia had inherited the cabin, the boathouse, and the three acres fronting the lake, but she never showed much interest in the property, preferring the more socially active scene in Old Greenwich or at the house Ainsley had bought for her up in Kennebunkport. Over the years, it became Kendra and Grady's place by default. They and their prep-school and college friends gathered there for long holiday weekends and summers and afterwards set down their thoughts and thanks in the guest book, a tradition started by Nora Alicia's mother back in the Forties.

Over the last twenty years, the winters had taken their toll on the cabin. There were tattered screens, a leak in the Fishbowl roof, loose planks on the thirty-foot dock, a rotten floor in the boathouse, mice in the chimney, and chronic problems with the septic system, to name only the most obvious wounds. And so it was that Morgan

Ford's one-night invitation to turn out the bat and haul in the firewood stretched itself into one week, then another, and another as autumn wore on and one home repair chore after another kept him there. Secretly calling him Mr. Fix-It, Kendra termed the sometimes unique ways he solved certain technical problems Morgan Ford Technology.

Kendra, who normally hoarded her privacy, found him a rather comfortable companion: silent and preoccupied with his own thoughts and projects during the day, as she was with hers. And at night over supper, which they ate at the small table before the fieldstone fireplace in the living room, amiable and able to lend himself to discussions on a range of topics, from the current art scene to the American theater to the varieties of bird life that came to eat at the big cedar feeder outside the kitchen window. On the subject of her own art, he kept his silence unless called upon to comment. Kendra's way of working was to finish a piece and then to turn her back on it and take a long walk, returning to it after a few hours with a fresh eye. Sometimes she invited him to join her in this appraisal. Unlike many people, he was unselfconscious about expressing his opinion, and she welcomed the extra set of eyes.

About her pregnancy he seemed shy and a little awed. A couple of times she had started to invite him to put his hand on her belly and feel some of the feistier kicks, but then thought better of it. It was, after all, the sort of intimate gesture only a father was permitted and Morgan was not, after all, as far as one of them was concerned, the baby's father. In fact, memories of their passionate sexual encounter had faded into distant memory along with many aspects of her pre-pregnant life. Although she was aware of being alone in the house with a fit and healthy male, it was as if the shadow of the fictitious investment banker husband had fallen between then, making anything more significant than a casual grazing of limbs as they handed dishes to one another, or passed each other in the hall, strictly taboo. Only at night did her libido awake and make itself known to her. After they had finished washing and drying the dishes, after he had stoked the fire and they had said good night and retired to their separate bedrooms, she would get under the covers and turn on her vibrator. Holding it to the tip of her oh-so-sensitive clitoris, she would close her eyes and imagine him coming into her room, unable any longer to stay away from her. As she pictured him moving above her, filling her as she opened herself to him, his shoulders bare and muscular, his wavy hair smelling of woodsmoke, she shuddered her way to nightly relief.

"It's a shame your husband never makes it up here."

They were out in the middle of the lake in the canoe, she in the rear ruddering, he in the front, providing the power. She was thankful he had his back to her so that he could not see her face as he made the first mention of her mythical husband. The lake was like glass, a wispy morning mist hanging over it, evaporating as the sun climbed higher into the sky. The hills on the opposite shore, only a few weeks ago a riot of colors, had dimmed to mauve bare trunks holding a few brown die-hard leaves.

"He's a busy man." She paused only briefly in her paddling.

"I guess he must be. I tell you one thing: If you were my wife I wouldn't stay away from you for even a day."

"Well, you see, it's like this. We—"

"Have an understanding," he finished for her.

"Right." She blushed and added, "Plus he's kind of married to his job."

"More than to you." It seemed like a statement instead of a question.

"I guess so—I don't know."

"Still, this is such a gorgeous place and you're so—what I mean is, I see the changes happening to your body every day. I mean, I can't help seeing. And it's so beautiful. It seems a shame he's missing it."

"Sort of like missing the high color?"

"Sort of."

"My shoulders are getting stiff," she lied. "Let's turn back."

"If you want to rest, I'll be happy to take us in."

"No, that's okay." She felt a sudden shrill tingling between her legs. His voice was so gentle, his stroke so strong. She felt her will weakening as she guided the canoe in a tight circle toward the boathouse.

"Hey, Kendra!" A man was standing on the boathouse roof waving his arms over his head in a wide arc.

"Is that your husband?" Morgan asked.

"No," she said, her heart quickening. "It's my brother, Grady." *The cavalry to the rescue*, she added silently, making steadily for the dock.

"Morgan's been fixing up the house."

"So I see." Grady tested one of the replacement planks on the dock with the toe of a soft Italian pump. "It so nice to have a man around the house," he added fatuously.

"Morgan even kicked out a bat for me."

Grady covered his heart with one hand. "Ye gads! I've been usurped! What did you use for a hat?"

"What are you doing up here, anyway, Grade?" Kendra followed Morgan across the lawn into the house. "You look like a fugitive from the Love Boat. I thought ascots gave you hives."

"I came to look after my little sister, the world's most ravishing Single Mom, and to check on the progress of my prospective niece or nephew."

Kendra gave him a sharp elbow to the ribs.

"That's my brother," she said. "Refusing to recognize my husband simply because he has the bad taste to work for a living."

"Your husband?" Grady mouthed the words, staring hard at Morgan's back.

"Grady looks down his nose at capitalists." Kendra strode into the kitchen and put on a kettle of water to boil.

"On the contrary," Grady defended himself, settling at the kitchen table, "some of my best friends are capitalists."

"So long as they don't marry your sister, right?" she persisted, wondering when he would get the hint.

Throwing up his hands, he finally gave in. "So how is the *old rogue*, anyway?"

"Oh," Kendra said, "investing away. You know old Bob."

"I think the dude's crazy." Morgan sat down at the table across from Grady to tinker with a lamp that had shorted out five summers ago during an electrical storm and never been fixed.

"Oh, definitely," Grady said, warming to the ruse at last, "out of his mind, old Bob is. Out of this world, if you ask me. Tell me, Morgan, what is it that you do...apart from mending country houses, fixing broken lamps, and rescuing damsels from bats?"

Without looking up from his work, Morgan said, "I build and design sets, stage manage, and generally bust ass backstage."

"Ah!" Grady said wistfully. "I once used to tread the boards."

"And...?" Morgan prompted him.

"I got terminal splinters. No, seriously, my sister's the artist in the family. I honestly don't think I have the stamina for it. You, on the other hand"—he eyed the other man significantly—"look rather robust."

"I earn a decent living," he said. "But I tell you, you spend time in a place like this and you realize what you've been missing locked up in theaters all these years, never seeing the light of day, never seeing the seasons change..."

"I don't know," Grady mused, "there's lots of regional theater springing up in the country. There's a little place in Saratoga, as a matter of fact, that Nana—that's our sainted mother, Nora Alicia—supports rather staunchly. You could work a little theater like that, live in a house like this, and have the best of both worlds."

Morgan looked up from the lamp and regarded Grady curiously.

"I think I'd miss the city," Kendra said hastily, wanting

to break up whatever bond was forming between the two men.

"And the city would miss you, too, Keddy, which is basically what brings me lakeside. I have come to fetch you and drive you back to the city. Nana has finished purchasing your layette and wants an official unveiling. And how convenient that Morgan is here! You can ride with me in a *real car* while Morgan coaxes the Saab, pronounced S-O-B, cityward. Not that I don't hate to break up this scene of tranquil—but obviously platonic—domesticity, but when Nana beckons, we Madisons run."

"I must say I heartily approve your choice of donor," Grady said, pulling onto the Quickway and heading south. Behind them Morgan Ford followed in the Saab.

"I don't know what you're talking about, Grade." Kendra sat with her eyes closed, the autumn sun warm on her eyelids and cheeks.

"Come on, Keddy. This is Grady here. You don't have to lie to me. Isn't he what you and your little girlfriend refer to as a GAS—genetically approved specimen?"

"Genetically acceptable. So I availed myself of his seed. Mea culpa."

"But why the investment banker husband?"

"I pulled that out of a hat when he showed up here five weeks ago. He was supposed to stay over in Europe for a year."

"The best-laid plans, eh? And he doesn't suspect?"

"I explained to him that he was a sort of last fling for me and I think he believed me. He's not of a suspicious nature, Grade. He's actually rather sweet."

"*Rather.* And comely beyond the call of duty, I'd say. Why don't you come clean with him?"

Kendra cast a look over her shoulder, wary that Morgan might be capable of eavesdropping at a distance. "Because it's not in the plan."

"I assume that your hormones have rendered you senseless or that you're as queer as I am and are planning to move in with the not-so-gay future divorcée, Jill."

"I might just do that. She miscarried, you know."

174

"If that wasn't merciful intervention, I don't know what is."

"That's a terrible thing to say, Grade. Even for you."

"It's the truth and you know it. That's a bum marriage if ever I saw one."

"And I suppose you want me to lose my baby, too?"

"Now *that's* a terrible thing to say. Of course I don't. It's different with you. With this Morgan fellow, you could be backing into a very good thing."

"Well, if anybody knows about backing into things, Grade, it's you."

"Keddy," he said, eyeing her askance, "it's not like you to fight dirty. Methinks I have hit a nerve."

Kendra found the Bowery unchanged except for the stained double box spring by the corner mailbox on which a couple of bums were curled up, snoozing away.

"I'm surprised Nana didn't have them hauled off," Grady said, sidestepping a huge cardboard box that looked as though it might be inhabited.

"I honestly don't think she sees things like that."

"Will Master Morgan be joining us?" he asked.

"Are you crazy? You think I'd let Nana lay eyes on him? Her radar is at least as sharp as yours. He had business at the Public Theatre. He said he'd call and tell me where he parked the Saab." She stopped at the front door and fished out her keys while Grady stood by, her bags in his hands.

Someone had obviously been collecting her mail, for she found only the latest Con Ed bill and a bank statement awaiting her in the entryway. What she didn't notice at first until Grady pointed it out to her was that someone had installed an invalid chairlift, the kind they advertise in the back of the Sunday *Times* magazine near the crossword puzzle: Inclinettes.

"What in the world...?"

"Remember," Grady said, flipping down the seat and switching on the mechanism, "no climbing stairs. Incline, do please."

"I couldn't," she said. Then she looked up the long,

steep first flight, which seemed to have gotten even longer and steeper in the six weeks she had been gone. "Well"—she hesitated—"I guess it wouldn't hurt to try this once."

"That's a sensible girl," he said.

"Talk about heavy cargo," she said as she rode up slowly along the electrical track.

"That's *precious* cargo, sister dear," he said, managing to keep pace with the moving chair.

On the next flight another chair awaited her.

"Two?" she asked, incredulous.

"Actually, three," he answered, "one for each flight."

"This is ridiculous." But she got on anyway and pushed the button.

"Yes, isn't it?" he agreed gleefully.

She waited for him at the top of the third flight, where he joined her, winded and pounding dramatically on his chest. "Remind me to use this thing next time I come to visit."

"For a man in your delicate condition," she said, "it's the only way to travel." She fitted her keys into the various locks and pushed open the fireproof door.

When she first looked inside, she was sure she had somehow gotten off on the wrong floor and entered someone else's space. She turned around and looked at Grady, opening her mouth but failing to produce any sound.

Smiling at her, he gave her a gentle nudge the rest of the way in the door.

"Surprise!" Nora Alicia stepped out from between a giant ficas tree and a painted screen, a glass of champagne bubbling in her hand. "And welcome home, Dolly!"

Bewildered, Kendra fell into her mother's arms. Over Nora Alicia's shoulder she saw that not a single square inch of the old 2,500 square feet remained as it had been when she left it six weeks ago. The splintered, patched, battleship-gray floors had been torn up and replaced by gleaming maple planks. The walls were freshly painted wallboard. Even the old, grimy wire-mesh windows had been replaced by combination storms and screens and bubble-style skylights. Only the old pounded tin ceiling remained, but it had been scraped and painted a pale robin's-egg blue. The kitchen, once relegated to a stingy four feet along one wall, had been expanded into an actual room of its own. New stove, refrigerator, and sink— all in matching robin's-egg blue—had been installed, along with a long L-shaped parquet counter complete with track lighting and overhead glass racks from which an assortment of brand new crystal goblets, snifters, and stemware now hung. Kendra wandered around in a daze. A gallery bedroom had been erected along one wall, dominated by a new queen-sized four-poster made up with Laura Ashley sheets and quilts, and next to it, a wicker bassinet with a long white lace skirt. Beneath the gallery was a full nursery, including changing table, and matching hand-painted Babar crib, chest of drawers, wardrobe, and Kendra's old wooden rocking horse with a refurbished mane and tail.

"My bay mare, Lady Jane Gray, donated the mane and tail," Nana said softly. "I hope you approve."

Kendra nodded, opening the wardrobe and the drawers. They were packed with neatly folded stacks of T-shirts, stretchies, nighties, booties, buntings, and blankets. In the center of the loft, where her bed had once been, Nora Alicia had designed a sort of conversation pit surrounding a Franklin stove: an arrangement of sectionals and combination easy chairs and hassocks— enough to seat at least twenty. Nearest the stove was a carved oak rocker Kendra recognized from the nursery at Whispering Laurels, and an old hooked rug that had belonged to her grandmother. Kendra wandered into the bathroom.

Once consisting of a tin shower stall, a stained birdbath-sized sink, and a leaky toilet minus the lid, it had been gutted and redone in shades of moss green. There was a separate shower and raised tub. The sink was large enough to bathe a baby in. Next to the sink, an arrangement of powders, diaper pins, lotions, and cotton balls was laid out on top of an antique oak washstand.

Kendra used the brand new toilet, flushed it, and emerged from the bathroom to find Grady and Nora Alicia watching her eagerly.

"Well ...?" Grady said.

"What do you think, Dolly?" Nana held her hands in front of her mouth as if praying. Her eyes were moist. "Is it too, too much?"

"Of course it's too much. But," she added quickly, "it's beautiful. There's only thing wrong with it."

"I know," her mother anticipated her, "there's no place to paint."

"Exactly."

"Well, now, Nana thinks of everything. I've taken over the loft across the hall from this one. All your painting equipment has been moved over there. It meant buying this red-brick fiasco, but I didn't mind. I think you'll find it rather resembles this place before I got my hands on it."

Kendra couldn't see her mother's face for the tears flooding her eyes. A year ago if Nora Alicia had pulled a stunt like this Kendra would have been furious. But now she felt only touched. After all, it wasn't for Kendra so much that Nana had done all this, but for her unborn grandchild. And who was Kendra to deprive her baby of a comfortable nest?

"Thanks." As Kendra again moved into the circle of her mother's arms, Grady, who had remained gloatingly silent up until now, moved in to join them in a three-way hug.

Grady chuckled. "Talk about your Power Showers!"

Carleen

Carleen couldn't believe she had walked in on another one of those ladies' room discussions. She had excused herself from an after-luncheon meeting in her office with Mitch Michaelman to go to the bathroom and freshen up when two assistant editors cornered her at the sinks.

"So, have you gotten the results of your amnio yet?"

"Not yet," Carleen said, as lightly as she could manage.

"It's been a long time, hasn't it?" one of them asked.

"You must be nervous," the other joined in. "How long's it been?"

"Only a few weeks." Carleen leaned close to the mirror and picked one long black lash out of her eye.

"Don't they usually know sooner?" one wanted to know.

"Maybe they lost it," the other suggested. "Wouldn't that be awful if they lost it and you had to go through it all over again?"

"A few weeks!" the other repeated, shaking her head. "I don't know if I could take it. I mean, so much hangs on it."

Carleen, who had made a considerable effort not to dwell too much on the test or the upcoming results, didn't appreciate being reminded.

"Are you going to find out the sex?" one asked.

"She doesn't need to," the other answered. "I already know, it's going to be a boy."

"How can you tell?" Carleen asked, not setting any particular stock by what the woman said, but curious as to her methods of divination.

"You're carrying heavy and wide. My sister-in-law, she carried light and real pointy-like. And she had a girl."

"Oh," Carleen said politely. "Pointy-like." Where were they recruiting young editors from these days, she wondered, vocational high schools?

"I'd ask, if I ever had amnio," the other said, "which I never would. Let somebody stick a needle in me? I mean, forget it. But if I ever did I'd ask to know the sex."

"I don't know," Carleen said, participating in the conversation in spite of herself. "I think it's a little bit like opening your presents before Christmas. Takes some of the fun out of it."

"I used to do that, too," the woman said, blending in her blusher. "Wherever my parents hid them, I'd track them down and open them weeks before Christmas."

"My girlfriend asked to know the sex of hers," the other said, "so she could pick out the name, decorate the nursery, buy the layette. I mean, you figure it's gotta be either pink or blue."

Carleen ran a brush through her ash-blond hair, dropped the brush back in her purse, and snapped it closed. "What's wrong with green? Or yellow, for all that matter?" And on that note, she returned to her meeting with Mitch Michaelman.

"There she is!" He turned from the window where he had been admiring her small V-shaped view of the East River visible between the two shoulders of the hospital complex two blocks over. "I was about to send in the troops."

"Sorry," she said, resuming her place on the sofa. "There were some women in the bathroom speculating on the probable sex of my child."

"Women!" He snorted and reached into his breast pocket for a thin breadstick. Out of deference to her, he had refrained from smoking cigars around her since learning of her condition. Breadsticks were his substitute. He poked one into his mouth as he sat down next to her. "I think it's a girl, for what it's worth. And I want you to know I guessed right on all four of my ex-wife's pregnancies. Of course they were all girls..."

180

She smiled at him and picked up the legal pad on which she had jotted down some minor quibbles she had with the rough draft of his new novel. "Where were we?"

"Hard to imagine, a big macho guy like me turning out nothing but girls," he said, puffing forlornly on his breadstick. "I suppose you'll be wanting a girl. Most of you liberated types do. Mold them in your own image and all that."

"Mitch," she said matter-of-factly, "I'll take anything I can get...so long as it's healthy. I think we were discussing the pacing in the submarine scenes. I think, because it's such a constricted space, you don't want to draw them out."

"You're right," he said, "health is absolutely everything. We lost our third daughter to bone cancer, I ever tell you that?"

"No," she said, dreading that he would tell her more. Since she had become pregnant, she couldn't bear to hear stories of sick or dying children, kidnapped or abused children, or children the victims of famine, war, revolution, or divorce.

"Stood by and watched her die," he went on morosely. "It broke up our marriage."

Hadn't Bill once said that if anything happened to this baby, he didn't know whether he could go on living with her? "I guess something like that either brings you closer together or drives you apart."

"In some ways, Marcie and I had been breaking up since the birth of our first. Maybe marriage is like life— from the day you're born you start dying? From the day you're married you start breaking up?"

"Gee," Carleen said, at a loss as to how to lead him back to business. The three whiskey-sodas he had downed at lunch were no help. "I'd sure hate to think that's true, Mitch."

"I guess I was jealous of the attention she showered on the kids. Before they came along, I was the sun, the moon, and the stars to my Marcie."

"They say that happens," she said lamely.

"It'll happen to you and your husband, too, you watch and see."

"Mitch, my husband wants this baby as much as I do. More, in fact."

"Yeah, but he won't be the one to fling a tit at it when it's hungry, or comfort it in the night when it cries out for the comfort of the womb."

"Actually, that's one of the reasons I've decided against breast feeding."

"Even still..." He waved this away. "Try as he might, he won't be able to relate to that baby the way you will. And for you, it will become the most important thing in the world. Bam! Overnight! Everything else—your husband, your job—yes, Carleen, even your precious job—will recede into mere background. It will be you and that little sucker, center stage. And speaking of which." He roused himself from his ramblings and turned bloodshot eyes on her. "What about us?"

"What about us?" Carleen asked carefully.

"Our working relationship, I mean. I mean, when I signed on board, I signed on for round-the-clock editorial expertise. I hope you don't think I intend to hang fire while you fulfill yourself as a woman."

"Mitch!"

"Don't Mitch me, darling, I'm telling you. I've been through it. It'll be so long, Grantley, so long, Mitch—hello diapers and soft milky burps, you mark me. What am I supposed to do meanwhile?"

"I assure you, Mitch," she said, trying to keep her temper in check, "except for a week or so when I expect to be out of commission, I'll be completely available to you as always. You already have my home number—"

"I was talking to that Elton John guy."

"You mean Elton Norton?" Carleen asked lightly.

"Yeah. We rode up in the elevator together this morning. He's read all my stuff, you know."

"Most red-blooded Americans have."

"Yeah, but with a keen eye, I mean."

"Bully for him."

"Anyway." He turned a second breadstick slowly in his

fingers, avoiding meeting her eyes. "He just happened to mention the Happy Event." He gestured toward her belly. "Hell, that's all anybody around here talks about these days."

"For which I apologize, Mitch, believe me. It isn't my—"

"Hey, you've got nothing to apologize to me for. Anyway, this Elton fellow, he said that if I needed, oh, an extra reader, or a sounding board while you were, you know, out of commish, he'd be happy—hell, *honored* was how he put it—to stand in for you. Not that he could ever hope to replace you."

Carleen smiled tightly at him and said, more to the absent Young Turk than to her prize author, "That's right. He hasn't a hope in hell."

"How dare you!"

Carleen stood over Elton Norton's cluttered desk, where he sat leaning back in his chair, feet resting on an open drawer, smiling innocently up at her.

"Carleen, calm yourself. You'll bring on premature labor and I'd never forgive myself."

"Elton," she returned, "fuck yourself."

His smile faded as, hastily, he removed his feet from the drawer and planted them on the floor, bracing himself for a fight.

"I didn't realize you were so territorial, Carleen. So insecure."

"You little shit. How would you like it if you went away to tennis camp and came back to find I'd taken your precious Bart Weston Ellison out to the Mudd Club and discussed his next book with him?"

"The Mudd Club's closed."

"You know what I mean."

He scratched his shaggy head in an effort to look ingenuous. "I guess I might be a little put out."

"A little *put out?*"

"Come on, Carleen, don't you think you're being a bit too sensitive? Raging hormones and all that?"

"You leave my raging hormones out of this."

"It was a casual chat in the elevator and you're trying to blow it up into a major poaching operation."

"That's certainly the picture Michaelman painted."

"Well, maybe it was wishful on his part. After all, Carleen, no offense, but you are a girl. He's a guy and I'm a guy. And he writes guy-type books. Capital G."

"So now you're telling me that I'm fit only to edit women's books, eh, Elton? Small w?"

"Not exactly." He had taken up his ivory letter opener and was running its point beneath each begrimed fingernail. "But you have to admit, he's a pretty macho guy."

"Unlike the author of *Minus Zilch and Counting?* We are what we edit."

"Leave Bart out of this."

"I will not leave Bart out of this. I have a good mind to start to appropriate your authors, one by one, if only in self-defense."

She moved around his desk and stood over him. "Look, you know as well as I do that ever since I've become pregnant you've been slowly but steadily moving in on me."

"That's just not true, Carleen. I'm trying to serve as your backup."

She shook her head. "Backup, indeed. I back up into you, I back into a knife. I know there's no easy way to be rid of you. But that doesn't mean I can't be pushed into giving it a try! Even though The Third seems inordinately impressed with your editorial élan—not to mention your backhand."

"Low blow, Carleen."

"Oh, my fair-haired boy, I can go *lots* lower than that. You—"

"Excuse me, Carly."

Randy poked his head into the half-open door of Elton's office, his face bland. "Thought you'd want to take this call. Dr. Hoo's on line two."

"Dr. Who?" Elton put in. "Who's on second. Dr. What's on first."

"Very funny," Carleen said to him, but she had already said what she'd come to say and put this scene behind her. "I'll take it." She walked quickly out of Elton's office and into her own, shutting the door behind her.

"Yes, Dr. Hoo!" Carleen's heart was beating so loudly she could barely hear the soft feminine voice speaking at the other end of the line.

"Good afternoon, Mrs. Donovan. This is Dr. Hoo calling. From the genetic counseling office? The results of your amnio are in."

"Yes?"

"And I'm happy to tell you they are normal."

If Dr. Hoo had been sitting there in the office with her instead of at the other end of a phone wire, Carleen would have picked her up and hugged her. "Oh, thank you, Dr. Hoo! You must really *like* making these phone calls!"

"Well, yes," the woman confessed, "I do. We'll be sending the results along to Dr. Fitzwater." She read out the address to confirm it.

"Well," said Dr. Hoo, as if hesitant to break contact with the recipient of such lucky tidings, "the very best to all three of you."

Carleen hung up the phone, a wide grin on her face, and immediately dialed Bill at home. When it had rung over seven times, she began to drum her nails on the desktop. If she didn't tell someone the news very soon, she would explode.

At last he picked up.

"Hi," she said. "It's me."

"Hello, You. What's up?"

"Dr. Hoo called."

"*Who?*"

"Hoo! And guess what?"

"What?"

"This is one waffle we won't have to throw away."

"Yeah? Well, listen, Carleen, I knew that all along."

"Did you really?"

"Absolutely."

"How?"

"Because you're your mother's daughter, that's how."

"In what way?"

"Perfect waffles, every time."

Jill

Jill's sister, Cheryl, picked her up at the train station at Port Jefferson, where she stood waiting at the platform along with a handful of students home for Thanksgiving. Jill found herself searching among them for a familiar face before she realized it had been almost twenty years since her own student days, and that these kids could easily be the children of her classmates.

"You don't look too much the worse for wear," Cheryl said, giving her a hug and the once-over in quick succession.

Cheryl was driving an International Harvester Travel-All with a wire grillwork behind the front seat. It smelled of dog fur and had NAGEL'S BEAGLES printed on the side door. She and her husband, Douglas Nagel, ran a beagle ranch farther out on the island.

"I feel okay," Jill said. "How's Dad and Ann and the kids?"

"He's okay. Slowing down. She's beginning to show her age, thank God. And if those little fuckers call me *Aunt* Cheryl one more time, I'm gonna haul off and belt them."

"What do you call a half-sister, anyway?" Jill asked, gazing out the widow, scanning the town she had grown up in for signs of change.

"Just plain Cheryl would do fine."

"So, Just Plain Cheryl, how's life treating you?"

"Not bad. Not bad. We're building two more kennels this spring. Our bitch got a ribbon at Westminster last winter."

"Congratulations."

"Dad's disappointed Warren's not coming."

Jill stared hard at her sister. "What's his problem? He thought maybe he could talk Warren out of it man to man?"

Cheryl shrugged. "Maybe he's just sad because he didn't get a chance to say good-bye. Who knows?"

Warren's father had actually called Jill from his bank in Philadelphia. "If it's any comfort, young lady," he had said, "you're the best thing that ever happened to that big fool." She wondered whether he had met Wendy yet and found her a "bimbo" like the women who had preceded Jill. Mr. English had even given her the name of a top-notch divorce lawyer in New York. "Stick him up for all he's worth," the old man had instructed her in fierce tones. Was this his way of making a man out of his son, like forcing him to pay for the abortion of that Mt. Holyoke freshman?

"I didn't tell Dad about the miscarriage," Cheryl went on. "I thought I'd leave that up to you."

"Since I never got around to telling him I was pregnant in the first place, I hardly see the point."

"I suppose you're right. Are you at least getting a decent settlement out of the Big Lug?"

"Sticking him up for all he's worth," she said with bitter cheer. "I think he feels guilty for dumping me so quickly after the miscarriage. And I suppose the money will be some consolation."

"Consolation for what?"

"Having an incompetent cervix."

"Are you kidding?" Cheryl asked, but they were already pulling into the driveway and there was no time for Jill to elaborate.

Jill sat at the kitchen table and watched her stepmother baste the turkey while her eight-year-old half-sister, Gretchen, sat on her lap having Jill weave her hair.

"I wish Jill could live with us all the time. Then my hair would always look excellent."

"I do, too, Gretchie," her mother said absently, bending over the turkey. It was a little unsettling for Jill that the distinctive-looking young woman who had married her widower father almost twenty years ago now bore an uncanny resemblance to her late mother.

"But divorce is so final, Jill." Her father came through the kitchen, dipped a finger in the mashed potatoes, and picked up the frayed thread of their conversation.

"I know it is, Daddy. But at least we realized our mistake before investing any more time."

"But where does that leave you, Jill? Thirty-six, divorced, jobless, without a future."

"Donald," Jill's stepmother said, "I wish you'd drop it."

"Damn it, Ann, I can't just stand by and watch my daughter throw—"

"I haven't thrown anything away, Dad," Jill said quietly. "I plan to go back to painting." She finished plaiting Gretchen's hair, attached a hot-pink barrette, and shoved her gently off her lap.

"So you're going to play with paint for the rest of your life?" When it came to contempt for art, her father and Warren had much in common.

"What's wrong with that, Dad?" she said. "Is it any worse than working for a computer company? Or raising beagles?"

"You leave my doggies out of this!" Douglas Nagel called from the next room, where he was conducting a lusty game of knock-hockey with Jill's two half-brothers, Gordon and Gilbert.

"I'm sorry I'm such a screw-up, Dad." She left him with that thought and went to the hall closet to get her coat. Halfway down the road on her way to the Sound beach, Cheryl caught up with her.

"He's a pisser, isn't he?" Cheryl said, lighting up a Benson & Hedges. "A real dog with a bone."

"Remember when you used to sneak those on the back porch and I used to tell?" Jill asked.

"Yeah." Cheryl grinned, remembering. "You used to call them Benches in Heaven. I was thirteen and you were

188

seven. You were such a brat." Cheryl flung an arm around her sister's shoulders and squeezed.

"I still am," said Jill.

"So what's all this hooey about an incompetent cervix?"

Jill hunched into the collar of her coat as they rounded the bend and came out on the road running parallel to Long Island Sound. Apart from a man running his greyhound, the beach was empty.

"I love those dogs." Cheryl shivered. "But they always look so cold come winter. Like deer, starving in the snow. So, tell me about your cervix."

"What's to tell? My four abortions wore out my zorch."

"What?"

"My uterus can't hold on to a fetus after a certain point because it's been pried open one too many times."

"You sure about that?"

Jill stepped through a gap in the cyclone fence and walked onto the beach, her eyes instinctively scanning the sand as in the old days for worn bits of beach glass, intact shells, lost coins. She found a flat stone and skipped it across the shallows before turning to her sister and saying: "Sure, I'm sure. That's what the good doctor told me. Why do you ask?"

" 'Cause doctors are a pack of fools. And because I'm no stranger to miscarriages myself."

Jill stared at her sister. Although they had not been particularly close during their adult lives, it was hard for Jill to believe that her sister could have kept a miscarriage secret from her.

"In the second trimester, too," she went on, "like yours. I had a real fuck-up for a doctor until I lucked out. This new guy did some poking around. Even got in touch with Mom's old obstetrician, Dr. Hardy. It turns out old Doc Hardy gave Mom that drug DES for nasty morning sickness, which she had with both of us. This doctor figures that, as a result of DES, I have, like you, Sis, an incompetent cervix, plus a tilted uterus. He told me if I wanted to have a baby, he'd see what he could do about helping me hold on to it. But by then I was closing in on forty, no longer the fertile maiden I once was in the days of good old Paul la Pipette. Besides, I just didn't have it in me to try again."

"How long have you known?"

"Years."

"Why didn't you tell me, Cheryl?"

"Hell." Cheryl plucked the cigarette from between her lips and flicked it into the water. "I figured you knew."

"How? By osmosis?"

"I don't know. You were always so much smarter than me. Me, I was just a dumb cunt, but you, I figured you'd put it all together."

"I'm sorry, Cheryl. I don't buy it."

"Well then, buy this." Cheryl turned on Jill fiercely. "You had one miscarriage, little sister. One! Imagine how I felt after *five* of them."

"Five!" Jill gaped.

"Boggles the mind, doesn't it? Not to mention the spirit *and* the body. It even made me feel ashamed. Inadequate as a woman, you might say. And I sure as hell didn't feel like *sharing* the experience...not even in the name of sisterhood, my sister!"

"Oh, Cheryl, I'm so sorry!"

"Hey, don't feel sorry for me. You'll see, you'll even get used to it. And when you do, you'll find you feel a certain sense of relief."

"Relief?"

"Look at it this way: If you don't have anything, you don't have anything to lose."

Jill turned away from her sister and looked out over the flat, gray waters of the Sound. Nothing to lose? On the contrary, she suddenly felt the loss so powerfully, it was all she could do not to open her mouth and howl.

PART IV

Third Trimester

Jill

Jill's hotel suite was on the second floor of a brand new unit built right on the beach. From the concrete balcony outside her bedroom she could feel the spray of the surf. Her first night there, finding the air inside dead and too new-smelling, she dragged her mattress, linens and all, out onto the balcony, where she slept—much to the chagrin of the maid who daily made up the room—every night of her three-week stay. Often, she would wake up in the morning to the sight of a small green lizard inches from her nose staring at her with black, shiny eyes. "My roommate," she came to call it.

The first day on St. Martin, she walked into a chic French boutique and bought herself a two hundred-dollar white knit bikini and a delicate silver chain carrying a single emerald, Warren's separation gifts to her. After all, her lawyer had told her to spare no expense on herself. Each day she awoke early and had her breakfast in her room: a bowl of fresh fruit and a croissant. The croissant she usually wrapped in one of the hotel napkins and saved to eat with her lunch, which was invariably a split of ice-cold champagne that she drank on the beach in the shade of her private cabana. Nights, she dressed up and went over to the hotel proper, where, sun-dazed and salt-parched, she ate and drank her fill, alone, signing her checks "Mrs. Warren English" and feeling every inch the mysterious, faintly embittered divorcée. After dinner she sat alone at the bar drinking champagne and kir and listening to the band which, seemingly caught up in a time warp, played "Yellow Bird" and "Feelings," to the exclusion of almost everything else.

Since most of the guests gravitated to the pool, Jill had the run of the beach, a pure white curve of sand bordered by a fringe of palms and hot-pink bougainvillea. The water, sheltered from sharks and tropical currents by a long man-made outcropping of rocks, was warm and lambent, the color of her own eyes, a pale and powdery blue. Day by day, she was able to work herself up to twenty laps, which she gauged must be a little over five miles. While she swam, her mind was reduced to a blessedly dependable blank. But as she staggered up on the beach and flopped down on her blanket, her head reeling from exertion, she often found herself weeping.

Why, she wondered, the tears? She thought of Warren, summoned his face, his bulk, his habits to mind and chartered the course of their relationship. True, she had been fond of him, but she had never loved him. Not the way she had loved in high school and college, so passionately that when the inevitable breakup came, she felt as if her world were coming undone. But the tears weren't for Warren. The tears were for her lost baby, whose faint but persistent kicks she had just begun to feel. In many ways she still felt pregnant. There were the prenatal vitamins, for one. Her doctor had suggested she finish them to help hasten her recovery. The sight of the bottle on the bathroom counter sometimes jarred her. And then there were her dreams. Night after night, she dreamt she was pregnant, only to wake up in the morning, aching with her loss. She found herself, after the first ten days on St. Martin, wishing she had someone to talk to. She bought a postcard in the lobby showing a plump local woman and a burro with a straw hat. "Guess which is me? Having a wonderful time and wish you were here," she wrote to Kendra on the Bowery. The next day, she brought a pad of stationery with her to the beach and, propping it on her damp knees, wrote Kendra a letter.

...Except for that one-woman show at the Paula Cooper Gallery, I've always got everything I wanted. I set out to get straight A's in school and I got them. Junior year, I took one look at the Smith catalog and wanted in and, sure enough, I got in. Any boy I've ever set my sights on, I got. Having children was something I knew I was always going to do. As efficiently as once I had aborted them, I would one day, when I was good and ready, spit them out. I've gone through life so damned cocky. Who knew I would have this *problem?* I feel like some poor slob must feel who is stricken, out of the frigging blue, with Hodgkins' or some other exotic disease. Why me, I keep asking? Why can't I have as much control over having a baby as once I had over aborting them? It makes me feel mortal and scared and humble—hey, all-new sensations for me!

But enough of me. What of you? I picture you, up there in the frozen north, getting bigger and more gorgeous by the day. I can't wait for this baby to be born. Have you heard of the nurse dolphin? Apparently, when a dolphin gets pregnant another dolphin, also female, begins to swim with her and look after her. After the birth, they take turns—the mother and the nurse dolphin—looking after the young 'un. Anybody who denies they are a more highly evolved species than us is, well, not very highly evolved, if you ask me. Anyway, if you'll let me, now that I am no longer with child myself, I would be honored to be your nurse dolphin. I'll be your Lamaze coach and your nanny and your baby's godmother all rolled into one lovable, indispensable Me.

Be well and see you sometime around Christmas.

Your humble, obedient Nurse Dolphin,
Jill

Mary Beth

Mary Beth sat in her studio and stared down at the sheet of vellum tacked to her drawing board. He was supposed to be a kindly looking old muskrat gentleman, but each time she drew him he came out looking like an evil rat. She exxed him out in bold pencil and turned away from the board to look at the clock: eleven. Only three more hours until she would be with Daniel again. She switched off the gooseneck lamp and went to run herself a bath.

As she lay in a nest of fragrant bubbles, she waited for the baby inside her to come awake as it usually did in response to extremes of temperature. When it didn't, she gave in to a few moments of stark fear, thinking what she always thought at such times: *My baby has died.* Why was it this fear surfaced only on her Daniel days? It had occurred to her as she left Daniel's apartment last week that the reason she had stopped having orgasms with him was that she was convinced that the contractions brought on by climax would cause her to expel the baby too early. Was it that if she felt no pleasure, she would risk no punishment? As if concurring with this theory, the baby began to kick, sluggishly at first, then more strenuously. From the position of the kicks, an arc below her ribs, she could tell its head had moved down into her pelvis. Very lightly, she scratched the hard spot above her pubic bone where its skull was now and the baby responded, in a cat-like fashion, by releasing a flurry of light kicks.

Mary Beth emerged from the bath, the steam having melded her freckles and given her complexion the temporary look of ruddy good health. Still, nothing could disguise the gauntness of her cheekbones. She oiled her body while it was still damp. Her arms and legs were scrawny, her belly bloated, like a starving child. She dabbed cologne between her legs, behind her ears, beneath each of her breasts, all the places where Daniel would come across and inhale it appreciatively later today. Then she dressed in a new purple maternity jumpsuit. It was a color she would never have worn while her father was alive. He had forbidden her or her mother ever to wear purple. "The color of madness," he called it.

She got on the train before the one she usually took, doodling on a small sketch pad on her lap, still trying to work the malevolence out of that poor muskrat gentleman while, out the window, there flashed past a steady procession of gaudy Christmas decorations: plastic Santas, Rudolphs, elves, and enough lights to illuminate a small city.

When she arrived at Grand Central she hailed a cab and gave him the address of the church three blocks south of Daniel's apartment. Passing its graffiti-scarred doors last week, she had happened to notice the hours posted for confession. She had deliberately avoided going to confession at her own church in Westchester. The new priest, a product of Vatican II, preferred hearing confessions face-to-face and giving counseling instead of Hail Marys. She missed Father Finnian, who had retired to Florida the year before last; Father Finnian, who had baptized all the O'Mallys, who had given her her first Holy Communion, who had been a golfing buddy of her father's. She wondered now if Father had ever taken Liam's confession about his affair with Dina. If he had, what had he thought of Liam O'Mally, as they strolled the country club greens together? That he was a wicked man or merely human?

"Forgive me, Father, for I have sinned."

The air in the confessional was stale as Mary Beth knelt and spoke as soon as the priest slid open the grill in the wall separating them.

"How long has it been since your last confession?"

"Two years, Father."

She remembered, as a girl, having to make up things to confess, such a good little girl was she.

"Very well, what is it that you wish to confess?"

Mary Beth dug her nails into the palms of her hands.

"I've been having an affair, Father, with a married man, and I myself am married." Once it was out, she relaxed. After all, it was a question of degrees. In a parish like this, confessions must run from knifing to shooting up to pimping for little sisters.

"Go on, my child."

"I'm carrying a child, and I don't know who the father is."

She heard the priest's breathing on the other side of the grillwork. He was either very old, or he had a respiratory condition.

"I'm afraid, Father."

"Of what are you afraid?"

And then it struck her, exactly what she was afraid of. She wasn't afraid of the Wrath of God. She wasn't afraid of the baby's dying for her sins. She was afraid that Frank would find out and divorce her. She was afraid, quite simply, of being discovered and of losing her two lovers. And her fear was undermining the intense enjoyment she once had felt. It was her very lack of a sense of guilt that made her so wicked.

She stood up and opened the door of the confessional. "I'm sorry, Father," she said, "but suddenly ... I don't see the point in this."

"You mind telling me what's eating you, Mary Beth? Apart from me, although not very effectively, I might add."

Without giving his little joke a trace of a smile, Mary Beth got up from the studio couch and pulled her winter coat over her naked shoulders. She stood at the window and looked out at Amsterdam Avenue in the gloomy winter light.

"Is it that you'd rather be somewhere else?" he persisted.

She shrugged. She didn't want to be here. Then again, she didn't want to be much anywhere else.

"You seem very angry," he ventured.

She turned to him quickly. The sight of his slightly haggard face, usually so dear to her, today disgusted her. Was estrogen actually dampening her ardor, or was she falling out of love with him?

"You *are* angry."

"No, I'm not." She looked back out the window.

"Don't you think you'd better vent it?" He ignored her denial. "I'm sure so much negative feeling can't be good for the baby."

Defensively, she covered her stomach. "I'm not angry," she said. "Just tired. I haven't been getting a heck of a lot of sleep lately."

"Anger, insomnia, fatigue, whatever it is, it's been making you a bloody bore in bed."

Shocked, she turned to him. "What a cruel thing to say! Is that all you care about? What goes on in bed?"

"We *are* lovers, after all."

"You don't care what's happening to me, what's going on in my life, so long as you get a satisfying roll in the hay, is that it?"

"Now you're feeling sorry for yourself."

She scowled.

He smiled. "You hate me right now, don't you?"

"I do not!" she said hatefully.

"I refuse," he said, getting up to put on his bathrobe, "to be reduced to arguing on this level with you. And I refuse, what is more, to allow myself to turn into some sort of running sore for you. Either you decide to work on your attitude so that we can recoup some of the old ecstacy, or we're going to have to rethink this thing."

She remained silent, his words having given her an oddly satisfying sting.

"What you've got to do," he went on, "is sit down with yourself and find out just exactly what it is that you want, my dear. Because, frankly, I'm tired of guessing."

And then she realized exactly what it was she wanted. Not to have an orgasm. Not to confess to some stranger behind a screen or to say ten Hail Marys. She wanted somebody to yell at her—just like this.

Kendra

Out of consideration for the models, the Life Studies studio was kept a semi-tropical seventy-five degrees. The steam from the five long, low radiators shot up in unison, fogging the high wide windows overlooking Cooper Square and drowning out the sound of charcoal scratching against coarse paper and the occasional rumblings of Josh Foreman, the drawing instructor, as he wandered among his thirty-seven students and offered his comments on their work.

As Kendra stood naked on the pedestal, hands crossed serenely over her high, sleek belly, she focused on the sprig of holly some wit had tacked up over the crotch of an adjustable wooden mannequin, in honor of the approaching holiday. Occasionally, she felt a tightening of the skin beneath her fingers as her uterus hardened into yet another of the so-called practice contractions named for a man called Braxton-Hicks.

"Two more minutes, people!" Josh bellowed over the radiators' racket. "Make the most of your time."

Kendra, only peripherally aware of the thirty-seven sets of eyes on her body, was just beginning to sense the strain in her lower back she always felt as she neared the end of a session. Only nine more weeks until her due date.

Lamaze classes would begin in another three weeks. Soon she would have to stop modeling. The weight of her stomach was simply too taxing. She began to feel an itch in her nose. Knowing she could do nothing about it, it began to fill up her entire consciousness until all she felt was One Big Itch. At least it detracted from her backache.

"That's it for this week, people!" Foreman shouted and clapped loudly. "Let's hear it for one hell of a model!"

Winking, he tossed Kendra her chenille robe while applause rippled across the room. "You're a wonder, Kendra Madison," Josh said. "Best model we've ever had."

Kendra was too busy satisfying her itchy nose to acknowledge the compliment.

"Hey, excuse me, buddy, but this is a closed class," Josh said gruffly.

As the students streamed out of the studio, a single man had come to stand in the open door, arms folded across his chest.

"That's okay, Josh," Kendra told him. "He's a friend." Hastily gathering her robe around her, she made her way toward the newcomer. She hadn't seen or spoken to Morgan Ford since the lake, having successfully eluded his many attempts to reach her by phone.

"Hi," he said.

"Morgan," she said. "Be with you in a sec, okay?" She stepped behind the screen where her clothes were hung and quickly dressed. "How did you know I'd be here?"

"Grady thought I might find you here."

"Grady!"

"Grady returns my calls."

"All right, all right, I stand accused."

"What does your husband think of your modeling?"

"Oh," she said evasively, "he welcomes the extra income."

"I wasn't aware that investment bankers were in need of pin money."

Kendra emerged from behind the screen wearing an L. L. Bean tartan plaid shirt of Grady's, a pair of black stretch pants, and low-heeled boots.

"Is that why you hunted me down here?" she said, quickly plaiting her hair into a single long braid. "To bust my chops about nude modeling? If so, you're worse than my father."

"I'm glad to hear somebody else objects. Actually, I didn't come for that reason. I came to give you your Christmas present."

She colored. "Morgan, how sweet of you!"

"You have any time for me? I've been tracking you down for so long, now that I've got you I hate to let you go right away. How about a bite to eat?"

"Actually, I'm ravved," Kendra confessed. "Making like a statue for two hours burns up tons of calories."

"Great," he said, and offered her his arm. He smelled familiarly of leather soap and lime aftershave.

They went to Phoebe's, an Off-Off-Broadway show-business hangout down the street from Cooper Union, where she ordered onion soup and a salad and he a grilled cheese and beer. Sitting across the small table from him, knee-to-knee, she had to restrain herself from telling him how good it was to see him again, how luscious he looked, how much those weeks up at the lake had meant to her.

He waited until their order came before handing her the gold foil-wrapped gift. On the jukebox, Bruce Springsteen rasped, "Santa Claus Is Coming to Town."

"I should warn you." He cleared his throat awkwardly. "My mother tells me I have a real knack for the sentimental gift."

As she unwrapped the small, flat package, she felt his eyes on her face, bright and expectant. She felt vaguely guilty for not having anything to give him in return.

"Oh, Morgan!"

It was a dried, pressed maple leaf of brilliant red tapering out to flaming orange and yellow at the tips. He had mounted it on deep maroon paper and framed it behind glass in honey-colored oak.

"Do you recognize it?" he asked.

She looked up at him in wonder. "The one I gave you last fall?"

He nodded, pleased.

Their last evening at the lake together they had taken a walk after dinner while Grady, tired from the drive, slept in front of the fire. She had found the leaf on the path near the dock and presented it to him at the end of their walk just before bedtime as a token of their time together.

"I figure giving it back to you sort of completes the circle," he said.

"Thanks. It means more to me . . . it means a lot."

"You don't have to cry."

"Who's crying? I'm just tired. But your mother's right about you. You've got a real knack for the sentimental gift."

After dinner, he walked her home down the Bowery, from whose wind-swept sidewalks the bums had all fled to the warmth of the shelters or subways. When she rode upstairs in the Inclinette, he commented: "Fancy new addition."

"My husband's idea," she said, feeling like a rat. To assuage her guilt, she had invited him up for a cup of Irish coffee.

She hadn't prepared him for the sight that would meet his eyes when she opened the door of her loft. Used to it as she was by now, she had all but forgotten the rather rustic place he had seen when he visited her here last May.

"Holy shit!" he said, looking around. "This, I gather, is your husband's doing, too?"

She nodded and walked over to switch on the Christmas lights on the small, plump potted Douglas fir she had trimmed with kumquats, cranberry chains, and nosegays. He shucked his leather jacket. He was wearing cowboy boots, dungarees, and a pale-blue cashmere V-neck with nothing on underneath. She had forgotten how lovely his body was, how tempted she always was to run her hands over the muscles rippling across his back and chest and down his arms.

"Very swanky," he said, walking up and down the loft's length. "Your taste or the banker's?"

She shrugged and opened the door of the Franklin stove, where this morning's embers still glowed. "A little of both, I guess."

"Let me do that." He stopped her hand as she was

about to reach for a log from the woodpile. For a minute, they stood facing each other, holding hands.

"You know, you really shouldn't spoil me," she said.

"What's the matter?" he whispered. "Doesn't your husband believe in spoiling you?"

She felt a flush staining her cheeks and turned away abruptly, wrenching herself free of him.

Throwing the log on the fire, he closed the stove door and swiveled open the vents. He would know just how to keep the stove working at maximum efficiency, as he had known how to handle the big fieldstone fireplace up at the lake. More Morgan Ford Technology. She was aware of him standing behind her, then felt his hands on her upper arms. Her flesh tingled. It had been almost seven months since she had been with a man. And here he was: the very man who had been fueling her fantasies.

"I said," he repeated, his lips very close to her ear, "doesn't your old man spoil you? Because if he doesn't, he's out of his fucking mind."

And then he was turning her around and she was in his arms and they were kissing, breathless with passion.

"Where is he?" he managed to ask between kisses.

"Gone."

"Gone...out? Or gone...gone?"

"Gone...gone." She settled more deeply into his embrace. "We're separated." Why not? If she created the lie, she could just as easily undo it. She wanted him so badly that at that minute she would have done or said anything.

He held her to his chest. "God. I can't tell you how happy that makes me."

Hand in hand, they climbed the stairs to the bedroom, where slowly, lovingly, they undressed each other and lay down on the bed.

"I have a confession to make," he whispered, reaching to kiss her forehead, the tip of her nose, her cheeks. "I stood outside the drawing class and peeked through the window this afternoon."

"Did you like what you saw?"

"Oh," he said, slipping his fingers gently inside her, "I loved it. I *loved* what I saw."

They were rolling back and forth across the big bed, their tongues tasting, their fingers exploring, eagerly reacquainting themselves with each other's bodies. After a while his hands came to settle protectively on her belly as if he had been waiting a long time to do just this.

"I love you, Kendra," he whispered, slipping himself into her at last.

Astride him, she smiled down at him over her belly and, before she knew it, she was coming—coming!—and without the benefit of her Mean Little Machine, which remained in her bedside table drawer, rendered obsolescent.

Carleen

In order to arrive in Puerto Rico on time for the sales conference, Carleen had to leave New York City half a week in advance of the rest of the staff. Bill came to Pennsylvania Station at four o'clock in the afternoon to see her off on board the Orange Blossom Special.

"Well," he said philosophically, "at least we don't have to worry about turbulence." He patted her stomach fondly, after moving her things into the sleeping compartment where she would be spending the next seventeen hours.

"Don't forget to order the goose," she told him.

"Don't worry. I won't."

For Christmas this year they were inviting a few of her Grantley colleagues—including Grantley himself and his current girlfriend, and her assistant, Randy. Goose, which came dressed from Truffles 'n' Stuff, was much in demand and had to be ordered three weeks in advance.

"I'm going to do my Christmas shopping while you're gone," he said, a gleam in his eye. "Boy, are you going to be surprised!"

The conductor came through checking tickets and told Bill he had three minutes to get off the train.

"I wish I were coming with you," he said wistfully, testing the mattress in the pull-down bunk.

"I know. But it's better you stay...just in case that big freelance job comes through. We really could use the money. And don't go overboard with the shopping, okay?"

"Would I ever go overboard?"

"Invariably." She hugged him.

"Remember to get up every once in a while and move around," he said. "Fitzwater said it's important not to sit too long in one place."

"I'll remember," she said.

"And when you get there, don't let the bastards get you down."

"I won't."

"Call me."

"I will."

"Don't drink the water."

"I won't."

"Miss me?"

"Already."

"Love you."

"Love you."

With a chuffing of air brakes, the train eased down the tracks, Bill running alongside waving until the platform ended and the train was swallowed up in the blackness of the tunnel.

Although Carleen had packed no manuscripts to read, she had brought a briefcase fat with work. There were the pitches for the books she was presenting to the sales force to be written, the schedules for Harvey's one-on-ones with the sales people to be gone over, and a dozen or so leisurely letters to authors she had been putting off for the last several months. As the train seemed to fly past the bleak industrial towns and parks of New Jersey, then Pennsylvania, then Maryland, she felt a gradual lightening of her spirits.

The sales conference, which she had dreaded as the last obstacle standing between her and the birth of her baby, was upon her. She had found a way to attend it without jeopardizing the baby. The five days, packed with meetings and meals, would melt away and, before she knew it, she would be back on this train headed toward the Christmas holidays, with their usual bustle and round of parties, and, within less than two months, the birth of her baby. How quickly the time had passed. It had not always been so. She remembered back to those first anxious days of early summer when she had scarcely believed she had actually managed to conceive. Then there were the weeks of morning sickness and anxiety preceding the amniocentesis and the equally anxious weeks following it while she awaited its results. Then she had been halfway there, and from then on the weight of time had tipped the other way, moving swiftly, her days fired by eager anticipation of motherhood and an energy she had never experienced before. Her hand flew, drafting notes for her presentation and letters, and before long the glass next to her had blackened and the porter was knocking at the door of her compartment.

"Don't mean to interrupt," he said, "but the dinner bell's rung, ma'am."

Carleen looked up from the legal pad in her lap and shook out her writing hand. "Could I have my dinner served to me here in my compartment?"

"You surely could, ma'am, but if you don't mind my saying, it would probably do you some good to get up and stretch your legs. The dining car's two down."

She narrowed her eyes at him. "If I didn't know better, I'd swear you'd been talking to my husband."

He shrugged innocently. "He did stop and have a word or two with me. Wanted me to keep an eye on you, if you know what I mean."

She smiled. "I'll be along directly."

The dining car was cozy and aromatic. Carleen sat down at a small square table covered with white linen and set with gleaming silver and china. She was only now realizing how hungry she was. As she peered out the window into the racing gloom, someone said, "I wonder if this seat is taken?"

Carleen looked up. There stood a rosy-cheeked old gent with white muttonchops, wearing a gray three-piece suit with watch chain and fob. His scarlet-striped silk tie was held in place by a pearl stick-pin. He bowed to her.

"I don't think so," said Carleen.

"If I might be so bold as to join you?"

She smiled her consent. Laying his mother-of-pearl-headed cane next to the window, he sat down.

"I was just wondering where we were," she said.

"South of Washington, D.C.," he said.

"You sound as if you know the route well."

"I've been taking the Special for thirty-five years. Used to take twenty-six hours. Barnabus B. Venable, at your service."

He handed her an embossed card on off-white stock: BARNABUS B. VENABLE. ANTIQUITIES. RARE FINDS.

"It takes one to know one," he said. "And you are ...?"

She responded by pulling out one of her own business cards. In order to make out the print, he produced a pair of gold wire-rim spectacles.

"Carleen Donovan," he said as the waiter came by, "if you will permit me, I will order for us. My knowledge of the menu is substantial and, I don't mind saying, I have friends in the kitchen."

Thanks to her dinner companion, Carleen enjoyed rare baby rack of lamb in mint sauce, julienned potatoes, and boiled carrots that were actually served *al dente*. By the time the fresh honeydew melon balls were brought around for dessert, Mr. Venable had regaled her with one story after another of beating around the flea markets and bazaars of the world in search of antiques. His speciality was fulfilling the cravings of wealthy, usually eccentric, collectors of the odd item. Tracking down an elaborate armoire once belonging to Marie Antoinette for a certain Hollywood film actress, a fourteenth-century Venetian *escritoire* for the prince of Lichtenstein.

"Believe it or not, I found the *escritoire* in a hock shop in Mexico City."

"Have you ever thought of writing down your experiences?"

He paused and stroked his snow-white handlebar moustache. "Strange you should ask me that. Thirty years ago, Alfred Knopf suggested that very thing to me. At the time, I was too busy with the hunt—I fancied myself something of a swashbuckler in those days—to sit down and put pen to paper, but now..." He laid down his napkin and stared at her quizzically. "Do you really think anyone would read it?"

"I've been listening to you for the last two hours and I've been riveted, Mr. Venable."

His bushy white eyebrows were furrowed in thought.

Carleen pressed on. "I think your memoirs would be interesting not only to antiques hounds but to gossip hounds as well. I mean, you've dropped more names— you'll excuse the expression—in the last half hour than any single issue of *Vanity Fair*."

"I'm something of an amateur shutterbug as well," he said. "I've been taking pictures of my expeditions and clients for fifty years."

"And we could bring in a professional photographer to shoot very glossy shots of some of your prize finds. That way, it's a coffee-table book." She wrinkled her nose. "I hate the term, but there is a substantial market for them. I think we could make a lovely book together, Mr. Venable. Why don't you come to my compartment tomorrow morning and we'll talk? I've brought a tape machine, and if you don't mind, I'll just run it while you reel off some of your more fascinating experiences. If I'm not mistaken, the tape will speak for itself. I'll play it for my colleagues and I'm sure they'll share my enthusiasm. When will you be back in New York?"

He consulted a small lizard-skin pocket diary. "I'll be in

Key Biscayne checking the authenticity of a collection of Ponce de Leon swords, scabbards, and spurs through the first of the year, but I should be back in early January."

"Good. We'll be able to lock you up in a contract then."

"Madame"—he bowed his head—"consider me your prisoner."

The train pulled into Miami just after noon the next day. She had spent the morning in her compartment taping Mr. Venable, who was not in the least inhibited by the machine. And, following a delightful brunch of cracked crab and salad, during which he continued to talk (and she continued to tape), she napped briefly only to wake to the Flordia sun blazing in her face and the porter knocking briskly at her door.

Since the cruise ship that would convey her to Puerto Rico wasn't scheduled to sail until noon the following day, Carleen checked into the suite Randy had reserved for her at the Princess Hotel, showered, and ordered a light dinner in her room. After calling the office, and then Bill, she fell asleep to the gentle but constant shifting of her baby in her womb and the air conditioner's throbbing white noise.

Before checking out the next morning, Carleen dropped in at the hotel's dress shop and spent over five hundred dollars. It wasn't until she felt the full force of the Florida sun that she realized most of the clothes she had brought with her were much too formal and confining. Although the shop carried no maternity wear, she was able to purchase some flowing sundresses with skimpy straps and low necklines that would show her newly improved bust line to advantage. Just because she was pregnant didn't mean she had to look frumpy. She also bought some low-heeled sandals—three pairs—realizing, too, that to wear pantyhose in this heat would be madness. If she was comfortable, she would feel better and do a better job.

On board the *Christina*, Carleen sat up on deck and sunbathed. Usually she found lying in the sun boring, but in her current state it was strangely lulling. She felt like a lizard sunning itself on a rock. In a tank top and shorts and slathered with sunscreen—for Fitzwater had warned her that pregnant women had a tendency to burn—she wiled away a good portion of the afternoon and was pleased to see that the face she saw in the mirror before dinner was minus its winter pallor. That night, as they sailed past Cuba, Carleen stood at the rail and sipped a nonalcoholic fruit punch, wondering whether her baby noticed any difference between being on land and being at sea. Perhaps floating in amniotic fluid was like always being at sea. She slept with the porthole open and a fine mist invaded the cabin, making her normally arrow-straight hair curl up at the ends. She dreamed she gave birth right there in the cabin to a baby boy and Barnabus Venable, who assisted in the birth, pronounced him "authentic."

The rest of the staff was just checking in when the jitney that had borne Carleen bumpily over the mountains from San Juan arrived at the Lomas Beach Club. There were the usual room mix-ups and snafus that Randy, standing at the desk with clipboard in hand, was patiently trying to sort out.

"You made it!" he cried as soon as he saw her. "And you even got a head start on your tan!"

"How's everything, Randy?"

"Chaos, but nothing for you to worry about. There's a whole passel of messages in your box and a million people have been asking for you, but I told them all to fuck off until drinks at five. In the Bougainvillea Room with The Third. Meanwhile, you go get checked in, freshen up, have yourself a nappy-poo, and I'll come pick you up at quarter to, all right, Mommy?"

She smiled sweetly at him. "That's Mommy *Dearest* to you."

As the bellboy opened the door to her suite, Carleen let out a small scream. Through the curtains leading to the balcony, she saw the figure of a man standing at the railing.

"There must be some mistake..." she began, but the words died on her lips as the man turned around and parted the curtains.

"Bill!" she cried.

"I hope you're not mad," he said, tipping the bellboy and seeing him out.

"Mad? How could I be mad?"

"I figured I'd only be in your hair on the train, but down here there's lots to keep me busy. Skin diving, wind-surfing, tennis, not to mention rhumba lessons and shuffleboard. And when you need me"—he grinned and hugged her—"I'm all yours."

"How long have you had this little trick up your sleeve?"

"Actually, I have to give The Third most of the credit. He's been feeling guilty as hell for making you come down. I think this is his little way of compensating. Now, how about a shower and a nap before your drink date?"

"I could use the shower," she said, "but about that nap, I don't know." She fiddled with his shirt collar. "I think there's *something else* I could use even more."

"Really?" he said, scarcely daring to hope. Their sex life hadn't been exactly overactive of late.

"Really," she said. "Something about this tropical climate's making me feel nice and loose and sexy."

"Then by all means," he said, unzipping the back of her dress, "loosen up."

Elton Norton, in navy-blue blazer, yellow ascot, and white linen trousers, stood chatting with Harvey on the terrace outside the Bougainvillea Room while Carleen, wearing a strapless sundress of flame-colored voile, discussed chain-store discounts with the West Coast regional sales manager and The Third stood by trying valiantly to mask his boredom.

"I was just telling Harv," Elton said, joining them at their table overhung with bougainvillea and overlooking the sea, "that Rod Haver's staying here."

"Here?" The Third perked up instantly. "The champion of this year's Wimbledon, staying at this very hotel?"

Elton nodded smugly. "I saw him out on the courts this morning."

"Did you introduce yourself?"

"Well, no. He was with this really gorgeous chick—"

Carleen cleared her throat conspicuously.

"Excuse me, *woman*, and it didn't seem to be the right time. I asked the hotel pro what his schedule was and he said Rod comes down every morning from nine to eleven."

"Nine to eleven, eh?" Grantley's little wheels began to grind into motion. Then he frowned. "I'm tied up with orientation of new sales personnel tomorrow morning."

"But I'm not," Elton said slyly. "And I know for a fact that Random's been wooing him for big bucks but so far he hasn't signed. They say he's shy. But I was thinking, with my persuasive ways and bewitching backhand—"

"Not to mention your unparalleled modesty," Carleen put in snidely.

"I might just land us a tennis pro on our list."

"Sounds good to me, Elton," The Third said just as Randy breezed out and informed them that their table inside was ready.

It was after midnight when Carleen tiptoed into the room and made for the bathroom. All those tropical punches— nonalcoholic though they were—were making regular trips to the loo an urgent necessity. Climbing out of her clothes and into a shortie nightgown, and laying out tomorrow's sundress—dark blue and white polka dots with band straps—she got into bed beside her sleeping husband, and was surprised to find he wasn't sleeping at all.

"Hi, Busy Executive." He wrapped his arms around her and snuggled up to her bosom. "Hmmm, Busy, *Pregnant* Executive. How did it go?"

"Pretty good." She yawned. "It's weird when everyone's drunk but you."

"Hmmm," he said. "Gives you a chance to feel superior. Not that you don't always feel superior."

"You know Rod Haver, don't you?"

"Know him? I used to change his diapers."

213

"Seriously."

"I covered him for *U.S. News* when he was on the college circuit."

"Well, Rod Haver's staying at this hotel."

"No kidding. I'll have to look him up."

"Elton's hot to sign him to do a book for us."

"Well, he'll need a ghostwriter. That boy's about as articulate as a sweatband."

"Have you ever thought of ghosting?"

"Whoooooooo!" he intoned eerily.

"Be serious."

"Sure," he said, "there's lots of bucks in ghosting."

"Don't I know it! Some of the ghosts we sign get half the points *and* half the advance. And you have the experience."

"Are you thinking what I think you're thinking, Carleen?" Bill sat up and stared at her, his eyes wide in the moonlight.

Carleen grinned conspiratorially. "It's not as if you and I don't work very well together."

"Hey, and there's no way I'd let a putz like Norton edit my stuff..."

"And I know you'd get a great story out of Haver."

"Hell, it would be the definitive tennis book. A how-to as well as a tell-all."

"Do tell."

"For starters, I know he had an affair with the daughter of a very prominent politician. An older woman."

"How prominent, and how much older?"

"As prominent as you can get and old enough to be his mother."

"Really?"

"Well, his big sister, maybe. He was bragging himself blue in the face last time I covered him."

"Could you be out on the courts tomorrow at nine? The hotel pro says he's out there every day."

"I even brought my racquet. But what about Mr. Elton?"

"Oh," Carleen said, snuggling under the covers, "Mr.

Elton *expects* to be out there at nine o'clock, too. But I have breakfast tomorrow with him and what he doesn't know yet is that breakfast is going to go on and on and on and on."

"Carleen," he whispered, hugging her hard, "did I ever tell you I'm very happy to be married to you?"

"Feel free to tell me again."

"Because if I wasn't married to you, I think I'd be scared of you."

On the evening of the last day of the sales conference, there was a banquet at which the sales force received little tokens of the publisher's gratitude—this year a Mark Cross gold matching pen and pencil set. Carleen was wearing a filmy aquamarine cocktail dress and a pair of elegant silver sandals. In her ears she wore an early Christmas present from Bill, a pair of uncut turquoise studs. Her tan was an even shade of mocha from the ten hours of sunning she had managed to stretch out over the last five days. And the conference had been, all in all, a success. The Third had just presented the Salesman of the Year award when he knocked his spoon against his glass, raising his voice above the congratulatory rumble.

"I have another announcement to make. One that gives me particular pleasure since it concerns my right-hand man here." He gestured to Carleen. "No, she's not making me the godfather of her child." The audience chuckled. "Although that would be a grand idea. But she has managed in her short time here in Puerto Rico to entice into the Grantley stable a truly super superstar of the sports world."

While he spoke, Carleen was careful to keep an eye on Elton Norton, who Randy had placed across the table from her and Bill. Knowing that Bill had managed to keep Haver away from Elton all week, and that she had with only a twinge of guilt destroyed with her own hands the messages Elton had left in Haver's box, her latest coup would come as a complete surprise to Norton.

"Not only has Carleen managed to negotiate a brilliant contract with Rod's agent, but she has managed to secure, as coauthor, a distinguished and talented sportswriter who just happens to be her husband, Bill Donovan. As the eponymous head of Grantley House, I'd be the last man on earth to poo-poo nepotism. So let's hear it for this lovely, lucky couple."

As the staff and sales force of Grantley burst into rowdy applause, Elton Norton pushed back his chair and, face ashen and hands trembling, walked out of the banquet.

Jill

"Well, Jill, I was right about you."

Sheldon Berry sat down at his desk across from Jill and beamed at her over her cherry-pink file folder.

"Right about what?" Jill fiddled with the emerald on the chain at her throat.

"That's one fabulous suntan you've got."

"You already said that," Jill reminded him sweetly, "but thanks, again." Now that Warren wasn't with her, she was more acutely aware than ever of the good doctor's dazzling good looks.

"I was right about something else, too," he added. "You're pregnant!"

Jill's jaw dropped. She had thought she had brought some sort of stomach bug back from St. Martin. She had come to Berry to be fitted for a diaphragm, almost a symbolic gesture, one of her first as a born-again single woman.

"Well, gee" was all she could think of to say.

"I'll bet that husband of yours'll be bursting."

Jill puffed up her cheeks and blew out slowly. "He'll be

bursting, all right. I'm in the middle of suing him for divorce. Talk about your parting shots!"

Berry's smile faded; a frown creased his perfect forehead. "Well, gee," he said. "I guess you'll have to think this one out then, Jill."

She looked down at her stomach and placed both hands over it. "Is there anything really to think out, Doctor?"

"Under the circumstances, with you and your husband on the outs—"

"No, I mean about the pregnancy itself. You saw the records I had sent up from Cape May. And I told you back in the examination room about my mother and DES. What I mean is, aren't I in danger of losing this one, too?"

He nodded, stroking his chin. "I'll tell you something, Jill. That bit about the DES was the best piece of news you could have brought to me."

Jill bugged her eyes sarcastically. "Glad I could make your day, Doc."

"What I mean is, our biggest enemy in chronic miscarriage is ignorance. Now that we know the cause of your incompetent cervix—though let's just call it your tendency to miscarry, shall we?—we can do something to prevent its happening."

"You mean plug me up and make me lie down for nine months."

He smiled. "It's not quite that bad, Jill. Call it four and a half months. Tell me, are you a reader?"

"Yeah," she said, suspiciously. What did this have to do with confinement?

"I'm a nut for books myself. The only problem is I never seem to have enough time to read all the books I want to read. Look at it this way, Jill. This is *your* time. Your time to catch up on all that reading you've always wanted to do. That is," he added, "if you want to have this baby in the first place. And, believe me, I understand your situation is fraught with more than its share of extenuating circumstances."

Jill looked back down at her hands cupping her belly. Did she have it in her, she wondered, to go through all of it all over again, and this time, to go it alone?

"But there's no guarantee, Doc, is there, that I wouldn't lose this baby, too?"

"Hey, Jill." He held his hands palm up. "I don't need to tell a savvy gal like you that nothing in this world—especially not that most precious gift of life—comes with an ironclad guarantee. What I can tell you is that if you're game, I'm game. And if you're in this, I'm in it, too."

No wonder she had felt pregnant on St. Martin! As the shock subsided, she realized this was exactly what she wanted more than anything else in the world.

Misinterpreting her hesitation, Berry said, "I always say, after you're thrown, there's nothing like getting back up on that horse—"

Jill nodded quickly. "Okay, Doc. You're on. Let's ride!"

She reached across his desk and shook hands with him, so pleased to have an ally that, for the moment, she completely forgot how good-looking he really was.

"How come the dinosaur doesn't have a penis, Dad?" Zack Rosen ducked beneath the wooden railing and peered up between the legs of the life-size skeleton of the tyrannosaurus rex on the fifth floor of the Museum of Natural History.

"I've heard of boners," Marty muttered, "but this is ridiculous."

"What did you say, Dad?" Zack asked.

"I said, it's a skeleton, Zack. The penis is an organ that doesn't really have a skeleton."

"Penisaurus rex!" Bruce called out in a shrill little voice that made the museum guard wince, not for the first time since the Rosen family happened on to his beat. The woman standing next to Marty gave him a nasty look and pulled her small daughter a few inches closer to her skirts.

"Put a lid on it, eh, Bruce?"

Bruce, who was standing next to him, made as if to slam a lid on his father's penis. Marty's eyes crossed and he opened his mouth to cry out in pain when Mary, nestled angelically in his arms, plugged up his mouth with the stub of the giant pretzel she had been working on since breakfast.

"All better!" she chirped.

Spitting out the pretzel, Marty looked around desperately for his wife and discovered her sitting on a bench in the corner near the pleiseosaur, peacefully sketching. "Can you talk to him? That's the third time today he's socked me in the nuts."

Without looking up from her sketch pad, Louise said, "Be nice, Brucie. Or Daddy won't take you to the museum again."

"Pwettel!" Mary cried out and beat at her father's face with her chubby fists.

Marty fended off her savage little blows with one hand while Zack began to climb over the railing.

"Pwettel!" Mary screamed.

"Wait just a minute, young man." Marty managed to grab Zack by the seat of his pants and haul him off the railing.

"Pwettel!" Mary howled, turning purple.

"You climb up there one more time, young man, and I'll break both your legs. Louise, talk to him. Mary, what exactly is your problem?" Mary was now so hysterical she could not catch her breath. "What's the matter with her? Louise, she's not breathing! Louise, she's turning blue!"

"But, Mom!" Zack protested. "I was just trying to get the stupid pretzel for my stupid sister."

"She does that," Louise explained to Marty, "when she loses her temper. She'll start breathing again in a minute. Zack," Louise went on patiently, "if you don't stay out of the displays, you won't get a souvenir at the museum shop. And don't call your sister stupid. Marty, why don't you save everyone a lot of trouble. Reach over the railing and get the pretzel."

"But it's on the floor, Louise."

Louise spoke as if to an imbecile. "Then rinse it off in the water fountain, Marty."

"But that's disgusting, Louise."

Mary, who, sure enough, had resumed breathing, had also resumed crying.

"Suit yourself," shrugged Louise, "but once she gets it into her head she wants something..."

"Like mother, like daughter," Marty grumbled, but he retrieved the pretzel and headed for the water fountain, both boys trailing, chanting, "We want water! We want water!"

Louise continued to sketch while, out in the hall, she heard the echoes of her children demanding equal time at the fountain.

In a few minutes, they straggled back in: Mary, tear-streaked but now happily gnawing her soggy pretzel, and all of them looking as if they had just run under a sprinkler. Zack stood in front of his mother, arms akimbo, grinning. Bruce came over to him and punched both cheeks, releasing the water Zack had been storing, hamsterlike, in his cheeks.

"Jesus Christ, Bruce!" Marty shouted.

"Shhhhh," said Mary, spewing pretzel crumbs.

"Zackie made me." Bruce shrugged, biting back a gleeful smile.

Marty set Mary on the floor and got down on his hands and knees to swab up the mess with his handkerchief. Mary squatted next to him and began to rub the pretzel in the puddle as if it were the dip dish at a party. Both boys jumped on their father's back and, pounding his shoulders and yelling, "Giddyap!" demanded to be taken on a tour of the gemstones.

"Mary, stop that! Guys, give me a break, will you? Jeez, Louise, can't you control these kids!"

"They're your kids, too, Marty," she said serenely, realizing, with something very nearly akin to pleasure, that she wouldn't have to divorce Marty Rosen to punish him for his infidelity. She simply had to make him spend every Sunday afternoon with his children.

JANUARY 21
L A M A Z E • • *The Second Lesson*

The plows had piled the snow so high on the sides of the narrow Village streets, it felt to Kendra as if the cab were hurtling down a long white tunnel.

"Heck of a night for a young lady in your condition to be at large," the taxi driver ventured.

"Don't worry," she assured him, "I have no intention of giving birth in the back of your cab."

"Jeez! Look at that, will you? Welcome to Aspen, Colorado!" He narrowly missed a man making his way across the intersection of Bleecker and Seventh on cross-country skis. "Tell you the truth, young lady, I doubt I could help you if you did. In my day, we men stayed out in the waiting room, where we belonged."

"Make the right onto Barrow," Kendra directed him.

"I know how to get to Bedford Street, young lady, I just don't know how to born no baby. Are they going to let your husband help?"

"Coach?" she supplied. "No, I don't have no husband."

"Well, excuse me for breathing."

"You're excused. It's right up here on the corner of Bedford and Grove. The stucco. She should be waiting outside."

Sure enough, Jill's curly head was just visible behind a high drift. She looked nut-brown, nestled in an ancient raccoon coat Kendra hadn't seen since Smith, a pair of fuzzy mukluks on her feet.

"If it isn't my nurse dolphin!" Kendra hailed her, leaning over to open the door.

"God." Jill bundled herself into the backseat and pressed her cold cheek to Kendra's. "Look at you! You're pregnant!"

"Where to now, ladies?" The cabbie scrutinized them in the rearview mirror. Kendra gave him the address of Hudson River General.

"Hey," he said magnanimously, "I'll take you all the way to Vermont, you want to go."

"Let me look at you!" Jill unbuttoned Kendra's coat. "You're carrying so beautifully. What does Morgan think? That you're a goddess?"

"That I'm a very nice woman with a very big problem."

"Not, however, *his* problem," Jill added.

"I am nothing, Jillsie my dear, if not an accomplished liar. How's the new place?"

"Shaping up. Like me. Slowly but surely. Can't seem to shake this bug I picked up on vacation, though."

"Your resistance is probably a little low," Kendra said, regarding her friend curiously. Was there something Jill wasn't telling her?

"So, tell me," Jill said, evading her glance, "what are we learning about tonight?"

"Breathing," Kendra said, "during the second phase of uterine contractions. And a tour of the facility, I think."

Jill grinned. "It's really going to happen, isn't it? You're really going to give birth."

"Minus five weeks and counting."

"Nervous?"

"Petrified. I feel like I'm about to go over Niagara Falls in a barrel."

"Never fear." Jill patted her hand. "Barrel navigation's my forte."

"As you can see, we're welcoming two new coaches here tonight," Nurse Maxi said. "Jill is going to be coaching Kendra. And Francine—"

"Is sitting in for Marty," Louise Rosen said. "He's a little busy at work these days," she added.

"And Bill here tells me that Carleen's running late at a meeting, but she hopes to make it eventually. Isn't that right, Bill?"

Bill Donovan blushed. "Sometimes I wonder whether she won't be too busy to stop and give birth."

"Somehow I think she'll find the time," Maxi said. "Tonight, the first thing we're going to do is take a tour of the maternity wing." She looked at her watch. "They're expecting us in about ten minutes, so we'd better head out. What with the elevators in this place, you never know..."

As they proceeded down the hall, Maxi continued, "How many primates do we have here?"

Everyone looked puzzled except for Jill, who cracked, "What is this, *Planet of the Apes?*"

Maxi smiled. "*Primates* are mothers expecting for the first time. *Multips* have given birth before. When you're in here for your stay, you might overhear nurses and doctors referring to you as such, so just so you're not mystified... Anyway, you multips are just along for the ride tonight. This tour isn't anything new for you—although I will be showing you our brand new delivery room, of which we are very proud."

Maxi pushed the elevator button and was surprised to find its doors opened to her touch. "Will wonders never cease?"

As she herded all eight of them onto the elevator, there were a few muttered comments about the elevator's capacity to hold three such pregnant women at once.

They followed Maxi through the double swinging doors marked "Maternity."

Jill whispered: "Abandon all hope, ye who enter here..."

When Kendra gave her a sharp look, Jill lifted her shoulders innocently and said, "What can I tell you? I hate hospitals. I always have and I always will. But for you," she added, smiling sweetly and batting her eyelashes, "I'll learn to love them."

"The first room you'll be seeing is the Birthing Room. Lucky for us, it's not in use tonight."

She pushed open a door marked "Birthing Room A" and the group filed in.

"The only ones of you who will be using this room are Kendra and Jill."

"Why is that?" Bill Donovan spoke up.

"Because Kendra is enrolled in the midwife program. If all goes well, Kendra will spend her entire labor in this room and give birth in it as well."

Kendra tested the bed. It looked like a dorm room, decorated by someone with not very adventurous taste. The bedspread and drapes were in matching bland brown stripes. A rocking chair stood in one corner with a crocheted seat cushion and, next to it, a floor lamp emitting a dim, pleasant glow. Nowhere was there a sign of any medical equipment.

As they left the room, Bill Donovan gave it a wistful look over his shoulder. Louise, waddling along behind him, chucked him on the shoulder.

"Don't worry, Bill. When Carleen's in labor, you won't care two figs about *atmosphere*."

"And here is the labor room," said Maxi.

All heads peered into the empty room. Two crank-up beds, two lockers, sink, and a small bathroom all in tones of gray.

"Looks like a regular old hospital room to me," Bill said.

"That's exactly what it is," Maxi said. "Here you will spend your entire labor up until just before expulsion, when you will be moved..." She led them out of the labor room and down the hall, through two more double doors. "Into the delivery room."

Everyone filed into the vast chrome-gleaming room and stood around blinking.

"It looks like it's never been used before," Jill said, gazing up at the big lamp suspended over the long, hard, narrow, cruel-looking delivery table.

"It's been used...only not very much. As you can see." She gestured to the spotless counters, rows of dials, and banks of equipment only a doctor or a medical technician

224

could love. "Everything here is state of the art. And this little thing here...," she said, pulling out a metal tray.

"Is a toaster oven," Jill put in.

"Actually, Jill, you're close. It's where the baby will be kept warm immediately after it comes out."

"I hate it," Kendra muttered under her breath.

Louise, who overheard her, shook her head and smiled. "I'm telling you, when the time comes, you don't really notice."

"And now, for the high point of our little tour."

Maxi led them down the hall to the nursery. The group stood before the big glass window and stared in at the rows of babies in their identical little metal carts on wheels. Most were wrapped mummy-tight in blankets. Pink and blue tags attached to the foot of the carts identified each baby.

"They look so constricted," Kendra said, pressing her face to the glass.

"When babies first come out of utero, they prefer to be wrapped up tightly. They're used to the tightness and warmth of the womb. When their arms and legs are loose, they tend to flail and fear they are falling."

Over in the corner, one little girl, her face purple with rage, had worked her way loose from her blanket and was waving tiny mittened fists in the air.

"What's with the mittens?" Bill asked.

"During your baby's stay in our nursery, it will be dressed in hospital-issue T-shirts, all of which come with built-in mittens. Babies are born with extremely long fingernails and we don't, per hospital policy, trim them. That's one of your first jobs when you take your baby home, giving it its first manicure. But while they're here, the mittens keep them from scratching their little faces."

"Mittens and straightjackets," Jill commented. "Charming."

Mary Beth leaned up against the glass before the raging baby and tapped it. "Don't cry, little baby. Please don't cry. Why doesn't somebody hold that baby?" She began to cough, a dry, painful-sounding hack.

225

As they came trooping back through the halls, they passed one of the labor rooms. The door was ajar. Lying in the bed nearest the door was a woman, her big belly exposed and girded by two belts. Beside her bed a fetal monitor beeped away.

"Oh, God!" the woman cried, gripping the bed's metal rails. "I can't stand it. I can't stand it another moment! Please, God, help me! Help me! Help me!"

"Shhhhhh," said the nurse standing beside her bed. "You don't want to scare these ladies, do you?"

"Who gives a shit," the woman cried out, "about any fucking ladies?! I'm dying here."

The "ladies" remained standing in a horrified half-circle outside the labor room door. A second nurse came sashaying down the hall, whistling, her surgical cap soaked with sweat, the front of her gown spattered with blood. "Looks like fun, doesn't it, gals?" she cracked. "Bet you can't wait."

Maxi directed a dirty look at her back. "Shall we move on?" she suggested brightly.

Like witnesses at an accident, the group seemed incapable of moving on. Then, one by one, they tore themselves away and headed back down the hall and out the doors of the maternity ward. They rode the elevator back up in stony silence, except for the sound of Mary Beth coughing.

"Hey," Louise chirped when they got back to the physical therapy room, "it's not really as bad as it looks."

Everyone stared hard at Louise, but nobody believed her.

"Right," muttered Jill under her breath, "it's probably even worse."

Mary Beth

Mary Beth took the decorations off the tree, wrapping the breakable ones in newspaper and tossing the nonbreakable into a large wicker hamper. The dried needles fell off the tree by the handful. It was well after Twelfth Night and the tree, a blue spruce they had selected and cut themselves at a Christmas tree farm up in Connecticut two weeks after Thanksgiving, had served them well for over a month. Tomorrow Frank would drag the tree out to the curb for the trashmen to pick up and Mary Beth would vacuum up the trail of needles. But she knew that, as late as next July, she would still be finding them beneath the rugs and the couch cushions, a fragrantly pleasant reminder of Christmas past.

Ever so carefully, she removed from one of the topmost branches the red rubber ball Denny had this year painted gold and decorated with an assortment of sequins, glitter, and silver braid. It looked like Liberace's idea of a baseball. She took down the red and green construction paper chain and the silver foil star he had made for earlier Christmases. Every so often she would start at a faint thundering sound, as fluffy avalanches of snow tumbled off the roof into the yard. While Christmas itself hadn't been white, it had snowed the Wednesday after and twice since then, ironically always in the middle of the week, before or on the day she was to have gone into the city to visit Daniel. But the roads had been bad and the railroad lines worse, and she had stayed at home assuming he would understand that only an Act of God could keep them apart. Last night, the third week in a row, it snowed again. When she woke up in the morning to a world white and muffled with the new mantle of snow, and heard the school-closing reports on the radio, she had been secretly relieved.

The phone rang just as she was untangling the Christmas lights and coiling them into a nest of crumpled newspaper. She got to the kitchen and caught it on the ninth ring.

"I was afraid you wouldn't be there."

It was him. He had never called her at home before.

"Hi," she said.

"I know I'm not supposed to be calling you there," he said.

She said nothing, wandering over to the counter to poke a finger into this evening's rib roast, still thawing. Outside in the backyard, Denny and Frank were building a snowman. Denny, stiff and barely recognizable in snowsuit, muffler, and ski mask, was struggling to push along the middle ball while Frank anchored the big one next to the birdbath.

"I wanted to hear the sound of your voice."

As if on cue, she began to cough, crossing her legs to prevent herself from having an accident.

"You still have that cough."

"I still have it," she said miserably.

"Over the holidays yet."

She coughed again. "It comes and goes."

"Did you have a good holiday anyway?"

"It was fun," she said. "We made wreaths and gave them to the neighbors. And I got really carried away and made an entire gingerbread village."

"My, my, you have been busy."

"Denny's friends decorated it. It was fun...if you like blue gingerbread. What did you do?"

"Oh," he said, sounding bored, "shopped, ate too much, drank too much. I miss the hell out of you. When am I going to see you?"

"Well," she said, feeling another bout of coughing coming on, "if the snow has its way...never."

228

She surrendered to the coughing.

"I don't like the sound of that."

"What?" she said, recovering. "The cough or never seeing me again?"

"Both."

Just then Denny ran in, bringing with him a fine snow-laden breeze.

"We need a carrot, Mom," he said breathlessly.

"For your snowman's nose? Wait on the mat by the door."

"Is that your son?" Daniel asked.

"He's making a snowman," she said, opening the refrigerator door and pulling out the crisper to get the carrot.

"Excuse me," said Denny, "but it's a snow *lady*, Mom. And, anyway, who are you talking to?"

"A friend. It's a snow lady," she told Daniel.

"So I hear."

"A *pregnant* snow lady," Denny went on.

"A pregnant snow lady?" Daniel repeated, having overheard.

"Get off the phone and come out and see her." Snatching the carrot, Denny ran back outside.

"Sounds like a cute kid," Daniel said.

"He is," she said. "Very cute."

"Bet the one you're carrying is even cuter."

Why? she almost asked. Because there's a chance it might be yours? But she didn't say anything. Instead, she coughed again, said good-bye, and hung up.

"You really should do something about that cough."

Daniel stared at her in consternaton as she rose up from the sheets hacking, then lugged herself off to the bathroom before she wet the bed.

"I'm so sorry," she said, coming back a few minutes later.

"Don't be," he said, trying to pick up where they had left off.

The last time they had been together, the week before Christmas, she had stolen time from a week of family ac-

tivities to be with him. Whether it was the holiday excitement or hormones, she had spent most of their time together crying. And when she wasn't crying, she was
coughing. All of which left very little time for lovemaking.
She couldn't remember the last time she had had an orgasm with him.

"What does your obstetrician think of your cough?" he
asked.

"She thinks it's psychological," she said, pleased that it
was he who had introduced the subject.

He frowned. "You feel like this bundle of bones around
a belly. Have you lost weight?"

She nodded. "Six pounds in the last month." She had
found the trip in on the train and the cab ride up through
the dirtied city snow totally enervating. Now that she
was here, all she wanted to do was curl up and go to
sleep.

"It's not good to lose weight when you're pregnant."

"I know that!" she snapped. Then, more easily: "It's
hard to have an appetite when you're coughing all the
time."

"Of course it is." He smoothed her hair. "I still think your
doctor could give you something for it—even if she does
think it's psychological. My wife took some medicines
when she was carrying the kids. Stuff that didn't cross the
placental barrier." Then, after a brief silence: "Mary Beth,
would you consider seeing my wife's doctor?"

She pulled away from him. "Why would I want to do
that?"

"He's a good man."

"And my doctor's a good woman!"

"If she's so good, why isn't she helping you to get well?"

"Who knows? Maybe because I'm not helping myself."

"But maybe you'd be helping yourself if you went to see
our man."

It was *our* man now, was it? she thought with a bitter-
ness that surprised her. Could it be that she was even an-
grier with Daniel than with herself for prolonging this
affair?

"Can I help it if I'm concerned about you? And I'm concerned about him—or her—too." He patted her round belly. "Our baby here. Our love child."

"*Ours?*" She blinked at him.

"Yes, ours."

"What makes you so certain it's ours?"

"Take it easy now. Don't get your Irish up. You know what I mean."

"Maybe I don't after all. I have no idea whose this baby is. Why should you be so sure all of a sudden?"

"Call it a gut instinct."

"Let's just call it *my* baby and leave it at that." She got up off the bed and went to the window.

"Mary Beth."

"What?"

He came up behind her and took her gently by the shoulders. "We're fighting again."

"People fight," she said sullenly.

"Not us. At least we never used to."

That's because we're not real, she said to herself. *We never have been.* To him, she only said, "Well, I guess we do now. What's the matter," she added in a hard voice, "can't you take it?"

He sighed deeply and said, "I'm afraid you're the one who can't take it."

"I don't understand what you mean."

"I mean this obviously has all been too much for you. Listen to you: You're snappish, overwrought. It's been a month since we've made love and today you were as cuddly as a snake. I never thought I'd be the one to say it, Mary Beth, but I think it's time."

"Time?" she asked, her heart beating wildly in time to her baby's kicking.

"To say Uncle," he said quietly.

She turned to stare at him for a long moment.

"Why are you smiling?" he asked, appalled.

Guiltily, she crushed her lips with a thumb and forefinger. "I didn't think I was. It's just that it suddenly occurs to me that *I* was the one who said Uncle the first time.

And the first time, it didn't take, did it? I guess maybe I wanted you to say it...to make sure it takes this time."

He arched an eyebrow. "Passive aggressive, eh? Is that what this has been about all along?"

"I don't know," she said, feeling exhausted. "All I know is that sooner or later one of us had to say it. We've always known that, haven't we?" Her eyes were suddenly brimming with tears.

He shook his head sadly. "I'm sure gonna miss our afternoons. I don't suppose it would be proper of me to ask you to drop me a line and tell me about the baby."

"You mean tell you whether it's yours or Frank's?"

"That's putting it rather baldly, isn't it? On second thought, maybe I'm better off not knowing. Maybe there is a more than conspicuous element of macho territoriality in all this. Maybe there has been, all along." He caressed her stomach.

"I should go," she said, abruptly going to fetch her clothes where they hung draped over a chair. "I forgot to mention before that I had to leave early. I thought it would upset you."

"You're right. It would have."

"The guys are going skating at the Rockefeller Center rink." As she dressed, her spirits surged at the thought that she would soon be joining her husband and son, and she heard herself almost chattering. "Denny's got new skates. His first pair of single blade. I promised I'd watch. Then we're dropping Denny off at my mother's and going out on the town."

"I'll give you a lift downtown."

"No, please," she said a little too quickly. "That's okay. I'll get a cab. They think I'm at the New York Public Library. I promised I'd meet them—"

"Don't tell me," he said. "Out in front by the lions."

Mary Beth nodded, running an Afro pic through her curls. Suddenly she stopped and stared at him. He would never make love to her again. At that moment, it seemed a small price to pay for this feeling of freedom and well-being coursing through her.

"What are you thinking?" he asked.

"Oh," she lied. "I'm fixing your face in my mind...so I can keep it with me, always."

His eyes filled; he didn't believe her. They stood at the door and kissed. In the hall, she turned and waved to him: a careworn, aging, smallish man in his underwear.

Jill

When she heard the knock, Jill had just finished wretching. She flushed the toilet, splashed cold water on her face, and went to let him in.

"Hi, Morgan," she said, "thanks for coming over. Do pardon my appearance."

Still in her robe and nightgown at midday, she stood aside and let him into her Mexican-tiled kitchen. On the windowsill, a bowl of white narcissi was just blooming, filling the air with sweet perfume.

"Nice place," he said, looking around. "Lots of light."

"Are you kidding? It's like a Hollywood set. I have to wear shades to read in bed. Let me take your jacket," she said. "And then if you don't mind, I'm going to go back to the couch and lie down."

"Are you okay?" he asked.

"I'll live," she said. "I'm afraid I don't have much to offer you in the way of refreshments. Water or ginger ale? I myself am going to partake of these yummy saltines."

"Ginger ale's fine. So, you still have that stomach bug?" He followed her into the sun-flooded living room, where she climbed beneath an afghan on the Pierre Deux-upholstered harvest bench and waved him weakly toward the love seat opposite. Before she went to St. Martin she had found this apartment in the oldest part of the West Village. It was expensive but the neighborhood was good and she thought it had the right karma. She was able to furnish it with the pieces she had bought for Warren's triplex; they had always seemed out of place there, anyway.

He took a swig of ginger ale. She watched his Adam's apple bobbing. His fingers around the glass were strong and capable-looking. Kendra, Jill thought, doesn't know how lucky she is.

"So," he said, "what can I do for you, Jill?"

"First of all, tell me—and forgive my nosiness, by the way—how are you and Kendra getting along? Pretty well?"

He nodded. "I've been spending almost every night at her place since New Year's."

"Very good," she said. "I'm glad. I want you to know, Morgan, that I always approved of you. From the first time I saw you at the Broome Street Bar."

"That's right! You were there with Kendra that first night."

"Yeah, back in the days when I was a married lady."

He didn't say anything.

"You know, I've sort of promised Kendra I'd be her coach in the labor room."

"Yeah, she's real excited about that."

"And I've already been to one Lamaze class with her."

"I know."

"And I'm sure I could do a good job of it."

He waited.

"But for health reasons, I'm afraid I'm going to have to bow out."

"Kendra's going to be disappointed."

"She'll be pissed as hell is what she'll be. So I've been giving a lot of thought to replacements."

"Replacements?"

"You know, substitute coaches. At first I thought of Grady. She and Grady are pretty tight, as brothers and sisters go."

"I like Grady," he said equably.

"Then again, I thought no, he doesn't really have the stomach for it."

234

He nodded. "You're probably right."

"And our other friend, Lane, is out in the 'burbs and pretty tied up with her own family. So, the only person that leaves is you."

"Me?" He seemed surprised.

"Why not?"

"Well, for one thing, I think Kendra was counting on having another woman with her. And what about her ex-husband? Wouldn't he—"

Jill closed her eyes and took a deep breath. "Morgan, I don't know quite how to put this. And I realize it's pretty presumptuous of me, and that Kendra may very well want to wring my neck, but I cannot stand by another day and see a smart, sincere, sweet guy like you walking around in the dark. Morgan, my friend, my man, read my lips: There is no husband."

"I know. They're separated."

"There never was any husband."

"Never?"

"Kendra set out intentionally to have this baby on her own."

"Really?"

"It was mostly to keep me company. See, I was already pregnant at the time. Who knew I would lose it? We've been through so much together. It seemed only natural that we should go through pregnancy together. Only Kendra wasn't interested in hooking up with some guy just to have kids. I want you to know, she shopped around for a donor very carefully."

"A donor, eh?"

"A father for her baby. Only the idea was not to involve him beyond the original act. You were perfect: a YUM as well as a GAS."

"A what?"

"Never mind," she said. "I'm telling you too much as it is. Anyway, when you came back from Europe early, Morgan, you totally screwed up her plans. Not that I don't think she hasn't adjusted admirably. Anyway, no one has more right to be in that birthing room with Kendra than you."

"Is that a fact?"

Something in his tone made Jill stop and stare at him. "Why do I have the feeling you already know all this?"

Morgan contemplated the toes of his boots in silence.

"You know already, don't you?"

"Maybe," he said.

"How long have you known?" she demanded.

He shrugged and looked out the window. "Maybe I've always known."

"And you let me sit here and rant?"

"Playing dumb can get to be a habit after a while."

"But...how did you know?"

"Kendra."

"She told you herself?"

"Not exactly." He grinned. "See, she turns this real pretty shade of pink when she fibs."

"You sly fox, you."

He dismissed this with a modest shrug.

"And do you also know that she's in love with you?"

"I've had my suspicions."

"Well, what do you know?" said Jill.

"Pretty much everything," he conceded.

"Are you going to marry her?"

"Maybe. If she's into it."

"By the way, who exactly are your people?"

"My people?"

"You know. Your mom and pop. What's your father do?"

"He's a studio executive out on the Coast."

"Studio as in *movie* studio?"

He nodded. "He used to be third banana at Fox. Now he's second at U.A."

"And your mother?"

"Your basic Beverly Hills homemaker and hostess."

Jill frowned, considering. "Not too shabby. It could be worse. You could be Jewish. Or black. I think you may just come up to snuff. And I personally think Nana will adore you."

Morgan finished his ginger ale and stood up. "If that's all, Jill, I've got to get to a rehearsal. Don't bother seeing me to the door. Oh, and by the way"—he stood in the living room doorway and zipped up his jacket—"when had you planned on telling Kendra about your pregnancy?"

"You know that, too?" Jill spit cracker crumbs.

"Hey," he said, "ginger ale, saltines, stomach bug? I guess you could say I'm a regular Sherlock Holmes."

L A M A Z E · · The Third Lesson

February winds roared against the new double-glazed windows of Kendra's loft as Morgan Ford sat cozily in the wing chair by the Franklin stove skimming Elizabeth Bing's *Six Practical Lessons for an Easier Childbirth*. When Kendra came down from the bedroom wearing a purple-and-red-striped leotard and yellow tights, he gave out with a long, low whisle.

"Love those stripes!"

She snorted in self-derision. "I feel like Tweedledum."

"In that case, you can steal my rattle any day."

"Very funny."

"Well, excuse me if I find you beautiful." He shrugged and returned to the Bing.

"Fascinating reading?"

He nodded. "Makes sense to me. Then again, I don't have to go through with it."

She went into the kitchen and put on a kettle of water to boil. "I want to thank you again for pinch-hitting for my coach tonight."

"I didn't have anything else to do."

"Where did Jill say she had to go?"

"To the doctor."

Kendra frowned. "I'm worried about that girl."

"I have a feeling she'll live."

"Do you think she's just trying to weasel out of being my coach?"

"Why should she want to do a thing like that?"

Kendra scrutinized him across the counter, but he remained absorbed in the paperback. Why did she get the feeling he wasn't telling her everything? Just then the downstairs buzzer sounded. She leaned over and depressed the intercom button.

"Hi," she said.

"Hi, it's Carleen and Bill. Freezing to death."

"To the left of the door as you step inside is the switch for the invalid chair. Sit down and throw it and save yourself the climb," she said, then buzzed them into the building.

"Those little chairs are sure going to get a workout tonight," she said, getting the bowl of fruit salad out of the refrigerator. In addition to two kinds of melon, bananas, oranges, and grapefruit, it had slices of fresh kiwi which Morgan had just brought. "Thoughtful of my ex-husband to install that gizmo," she added.

Morgan looked up from the book. "If you don't mind," he said, "I'd just as soon not talk about him tonight."

"Fine with me," she said, going to open the door. "You know I'd just as soon pretend he never existed."

Frank and Mary Rapasardi arrived fast on the heels of the Donovans. The three tiers of Inclinettes were kept busy shuttling up and down the steep stairs. At the end of the second Lamaze class last week, they had unanimously agreed, at Nurse Maxi's suggestion, that since they were a small group, they would hold classes, on a rotating basis, in each other's apartments instead of at the hospital.

Kendra introduced Morgan as a friend standing in for Jill, who was ill, then returned to the kitchen to brew a big pot of herbal tea. While Carleen, who was interested in publishing a book on the subject of the great Off-Broadway producer, pumped Morgan for Joseph Papp stories, Frank wandered around the loft admiring the carpentry and Mary Beth came to help Kendra in the kitchen.

"These are gorgeous," she said, taking the fruit bowls down from the cupboard shelf. "In fact, everything about this place is gorgeous. And it's such a surprise, considering..."

"It's such an ugly neighborhood?" Kendra finished for her with a grin. "Thanks. Actually, if you'll keep it a secret, it's all my mother's doing. And speaking of gorgeous, you're looking really well tonight."

Mary Beth, wearing a kelly-green knit jumpsuit, blushed. "I got rid of my cough."

"That's it!" Kendra nodded thoughtfully. "I knew it was *something*."

"I was beginning to think that cough was a permanent part of me."

"How did you finally shake it? Drugs?" Kendra asked.

"Oh," Mary Beth said casually, "actually, I got rid of a certain source of tension in my life and just like that"— she snapped her fingers—"the cough disappeared."

Kendra gave Mary Beth a quick hard look. With her halo of russet curls and her bright Irish eyes, she looked so innocent. Was it possible that beneath the parochial-school exterior there existed another, more complex, Mary Beth?

"Well, whatever you did, it worked."

By the time Maxi, Louise, and Francine had arrived and everyone had sufficiently admired and complimented Kendra on her loft, the tea was brewed and the fruit salad spooned out into the hand-painted French fruit dishes. They sat around the Franklin stove, sipping and eating while Maxi, apropos of tonight's lesson, described the plight of the woman she had helped deliver last night—a woman who had been in back labor for eighteen hours.

"Back labor," Maxi said, setting aside her empty fruit dish, "is a bitch. There's no telling who will fall victim to it. But about twenty-five percent of all women experience it."

"What exactly is back labor?" Kendra asked.

"Well, quite literally, it's labor you feel in your lower back and upper thighs, instead of in your pelvic region."

"What causes it?" Francine wanted to know.

"There's no one cause," Maxi answered. "But it does usually occur when the baby lies in a posterior position, which is to say when its head is pressed against your spine."

"Ouch." Carleen winced.

"Yes, well, there are ways of dealing with it," Maxi went on. "One way is for your husband or coach to apply pressure to your lower back, where you'll be feeling the most pain. Don't be afraid—especially you men—of really pressing hard. The harder the better. You can also massage her thighs. But just in case this goes on for hours and hours and hours and hours, as it did with this poor woman last night—whose husband's knuckles really ached after a while from all that rubbing—I'd like to suggest that you include in your Lamaze bag a couple of tennis balls, or a cylinder of tennis balls. Lying on the tennis balls, or even on the container itself, will put pressure on your lower back and offer you some relief.

"Another thing you can do is change your position. Lie on your side or, better still, in the knee-chest position, like this. Why don't we all try the knee-chest position?"

She knelt on the hooked rug and rested her body on her lower arms and hands, the others following suit.

"This way, you can, quite literally, get that baby off your back."

After that, Maxi went on to demonstrate the next breathing technique to be used during the second part of the first stage of labor, when the cervix dilates from three to eight centimeters.

"Contractions are stronger now," she told them, "lasting from forty-five to sixty seconds with sometimes no more than two to three minutes of rest in between. First-phase breathing—the technique you've been practicing all week—won't be much help now. You'll need to shift up to a shallower, higher breathing."

As the coaches helped the women simulate their contractions, she walked among them, giving them gentle hints and suggestions.

"Release your neck, Carleen. You're holding tension in your neck. It's important that you don't expend any extra energy. Tension is energy wasted."

"Francine, try to maintain eye contact with Louise. Same for you, Morgan. Don't be so fascinated with your watch. It's your partner who needs you, not your Timex."

Then Maxi went on to describe transition, the final, shortest, and most grueling phase of labor, when the cervix dilates from eight to ten centimeters.

"You may become very wet and bloody at this stage, but don't be alarmed."

Carleen and Kendra exchanged rueful looks.

"It's a sign that the baby's head is descending. You may feel nauseated. You may even throw up. And, warning to you coaches, your charge is apt to become highly irritable at this point. She may not be able to tolerate your laying a finger on her. She may scream and curse and beg for drugs. She may simply say she's had it, that's it, she's ready to give up." She looked around the room at the faces of her pupils, serious and pale in the light from the stove. "But don't despair." She grinned. "That's a good sign. It means the end is near. Many women begin to shake uncontrollably at this point."

"That's what happened to me," Mary Beth burst out. "Remember, Frank? My legs started trembling. The whole bed was shaking. Like in *The Exorcist*. It would have been funny except I had this awful urge to push."

"Exactly!" Maxi said. "And it's of vital importance at this stage to fight that urge. If you push now, it will be wasted energy. Worse yet, it might even cause your cervix to swell. To fight the urge to push, you have yet another breathing technique at your disposal."

The lesson went on a half hour longer than usual, during which they practiced transition breathing. As the women and their coaches got their wraps and prepared to descend once more into the frigid winter night, there was less chattering than usual. It was as if the subjects discussed tonight—painful back labor, swift and concussive contractions, and the dreaded Transition—coupled with the rapidly looming advent of their giving birth, had plunged them all into a serious and pensive mood.

Kendra let Morgan do the dishes and straighten up while she retired to the bathroom for a long, hot bubble bath and a cup of camomile tea.

She was almost nodding off when Morgan shyly poked his head around the door.

"Are you okay?" he asked.

She opened one eye; she felt drugged, her heart thudding heavily in her chest, her baby knocking relentlessly against her lower ribs.

"Sure, I guess so," she answered groggily.

"It's all pretty awesome," he said, sitting down on the closed lid of the john.

"Ain't it though?" she said, sighing. "Almost enough to make me wish I was doing it the good old-fashioned way. With lots of drugs to knock me out and those handy little forceps."

He looked alarmed.

"Just kidding," she said lazily. "It's a shame Jill didn't make it tonight." She yawned. "The other lesson she missed was no big deal, but tonight was pretty important, don't you think?"

"Tonight was very important," he agreed softly. "But I think...I don't know...I think I could handle it. I think I could really be of some help to you."

Kendra opened her eyes again. He looked so sweet and earnest.

"You mean help practicing?"

He nodded. "That and for the real thing, too."

"But Jill—"

"Look," he cut in, "can we stop playing this game? It's getting a little old."

She sat up in the sudsy water and stared at him, wide-eyed. "What game?"

He widened his eyes to match hers. "The Investment-Banker-Husband Game."

"Oh." She swallowed. *"That* game." Then after a long, awkward silence: "How long have you known?"

"You know, Jill asked me the exact same question. What

do you girls do? Share the same scriptwriter? But, in answer to your question, I think I've always known."

"Always?"

"Since I first saw that gorgeous pregnant stomach of yours. Simple mathematics."

Kendra frowned.

"Besides," he went on, "you and an investment banker? Now, if you'd said he was a conceptual artist who glued macaroni to down coats, maybe..."

"And to think I thought I was so clever."

"You are clever."

"I am not."

"Clever enough to get me to marry you."

"Who says I want you to marry me? I don't want you to marry me."

"Yes, you do."

"No. I don't."

"Do."

"Don't."

"Fine!" he said. "Then I'll just get my jacket and go." He got up and left the bathroom.

"No, wait!" she called after him.

He came back into the bathroom and stood over the tub. She held her soapy hand out to him.

"Yes, I do," she whispered.

"He knows."

"I know he knows." Jill, who had gotten out of bed long enough to let Kendra in the door, climbed back under the covers.

"You know he knows?"

"I knew he knew before you knew he knew."

"Just goes to show you, you never know." Kendra, who hadn't taken off her coat, paced back and forth at the foot of the bed.

Jill blinked at the ceiling. "Maybe it's just me but so far I'm finding this conversation very strange."

"You didn't tell me this was such a nice apartment." Kendra stopped pacing and looked around.

"I like it."

"It's homey and very pretty."

"That's the idea."

"You, on the other hand, look like shit."

"Thanks, Kendra. I *feel* like shit, but it's always nice to hear it confirmed by a close personal friend."

"Is that why you're punking out?"

"Punking out of what?"

"Being my nurse dolphin."

"Listen, honey, you've got a man. You don't need a dolphin."

"True," said Kendra. "I thought maybe that tour at the hospital freaked you out."

"It did, but that's beside the point. Anyway, over the next few months I'm going to be seeing so much of hospitals and doctors, I figure I better start loving it."

"Jill, is there something seriously wrong with you that you haven't told me about?"

"About as serious as it can get."

"Oh God." Kendra sat down hard on the bed. "I knew it."

"You knew I was pregnant?"

"You are?"

"I am."

"Again? How?"

"Sexual intercourse," she said darkly. "But I thought you knew."

Kendra nodded slowly. "When?"

"I'm due the end of August."

"Who? Don't tell me you picked somebody up in the Broome Street Bar."

"No, with my luck I would have gotten somebody with AIDS or a long family history of madness or hairlip. Actually, it's Warren."

"Does he know?"

Jill nodded wearily. "I broke the news to him the other day. Let's just say he practically wept, and it wasn't with joy."

"He doesn't want custody or anything ugly like that?"

"*Au contraire*, I'm sure he'd love it if I lost this one, too, which, by the way, I have no intention of doing. Wendy—sweet, sensitive, understanding Wendy—is royally pissed off at him for knocking me up. Naturally, she wants her own perfect babies."

"Well, good then. He'll have to support you while you have this one. Serve the Bag of Dirt right."

"He is rather a BOD, isn't he?" Jill said thoughtfully. "His insurance is giving me full coverage. Plus I'll be getting alimony and child support. Plus my lawyer's getting him to spring for weekly maid service, plus a VCR and a brand new color tube since from May on I'll be pretty much flat on my back and there's only so many hours a day I can spend with my nose in a book."

"It sounds as if you've set everything up just right."

"The only thing I'm missing is a nurse dolphin. Cheryl says thanks but no thanks. Maybe if I were a beagle, it would be different."

"I know an absolutely marvelous nurse dolphin. I think she should be able to tear herself away from the lake in order to pack your Lamaze bag."

"Really?"

"Really."

"But I warn you, I'm bound to be a real bitch after five months on my back."

"Don't you mean even *more* of a bitch?" Kendra asked.

Jill sighed. "It's nice to be appreciated for your real self."

Louise

"Hey, what's this?"

Marty picked up the Wonderwear catalog that Louise had deliberately left lying around on the living room coffee table for him to see.

"The first of many fabulously successful catalogs, I hope," she said, casually looking up from some embroidery she was doing on a prototype for a new bunting.

Marty thumbed through the glossy full-color pages. In addition to professionals, she had used their own three children as models.

"Hey, look at this!" Marty grinned proudly. "Our own little Mary! Mary looks so pretty! She looks just like her mother."

Louise smiled. Marty smiled. Then they both turned quickly away, she back to her sewing, he to the catalog.

"So it looks like my money was put to good use, after all," he said a few minutes later.

"I told you it would be," she said.

"But I guess we'll have to see what kind of orders you get, huh?"

"The mailing just went out," she said, "but don't worry, we'll get the orders. We purchased a very good list. And everybody is pregnant these days. It's a major mini-boom, they're saying."

He nodded thoughtfully. "You're turning out to be a good little businesswoman, Weezie. You know what I'm saying?"

Weezie. It seemed months since he had called her that. "Little?" she said, patting her belly.

"Oh, that!" He waved his hand at her. "You'll get your old bod back, babe. You always do. When is it you're due, anyway?"

With multiple births, she almost told him, you're lucky if you make it to the thirty-sixth week. And if my blood pressure keeps going up, I may have to go in for an early c-section. Instead, as lightly as she could, she said, "A few weeks."

He glanced back at the catalog. "Hey, I'm sorry I've been missing your Lamaze classes."

"I know you're busy," she said. "Besides, I think Francine's been enjoying them."

"Well," he said, slapping his palm with the rolled-up catalog. "She better not enjoy herself *too* much. 'Cause when it comes to El Big Day, I'm gonna be the one to see you through."

She looked up at him. "I never thought you wouldn't, Marty."

"I mean, haven't I always been there for you before?"

"Yes, you have, Marty."

"And don't I do a dynamite job? I mean, you couldn't ask for a better coach."

"No, I couldn't, Marty."

"Good," he said, as if the matter was settled. Then: "Say, who says I have to go back to the store tonight? Why don't you and me go out and grab ourselves some chow. It's been ages."

"Oh, Marty," she said, genuinely sorry, "I'd love to, but I invited Patsy and Agnes over and—"

"The Bitches of Bridgehampton! Say no more!" He threw down the catalog and grabbed his shearling coat, heading straight for the door. "I'm outta here, baby. I mean, *I am outta here!*"

"You weren't kidding." Patsy stood on the threshold to Louise's apartment and pushed her nighttime sunglasses down on her nose. "You *are* a little butterball."

Patsy and Agnes had come over for their annual mid-winter drink and gab fest after Louise called them and told them she was too fat to roll over to Elaine's. Even in the dead of winter, Patsy still maintained her beach color, thanks to thrice-weekly trips to a tanning salon and skiing in St. Moritz.

"Isn't she the little butterball?" Patsy repeated to Agnes, who had arrived a few minutes earlier and was lounging on the living room couch, her long legs folded beneath her, a goblet of red wine in her hand as she stared out the window at the ice forming on the Hudson River.

"I don't think she's a butterball at all," said Agnes, "considering."

"Considering?" Patsy lifted a suspicious eyebrow.

"Considering she's carrying triplets."

Patsy dropped her silver fox on the floor behind her and grasped Louise's fingertips. "She's *kidding*, Lou Lou. Tell Patsy she's kidding. Triplets?!"

"Shhhh," said Louise. "The kids don't know."

Francine had read to them and bedded them down, but there was always the chance one of them might be awake and listening.

Patsy went immediately to the bar cart to fix herself a large stiff Scotch. "What does Marty think of this? If I know him, he's been strutting all over the place. Multiple births are a real badge for studs."

"He doesn't know, either," Louise said miserably. She followed Patsy to the bar cart and poured herself a glass of cream sherry, the first drink she had had since last spring.

"Ought you to be drinking?" Agnes asked, worried as ever.

"Hah!" Patsy threw back her head and half of her Scotch along with it. "If I were her, I'd be soused from the moment I woke up in the morning. Three in one shot. Poor Weezie!"

Louise sipped the sweet sherry as tears of self-pity stung her eyes. "The worst part of it is I haven't slept with Marty since July."

"Fucked or *slept,* dear? It's important to be precise in these matters," Patsy said gravely.

"Fucked," said Louise, bowing her head over her drink.

"Yes, well, considering the consequences," said Patsy, "I'm not surprised."

"But I miss him!" Louise sniffed. "I'm all alone on my side of the bed. And where I sleep, there's this big, deep dent in the mattress."

"Poor baby." Agnes and Patsy both took up places on either side of Louise as she settled, with great difficulty, onto the nearest couch.

"Well, *some*body ought to tell him," Patsy said to Agnes over Louise's head.

"I've tried"—Louise's head popped up—"I really have, but I just can't seem to create the right...*ambience.*"

"What exactly is the right ambience," Patsy wondered aloud, staring at the ceiling, "in which to tell a man you're about to double the size of his already sizable family?"

Agnes drained her goblet and got up to refill it. "I wonder what they'll be? Kroger didn't want to know the sex of any of ours in advance. I always asked to know as soon as I got my amnio results. I figured—why be coy? But he wanted his little surprise. All the nurses and the doctor always knew. Kroger had to clap his hands over his ears every time somebody started to let it slip. Maybe you should just wait, Louise, and surprise him in the delivery room."

"Don't you think that's cutting it a bit close?" Patsy asked. "I mean, it's bound to get a bit hairy, don't you think? Did the Dreamboat Doctor say it would be a vaginal delivery? I personally always preferred c-sections. So much less fuss and bother. And those five days on the I.V. really melt away those unwanted pounds."

"Shelly thinks we should *try* for a vaginal delivery. He looks as it as a sort of challenge."

"He would," Patsy said grudgingly. "You poor, poor thing. And Marty being a perfect cad about the whole thing."

Louise sighed and shook her head. "It's all my fault."

Patsy rolled her eyeballs at Agnes. "Those triplets must be draining her brain."

"You might as well tell her the whole story," Agnes said to Louise.

"What, *what?*" Patsy sat up a little taller. "Have you girls been holding out on me?"

"Go ahead, Louise," Agnes said. "It will probably do you good to talk about it."

Louise got up, with considerable assistance from the women on either side of her, and made for the sherry decanter. "Marty's been running around on me." And she went on to repeat the story she had told Agnes before Patsy arrived, of her "surprise" trip up to the Ritz Carlton in Boston, and the "other" Mrs. Rosen who liked expensive French wine.

"Now *that,*" said Patsy when Louise had finished, "is about as low as a man can get. Cuckolding a woman in *this* condition."

"I brought it on myself, I tell you," Louise insisted. "I was the one who wanted him to make do with jerking off."

"Yes, but we all know you didn't really *mean* it. You were just grandstanding, weren't you, lovie?"

"I don't know what I was doing anymore," she said. "All I know is that it hurt to do it and I hated giving head—"

"Who doesn't!!" said Patsy.

"Speak for yourself," said Agnes, sipping from her goblet.

"Since when have you liked doing *that?*" said Patsy.

"Let's just say I've lately acquired the taste," Agnes said evasively.

"Hmmmm," said Patsy, "another victim of our phallic-maddened society."

"And what's more," said Agnes, squaring her shoulders, "I'm afraid I have to agree with Louise."

"Agree with Louise *how,* dear?" Patsy asked brightly.

"That it's her fault that Marty ... wandered."

Both women turned to stare at Agnes as color crept into her fair, chiseled cheeks.

"You can't really expect a man like Marty Rosen to go *without* ... especially after having sex with his wife two, sometimes three, times a day for the last seven years," she stammered.

"And how, pray tell, do you know it's *two, sometimes three, times a day?*" Patsy said accusingly.

Agnes began to sputter. "Because Louise said so." She turned to Louise hopefully. "Didn't you, honey?"

But Louise, too, was staring hard at Agnes, trying to figure out why it was that her friend was so flustered all of a sudden. "I might have," she said faintly.

"See?" Agnes said to Patsy, but the conviction ebbed from her voice. With a shaking hand she set her goblet down on the coffee table and pushed back her sleeve to look at her wristwatch.

"Got a heavy date, dear?" Patsy asked.

"No, not really. It's just that I've got this excruciating headache. Any my youngest's had the most grueling case of the flu and I've got a new babysitter tonight sitting in for Mrs. Sherman, whose sister in Camden is wasting away from cancer, poor thing." She heaved her shoulders helplessly. "I really don't feel right being here. I feel like I ought to be home."

"You run along then, dear," Patsy said tightly. "Louise and I will be just fine."

Grabbing her mink and flinging it over one shoulder, Agnes threw kisses to the air above their heads and made a dash for the door.

"Well!" said Patsy as the door's closing echoed clear down the hall.

"Well," said Louise, knowing as surely as this sherry was making her tipsy that her friend Agnes had been sleeping with her husband. She wondered how many of her friends Marty had tapped over these past months.

"I'm sure this is the naughtiest she's ever been," said Patsy, as if trying to convince herself.

Louise, imagining Marty in bed with Agnes, who, even though she had a good fifteen years on Louise, was nevertheless long and lithe and silky of limb, burst into tears.

"There, there," said Patsy, thumping her friend on the back as if she were choking instead of weeping. "It's shabby of Agnes, but you said yourself that you threw Marty into it and we all know that Agnes does her own shopping and positively jumps at the discount Marty offers her."

"You think that's how it happened?" Louise pulled away and wiped her tears on the sleeves of her hot-pink maternity sweatshirt. She was remembering that terrible day a few weeks just after Christmas when she had gone over to the store to pick up a fruit basket for one of her park friends who was in the hospital for a gall bladder operation. She had gone back to Marty's office to say hi, to let him know she was there since she came to the store so seldom these days, when she was surprised to find his office door closed. Normally, he had an open-door policy. She was just about to knock when a sound she heard on the other side of the door brought her up sharply. It was a sound she knew as well as the crying of her own children. It was the sound Marty made when he was holding himself back from climax: a sort of helpless cringing, as if someone were dragging him to the edge of a precipice and were about to push him. "No, oh no, oh wow, no!" And then she heard another voice, a female voice—rendered unrecognizable by passion—crying out, "Oh, you stud, you lovely stud. Fuck me, fuck me, fuck me."

She had turned around and walked out of the store, leaving the fruit basket by the cash register, and gone directly home to bed. There, with the sound of her children playing in the other room, she had stuffed the edge of the bedspread in her mouth and wept.

"I never thought it was Agnes," she was saying to Patsy through her tears. "I thought it was one of the cash register chippies."

"Well, they were two lonely people thrown together by circumstances. And try and look at it on the bright side, dear: At least we know *she* won't give him any exotic diseases."

Louise would have laughed if she weren't so unhappy.

"And I'm sure Agnes never meant to hurt you," Patsy went on. "She probably felt sorry for Marty, saw her opportunity, and pounced on it." She chewed on the ear-piece of her sunglasses and looked, to Louise, as if she regretted, however guiltily, that she hadn't gotten in there herself while the going was good.

FEBRUARY 7

L A M A Z E · · *The Fourth Lesson*

Out of deference to Louise, who had been ordered by Dr. Berry to stay off the icy sidewalks and, in fact, off her feet altogether, the class came to her apartment, instead of to Carleen's as scheduled, for the second to the last Lamaze lesson. As Louise waddled down the hall from the kids' bedrooms, where she was bidding them a final good night, the other three women and their partners were in the living room flipping through the inviting pages of the Wonderwear spring catalog. Since Louise had offered her classmates a generous discount, they were eagerly filling out their orders for colorful stretchies, terry diaper covers, side-snap T-shirts, and rompers. Along the window ledge Maxi had set up a series of diagrams showing a baby descending through the birth canal, a baby's head crowning, a baby's shoulders emerging and being turned by an unseen physician's hands, and a baby's head completely delivered. Of those present only Morgan, who had taken on his new responsibility as coach with a solemnity bordering on obsession, was studying the diagrams and now and then asking Maxi questions.

"Teacher's pet," Kendra chided him, looking up from the catalog with a grin.

"Hey," said Morgan, "it's the miracle of life and all that."

Louise met Francine in the hall as she carried in a diet cheesecake—courtesy of Truffles 'n' Stuff. As Louise, unseen by everyone but Francine, filled her cup with cream

253

sherry instead of the herbal tea they were offering the guests, Francine dealt her a severe look.

"There's nothing to worry about," she whispered, patting her enormous belly. "I figure these kids are old enough to drink by now." But as they both knew, it was her third drink since dinner and she had been hitting the sherry fairly steadily for the past week. Francine had reported her drinking to Berry, who had not appeared overly concerned.

"The fetuses are fully formed now," he had told her. "And Louise probably needs it to calm her nerves. I just hope she doesn't slip and fall." Hence the admonition to stay indoors and supine.

After reviewing with the class the three kinds of breathing they were to use for the three phases of labor—latent, accelerated, and transiton—as well as going over back labor and how to handle it, Maxi said: "Tonight we get to the good part. The second, and most rewarding stage of labor—*expulsion.*"

On the floor, Louise, leaning on a bank of pillows against Francine's legs, belched and let out a groan.

"Sorry," she said, clapping a hand naughtily over her mouth as Maxi directed her a swift, curious glance. "Must be the tea." And, so saying, she took another swig of her "tea."

"Expulsion," Maxi went on, "is what all these long hours of labor—of riding out your contractions through breathing—have led you to. Expulsion is when, after being told by your doctor or the resident or the nurse not to push, you can finally push. It's the hardest work you'll ever do."

Louise hiccoughed but this time Maxi ignored her.

"But it's also the most wonderful work you'll ever do. And believe me, it feels great."

"Oh, swell!" Louise muttered sarcastically.

This time, everybody looked her way. Her face was flushed, her eyes were shining, and she seemed to be breathing with difficulty.

"This stage is shorter than dilation and many women feel a renewed energy."

"Heave ho!" Louise grunted and, covering her mouth, commenced to giggle.

Carleen nudged Bill, but Bill shrugged his shoulders. While Frank and Morgan kept their attention glued to Maxi, Kendra and Mary Beth were beginning to catch the giggles from Louise and had to stifle them quickly. Francine just shook her head gravely and looked old before her time.

"You'll be doing your pushing in two places. In the labor room, for ten to thirty minutes. And then in the delivery room for another fifteen or so. You primates will be spending a bit more time in the labor room than you multips"—her eyes flickered over Mary Beth, then Louise, who was draining her cup—"who will be transferred to the delivery room as soon as a dime-sized portion of your baby's head is visible."

"Why is that?" Morgan wanted to know.

"Because the baby slips out much more quickly the second time around."

"*Boing!*" said Louise and laughed uproariously.

"And of course," Maxi added, frowning, "you and Kendra will be remaining in the birthing room for the whole of the expulsion process."

"Well, throw them a fish!" Louise crowed.

"Now, how do we practice pushing in the labor room?" Maxi asked rhetorically.

"Lean against your partner's legs at a seventy-five-degree angle, feet flat on the floor, knees comfortably separated, elbows out, head thrust forward. It's important not to rush into pushing as soon as a contraction begins. You'll want to take advantage of the contraction at its peak. Let it build a little first. And while it builds, you'll be fortifying yourself with a series of three cleansing breaths. Let's all try it now."

The four couples, all positioned as directed, began their first cleansing breath.

"Then breathe in and out for a second deep cleansing breath. That's it. Then breathe in, but only let out a little breath this time, hold, relax your jaw and *push*, directing your strength down through your vagina. Of course, when you practice, you won't really push. And during actual labor, you'll have to push for a longer period of time. Usually three breaths and three pushes per contraction. Each time you push, the baby will come down another few inches. Each time the contraction subsides, the baby will slip back up an inch or so. It's two steps forward, one step back. The harder you push and the more relaxed you make your pelvic floor, the quicker your baby will be born."

Just then, Louise let out a shriek. "Help me up!" she cried, holding out her arms.

Francine pushed and Maxi pulled and together they managed to bring Louise to her feet, whereupon she toddled off in the direction of the bathroom as fast as her legs could carry her.

"I think I will go check on her," said Francine, scurrying after her.

They all heard the unmistakable sound of Louise throwing up, the toilet flushing, then water running in the sink.

In a few minutes, Francine was back, looking pale and nervous.

"Is she all right?" Maxi asked.

"She's a little drunk, if you want to know the truth," Francine confessed.

The others began to whisper among themselves.

"I *thought* she was acting strange," said Maxi. "Is there something the matter?"

"Well," Francine said, gnawing on her lower lip, "I'm not one hundred percent certain, but I think she is going into her labor."

"Holy cow!" said Morgan.

"Well, I don't know about holy," said Kendra.

"Talk about your timing!" said Bill.

They fell silent as once again they heard Louise throwing up.

"I think I'd better look in on her," said Maxi.

"I think we should take her to the hospital," Francine said.

Maxi looked at her thoughtfully. "But her labor's only just beginning. Remember, Francine, you were here for the lesson when we discussed the pitfalls of going to the hospital too early on in labor."

"I know, I know." Francine nodded impatiently. "But Berry said he wanted her in for observation for the whole thing. You see, Maxi"—her eyes darted around the room at the other women—"Louise is having triplets."

Even Maxi's eyes bugged in astonishment as everybody else in the room gasped.

"She didn't want anyone to know," Francine explained, "for personal reasons."

"Well, we know now," Maxi said grimly as she went off to the bathroom to check on Louise.

The others waited in silence, staring dumbly at the diagrams of labor and listening to the Real Thing getting under way in the next room. In a few minutes, Maxi returned.

"You were right, Francine. Her water just broke."

"Yikes," someone said.

"Someone should call Berry," said Maxi. "Would you like me to?"

Francine sagged gratefully against her. "His number's on the board by the kitchen phone."

As Maxi went to phone, Carleen came up to the rattled Francine. "If you need someone to stay here with the kids," she said, "Bill and I would be—"

"Thank you," said Francine, "but I will be staying here with the kids."

"But you're her coach!" Kendra said.

Just then Maxi returned. "You were right, Francine. Berry would just as soon keep an eye on her. Labor for multiple births is endless, but he wants to watch for complications. Is her bag packed?"

"Oh!" Francine's hand flew to her mouth. She looked around wildly. "What goes in the bag? I have completely forgotten." And she lapsed into incoherent French.

"Chapstick!" Kendra volunteered.

"Facecloth," Mary Beth joined in.

"Paper bag and talcum powder," Morgan said.

"Tennis balls," said Bill.

Francine assigned each of them an item and told them where he or she could find it. While Maxi went to keep Louise company in the bedroom, the others ran around like people at a scavenger hunt, colliding into each other and trying to keep their voices down lest they wake the children. As Kendra deposited a facecloth into the bag Francine held open, she said, "I still don't get why you're not going to the hospital, Francine. I thought you were her coach."

"Kendra, would you please telephone Marty at Truffles? Tell him his wife is in labor and that he is to meet her at Hudson General as soon as possible."

Nodding, Kendra headed for the phone.

"But don't tell him about the triplets!" Francine called after her.

Kendra turned, her jaw dropping. "You mean *he* doesn't know?"

In the kitchen, Kendra dialed the number of Truffles and asked for Marty Rosen. As she heard Louise pay yet another agonized visit to the bathroom, Marty came on the line.

"Yeah."

Taking a deep breath, Kendra said, "Marty, you don't know me. I'm in Louise's Lamaze class. Well, a funny thing happened while we were practicing expulsion ..."

"I'll be right there," he said.

"No!" said Kendra. "She's just about to leave for the hospital. You're to meet her there."

"Can she come to the phone?"

"I'm afraid not. She's ... she's sick in the bathroom."

"That's how she usually gets started. Listen, do me a favor: Tell her to hang on, I'm on my way. And tell her ... tell her I love her."

PART V

Birth

$\mathcal{L}$ouise

It was nine-fifteen when Marty arrived at the hospital. Maxi was waiting for him by the desk in the maternity ward.

"Where is she?" he demanded to know.

Handing him Louise's Lamaze bag, she said, "Her overnight bag is in the locker in her room. She's all signed in. They gave her an enema a while ago and she's got another five minutes or so to put in on the john. Let the nurse at the desk know you're here and she'll tell you when you can go in."

"Where are you going?" he asked as he watched her push the button to call the elevator.

"Home," she said blithely. "I don't go on duty until seven o'clock tomorrow morning. I'd say I'm sorry I'm going to miss the show, but I have a feeling you may still be in the labor room when I come on duty."

"Hello?" he said. "This is Louise Rosen we're talking about here. She had Mary in *three hours.*"

Maxi patted his wrist. "In these kinds of situations, Marty, a long, slow labor is fairly common."

"In *what* kinds of situations?" Marty asked.

Smiling enigmatically, she pointed to the Lamaze bag he clutched in his hand. "There's a book in there you might want to take a look at. It's never too late to start preparing." She stepped into the elevator and the doors closed on her Cheshire grin.

Before Marty could make any sense out of what Maxi had just said, a nurse he had met during one of Louise's previous labors bustled past and said to him, "*There* you are, Mr. Rosen! I didn't think you'd want to miss out on this one, you rascal, you!"

Perplexed, Marty opened the Lamaze bag and peered inside at the book.

"Coping with Multiple Births." He read the title aloud. "What!" he exclaimed and marched immediately to the desk.

"Why is my wife here?" he asked the nurse on duty.

"Well, sir," the nurse said guardedly, thinking she was dealing with *one of those husbands,* "I imagine she's having a baby."

"I know that!" His hand came down on the counter with a bang. "How many?"

"Oh!" Comprehension dawned on the nurse's face and she gave him a patronizing smile. "You must be Mr. Rosen. Your wife is having *supertwins,* Mr. Rosen!"

"What the hell are *supertwins?*"

"Why, triplets, Mr. Rosen—but you know that!"

Marty staggered backwards and bumped into yet another nurse.

"Well!" she said. "If it isn't the proud father-to-be-and-be-and-be! We were wondering when you'd show up!"

It was the big bulldozer of a blonde who had attended Bruce's birth.

"You're looking a little peaked, Mr. Rosen!" she said. "Think you'll be requiring medication?" She winked at the nurse behind the desk, who giggled into the palm of her hand.

"Where's my wife?" Marty said vacantly. "I want to see my wife."

"Well," said the blonde, "it just so happens she's ready to see you. Step this way, Mr. Rosen."

And, like a sleepwalker, Marty Rosen followed the nurse down the hall to a private labor room.

They had cranked up the bed to its maximum height and Louise was sitting up, cross-legged, wearing a shortie hospital gown that tied in the back and a pair of bright purple knee socks. She was working busily in a sketchpad propped up on a pillow before her, but when she saw Marty she put the lid on her marker.

"Hi, Marty," she said softly.

He pulled up a chair next to the bed and, sitting down heavily, took her hand in his.

"How are you, baby?"

She shrugged. "So far, I don't think much of these contractions. They say this could take all night. I hope you brought something to eat."

"I'll call the store," he said. "They'll send stuff down. Why didn't you tell me, Louise?"

"Dr. Berry says he may not even have to do a cesarean. He said he'll see how the labor progresses. But he can feel them in there. All lined up to come out, like peas in a pod."

"No wonder you didn't want that abortion."

"Could we please not talk about that right now, Marty?"

"You must have known," he continued, undeflected. "Somewhere deep down inside you, your mother's instincts must have told you that you wouldn't be wiping out just a single fetus, but an entire population!"

"Honest, Marty, I had no idea at the time."

"And when you said it hurt to make love," he went on. "Christ, I thought you were just being bitchy."

"Dr. Berry said the incidence of miscarriage is four times greater with multiple births and that it was just as well we didn't—"

"And when you got so big, all I could do was criticize you."

"He's been watching for toxemia. And taking blood every visit. I've been going to him every week for the past fifteen weeks. I bet I've seen him more than I've seen you. He says I've done real good and he's amazed I've carried them this long."

The tears were rolling down Marty's cheeks, yet his voice remained level. "I wouldn't blame you," he said. "I wouldn't blame you one bit. In fact, you'd have a perfect right, Louise, never to forgive me."

"Believe me, Marty, I felt that way once, but now ... I'm not so sure."

He had slipped off the chair onto the floor and was looking up at her with large, sorrowful eyes.

"I'm begging you, Louise. See me? I'm down on my knees begging you to forgive me."

"Marty, please, I forgive you, already!"

At this, Marty struck the mattress with both fists. "God, Louise, I can't believe what I've done!"

"I know all about Agnes, if that's what you mean."

He looked up at her, incredulous. "You *know?* And you still forgive me?"

She hesitated. "Not exactly *gladly,* but I'd rather it was Agnes than one of your cash register chippies." She narrowed her eyes at him. "Or did you get it on with them, too?"

"I'd never mingle with the help!" he said righteously. Then, crossing his heart: "Agnes was *it,* believe me. It was a mercy fuck on both sides."

"And you swear you'll never..."

Louise became distracted as she put both hands on her belly to feel the contraction.

Marty went on, "I swear I'll never touch another woman, ever, ever, ever, ever again."

The blond nurse bustled in to take Louise's blood pressure. "What's with you?" she asked, seeing Marty down on the floor. Then to Louise: "Arm, please."

Louise, eyes closed, didn't respond to her command.

"Christ, woman," Marty said, "can't you see she's in the middle of a contraction?"

She gave him a haughty look. "Christ, man, can't you get up off your knees and make yourself useful by timing these things? This could go on for hours, you know, and I can't be in here every five minutes."

Louise emerged with a mild smile. "Now *that,*" she said, "was more like it." Obediently, she held out her arm for the blood pressure cuff.

They were all quiet as the nurse looked at her watch, then at the sphyg dial. "One twenty over seventy. Not bad," she added grudgingly.

"Of course it's not bad," Louise said, taking Marty's hand and giving it a little kiss. "My husband and I have finally made up."

* * *

From eleven o'clock to one, Louise walked the corridors of the maternity wing, Marty holding the back of her gown modestly closed, Louise stopping to lean on Marty's arm whenever she had a contraction. In between contractions, they discussed the logistics of supertwins.

"We'll send Brucie to nursery school. He wants to go anyway to be like Zack. That way, it'll just be Mary and the triplets."

"Sure," he said.

"I've been buying and stashing three of everything," she continued. "And, incidentally, in case you're worried, Francine's staying on. We'll give her a good raise, of course."

"Of course."

"And I was thinking maybe we'd hire her friend Laura just for the first year or so. They can room together and take turns taking the weekend off."

"Anything you say, babe."

"We'll also have to be extra nice to Francine, Marty. Not just because of the triplets, but because she's been such an angel to me these past months."

"Unlike your bastard husband."

"Stop it, Marty," she warned. "No more talk like that."

"All right. No more talk like that. I don't know," he said glumly. "I guess I feel like I should be punished or something."

"I *am* punishing you." Louise stopped suddenly to ride out a contraction. Marty looked at his watch. They were coming two minutes apart now and lasting almost fifty seconds.

"Forty seconds," he told her, having settled easily into the old routine. As of ten minutes ago she was out of preliminary and into accelerated labor.

Louise let out a cleansing breath and opened her eyes, resuming both their conversation and their walk. "I'm punishing you with triplets."

"Hey!" Marty said expansively. "You call that punishment? Like the man says: It's an embarrassment of riches."

Just then the big blonde caught sight of them. "There you are, you two!" she called down the corridor to them. "Dr. Berry wants to check you."

"A hundred bucks says you're five centimeters dilated," Marty said.

"You're on," Louise rejoined. "I say I'm seven if I'm an inch."

"Marty," Berry said as he peered between Louise's legs, "you owe your wife a hundred bucks."

"Really?" Louise's face shone. "Seven ... already?"

"Going on eight." Berry grinned. "See, normally, labor with multiple births takes much, much longer because the contractions have to work their way through the other two babies before they can get to the first one due to be expelled. But even with the unaccustomed load, your body seems to know the way it's done. You'll be going into transition soon, Weezie, any time now. I'd like you to stay put from now on. I'm gonna have them hook you up to the I.V., just in case."

"Don't worry," Louise said, taking a deep breath signaling the onslaught of the next contraction, "I'm not going anywhere."

As Marty began to rub her belly in small circular movements, Berry nudged him: "Any bets for delivery time of number one baby?"

Louise had become so bloody that a nurse came in every five minutes to change the pad underneath her. Marty had climbed into the bed behind her and was supporting her, putting pressure on her coccyx during her frequent severe contractions and sticking a sour lollipop into her mouth during her all too brief—in fact, virtually nonexistent—rest periods. They were both drenched in sweat and blood and mucus, and the nurse had already warned Marty he would have to change into clean scrubs before they would let him into the delivery room.

Louise bellowed as the desire to push overwhelmed her, and Marty had to remind her to do her special breathing to resist the urge. At last, at a quarter to four, Berry breezed in and checked Louise's cervix.

"Okay, Marty. I think it's time you changed into those scrubs. I'll have a nurse bring in a set of mediums and you can throw them on in here."

Louise gasped. *"Oh, my God!"*

"Don't push yet, Louise," Berry said. "I want to catch these little suckers in the delivery room."

"Cleansing breath," Marty said. "Blow, blow, blow, blow, blow, blow, blow, you're almost there, baby, you're almost there. Good work, baby! That's my girl."

Two orderlies came in and, looking at the two of them in bed together, one of them joked, "Gee, which one we supposed to move?"

Marty clambered out of the bed.

"Move her now," he directed them, "while she's between contractions. Be gentle, guys."

While the orderlies transferred her I.V. bottle to a mobile pole, Louise lay limp and lifeless on the bed. Then, one of them taking her shoulders and the other her knees, they moved her to the gurney.

"Where are my scrubs?" Marty shouted, fearful of being left behind.

Seconds later, a nurse opened the door and tossed Marty his change of clothes. As he tore off his bloodied clothes and scrambled into the scrubs, they wheeled Louise out of the room and down the corridor toward the delivery room. He could hear her calling out to him pitifully.

"Don't push yet!" He grabbed the two pillows from off the bed and raced down the hall behind the gurney. Seizing her hand, he said: "Blow, baby. Blow, blow, blow, blow, blow, blow, *blow!*"

"We'll be fine," Berry explained to the attending nurse, "so long as they don't get in each other's way."

They were trichorionic, which meant they each had grown from a separate egg and therefore had separate placentas. The first baby came out on the third push.

Berry was so busy congratulating Louise on her superb job of control that it wasn't until a few seconds later that someone called out:

"It's a girl!"

Louise smiled and sagged back against the pillows. "How sweet," she said breathlessly.

"Okay now, Louise," said Berry. "I'm going to puncture the membrane of the next in line. Then I'm going to give you ten minutes' rest and we're back in business again. Okay?"

Louise nodded and immediately dozed off. She awoke to someone showing her her baby daughter before whisking her off again. When Berry said, "Okay, Louise, it's time to push again," it sounded to Louise as if he was speaking to her from a great distance.

"I'm tired," she whined. "Can't I just rest a little while longer? Besides, I don't *feel* like pushing."

"Never mind if you don't feel like pushing, Louise," Berry said, "push anyway. Marty, help her. If we don't get these babies out of there, we'll have to do an emergency delivery. Come on, now."

Louise came to her senses with a scream. "Don't cut me! Please, don't cut me. Marty!" She clutched at his sleeve. "Don't let them."

Marty shook her lightly. "Listen to me, Weezie, nobody's going to cut you. Take a deep breath. That's it. Let it out. Take another. Good. Let it out. Take another. Good. Let it out. Another, release a little, hold it, now push, damn it. Bear down with all your might, like you're shitting a watermelon. Louise, come on now, babe, I know you can do it."

"One more should do it," Berry said from behind the tent over Louise's knees. "Okay, go for it now, Louise."

And once more, Louise primed herself and squeezed with all her remaining strength. She heard a baby crying and wasn't sure whether it was the one she had just pushed out or the one in the bassinet across the room where a nurse had suctioned its nostrils and wiped off the blood.

"Hey, what do you know?" Berry cried. "Another girl!"

The third, which came out five minutes later, was a boy.

As Berry stitched up Louise's episiotomy, she held a boy and girl bundled up in each arm while Marty held a girl.

"Huey, Louie, and Dewie," said Marty, grinning broadly.

"They're so *tiny!*" Louise exclaimed.

"Six pounds each isn't exactly tiny," the nurse commented dryly, "*considering.*"

"Oh, Marty," Louise said, turning to her husband, "I love you, but I don't want to have to do this ever again."

He kissed her lightly on the lips. "Don't worry, babe, you won't. Say, Doc," he called to the man on the other side of the surgical tent.

"Yes, *Superdad?*" Berry answered.

"You do vasectomies?"

Berry chuckled. "Not normally, Marty, but in your case, I think I could make an exception."

FEBRUARY 13
L A M A Z E · · *The Fifth Lesson*

For the last lesson, they decided to meet back in the physical therapy room. They were all feeling far too pregnant to play hostess, and besides, they wanted to see Louise and her babies, who were spending their last night in the hospital before going home. Maxi had promised to sneak them down after class for a quick look at the babies and a visit with Louise, who, Maxi reported, had been enjoying all week her undisputed reign as Queen of the Ward.

Since it was the day before St. Valentine's Day, Carleen had splurged and bought a big box of Godiva chocolates and a gallon of cold milk. They sat around in a circle on the carpet, the pregnant ones leaning against their coaches, eating chocolate as Maxi, ever attendant to her lesson plan, reviewed what they had learned over the previous weeks and sketched in what they would be covering this week: how to recognize the signs of early labor and when to go to the hospital.

It had been a mild, sunny day, the temperature rising to fifty degrees, and everyone was feeling a touch of spring fever. Toward the end of the lesson, talk drifted to other, albeit related, topics. Carleen, who had vowed she would continue going into the office until the onset of labor, had played hookey from work this afternoon and walked up to Lewis of London to invest a small fortune in baby clothes. Mary Beth had finished the last illustration of a picture book about a little muskrat and his new baby sister. Just before leaving the house this evening, she had called the diaper service. But it was Kendra who had the most exciting news to tell. She and Morgan had, three days ago, when they went in for her weekly checkup at the midwife clinic, gotten pre-nuptial blood tests. And today they had walked down to City Hall and obtained their marriage license.

"You should have seen the look on the face of that civil servant. I could tell she was just itching to make a comment like, 'Not a moment too soon!'"

"Congratulations," Maxi said, raising a paper cup of milk. "It's enough to make me wish I had a bottle of champagne handy."

"Did someone say champagne?"

Everyone looked up.

"Jill!" Kendra cried, and struggled to her feet.

Jill stood in the doorway, looking pale and pregnant, grinning broadly and carrying a big bouquet of yellow roses in one hand, a brace of heart-shaped balloons in the other.

"Grady!"

Behind Jill, Kendra's brother, Grady, appeared in a black tie and tails, hefting a magnum of Perrier-Jouët and a giant bottle of Pepsi.

"Some catering hall!" he commented.

And then came the deluge. It was all the circle of pregnant women could do to scramble out of the way, for there next arrived a fleet of white-tied waiters bearing trays and pushing steaming chafing tables, followed by a professional photographer, a couple of coverall-clad men wheeling a piano, and six maids in short black dresses and heart-shaped aprons carrying flowers and garlands with which they proceeded to deck the physical therapy room. The pianist came next and sat down immediately to play a medley of Beatles songs. Swaddled in silver mink and sapphires, Nora Alicia Madison arrived with her husband in tow, followed by the pastor from their Old Greenwich congregation and several of the staff of Whispering Laurels, even Angus, the groundskeeper.

Kendra and Morgan stood in the middle of this festive mob and stared at each other, open-mouthed.

"I swear on the head of our unborn child," said Kendra, "I knew nothing about this."

"I have to confess," Morgan said uneasily, "I did. That is, Jill called me yesterday, but I never imagined..."

She gave him a look of mild reproof. "Traitor!"

"You leave this handsome young man alone," said Nora Alicia, having spied her prospective son-in-law in the crowd and staked her claim. "So very good to meet you at last," she said, offering him her cool, rouged cheek. "And welcome to the family!"

To Kendra she whispered: "Then again, it's never been your *taste* I've called into question. Ainsley, come here and be nice to your new son-in-law."

Ainsley Madison, dashing and tanned in morning suit and gray tie, shot out a rugged hand. "Good to meet you, young man. It so happens I know your father. He and I have met at breakfasts, luncheons, that sort of thing, over the years. Plays a mean game of racquetball, from what I hear."

"The Fords wanted everyone to know," Nana announced, "that they were so sorry they couldn't make it on such short notice. Some Hollywood function or other has claimed them in advance. But they will be coming east, they assured us, when the baby is born."

"Speaking of which," said Grady, who had been circulating, introducing himself to "the Lamaze ladies and their stalwart coaches," as he put it, "hadn't we better get on with it before the baby *is* born?"

"I hate to disappoint you, but I don't think it's going to happen tonight, Grade," Kendra told him. "It's ten days till my due date and first babies are usually late."

"I hear you've already lost one of your rank to premature delivery."

"You'd deliver prematurely, too, if you were carrying triplets."

"Heaven forfend!" Grady's eyes rolled heavenward.

Ainsley nabbed Morgan, for whom he had brought a tuxedo, and they went off to the men's room to dress and indulge in a bit of man-talk. As for Kendra, who was not to be spared, she was borne off to the ladies' room with Nana, Nana's maid, and Jill, there to don what Kendra could only describe as a monumental waste of money, a pale lavender maternity wedding gown set with embroidered yellow roses and thousands of seed pearls.

"There's enough room in here for *two* normal-sized brides," Kendra said, fitting it on over her head.

"Well, I couldn't very well schedule you for fittings, now could I," said Nana. "Besides, you'd only keep on getting bigger and bigger."

The first spare moment, Kendra turned to Jill. "You devil, you."

"It was mostly Nana's idea," she said. "I merely mentioned to her your little trip down to City Hall, and she dreamed up the rest."

"Is it okay for you to be up and about?"

Jill nodded. "Berry said it's okay for another few weeks. Besides," she confided, "I want to get around as much as possible before the curfew sets in."

"You'll be fine," said Kendra, hugging her.

"I know I will. One out of every five mothers in America is a single parent."

"Hey, that's my line."

"Not anymore it isn't."

* * *

The "Lamaze ladies" and Jill had been accorded the positions of maids of honor. Carrying nosegays of baby yellow roses, they led the procession. Grady, as best man, was in charge of the ring, a simple gold band set with a single moonstone, which Morgan had picked up on Eighth Street that morning. As the pianist struck up the chords of the wedding march, Ainsley led Kendra down the "aisle," which was to say, through the open doors of the physical therapy room and to the flower-decked "altar" that was the counter that normally held the little rubber squeeze balls and the nesting blocks. Marty and Francine arrived soon after, pushing Louise in a wheelchair. Someone tossed Louise and Francine their own nosegays and they took their places with the other maids of honor flanking the bride and groom. Kendra alternated between wishing she weren't there to moments of such intense happiness she thought she would burst the seams of her gown.

"We are gathered here this evening in the sight of our Lord—"

"Not to mention," added Grady out of the corner of his mouth to Jill, "the family lawyer who just happens to be president of the hospital board."

Just then, the P.A. system clicked on and a voice said, "Paging Dr. Hamirabi. Dr. Abdul Hamirabi. Come to the fourth floor nurses' station, stat." Everyone burst out laughing. Thereafter, there was never a time during the brief ceremony when someone was not giggling. Even Nana's lips were tugged by the occasional faintly bemused smile. It was, after all, what with one thing and another, not an occasion to be taken entirely seriously.

Mary Beth

"Oh!" Mary Beth groaned and slid into the passenger seat of the Toyota truck in the underground parking lot of Hudson General Hospital. "I ate too much."

"Best wedding food I ever had," Frank declared, getting in behind the wheel.

"It ought to be." Mary Beth rubbed her stomach. "Lutece catered it."

"Those bridesmaids' gifts were pretty snazzy, too."

Nana had given each of the pregnant bridesmaids a Tiffany's gift certificate entitling them to a silver monogrammed diaper-pin tray, pins, brush, comb, cup, and spoon. Francine got a silver and ivory brooch which she immediately pinned on her T-shirt.

"Obviously," said Frank, maneuvering out of the lot, "the woman does nothing halfway."

"I really did eat too much," Mary Beth sighed. "That salmon mousse was amazing."

"The wedding cake wasn't bad, either."

"Did you remember to pack a slice for Denny?"

"I tucked it in your bag."

"How do you think Morgan took the whole thing? I mean, it's got to be a shock getting inducted into that family *just like that.*"

"I think he's a pretty cool dude," Frank said. "I was talking to him. He's going to be working some gig up in Saratoga this summer. They're staying at the family place on Lake George."

Mary Beth shifted her bulk. "Sometimes I wish we had a place on the water."

"I told you," he said, "we can rent a place this summer for a couple of weeks. See how we like it. Fire Island."

"Not Fire Island," she said quickly.

"Okay, then, the Hamptons." They were heading crosstown on 59th Street toward Third Avenue, where Dennis was staying with Mary Beth's mother, Audrey O'Mally. They had called her earlier to tell her that their Lamaze lesson had turned into a wedding party and they wouldn't be picking up Denny until after midnight. "Don't Marty and Louise have a place out in the Hamptons? Maybe they could give us some tips."

"Stop the car," Mary Beth said.

He gave her a double take.

"I said stop the car."

"What's wrong?"

"I think I'm going to be sick."

Frank took Mary Beth to her mother's apartment, not to pick up Denny, but to wait out regular mild contractions spaced five minutes apart, which Frank dutifully phoned in to Dina.

Audrey O'Mally, who had been up watching the Letterman show when they arrived, was delighted. She busied herself speculating on who the baby would look like and running around collecting the items her daughter would need for her bag. Frank sat on the couch with Mary Beth and kept track of her contractions. While they weren't severe enough yet for Mary Beth to have to do the special breathing, they were too painful for her to be able to move around.

By two-thirty, the contractions were coming harder and Mary Beth was now breathing to avoid crying out. Frank placed a call to Dina, and Dina told Frank to bring Mary Beth to the hospital right away.

"Really?" Frank asked. "It seemed like we went through hours and hours of this with Denny."

"Denny was a first baby," Dina reminded him patiently. "Second babies tend to come quicker."

When they arrived back at the hospital at three-fifteen,

Mary Beth was swept off by a nurse to be prepped while Frank took care of the remaining paperwork and changed into scrub clothes. When Dina checked Mary Beth in the labor room, she found that Mary Beth was six centimeters dilated.

"You're going to be a father, Frank," Dina told him, "within the hour."

"So soon?" Frank asked, amazed it was all happening this fast.

But there wasn't time to dwell on it. Mary Beth was caught up in accelerated breathing. Frank rubbed talc on her belly and, in the absence of lollipops, gave Mary Beth shaved ice to suck on. The nurse came in to take blood. Mary Beth went into a contraction while the needle was in her arm, and it was difficult for her to control the next few contractions.

At four-thirty, Mary Beth began having really strong contractions and had to switch to blowing breaths. Dina came in and examined her, then called to the nurse.

"Let's get her to the delivery room, stat."

By the time Frank got to the delivery room, Mary Beth was already transferred to the table and was being hooked up to an I.V. containing glucose. Someone handed Frank a cap and mask.

The anesthesiologist stood by in case he was needed, but the atmosphere in the delivery room was relaxed, as if everyone were on a coffee break rather than awaiting the birth of a baby.

In the midst of it all, Mary Beth was oblivious. Caught up in one contraction after another, she was blowing out fiercely. Suddenly, a gush of water spouted across the room, drenching the front of Dina's surgical gown.

"All right!" Dina told Mary Beth that on the next contraction, she could push.

Frank held Mary Beth's head as she fortified herself for the push.

"Let me tell you," said Dina. "This kid's got some head of black hair. Look up in the mirror, Mary Beth, and you'll see."

But Mary Beth was too busy to look in the mirror, something she would later regret, missing that first look at her baby's thatch of black hair.

"Three more should do it, Mary Beth. Okay. Ready," she said quietly. "*Push.*"

Mary Beth took two breaths, then held the third and pushed, gripping the metal bars of the table.

A strange gurgling sound preceded a long, bluish, wrinkled body sliding out between Mary Beth's legs.

"It's a girl!" Dina cried.

The baby let out an outraged scream as Dina clipped its umbilical cord.

"Okay, Mary Beth, one more push and you're through."

"You hear that?" Frank whispered in her ear. "You did it. She's a beaut."

After expelling the placenta, Mary Beth lay with her baby on her chest while Dina stitched up the episiotomy.

"She is beautiful, isn't she, Frank?" she breathed. "Happy Valentine's Day."

Frank gave them each a gentle kiss. "You're both beautiful."

"Go call my mother, would you, hon?"

"If you're sure you don't need me," he said hesitantly.

"Go," she said. "She'll be waiting by the phone."

Frank paused at the door. "What shall I tell her when she asks me who she looks like?"

Mary Beth took another look at her black-eyed girl with her head of wild black hair and then at her dark-eyed, black-haired husband. "I never thought I'd say this, but tell her she looks just like her father."

"She sure does," Dina agreed. "All she needs is a little black handlebar moustache. Kiddo..." she said to Mary Beth as soon as Frank left. "I don't know quite how to say this, but your father would have been proud of you tonight."

Kendra

"Oh, it's you." Breathless from lumbering across the studio to pick up the phone on the third ring, Kendra pressed a hand over her thudding heart.

"You expecting maybe the curator of MOMA?" Jill asked.

Now Kendra braced her lower back where it felt as if someone had just zapped her with a cattle prod. "It's just that if one more person asks me why I haven't had this baby yet, they're going to have to drag me out of here screaming in a straitjacket."

"I wonder if they make maternity straitjackets?"

Kendra eased into a chair as the pain shot from her lower back down into her thighs.

"Nana's been calling twice a day. She's leaving for Gstaad tomorrow night and she wants me to have the baby *now*."

"Lifestyles of the pushy and obnoxious."

"She's already rescheduled twice and she says she can't do it a third time, so would I please stop being so stubborn?"

"You've got a lot of nerve."

"I don't know how much more of this I can take."

"Try twenty years."

Kendra sighed.

"Cheryl and I were both late. My father took my mother on this very long, very bumpy car ride to get Cheryl to come out. To have me, she dragged around a bunch of rocks in a wheelbarrow."

"That sounds effective."

"I always thought that getting naked and scrubbing the kitchen floor was the best method."

"Why naked?"

"Who knows? It's part of the charm."

"Actually, now that I think of it, I know why naked. The sight of your naked body is so gross you go into labor."

"You're not gross."

"Trust me. I'm gross."

Kendra was across the hall in her studio working on a piece when she first began to feel the contractions. It was mid-afternoon, nearing the end of the first week in March, and she was ten days past her due date, so she wasn't surprised. Three times in the last week she had construed vigorous clusters of Braxton-Hicks contractions as the onset of labor, only to realize, after an hour or two of close monitoring, that she had been fooled by a false alarm. Just in case this, too, proved to be false, she continued to work on the piece, not giving the clock so much as a glance.

At six o'clock, Morgan, returning from work at the Public, dropped in to see how she was doing and to ask whether she felt up to dinner at the new seafood restaurant that had just opened over on University Place. For the past two weeks it had been impossible for Kendra to eat more than a few bites at a time, so constricted was her stomach by her growing uterus. But tonight, for some reason, she felt genuinely hungry.

"Just let me clean up," she told him, "and I'll be right with you. I'm actually starved, for a change."

"Maybe you've dropped?" he said, eyeing her stomach hopefully.

"Dropped-shmopped," she said. "What I've dropped is all hope of ever giving birth."

"Don't say that."

"Watch. This will probably be the first kid ever to attend college in utero."

She washed and changed out of her paint-smeared overalls into a denim tent dress over which she threw a light denim jacket. Although she hadn't set foot outside all day today, the breeze blowing through her studio windows had been almost balmy. Arm in arm, Kendra and Morgan ambled across town. Every second block or so, Kendra had to stop for a minute to rest.

"Interesting," she said, after the third stop. "They seem to be regular."

"Since when?" Morgan tried to keep the excitement out of his voice.

"I don't know." Kendra shrugged. "Maybe for the past three hours."

"Three hours!" Morgan echoed. "Shouldn't we report this to the midwives?"

Smiling indulgently at him, she patted his arm. "I've already called them twice last week. I'm beginning to feel like the boy who cried wolf." But after resuming her pace, she added, "Maybe after dinner I'll call."

It was midweek but the restaurant was full and there was a line of three couples waiting for tables. The blown-up photostat of a review in last week's *Times* Weekend section—and the springlike weather—explained the rush.

Without the slightest compunction, Morgan explained to the couples standing ahead of them that his wife was probably about to go into labor and would they kindly let them cut ahead? Giving Kendra's distended stomach an anxious look, they stood aside without argument.

Kendra ordered the lobster and Morgan the Fisherman's Platter. Morgan had a beer but Kendra opted for water. "Just in case."

Morgan had to break up Kendra's lobster for her. It seemed that every time she started to use the cracker, she began a contraction. "Sympathetic reaction," she said.

"Do you think you should be eating at all?" Morgan asked, forking her over yet another tender morsel of meat dripping with melted butter.

"I'll need my strength, won't I?" Kendra said, and proceeded to polish off the lobster right down to the swimerettes. She ordered chocolate mousse for dessert, also for "energy."

The walk home took twice as long, as Kendra had to stop almost twice as often.

"I feel a little queasy," she said, riding up in the Inclinette.

When Morgan unlocked the door, Kendra went immediately to the bathroom and discovered that her underpants were damp and a little bloody.

"I think I'll call the midwives now," she said, casually picking up the phone.

Over the phone, she explained to the midwife on duty that she had had contractions since three-thirty that afternoon. Morgan watched anxiously as Kendra answered the midwife's questions in monosyllables. When she hung up, Morgan asked, "Is everything okay?"

"Sure," Kendra said thoughtfully. "They seem to think my water may have broken."

"*Seem to think?* I thought it was supposed to make a big mess, like a punctured water balloon."

"Apparently not always," Kendra said. "Sometimes it just gets a slow leak. Honey," she said, "you'll have to run out and get me some castor oil."

Morgan made a face. "Why?"

"To clean me out," she said matter-of-factly. "And maybe it will help make my contractions stronger."

Morgan left immediately to get the castor oil. Kendra paced the loft, feeling nervous and nauseated. None of this so far sounded like any of the descriptions she had read about in any of the books or heard about in any of the discussions they had had in Lamaze class. Then again, questions about the signs of early labor had been cut short by Nana's absurd, eleventh-hour wedding bash. She found herself wishing that Nana were here, then remembered that blood and Nana did not mix.

Morgan came back in five minutes with the bottle of castor oil and a box of sanitary napkins. Unsheathing the bottle grimly from its drugstore bag, he said, "They didn't have any flavored. Sorry, honey. How much of this junk are you supposed to take?"

"As directed," she said, reading the label with distaste. Morgan went to get a teaspoon.

Gagging, grimacing, and groaning, she managed to choke down two teaspoons. Five minutes later, she had thrown up all of her dinner. A half hour later, she was emptying her bowels. Morgan stood outside the bathroom, offering her encouragement and a damp facecloth. After two more trips to the bathroom, Kendra felt that her contractions had sharpened. They sat on the bed, Kendra propped up by pillows, and watched a movie on late-night television. Neither one of them could follow the plot. The things happening on the screen seemed far away and pale. At twelve-thirty, the contractions were lasting from fifty to sixty-five seconds and coming every five or six minutes.

"Why aren't I nice and regular like in all the books?" Kendra wailed.

"I think we should call the midwives again."

After a two-minute discussion with the midwife, Kendra hung up the phone. "They say to come in."

Morgan sprang for his jacket and keys. "I'll get the car. Will you be all right here alone?"

"I'll be fine," she reassured him. "I'll get my stuff and be waiting for you out front."

"No way," he said. "I don't want you out on the Bowery alone at midnight in labor."

She shook her head. "An unregenerate gentleman you turned out to be, Morgan Ford."

"I love you." Kissing her on the forehead, he bounded downstairs.

They arrived at the hospital at one o'clock in the morning. Kendra's contractions, though strong, were not always severe enough to necessitate Lamaze breathing. She undressed and put on a gown and lay down on the bed in the birthing room. The birthing room, which had struck her on her tour of the facility as so cozy in contrast to the labor rooms of the physicians' patients, now looked to her, with its matching striped drapes and lampshades, like a room in a Holiday Inn. The midwife examined her and said cheerfully:

"You're one and a half centimeters dilated."

Kendra shook her fists at the ceiling.

The midwife patted her sympathetically. "You've got a ways to go yet. Get dressed and we'll talk."

Feeling thoroughly discouraged, Kendra climbed back into her denim tent. Holding Morgan's hand, she sat on the edge of the birthing room bed while the midwife made her recommendation.

"You like booze, Kendra?"

Kendra shrugged. "Sure, but I thought the hard stuff was off-limits."

The midwife smiled reassuringly. "I don't think you're in danger of inflicting fetal alcohol syndrome at this stage. The important thing is to get this baby born. I recommend that you go home—"

"Home?" she echoed plaintively.

"Believe me," the midwife said, "you don't want to spend the next twenty-four hours here. You need rest, Kendra, for the long haul ahead. Morgan, take her home and mix her a couple of stiff Bloody Marys—you like Bloody Marys, Kendra?"

"Sure," she said listlessly.

"And call me when you wake up in the morning."

"Sure," she repeated, feeling like a total failure.

Kendra passed out at three o'clock in the morning stoned out of her mind and woke up at ten-thirty to contractions that felt like a battering ram aimed at her midsection. She called out to Morgan, who surfaced blearily from the rumpled bedclothes.

"These contractions are all business!"

Morgan struggled into his dungarees and fumbled for his wristwatch. Kendra, who had scrambled to a sitting position, rubbed her belly while Morgan looked at the sweep hand of his watch.

"Sixty seconds—*I think*," he said when he heard her expel a cleansing breath.

"This is it, isn't it?" he said.

She nodded. "And me with a hangover." And grimaced.

Five minutes later, the next contraction hit. They continued in a similar pattern for the rest of the morning. By noon they were so strong, Kendra could no longer talk. Morgan called the midwives for her, reporting her condition. The midwife suggested they come in to the clinic immediately. Morgan went to Kendra's closet and took out his favorite dress of hers, helped her put it on between contractions, and sat her in a chair by the door while he sprinted down to bring the car around.

When they arrived at the clinic at one o'clock, exactly twelve hours after their first visit, the midwife on duty examined Kendra and was pleased to report her six centimeters dilated.

At two-thirty Morgan had to hold Kendra's legs, they were trembling so violently. He gave her ice to suck on between contractions, swabbed off her forehead with a wet towel, and helped her overcome hyperventilation on three occasions by making her breathe into a paper bag. Every ten minutes, the midwife, who was also attending a woman in the adjacent birthing room, came in to check on Kendra's progress.

"Terrific," she said at five minutes after three. "Only one centimeter to go."

"I feel like there's a bull inside of me," Kendra rasped, her voice almost gone, "trying to kick its way out."

The midwife smiled. "Try and think of a friendlier metaphor. And try lying on your left side for a bit." Then to Morgan: "If she wants to push, don't let her. And see if you can't get her to slow down her breathing. She's rushing ahead of herself."

Morgan helped Kendra roll onto her left side. She found herself facing a pastel pointilistic poster on the wall, of a garden with a gravel path. As her contraction began, she breathed slowly and regularly and, with each breath, moved herself farther down the garden path. She reminded herself that it was important that she stroll, not run, down the path. And in this way she kept her breathing from getting too hurried and panicky. Each time a contraction came, she took herself down that path.

284

"Tell her not to push," she heard the midwife say to Morgan. "She sounds like she's bearing down a little hard at the end of each contraction."

"Don't push, honey," Morgan whispered in her ear.

She looked up at him, barely able to keep his face in focus.

"Do I blow now?" she asked him. "I feel like I should."

"Can she start blowing now?" she heard Morgan ask. It was as if she were in a foreign land and Morgan was her only link to the natives. Her trusty interpreter.

"She says go ahead and blow, honey."

With the next contraction, she found she hadn't the slightest idea how.

"Give me an image!" she cried out to Morgan.

He blinked and looked around as if searching the room for that elusive image.

"You've got a sailboat," he said. "In a bathtub," he added. "And you're blowing it across the tub each time."

And so Kendra spent most of transition blowing that little sailboat back and forth across an imaginary bathtub. Sometimes the sailing wasn't so smooth. At one point she gave up altogether.

"Remember the breathing," Morgan said. "The little sailboat." He demonstrated. She bared her teeth at him.

"Fuck you and your little sailboat, too."

Her braids had come undone and her hair stood around her head in a wild golden mass. "Oh, no!" she cried. "Oh, God, here it comes again. I'll never make it. Never. Never. Never."

"Yes, you will, Kendra," Morgan said. He trapped her face between his hands and blew in her face. "Do what I do." After the third breath, Kendra fell into a rhythm with him, and by the time the contraction was over, she had regained enough presence of mind to be ready for the next bout.

"They're overlapping!" she cried when the next one hit no sooner than the last one had faded.

He nodded and motioned for her to begin her cleansing breath, depressing the button for the midwife.

285

The midwife bustled in and, examining Kendra, said, "Way to go! Let's get this baby born."

With Morgan's help, they converted the bed for the delivery.

At the next round of contractions, Kendra was allowed to push. Morgan and the midwife were like a cheering section.

"Come on, Kendra, you can do it, you can do it. That's it. Good girl!"

After fifteen minutes of pushing in a squatting position, Kendra fell back and Morgan caught her.

"There's your baby's head!" the midwife cried out.

Five more rounds of cheers and five more pushes and the baby squeezed out.

With the baby resting on Kendra's stomach, the midwife waited while the blood flowed out of the placenta into the baby's body. They watched as the baby went from bluish white to pink.

Then, clipping the cord, she handed the surgical scissors to Morgan and gave him the honor of cutting his own son's umbilical cord.

"Jeremiah," Kendra whispered as the baby rooted around for her breasts and blinked at her with wide dark eyes. "You gorgeous little thing, you."

"Little, my foot," said the midwife, taking him away to weigh him. "He's at least ten pounds!"

Morgan smoothed the hair away from Kendra's face.

"I must look like the wrath of God," she said weakly.

"I've never seen anyone look more beautiful in my entire life" was her husband's reply.

Carleen

Carleen was in her office on a Monday afternoon in March three weeks after her due date, when Dr. Fitzwater called.

"There you are!" he said, as if he had been running around looking for her all over the city.

"Hello, Sam," said Carleen, swiveling her chair around to look out the window at the buds sprinkled over the maple tree in the lot across the street.

"I thought I'd be hearing from you over the weekend," he said.

He had her in regularly to strap on the fetal monitor and make sure that her overdue baby was not in any distress. In the last three weeks she felt as if she had been spending entirely too much time with Dr. Sam Fitzwater.

"Really?" she said politely. "Why did you think you'd be hearing from me over the weekend, Sam?"

"I don't know what it is, but you career girls somehow always manage to go into labor on the weekends."

"Well, not this career girl," she said flatly.

"I think it's time we did something about that," he said jovially.

"Did something?" Carleen disliked circumlocutious conversation. "You mean induce me?"

"When there's some doubt as to the maturity of the fetus, we like to wait, but in your case, well, we know the week, day, and hour of your gestation, don't we, Carleen?"

"You were there, Sam." Carleen swiveled back to her desk and looked at her calendar. "When?"

"How does tomorrow sound?"

"It sounds like Tuesday," she said without humor.

He chuckled. "I'll reserve you a bed. Do you know what oxytocin is, Carleen?"

"Yes," she said, "it's the hormone that triggers labor."

"That's what I like," he said with rousing enthusiasm, "a well-informed patient. I'll be giving you an intravenous drip containing pitocin, which is man-made oxytocin. That should get you started."

Carleen sighed and found herself marking tomorrow's calendar with the word "drip" in large block letters. "I guess I'll see you tomorrow, then," she said.

"Unless you decide to beat me to it tonight, nine o'clock it is. And Carleen," he added, "don't eat anything after eleven o'clock. And remember—"

"I know," Carleen said dully, "attitude is everything." She hung up and dialed Bill at home. From the eager way he picked up, she could tell he was expecting *the* call from her, as he had been, in vain, for the past five or six weeks. When she told him about her talk with Fitzwater, he sounded both anxious and disappointed.

"It'll be fine," she said, trying to reassure herself as much as him. "This is just to give me a little jump start. Besides," she couldn't resist adding, "medical science has been with us from the start. Why should it abandon us now?"

That night, Bill and Carleen had a quiet supper out on the terrace, which Bill had, as a surprise while she was down in Puerto Rico, glassed in with a greenhouse roof and walls. As the lights of Manhattan twinkled below them, Carleen couldn't help but begin to feel excited. After all, chance had been thrust aside. Tomorrow their baby would be born. As they were clearing away the dishes, the intercom buzzer sounded. Bill went to answer it. Carleen, who now found it necessary to lie down after eating, went to bed.

"Who is it?" she called from the bedroom.

Bill stood in the doorway, puzzled. "Some moving men."

"Who's moving?"

"They're delivering something...to us."

"What could it be?" she wondered aloud.

"Something from Mr. Venable."

"Augustus?" Carleen rolled off the bed and plodded to the front door. "This I've got to see."

Bill let in the moving men and they both watched as the two uncrated a complete set of Edwardian oak nursery furniture: wardrobe, bassinet, crib, bureau, highchair, and, last but not least, the most exquisite rocking horse Carleen had ever seen.

"My God," said Bill, inspecting the pieces. "This stuff must be worth a small fortune."

One of the men handed Bill a slip to sign, the other gave Carleen a small square envelope. Carleen read aloud the note inside.

"I know, from our numerous bookish luncheons, that you are an avid Bloomsburyite. This set belonged to the *Leslie Stephens* family, although I cannot vouchsafe that the tiny teethmarks on the crib rail were made by the infant Virginia Woolf herself. May your own child grow up healthy and wise amongst these lovely pieces. Your obedient servant and grateful author, Augustus Venable."

At eight-thirty the next morning, Carleen sat in Bill's Triumph with the motor running in the loading zone in front of the Grantley Building while Bill ran upstairs to deliver the manuscript she had finished line-editing in bed the night before. There was barely enough room for her in the passenger seat. Bill had had to wedge her in gingerly since she had, perversely, not wanted to take the trip to the hospital in some stranger's cab.

As she sat waiting, she felt a flush as a Braxton-Hicks contraction came on and she leaned over to look at herself in the rearview mirror. She was huge and moon-faced. She felt as if she had been pregnant for five years. Then she saw it: a meter maid copying down the number on the rear license plate. Carleen rolled down the window and called out sweetly:

"Excuse me," she said to the woman, "but my husband's just run upstairs to make a delivery."

"I can't help that, miss," said the woman, continuing to write up the ticket.

"But you don't understand...we're on our way to the hospital to have a baby."

At this, the woman looked up. "Sorry," she said, nicely enough, "but it's too late now. I've already written you up."

"Shit," Carleen said under her breath. A fine way to start the day. She took the ticket with a sour smile, rolled up the window, and cast an eye at the building entryway. Where the hell was Bill?

A horn honked behind her and she jumped, bumping her head on the low ceiling of the car. A panel truck had pulled up next to her. The driver was gesturing for her to move up. When Carleen tried to ignore him, he only stepped up the rhythm of his horn-honking.

"Shit!" Once again, Carleen rolled down the window.

"Move, lady!" the man shouted.

There was no way she was going to get out of the car and squeeze herself into the driver's seat to satisfy this man.

"No!" she shouted.

"Lady, I gotta delivery to make. Move your car!"

"I gotta delivery to make, too," she said. "I'm about to have a baby."

The driver sneered. "Oh, sure you are, lady!" And proceeded to lean on the horn once more.

That did it. First the ticket, now this obnoxious asshole. Carleen struggled with the door handle and worked her way out of the car.

When Bill emerged from the Grantley Building a few minutes later, he found his wife out on the street hysterically pounding on the window of the panel truck.

"You fucking asshole! Have you no decency? I'm in labor. See this? This is a baby and I'm about to have it, you stupid fucking—"

Bill pulled her away from the truck. Shaking and crying, holding the crumpled parking ticket in her fist, she managed to tell him of the horrors that had befallen her since he had gone into the building not five minutes before. Gently, he helped her back into the car, then went over to the panel truck. Putting on his most amiable smile, he tapped on the driver's door. The man rolled down his window, prepared to accept Bill's apology for his wife's irrational behavior.

"If I didn't have better things to do right now, Mack," Bill told him, "I'd drag your ass out of that truck and beat the living shit out of you."

As Carleen watched the solution begin to drip into the long clear tube leading to her right arm, she felt slightly faint.

"Are you okay, sweetheart?" Bill asked. "You look a little pale."

"It took them a while to find a good vein," she said. "And I guess I'm a little tired." What with the fullness of her belly and the pressure on her bladder, Carleen had not gotten a full night's sleep in over a month. The weeks of waiting had taken their toll.

"Just rest," Bill said, smoothing her brow. And, as if the I.V. were administering a sleeping drug, Carleen found herself floating off.

As soon as the contractions began, around mid-morning, a nurse came and strapped the two belts of the fetal monitor around her midriff. As she and Bill learned to read the two lines on the printout—the top line representing her contraction, the bottom the baby's heart rate —Carleen began to feel almost cheerful. She was on her way!

"At least something's happening," she said to Bill.

By early afternoon the contractions were stronger. Carleen had to lie on her side while Bill massaged her lower back and thighs.

"Figures I'd get all this and back labor, too," she said between contractions.

At one o'clock a nurse came in and checked her cervix, shook her head, and clucked.

"What?" Carleen said. "What's wrong?"

"You're only two centimeters dilated," the nurse said, frowning, as if it were Carleen's fault. "I'll ask the doctor if we should step up the pitocin."

As the nurse left, Carleen said between clenched teeth, "I hate her. Why can't Maxi be on duty?"

Bill shrugged. "The luck of the draw, I guess."

Fitzwater came in a few minutes, his usual jolly self. As he examined Carleen internally, he shrugged and said, "So? We'll give you a stronger shot." And he adjusted a clamp on the I.V. bottle.

"Fire away," Carleen said.

"That means we'll be having to hook you up to the internal monitor as well, Carleen," he said. "And in order to do that, I'll be puncturing your membranes. You should begin to feel some serious contractions then."

"How come these feel so serious already?" she wanted to know.

"Because you're having back labor, you lucky girl, you!"

Carleen winced when Fitzwater took the rosewood stick and punctured her bag of waters. For a few seconds, before the nurse was able to change the sheet beneath her, she lay in a warm puddle. A second nurse arrived and catheterized her urethra, an extremely uncomfortable procedure. But it was nothing compared to what she felt when Fitzwater shoved the internal fetal thermometer up her vagina. Between the belts around her waist and the hard piece of metal up her vagina, the smallest movement was excruciating for Carleen.

"The Spanish Inquisition missed out on a wonderful means of torture," she gulped to Bill.

And when the new, harsher contractions began to come on, she was helpless to fight them and no longer inclined to joke.

Bill, who had stood by grim and helpless while his wife was hooked up to one gizmo after another, tried to make her as comfortable as possible. But while he attempted to hold her to her breathing, Carleen, trussed as she was and forced by the machinery to endure her back labor on her back, soon became lost to the pain. After twenty minutes of watching her writhe, he left her in a nurse's care and ran down the corridor to find Fitzwater.

"Please," he begged the doctor. "You've got to give her something for the pain."

"That pain," said Fitzwater, looking up sternly from a chart, "is dilating her cervix."

"But she's in agony," said Bill.

"Has she asked for relief?" the doctor asked.

"She can't even talk, Doctor. She doesn't even know I'm here. Please, you've got to help her."

Fitzwater returned with Bill to Carleen's room.

"Carleen!" Fitzwater raised his voice to get through to her. "Would you like something for the pain?"

Carleen nodded energetically.

"Open your eyes and look at me, Carleen," he commanded.

Carleen's eyes fluttered open. "Just a little something," she begged. She felt like a little girl—a pathetic little girl.

"Okay," said Fitzwater. Then to Bill: "Too much could impede her labor, so I'm giving her just enough to ease the pain. Maybe enable her to get on top of her contractions."

Carleen, who was clearly pinned beneath them, screamed, "Hurry up, for Chrissakes! *I'm dying.*"

Bill looked at Fitzwater in alarm, but the doctor only smiled. "She's not dying, Bill. She's in labor. And remember, A is E."

As he left the room, Bill punched the palm of one hand. "He says that one more time, and so help me ..."

A nurse came in and injected a syringe of Demerol into the I.V. and in a few minutes Carleen had calmed down. "Oh," she said dreamily, "that's so much better. Why didn't somebody think of that before?"

But in under fifteen minutes, the contractions, having nearly doubled in severity, had pulled her out of her drugged trance and flung her once more on their ragged shoals. Bill, watching in despair, had to be told by a nurse to breathe with his wife.

"What kind of breathing?" he asked.

"That's accelerated labor she's in, sonny boy," said the nurse. "Try shallow chest breathing."

Bill was able to get Carleen to breathe through every third contraction. But each time he felt she was with him, she gave in to her fear and pain and began to cry and moan and thrash about.

"Stop that!" said the nurse. "Carleen, breathe, don't fuss."

Fitzwater came in every half an hour and reached up Carleen's anus, causing Carleen considerable pain, in order to check her cervix.

"Good girl," he said on the third examination.

"What's so good?" Carleen asked weakly.

"Take a look at the clock, Carleen."

Carleen blinked at the big clock on the wall.

"It's going on five-thirty, Carleen. You're going to be giving birth by six o'clock. Isn't that terrific!"

"No, it's not!" Carleen screamed as a contraction hit her.

By the time Fitzwater told her she could push, Carleen had very little wind or strength left. It took Bill and a nurse to support her as she sat up. Her breath was reedy and her energy sapped. And as she began to push, the expressions on the faces of the medical staff were not hopeful.

One of them checked the printout of the fetal monitor and, shaking her head, showed it to Fitzwater.

"Let's try again, Carleen," said Fitzwater, sounding sorely disappointed in her.

Carleen tried but it was like having to sprint in the last leg of a marathon for which she had been inadequately trained.

"She's swollen," Fitzwater said, peering between her legs. "The baby's head will never make it." He held out a hand and one of the nurses showed him, yet again, the latest printout from the monitor. Passing it to Bill, he said, "See this?" He pointed to the red line. "The heartbeat's dropped fairly drastically. I'm afraid we're going to have to do an emergency delivery."

Bill covered his eyes and turned away, but Carleen piped up almost cheerfully, "Terrific! Hurry up, Sam. This baby and I have *had* it."

Bill was allowed into the operating room because they had chosen an epidural block over complete anesthesia. But while they administered the anesthesia, they made him wait in the doctors' lounge down the hall. A nurse helped Carleen sit up on the operating table while the anesthesiologist injected a needle into the base of her spine.

"Your contractions should be leveling off soon," one of the nurses said.

"Great!" Carleen breathed.

She lay back down and they taped her arms onto two long boards.

"I feel like the crucifixion," Carleen said when Bill came back in.

Bill, who could no longer hold Carleen's hand, merely patted her shoulder and whispered, "It'll be over with soon."

Every so often the anesthesiologist or his assistant would prick Carleen's toes or knees with a pin and ask her if she could feel it. When she could no longer feel anything below her breasts, they erected a surgical tent over her waist and disappeared behind it.

Carleen lay there trembling.

"Feel that, Carleen?" Fitzwater asked from behind the tent.

"Yes, but it doesn't hurt." She felt a peculiar tugging, as if fabric were being ripped, and a tension in her shoulders and neck and lips as if those parts of her body that retained feeling were registering the pain being inflicted on the parts of her body that couldn't.

"You have a beautiful son, Carleen."

Carleen had to take his word for it.

She felt another tug. She closed her eyes. When she opened them, someone had laid him across her belly, wrapped tightly in a white hospital blanket: her baby.

295

Since her arms were still bound and numb, she couldn't hold him herself, and Bill had to do that for her, steadying him on her chest. But her eyes locked with those of her son. Except for a small red mark on his forehead where the fetal monitor had touched him, he was perfect, and so familiar-looking, she felt as if she had always known him.

"Oh, welcome, little one," she said in a soft, gentle voice she had never heard herself use before. A mother's voice.

PART VI

Postpartum

Carleen felt herself being dragged upwards through dense layers of sleep by the high, shrill cry of her five-week-old son, who, from the moment he had come home from the hospital, had failed to clock more than three consecutive hours of sleep.

Her eyes burned as she brought the glowing red numerals on the digital clock into focus: 3:41. Two hours since the last feeding. She rolled out of bed and staggered into the bathroom. From the bassinet next to their queen-sized bed, Jackson Donovan wailed on with all the desolation of an infant abandoned on a doorstep. She groped for her warmest robe. In the dead of this spring night, winter could still be felt. Leaning against the sink, she filled up a glass with cold tap water and splashed a few droplets on her face just so she wouldn't fall asleep on the job. Then, for the third time in six hours, she reported for duty to the bedroom "nursing station": a rocking chair, a footstool, and a TV tray set two feet away from the television screen.

Enviously, and a little resentfully, she gazed over at Bill, who slept on, as he had during the two earlier feedings, as he did every night. Looking at her ravaged face in the light of day, he was often prompted to say: "Why don't you let me give him a bottle every so often? Give you a chance to get in a whopping five hours of sleep."

To show that he meant business, he had even gone out and bought a can of infant formula and a baby bottle that claimed to be "the next best thing to Mother." Carleen had taken one look at the thick, yellowish, foul-smelling substance, at the PCB-impersonation of her nipple, and rejected his offer. Jack would get nothing but breast milk for as long as Carleen could hold out.

She set the glass down on the TV tray, slung a diaper

over one shoulder, turned on the television by remote control, put on the earphones, and reached into the bassinet for the baby. Like a blind puppy, he wriggled in her arms and rooted at her nightgown where her right breast had already begun leaking through the fabric.

"Hold on, Sport," she whispered to him. Any anger she might have felt toward this tiny robber of her sleep ebbed away as she laid eyes on his desperate little face. He fastened onto her nipple and began to suck, his features softening as her milk let down. Then he stared up at her in relief and gratitude and, yes, adoration. Cupping his downy skull in one hand, she leaned back in the rocker and, sipping her water, watched on old MTM rerun already in progress. She was cultivating a grudging appreciation for the nocturnal underbelly of television programming: the reruns of sitcoms from "Mork and Mindy" back to "My Favorite Martian," from "Happy Days" to "Ozzie and Harriet"; the reruns of bad made-for-TV movies and even worse old movies not good enough to be rented out in video stores; and the talk shows, the news shows, and the rock video shows—all with their nightshift, insomniac, crackpot constituencies out there somewhere, just like Carleen, wide awake while everyone else slept.

She lifted Jackson up on her shoulder to burp him. Murray was giving Mary a pep talk and Mary was getting up the nerve to go into Mr. Grant's office and ask him for that promotion. There was something in the timbre of Mary Tyler Moore's voice that Carleen had never really noticed until now. Something high and brittle and *out on the edge*—exactly where motherhood had thrust Carleen.

As she patted Jackson's back with a flattened palm, he worked himself loose from the blanket in which she had swaddled him, papoose-style. In the cold night air, his little body felt warm and smelled like a damp meadow steaming in the sunshine. The next moment, he managed to burp and fill his diaper all in the same breath. As she went to rewrap him, he landed a kick in the stitches running across her lower abdomen. It no longer hurt unbear-

ably as it had in the first few weeks when he would bully
her with kick after kick there, as if he knew instinctively
that this was the way back in. With every day, the shock
of the operation was diminishing. Apart from the scar—a
smile-shaped seam above her pubis—only a tightening
around her mouth and a slight twitch in her left eye remained of the trauma. But lately she had developed a
new pain in her shoulders and upper back, which she sus-
pected came from nursing and holding the baby. It wasn't
that Jack was heavy, only that she was not used to holding anything quite this precious for so many hours of the
day.

If she was careful with the baby, a corresponding care-
lessness had set in elsewhere. Sleeplessness having destroyed her coordination, her fingers were riddled with
little cuts from slipped kitchen knives and burns from
mishandled irons and pots and pans. Her grooming had
fallen off as well. She no longer made herself up with care
every morning. Jackson sucked on her face whenever he
wasn't sucking on her breasts, so what was the point? She
now pulled her luxuriant ash-blond hair back in a severe
ponytail beyond the reach of his tugging, tearing little
fists. Her working clothes consisted of old sweats and
shirts of Bill's because Jackson spit up with such astonishing regularity, no decent garment was safe. And when
he wasn't heaving little cascades of curdled milk down
her shoulders, he was pissing or shitting in her lap. Being
a mother made her feel utterly *lived in*. When Bill walked
in the door at six, she thrust the baby into his arms and
went off to the bathroom to hose herself down.

Nor was she the intellectual companion that she once
had been. Her powers of concentration had so dwindled,
it was all she could do to read the instructions on a box of
pasta, let alone a magazine article, and the mountain of
manuscripts the office so optimistically had sent over remained unassaulted.

Once a reserved person, she now wept with little provo-
cation. A story on the news of a family burned out of their
tenement building could send her into a jag. If the eleva-

tor man closed the doors just as she entered the lobby with two shopping bags and a ravenous Jackson bawling in the Snugli, the tears coursed down her cheeks, in full view of the lady down the hall, who looked on Jackson with pity that he should be saddled with such greenhorn parents.

And yet when Hugh Grantley called her two weeks ago to ask her when she was planning to return to work, she heard herself telling him he had better start looking for a replacement. She might take on some light editing at home when she started getting more sleep, but for now she belonged to Jackson...and the night.

Hugh had sputtered. Hugh had stammered. Hugh had even offered to pay for her nanny. But Carleen would not budge.

"It's taken us eight years to have this baby, Hugh. What kind of sense does it make for me to hand him over to some stranger to raise?"

"But you just finished ranting about baby puke on your silk blouses and you've got the DT's from sleep deprivation. It sounds like hell to me."

"It is," Carleen admitted ruefully, then added, "but it's heaven, too."

It was during the "Life of Riley" feeding at five o'clock one chilly morning that it occurred to Carleen to suggest Bill as her replacement. She had even shaken him awake to broach the idea.

"Great," he mumbled into his pillow. "I'll call first thing."

And, sure enough, Hugh took to the suggestion with gusto. Hugh was a creature of habit, and having a Donovan in the office was as close to habit as he could expect to get under the circumstances. Besides, *this* Donovan had a superb backhand.

In the dark, Carleen stood over the changing table with her son's feet gathered in one hand while she swabbed off his bottom with the other. The postpartum reunion for their Lamaze group was meeting today. Today, that is, after the sun rose; this afternoon: *a lifetime from now.*

When Maxi called the other day to invite her and Bill and Jackson, Carleen had positively bubbled at the prospect.

"Ah, the naked enthusiasm of the shut-in," Maxi observed airily.

By the time Bill came home that night from his first day at Grantley House, Carleen was in tears.

"I don't want to go to that reunion," she told him. "Why did I say we'd go?"

"You were probably just being polite."

"What do you want to bet I'm the only one in the class who had to have a cesarean?"

"Is that what's bothering you?"

"Even Louise, with triplets, didn't have one."

"A c-section is nothing to be ashamed of, Carleen."

"The hell it isn't. The fact is that if I'd been living a century ago, Jack and I would have both died on the table."

"C-sections are older than the Caesars. Don't you think you're being just a little melodramatic?"

"We're freaks of modern medicine!"

Gently, Bill took the baby from her and held him over one shoulder, pulling Carleen against the other and patting her. As Carleen calmed down, a smidgen of rationality returned.

"It's just that I'm used to a certain degree of success. Maybe, in a way, this is my first experience of failure. And I don't like it."

"Look at him." Bill held up Jackson and forced Carleen to look at her son, who was drooling and smiling and totally unperturbed by his mother's carrying on.

"You call this a freak? You call this a failure? This, Carleen, is a miracle! And you are the miracle's mother."

After nine weeks, it still amazed Louise how much the "trips"—as Marty referred to their triplets—reminded her of a litter of kittens. No matter how far apart in the crib she tucked them in, they always woke up in a mewing little heap. This morning, Melissa and Franky (named after Francine) were still asleep, arms slung over Martin

Jr., who stared up imploringly at his mother. The reluctant brother sandwich.

"Are you hungry, little guy?" she whispered, extricating him from the pile. She parted her robe, put him to her breast, and continued nursing him as she walked down the hall to wake up Zack and Bruce for school. Since Francine had gotten up for the four o'clock feeding, and it was a little past six now, Louise would let her sleep just a little while longer.

"Wake up, Zackie." She mussed the hair of her firstborn and he sat up and rubbed his eyes.

"Marty-Farty!" he cried, setting delighted eyes on his littlest brother.

"Don't call him that!"

"He's so cute," Zack said. "Let me kiss him."

Louise pulled Marty off the breast long enough for Zack to plant a wet kiss on his cheek, then reattached him and said: "Do me a favor and wake up Bruce, will you?"

Zack leaned over the side of the bunkbed and called down to his brother in a cloying falsetto: "Wake up, Shriveled Dork!"

"Zack!" Louise frowned. "Don't call him that!"

"Well, I can't help it if that's what he is." Being the eldest of the instantly prodigious tribe had given Zack a certain wizened toughness.

Bruce sat up and complained groggily, "I only just got to sleep a few minutes ago!"

"Liar. Lying Dork."

"Zack, *don't call him that.* If you didn't sleep last night, Brucie," she said, "what were you doing when I came in here to check on you at one o'clock this morning?"

"Thinking," said Bruce.

"With your eyes closed?"

"I think better with my eyes closed."

"Yeah? What about?" Zack wanted to know.

"Dead Smurfs."

In the kitchen, Magda had already brewed a pot of coffee and squeezed a quart of orange juice. The table was set for six and the three baby loungers—green, gray, and yel-low—were lined up on the counter. Mary, who always woke at five with Magda, sat on the floor dropping plastic cookie cutters into a tin cannister and taking them out again. On the stove next to where Magda was making silver-dollar pancakes for Marty, two baby bottles stood warmed and ready. On top of the refrigerator in neatly rolled brown bags, Zack's and Bruce's lunches were set to go. Five boxes of dried cereal were on the table next to a bowl of fresh strawberries, which Mary, judging from the evidence on her face, had already plundered.

Louise sat down at the table. Magda set down a mug of milky, sweetened coffee, which Louise emptied in several gulps before requesting a refill. She sometimes felt as if caffeine alone got her through these days. Switching Marty Jr. to her left breast so that her right arm was free to use a pen, she wrote down tonight's menu for Magda.

"Francine and I will be needing a picnic lunch for the park," she told Magda.

Bruce and Zack skated into the kitchen in their stock-ing feet and made for the row of cereal boxes. They had the vaguely low-comic look of children who had dressed themselves. Louise had planned their wardrobes so that almost everything matched and very little of it had to be snapped, zipped, or buttoned. Still, Bruce's shirt was on backwards and Zack's pants were crooked.

"I want the magic pencil!" Bruce said, lunging for the cereal box in Zack's hand. The copy on the box promised a free magic pencil inside.

"No, *I* get it!" Zack said, holding it out of his reach.

"You don't even like that cereal, Zack," Louise inter-vened. "You said yourself it's not sweet enough."

"Yeah, but I like the pencil."

"If you don't eat the cereal," she told him, "you aren't entitled to the prize."

Scowling, Zack relinquished the box to his little brother, who, failing to fish out the prize for himself, hol-lered to Magda. Stoically, Magda dumped out the entire contents into a mixing bowl, gave the prize to Bruce, and refilled the box with a patience that inspired gaping admiration in Louise.

She was just burping little Marty when big Marty appeared in the kitchen doorway grinning.

"Look what Daddy found!" He stood holding a newly wakened, freshly changed, screaming purple daughter in each arm. For the first time in over a year, he and Louise had made love last night. Almost nothing in the world could lay low his soaring spirits this morning.

"I'll trade you." Louise held out the little boy to him, and with some skillful juggling they succeeded in swapping the fed for the unfed. It had hurt like hell, having sex with her husband last night, but then it always hurt after giving birth, for at least six months. She would get used to it as she had before and, at least now, she would not have to worry about getting pregnant...ever again. Marty had gone and had the operation last week. And, contrary to his fears, it had not affected him.

Big Marty took little Marty onto his shoulder and continued to burp him while Louise, criss-crossing the girls on top of each other, nursed them simultaneously, one to a breast. Marty deposited his small son in one of the loungers and coaxed Mary into sitting on his lap and sharing some pancakes with him. Meanwhile, Zack and Bruce had finished their cereal and retired to their room for a few last precious minutes of play before Marty dropped them off at school on his way to the store. While she continued to nurse the girls, she dictated to Marty the list of fresh produce she wanted Truffles to deliver. As Marty set Mary back on the floor and grabbed the list and the boy's bag lunches, Louise mentioned the Lamaze reunion.

"I'll give everyone your regards."

"Are you kidding?"

"I knew it wasn't your kind of thing, so I asked Francine to come with me."

"Tell Francine she's off the hook," he said, taking Melissa onto his shoulder to burp while Louise tended to the gassier, crankier Franky.

306

Louise stared at him. "Really?"

"I wouldn't miss out on the chance to be Superdad."

"Okay, if you say—"

Just then, Bruce and Zack tore into the kitchen, tripping over Mary and her cookie cutters. Bruce had just remembered he needed to bring in an old shirt for arts and crafts.

"And it has to be yellow, Mom. I hate every other color there is."

Zack could not find his backpack. "You had it last, Mom."

Mary was sobbing from being trampled by her big brothers and tugged at Louise's skirt for sympathy. One triplet screamed in Louise's ear, the other on Marty's shoulder, and the third over in the lounger. Marty was trying to explain to Magda about the replacement bulb for the refrigerator. Something was sizzling on the stove and the exhaust fan hummed. As the roar rose up around her, engulfing her, Louise closed her eyes. The screaming of infants and children was the medium in which she moved these days, the medium she had chosen, and she would not have traded places with any other woman. Still, there were times when it made her so tired, all she wanted to do was go to her room, lock the door, crawl under the covers, and stay there for a very, very long time.

"Weezie?"

"What is it, Marty?"

"You okay?"

"I'm fine."

"How come your eyes are closed?"

"I'm thinking."

"About what?"

She opened her eyes and smiled up at him. "Dead Smurfs."

It was turning out to be one of those early spring days so clear you could see the individual particles of pollen borne on the breeze. Drowsy from the antihistamine she

307

had taken after breakfast, Mary Beth lay on the chaise lounge on the flagstone terrace in her backyard and watched a blue jay peck at the seeds in the feeder hanging from a low branch of the sugar maple. Denny was at school, Frank was out injecting fertilizer into a grove of ancient oaks at a nearby estate, and Dania, eight weeks old and apple-cheeked, slept in the stroller in a pool of morning sunshine.

In the kitchen, a leg of spring lamb marinated in red wine, Greek oregano, shallots, and garlic. Tiny russet potatoes soaked in a bowl of cold water and, in her vegetable garden, two dozen tender shoots of asparagus were waiting to be picked for tonight's supper. As soon as the sun crept a little higher in the sky, she would go inside and put on her bathing suit, get herself a little color, and maybe sleep off her antihistamine before she had to go into the city for the reunion. She looked down at her body. She was just beginning to shed the extra layer of incubatory fat. Since she had chosen not to breast-feed Dania, her breasts had returned to their normal size. Dania was a good-natured baby who slept through the night and seldom fussed. Except for this allergy attack, Mary Beth felt strong. She felt rested. She felt absolutely contented with her life.

The phone rang. For the first few rings, she thought she would let it go unanswered. Whoever it was could call back later. Then it occurred to her that it might be her mother, who was coming to dinner tonight with her new boyfriend, an ob-gyn with a practice in New Rochelle. Taking a quick look at Dania to make sure she was still sleeping soundly, Mary Beth heaved herself up out of the chaise and made a dash for the phone.

"Hello."

She leaned on the kitchen counter and caught her breath. There was no sound. There never was, although she thought she could detect the faint rhythm of breathing at the other end.

"Hello. Who is this?"

More silence. Then the line went dead.

Whoever it was called once every few days, held on briefly, and then hung up. She had had her suspicions before but now she was absolutely positive, although she could not have said exactly why, that the person on the other end of the phone line was Daniel.

Heart pounding, Mary Beth dialed Daniel's office number. As if he had been waiting there for the phone to ring, he picked up immediately.

"Hello," he said.

"Her name is Dania," she said, her voice catching, the phone slippery in her hand. "She was born on St. Valentine's Day. She weighed seven pounds and eight ounces and measured twenty-three inches at birth. Her blood-type is O positive. She is the image, I repeat, *the image of my husband, her father*, whose blood type is also O positive. I love her and I love him very, very much."

The line went dead in her hand.

As she walked back out onto the terrace, her legs buckled beneath her and she had to lean against the house and take a few deep breaths. Behind her, the back door slammed, waking Dania. Dania began to cry. Mary Beth began to cry. She lifted her daughter out of the stroller and held her against her face. As she wept, an image of herself rose in her mind. She was holding a fireplace poker in her hand and beating out some embers smoldering on the rug.

"It's over," she crooned to Dania. "It's okay now. It's over. It's over. It's really over. I promise."

God might have let her get away with it once. But she knew she would never be so lucky again.

Jeremiah Madison Ford, a strapping fourteen pounds at seven weeks, wore a miniature New York Mets cap backwards to keep the paint from spattering his bald head while Kendra worked with him strapped in the Snugli. She had come up with a new method and medium to accommodate the baby's rhythms and needs, forsaking the white lead and turpentine of oil paint for more benign, quickly realizable watercolors. On a three-by-three-foot sheet of heavy-duty rag paper wetted so that it adhered to a drawing board, she lay down a series of bright, colorful sweeping strokes. After working briskly for almost forty-five minutes to a Bach fugue playing on the radio, she stood back to look at her work. The baby, as if on cue, lifted his slightly mashed, sleepy pink face from her chest and began to smack his lips.

"Your timing is perfect," she told him as she went over to the sink to wash her hands with soap and water. When she lifted Jeremiah out of the front-carrier, she saw that, despite her best efforts, his face and hands were freckled with pale spots of watercolor. Locking her studio door behind her, she took him across the hall to the loft.

"We have to clean you up," she told him, "else the Lamaze ladies will think I've been using you for conceptual art."

As the tub filled, she undressed them both, savoring the feel of the baby's nakedness against her own. Putting him to the breast, she gave him a sip while she phoned the theater and left a message to remind Morgan of the reunion.

"How's that adorable little critter doing?" asked the woman who answered the phone.

"Getting more adorable by the day," Kendra told her. "Aren't you?" she asked Jeremiah, who stopped sucking abruptly and regarded her gravely with midnight-blue eyes.

In the warm tub, Jeremiah floated on his back between his mother's legs like an upturned frog, staring up at her in absolute wonder. Usually he got his bath at night, after dinner, when she and Morgan bathed him together and then, on a blanket near the stove, rubbed his little body with oil. Still later, they would let him sleep between them in their bed, ignoring warnings from his mother— *"You'll roll over and smother him"*—and warnings from hers—*"Once you let him in your bed, you'll never get him out."* But both she and Morgan liked having him there with them in the warm nest between their bodies. And Jeremiah certainly seemed to like it. It was so cozy and convenient. He could nurse during the night whenever he liked without even disturbing his mother's sleep. And when she and Morgan made love, all they had to do was move him down to the foot of the bed, where the gentle rocking of their bodies never failed to put him to sleep.

On the way up to Hudson River General, Kendra stopped off at Jill's apartment in Greenwich Village to bring her a pint of the raspberry sherbet she constantly craved and a rose geranium. Jill was reclining on the Pierre Deux-covered harvest bench in the living room, looking bloated and disgruntled.

"I didn't think reunions were your style, Kendra. I'm frankly disappointed in you." She was eating the sherbet right out of the container. Since she was spending most of her gestation off her feet, she had resigned herself to gaining at least a half a ton.

"It'll be fun," Kendra said, lifting Jeremiah out of the Snugli and parking him on the bench next to Jill. "Hand-delivered by a midwife," the lettering on his T-shirt proclaimed. "I guess we'll swap labor stories, compare babies, that sort of thing."

Jill was not impressed. "Did you ever stop to think that we—the Baby Boomers, you should excuse that loathsome expression, who are having our own baby boom—are just too goddamned self-conscious about the whole process? I mean, why don't we just have our babies and shut up about it? Why do we have to make it such a big, fat deal?"

Kendra leaned over and picked at a spot of green paint she had missed near Jeremiah's right ear. "Maybe it's because we've become such a nation of consumers and having babies is a major consumer event. Or maybe our mothers made a big, fat deal, too, only they just never told us. Maybe it's always been a big, fat deal, and each new generation of women discovers it for themselves. I mean, think of the Stone Age Venus of Willendorf. Fertility lies at the center of everything. It always has and it always will. The survival of the race depends on it."

Jill sucked on her spoon. "I'm telling you, Kendra, sitting here day after day, week after week, is beginning to drive me batty."

"Only two and a half more months," Kendra said. "You can do it. Take it from your nurse dolphin."

"Two and a half more months and then what? The hard-luck life of a single parent? I mean, why am I going to all this trouble? Am I some sort of a masochist? Is it really worth it?"

"Trust me, Jill, it's worth it. Isn't it, Jeremiah? Tell Aunt Jill it's worth it. Go ahead. Tell her."

As if he understood exactly what his mother was saying, Jeremiah turned and looked directly at Jill. He arched his back and kicked his legs and flapped his arms up and down. And everything about him seemed to be saying *yes. It is. It really is.*